O9-AID-343

RAVE REVIEWS FOR RICHARD LAYMON!

"A brilliant writer."

—*Sunday Express*

"Plenty of teasing sex, outrageous violence and dawn-fresh writing that Laymon fans love."

—*Publishers Weekly*

"Laymon doesn't pull any punches. Everything he writes keeps you on the edge of your seat."

—*Painted Rock Reviews*

"One of the best, and most reliable, writers working today."

—*Cemetery Dance*

"Laymon is incapable of writing a disappointing book."

—*New York Review of Science Fiction*

"Laymon always takes it to the max. No one writes like him and you're going to have a good time with anything he writes."

—Dean Koontz

"If you've missed Laymon, you've missed a treat."

—Stephen King

"Laymon is an American writer of the highest caliber."

—*Time Out*

"Laymon is unique. A phenomenon. A genius of the grisly and the grotesque."

—Joe Citro, *The Blood Review*

"I've read every book of Laymon's I could get my hands on. I'm absolutely a longtime fan."

—Jack Ketchum, author of *Peaceable Kingdom*

RICHARD
LAYMON

BODY RIDES

LEISURE BOOKS   NEW YORK CITY

LEISURE BOOKS ®

March 2004

Published by

Dorchester Publishing Co., Inc.
200 Madison Avenue
New York, NY 10016

ISBN 0-8439-5182-6

The name "Leisure Books" and the stylized "L" with design are trademarks of Dorchester Publishing Co., Inc.

Printed in the United States of America.

Visit us on the web at www.dorchesterpub.com.

BODY RIDES

Chapter One

Neal Darden, alone in his car, took back roads to stay away from Robertson Boulevard. He wasn't worried about too much traffic on Robertson; he was worried about getting shot for no good reason.

After all, this was night in Los Angeles.

Anybody could get shot at any time of the day or night, but night was worse. And the well-traveled boulevards such as Robertson seemed more dangerous to Neal than the hidden roads that twisted through quiet, residential neighborhoods.

His theory was simple: the fewer cars in sight, the less likely you are to encounter a load of trigger-happy gangsters.

The very best way to stay alive was to avoid going out at all. Especially at night. Especially *late* at night. He refused to live that way, though. He was only twenty-eight years old, too young to become a hermit. For safety's sake, he might make a few concessions—but he wouldn't surrender and stay home for the rest of his life.

You take precautions and you go anyway.

Even if it's just to return the video rentals.

The two movies were due before midnight. Marta had stayed later than usual, actually changing for work in his bedroom so she wouldn't have to leave until the very last moment. By the time she'd gone and Neal had finished rewinding the tapes, it had been nearly 11:30 P.M.

Plenty of time to reach the store.

But a bad time to be out in your car on the streets of Los Angeles.

Neal knew that he could've waited and returned the videos tomorrow. There would be a late charge. Five or six bucks, he supposed. A small amount to pay, compared with the risk of taking them back at this hour of the night. But there was a larger price in waiting for daylight: a payment made in freedom and self-respect.

What kind of chickenshit's afraid to drive five miles? he'd asked himself.

Marta, who worked the graveyard shift at LAX, had to drive *thirty* miles, five nights a week. What would she think if she found out that Neal was afraid to take the videos back?

She'll never find out, he'd told himself.

She might. Anything's possible.

It's a moot point, he'd thought. I'm taking them back tonight, even if it kills me.

Now, driving along the empty streets on his way to the video store, Neal smiled and shook his head. He was pleased with himself. He felt fairly brave and reckless.

In the great scheme of things, the real danger in making a midnight run to Video City was slim. Nevertheless, a prudent person wouldn't be doing it. He was needlessly putting himself at risk.

If his mother found out he'd done such a thing, she would pitch a fit.

He smiled and shook his head.

What a way to go, he thought. Killed in the act of returning *Straw Dogs* and *I Spit on Your Grave* to the local video store. Oh, the irony.

He laughed softly.

He didn't feel particularly nervous until after he'd crossed National Boulevard. The freeway underpass, just ahead, never failed to worry him. It was too long, too empty. Driving through it, he always felt cut off from the world, vulnerable.

He had walked through it many times in daylight.

Seen disturbing graffiti under there.

LAPD 187

KILL OFAY

He sure would hate to run into the taggers who'd scribbled those charming tidbits. He wasn't a cop. He was white, though. Anyone who enjoyed writing such shit might very well try to kill him.

And such shit got written at night.

He thought about turning around. He could easily go back and take National over to Venice Boulevard. Avoiding the underpass. Avoiding the even creepier area on the other side of it.

As he neared the underpass, though, his headlights showed it to be empty. A broad, barren tunnel.

Nothing to be afraid of.

As he entered, he picked up speed. The engine noise swelled, reverberating off the concrete. On both sides, taggers had left their spray-painted names, symbols and threats—a jumble of secret codes, symbols and bizarre spellings. He'd seen them before, so he'd didn't try to study them now; he tried to ignore them.

I really should've stuck to the main roads, he decided. *This was stupid.*

He left the underpass behind.

On both sides, embankments slanted down from the freeway. The lower areas of the slopes were thick with bushes and trees. Then came the old railroad right-of-way. Unused for years. Overgrown. Scattered with every kind of garbage. Bordered by a ragged chain-link fence that obviously did little good.

Neal didn't even want to *think* about what sort of people might be lurking in there.

Not very long ago, a police officer had been murdered somewhere in that odd little strip of wilderness. Late at night.

LAPD 187

He looked both ways. He saw nobody wandering around. But nearby streetlights showed enough dense foliage to hide a legion of mad predators.

His car bumped over the tracks.

Time for another decision.

Make a left onto the back road or go straight ahead to Venice Boulevard? If he didn't make the left here, he would find himself at Venice on the wrong side of the video store. Also, he would have to turn into the drive-through lane of the Burger Boy where that teenager had gotten murdered last month.

He shook his head and sighed.

One way was probably as bad as the other.

The back road would be more direct.

Narrow, much of it dark under trees that blocked the street-lights, it ran for about half a mile alongside the abandoned rail-road right-of-way. Where God-knows-who might be lurking. Where the cop had been gunned down.

Neal made the turn and stepped on the gas.

To his left, the wilderness. To his right, a row of shabby dwell-ings.

Fun and games if the car breaks down.

His car seemed to be working fine.

Next time, he told himself, just take Robertson and forget about all this back-road crap.

Right. Next time, just forget about returning the damn videos in the middle of the night. You're asking for trouble with this.

Blowing it all out of proportion, that's what you're doing. Better just hope to God nobody ever finds out what a wimp you really are.

Through his open window—mixed in with the mild night air and the sounds from the freeway—came the far-off but distinct cry of a woman shrieking, "Hellllp!"

Neal's stomach clenched.

He looked to the left.

For a moment, his view was blocked by a van parked across the road.

After passing the van, he saw the strip of wilderness leading to the embankment. He slowed down and gazed out his window. High in the distance, cars and trucks sped along on the Santa Monica Freeway. He saw nobody by the side of the freeway, nobody in the grass and weeds of the embankment, nobody in the darkness among the trees and heavy bushes that cloaked the base of the embankment, that spread out toward him over the field of the long-abandoned right-of-way. He saw nobody on the railroad tracks.

He saw no lights over there.

The yell could've come from anywhere, he told himself. He

was fairly used to hearing distant cries and screams. He would sometimes step outside his apartment, glance around and listen for a while. But he had never done more than that. Most such cries, he suspected, came from kids goofing around.

"No!"

Goosebumps prickled Neal's face.

He swerved to the left, swung off the road, hit the brakes, killed the engine and headlights, and yanked his key out of the ignition. Clamping the key case in his mouth, he used his right hand to fling up the lid of his console beside his seat. He fumbled through the compartment, reached under the notepad, change purse, and a stack of napkins and snatched up his Sig Sauer .380 pistol.

He thought about the spare magazine. Down there somewhere. Couldn't afford the time to search for it.

Keys still in his mouth, the pistol in his right hand, he threw open his door with his left and leaped out of his car. He rushed to a gap in the chain-link fence, ducked through it, and ran straight for the deepest, thickest part of the darkness at the bottom of the freeway embankment.

As he ran, he plucked the leather key case out of his mouth. He shoved it into a front pocket of his shorts. Loose down there, it whopped against his thigh with every stride.

His baggy gray shorts looked pale in the night. His legs looked brighter than the shorts. His white socks glared. Only his shoes and shirt were dark.

Should've worn black.

Yeah, he thought. Right. Gotta dress proper for my midnight rescue missions.

He couldn't believe he was doing this.

Must be nuts.

He had never in his life rushed to the rescue of anyone. The opportunity had never come up. He'd never really expected it to come up.

The pistol in his console was meant for self-defense, a last resort in case of attack. He'd bought it after watching news coverage, telecast live from a helicopter, of people being dragged from their cars and beaten nearly to death at the corner of Florence and Normandie back in '92.

You just never know when you might suddenly find yourself in the middle of a riot, or jumped by a thug who wants to jack your car and possibly kill you in the process.

So you carry a gun, just in case.

Illegal as hell, but worth the risk.

Better to be tried by twelve than carried by six.

He wondered if he would be doing this if he didn't have the gun.

Not a chance.

This is nuts, he thought.

But he kept on running, kicking out his legs, pumping his arms, leaping over the dim obstacles of railroad tracks, brambles, ruts, an old tire, a sofa cushion, a collection of crushed cans that smelled of motor oil. He dodged the larger bushes, and a car bumper, several trees, a toilet that smelled as if someone had used it not very long ago, and an old door that lay on the ground like an entrance into the dirt.

Then something snagged his foot.

A root, a strand of barbed wire, maybe an electrical cord from a buried appliance.

He didn't know what, but it grabbed his left foot and held it back. He fell headlong.

On the way down, he almost yelled, "Shit!"

He kept his head, and yelled it only in his mind.

The landing hurt. He whammed down on an unseen mixture of foliage, dirt and junk. Things beneath him crackled, mashed, crunched, scratched him and gouged him. His breath got knocked out. His balls took a hit. He had hot, painful places on his knees and arms and chest. He thought that he must be bleeding here and there.

He wanted to get up fast.

No telling what horrible things might be under him. He easily and quickly imagined plenty: rusty nails, broken glass, a used condom or diaper or sanitary napkin, canine or human turds, spiders, snails or snakes. A half-mashed rat might roll over under his belly and give him a nip.

For a while, though, he was unable to move.

Then he pushed himself to his hands and knees, and stood up. He couldn't stand up straight—too much pain for that. He had to bend over, and it hurt to breathe.

This is what I get for trying to be a hero, he thought.

He felt as if he'd been clubbed in the groin and chest.

Warm trickles were running down from his right elbow and both knees.

"Don't," he heard. "Please."

Not an outcry, more of a sobbing plea.

From somewhere in the darkness of the trees up ahead and off to the left.

Eyes fixed on the area, Neal clenched his teeth and started hobbling. He tried to be quiet about it.

"What'll you give me?" he heard a man say.

"Anything. Please."

A soft chuckle. "That's what I thought."

"I don't want to die."

"Glad to hear it. Know what? I don't want you to die, either. Not for a few more hours, anyhow." More chuckling.

Then came a quick hiss.

"That didn't hurt, did it?"

"Yes." The sad and hopeless tone of her voice made Neal's throat tighten.

"Aw, tough tittie," the man said.

Then came a gasp.

"Or not so tough."

"Please." She wept.

"Awwwww."

"Ow!"

"Hurt?"

"Please."

"Tell me something."

"What?" she sobbed.

"Tell me you're a filthy, stinking slut."

"I'm a filthy, stinking slut."

"You need to be cleansed with pain."

"I need to be . . . cleansed with pain."

"I'm your salvation."

"You're my salvation."

"Please, make me scream."

"Please . . . make me scream."

"You don't sound like you mean it."

"I mean it!"

"Do you?"

"Yes!"

"Liar."

She squealed.

Limping past a tree, Neal saw them ahead and still a distance over to his left—maybe twenty feet away.

Dim, vague shapes that seemed to be facing each other. One blacker than the darkness, one pale. Both mottled by random flecks and dabs of light that reached them through the foliage.

The pale one, definitely the woman, was facing the dark one. She didn't seem to be wearing any clothes. She had her back to a tree trunk. Perhaps she was tied to it. Neal could see her squirming. He heard her sobbing.

The man's dark arm reached toward her. He held something shiny. A small tool of some sort.

Pliers?

"No!" the woman gasped. "Please!"

"Oh yes, oh yes," the man said.

The tool moved toward her left breast.

Neal yelled, "Drop it!"

Both heads turned fast.

The man had a white face masked by wild black hair.

"Drop the fuckin' pliers, Rasputin!" Neal yelled. "I'll blow your head off!"

He flung his arms high. "Don't shoot!" he yelled. "I give! Don't shoot!"

Above his head, speckled with moonlight, Neal saw the pliers in his right hand and a knife in his left. The slim, tapering blade of the knife looked almost as long as the man's forearm.

"Drop that stuff," Neal said, aiming his Sig at the dark figure. Shaking.

Heart racing, pounding.

Mouth as dry as a handful of sand.

The man turned toward him, arms still raised, knife and pliers still in his hands. He looked cadaverous. His black hair and beard hid most of his face except for pale knobs of cheekbones. His long-sleeved black shirt seemed to cling to the bones of his arms and rib cage and hug his sunken belly. The way his black trousers gleamed, they were probably leather. His black gloves appeared to be leather, too.

"Drop the knife and pliers," Neal said.

"Get outta here. Go on. This isn't any business of yours."

"Wanna bet?" Neal said.

"It's just between her and me."

"Not anymore."

"She's my wife."

"It's a lie!" the woman blurted. "He grabbed me! Kidnapped me!"

"See how she lies?"

"You shut up," Neal told him.

"Want in on her?"

"No."

"Just you and me. We do her when we get done, nobody'll ever know the difference."

Neal shook his head.

"Sure you do." In the blackness of the man's beard, teeth appeared. "You a *man?*"

"Please," the woman gasped. "Help me."

"You'd better drop that stuff," Neal said.

"I'll let you fuck her."

"No."

"Then fuck *you*, Charlie," the man said, and threw the knife at Neal.

Neal fired three times as he ducked, the blasts crashing in his ears, the pistol jolting his arm. The man in black, hit, staggered backward a step just as the knife whipped past the side of Neal's face. A couple more steps. Then a hard sit-down. He sat there, arms hanging, the pliers still in his right hand, his legs stretched out and twitching as if he wanted to kick off his boots.

Neal aimed at the shaggy black head and fired again.

The man's head jerked as if kicked under the chin, and he flopped backward.

Chapter Two

"Hello?"

He turned his head toward the sound of the voice and saw the vague, pale shape of a woman standing in front of a tree.

Oh, he thought. Yeah. Her.

The man Neal had shot, stretched out straight on the ground, looked like a black shadow. He hadn't moved in a long time. He hadn't moved at all, in fact, since flopping backward from the head shot.

"Hello?" the woman said again.

Neal looked at her again.

"Are you all right?" she asked.

Sure I am, he thought. Why shouldn't I be? *He's* the dead guy, not me.

"Mister? Are you okay?"

Am I okay? he wondered. After a while, he answered, "Yeah." His voice sounded dull and far away.

"Can you get up?"

Up?

He realized that he was down on his knees. It startled him, upset him. Quickly, he stood up. "I'm fine," he said. "Just . . . I don't know . . . I've never . . . how are *you?*"

"I want to get out of here."

"Are you okay?" he asked.

"Not exactly. Come here, okay? Come over here?"

"Yeah. Okay."

Neal walked toward her. He felt trembly and weak. His right arm, hanging limp by his side, swung with the weight of the pistol.

The woman was naked, just as he'd thought. Her skin looked ghostly pale except for the dark smudges of her eyes, nostrils, mouth, nipples and navel. And except for the blood. He supposed it must be blood—those black and crooked strings that led down her skin from several wounds.

"He cut you," Neal said.

"That's okay. I'll live. Can you untie me?"

"Sure." He started to slip the pistol into the pocket of his shorts, then stopped and looked over at the man he'd shot.

"Don't worry about him."

"Is he dead?" Neal asked.

"He hasn't moved."

"Jesus."

"It's all right. You did the right thing. He was some kind of a maniac."

"Keep an eye on him, okay?"

"I will."

Neal went ahead and slipped the gun into his pocket. Then he stepped past the woman's side. Her left arm slanted away from her shoulder toward the back of the tree trunk. A rope, wrapped around her wrist, was stretched around behind the trunk to the other side, where it bound her right wrist.

Neal decided to stay at her left side, where the woman and the tree blocked his view of the man in black.

She'll tell me if he moves.

With his fingertips, Neal started to pluck at the tight cluster of knots near the woman's wrist. His eyes were no help with the work, so he looked at her.

Beyond her upper arm, her left breast swelled out. Neal had a wonderful view of it, in spite of the poor light. It was rather small and nicely shaped, and the nipple jutted out. It was near enough to touch.

He kept his hands busy with the knots.

"I'm Elise," she said.

"I'm Neal."

"Thank God you came along when you did."

"I heard you yell for help."

"*He* said it wouldn't do any good. He said nobody'd ever hear me. And if they did, they'd ignore it."

"I almost did."

The knots felt hard as iron, but he didn't give up.

He watched Elise's chest expand, breast rising, as she took a deep breath.

"I was taking a couple of movies back to Video City," he explained.

"At this hour?"

"They're due before midnight."

"Are you going to make it?" she asked.

"I don't think so. It doesn't matter."

"Sorry I ruined things for you."

"Are you kidding?"

"I'll be glad to pay your late charges."

"Forget it. Really."

"You saved my life," she said.

"Yeah, I guess so."

"No guessing. My God. Getting killed . . . that wouldn't have been the worst of it, either, I don't think."

"Well, you'll be okay now. Except I can't get the knots undone."

"Maybe you can use his knife."

He remembered the big knife whipping past his ear. "I don't know if I can find it. Anyway, I shouldn't touch it, you know? It'd mess up his fingerprints. We should probably leave everything the way it is, so we don't disturb any evidence."

"Including me?" she asked.

"Well . . . I hadn't actually thought of that. Might not be a bad idea. If they see how he tied you up like this . . ."

"I don't want any cops seeing me." She turned her head as if trying to look at Neal over her left shoulder. "I don't want *anyone* seeing me this way."

Neal blushed. "Sorry," he murmured.

"You're different," she said. "You saved me. Look to your heart's content."

"Uh. Anyway . . ."

"Anyway, are you sure you want the cops getting involved in this?"

"They'll probably show up any minute."

"I don't think so," Elise said.

"Somebody must've reported those gunshots." Even as he spoke the words, he realized how naive he was being. Rarely a night went by when he didn't hear a few distant banging noises that might be gunshots. Or might be, instead, the sounds of slamming doors, automobile backfires, firecrackers, whatever. Some of the noises *had* to be gunfire, but he'd never called the police about any of them.

In this case, the shots had been fired in a strip of thick woods below the Santa Monica Freeway. Nobody passing along on the freeway was likely to have noticed them.

The nearest homes were those shabby places across the field and railroad tracks, beyond the chain-link fence, all the way over on the other side of the road. People living there were probably used to strange noises coming from this direction. Especially backfires.

"If someone called the police," Elise said, "where are they?"

"On their way, maybe. It takes a while . . ."

"It's probably been fifteen or twenty minutes since the shots."

"No," Neal said. "Not even five."

"I haven't exactly checked my watch," Elise told him. On the side of her face that showed above her left shoulder, the corner of her mouth seemed to rise. "It's been a lot more than five minutes, though. You zoned out. You must've been on your knees for at least fifteen minutes."

"No."

"It's true. I just stood here and waited. Tried to pull myself together. But I finally figured we might end up here all night if I didn't speak up. Looks like we're going to be here all night, anyway, unless you go find the knife, or something."

"Not the knife," he said. "I shouldn't touch it."

"Well, find something. Okay?" She sounded about ready to cry again. "I don't *like* this. I want to get *out* of here."

"I'll get something," Neal said. He stepped around to the front of the tree. He looked toward where the knife must've gone after flying past his face.

It should stay where it is, he told himself. Wherever that might be. Let the cops be the ones to find it.

He thought about making a quick return to his car. Probably something there . . . Sure. There should be a pocketknife some-where in the console.

"I could go to my car," he said. "I've got . . ."

"No, don't. Don't leave me alone. Please."

"It'd just take a few minutes."

"Something might happen. Please. Maybe . . . See if *he* has something."

Pliers, Neal thought. Pliers, if nothing else.

"Okay," he said. He walked slowly toward the body. He felt crawly inside.

What if the guy's not dead?

What if he is dead?

Either way, Neal didn't care for the idea of going in close to him.

He pushed a hand deep into the right front pocket of his shorts, took hold of the pistol, and pulled it out. He was fairly sure that he had fired three shots.

No, four.

Three quick ones, plus the head shot.

He was almost certain he'd started off with six cartridges in the magazine, and none in the chamber. He should have two rounds left.

It was a double-action pistol and had no safety, so . . .

Grimacing, he raised the gun close to his face. Not enough light. With his left hand, he fingered the rear area of the slide, searching for the hammer.

He found it all the way back.

In the dark, after blasting the man to the ground, he'd ob-viously forgotten to use the decocking lever. He had dropped the weapon into his pocket, at full cock with a round in the chamber.

Jesus, he thought. Could've blown my leg open.

Keeping the pistol cocked, his finger light against the trigger, he stepped past the man's feet and crouched down. The pliers lay on the ground near the man's right hand.

"Is he dead?" Elise asked.

"I guess so."

"Shouldn't you make sure?"

"You mean like shoot him again?"

"No! Check his vital signs."

"Like his pulse?"

"Yeah."

"I'd have to touch him." Quickly, he added, "Anyway, I don't think it's necessary. He isn't moving. I don't hear any breathing, either. I'm pretty sure he's dead. I mean, I shot him in the head."

For a few moments, Elise was silent. Then she said, "You're going to check his pockets, aren't you?"

"What for?"

"Maybe he has a pocketknife or something."

"I think the pliers'll work fine." Keeping his pistol aimed at the body, he reached for the pliers with his left hand. He watched the man's gloved hand. He half expected it to make a grab for him. But it didn't move. He picked up the pliers and hurried away. After a few steps, he glanced back.

"He isn't coming," Elise said.

"I know."

The pliers in his hand felt contaminated. As if they'd been soiled by all the suffering they'd caused, and might pass the filth to him.

He imagined himself suddenly clamping their jaws on Elise's nipple, squeezing hard, making her scream.

The fantasy sickened him.

Possessed pliers.

They're just a tool, he told himself.

Like my gun.

Stopping by Elise's side, he clamped the pliers under one arm and decocked his pistol. Then he dropped the pistol into his right front pocket. He took the pliers in his right hand.

"Watch out with those, okay?" Elise said.

"Don't worry."

"They can really hurt."

"I bet." Left hand holding her above the wrist, he caught a loop of the knot in the jaws of the pliers and tugged.

And felt the hard knot soften.

"It's coming," he said.

"Thank God."

"Keep an eye on him."

"I am."

Continuing to work on the knot, Neal said, "I mean, I know he's dead, but . . . That's what they *always* think, you know? In the movies? Like *Halloween*, that sort of thing. You always think the bad guy's dead, and then he gets you. I know it's just the movies, but . . ."

"Sometimes life's worse than the movies," Elise broke in.

"Yeah. You can say that again."

"And sometimes it's better."

"Think so?"

"And it's always stranger."

"Stranger?"

"I think so. Yeah."

"Well," Neal said, "all *this* is sure awfully strange. Me just happening to come by at exactly the right time and saving you."

"A few minutes earlier couldn't have hurt."

"Yeah. God. I sure wish . . ."

"I was kidding," she said. "I mean, it *would've* been nice, but on the other hand, I might not've yelled just as you drove by. I wouldn't exactly like to go back in time and give it another whirl. You might miss me altogether, and then where would I be?"

"Good point," Neal agreed.

"I'm not about to quibble about how it turned out. It's like a miracle."

"Or a bunch of lucky accidents."

"I don't believe in accidents," Elise said. "Everything happens for a reason."

"Well . . . I guess you weren't meant to die tonight. And he was."

"And *we* were meant to meet."

He blushed. "Guess so." Then the last twist of rope yielded to the pliers. "There," he said.

Elise sighed. Her wrist shoved against his hand, so he let go. She swung her arm forward, shaking the loose circle of rope off her hand. Then she stepped away from the tree. With a swing of her right arm, she whipped the rope out from behind it.

She hunched over slightly, head down.

Neal looked at her back and the curves of her buttocks and her slender legs.

We were meant to meet.

"Could you help me with this?" she asked. Turning toward him, she held out her right hand. It was still bound with knotted rope.

"Sure."

When he reached out, she took hold of his hand. She gripped it firmly while he used the pliers in his other hand to grab and rip at the knots. He tried to avoid staring at her body. He couldn't help it, though. Sometimes, when he jerked hard with the pliers, her breasts joggled. He could see that happen, even with the bad light. He could also see the neat little patch of hair at her groin.

After a while, he forced himself to look away from her.

He looked toward the body of the man he'd shot.

"Still there?" Elise asked.

"Yeah."

"Thought so." She lifted her left hand away from her side and put it on Neal's shoulder. "Still no police," she said.

"Not so far."

"I don't think they're coming. Not unless we call them ourselves. Which I don't think we should do."

"We have to," Neal said.

"No, we don't."

"Sure, we do."

She squeezed his shoulder firmly, but not so hard that it hurt. "Listen," she said.

He gave the rope a rough tug with the pliers. The jaws slipped off and the pliers leaped sideways. "Damn!"

"Stop it for a minute. Listen. Nobody has to ever find out about any of this."

"He was going to *kill* you."

"Yeah. And he's dead. So it's not as if he has to be apprehended or put on trial or anything. He's already been . . . brought to justice. He's never going to hurt anyone again. So what'll we accomplish by bringing in the cops?"

Neal shrugged. "I'm not sure, but . . . You don't just walk away from something like this."

"Why not?"

"I *killed* this guy."

"In self-defense," Elise reminded him.

"Maybe it won't look like self-defense if we run away. It'll make *us* look like the criminals."

"How will you explain your gun?"

"Tell the truth."

"Do you have a permit, or whatever?"

"Not to carry. Are you kidding? In L.A.? Nobody gets a carry permit. Not unless you happen to be the chief of police, or something. That's why crime's so out of control around here."

"The thing is, are you going to be in trouble?"

"Maybe. They won't prosecute me for killing the guy, I'm pretty sure. Though I guess his family could always sue me. You know, for wrongful death."

"Yeah."

"I guess that's very likely, if he has family. Not that they'd win. But I'd be up to my neck in legal stuff . . ."

"And what about the gun?" Elise asked.

"Carrying a loaded gun in my car . . . I'm pretty sure it's a felony."

Her hand tightened. "You could go to *jail?*"

"I guess it's possible."

"My God. For saving my life?"

"Well . . . The main thing is, I did what had to be done. If I have to go to jail for it . . . those are the breaks. I mean, I sort of assumed that risk when I started carrying the gun. But I'll probably just end up with a suspended sentence and a fine."

"What sort of fine?"

"I don't know. A thousand bucks, maybe."

"Okay, get this rope off me."

He lifted the pliers, clamped the knot, and started tugging again.

"I didn't think it'd be *that* bad," she said.

"What?"

"The trouble you could get into."

"Hell. The way things work these days, you're in trouble if you *look* at someone funny."

"I wasn't going to mention that." A slim crescent of teeth appeared in the blur of her face, then vanished. "Anyway, none of that will happen if we keep quiet about all this."

"I'm the one who'll be in trouble. You haven't done anything wrong."

"Do you think that'll matter? By the time the media gets finished with us?"

Neal grimaced. "You've got a point, there."

"You know exactly what'll happen. They do it to everybody. Doesn't matter how good a person you might be, they won't quit till they make you look like the scum of the earth. If they can't find dirt on you, they'll make something up."

"Yeah. That sort of thing happens."

"All the time," Elise said.

"Well, most of the time." As he said that, the knot gave a bit. He pulled harder. The tight bundle of rope came apart. "There."

"I'll get it." Elise let go of him and worked on removing the rope.

Neal watched her.

She said, "Even if they *don't* try to trash me—and they will—I don't much like the idea of suddenly being known throughout the world as the woman who got abducted and tortured by some sadistic maniac. That I was found naked and tied to a tree. It won't just be strangers who find out about it, either. It'll be everybody who knows me. All my relatives and friends . . ."

"Doesn't sound very pleasant," Neal admitted.

"There'll be pictures of me everywhere. Guys will probably look at them and have daydreams about stripping me and using pliers and knives." She threw the rope down and rubbed her right wrist. "I want to keep my life," she said. "I don't want to become public property."

"You talked me into it."

"You're with me?"

"Yeah. I don't want to end up in court or on *Hard Copy*."

Chapter Three

"Are your clothes around here someplace?" Neal asked.

Elise, still rubbing her wrist, shook her head.

"Here, you can wear this." Neal took off his shirt and gave it to her.

"Thanks." She put it on. As she fastened the buttons, she turned away and walked toward the body. The tail of the big, loose shirt draped her buttocks.

Neal followed her, the pliers in his hand. "What're you going to do?" he asked.

"Borrow his shoes, for starters." Crouching by the body, she started to pull them off. "Don't want to wreck my feet on the way out," she said. "He carried me over here."

He carried her naked?

"I'll carry you out, if you want," Neal offered.

"Thanks, but you don't have to do that."

I wouldn't mind, he thought.

She stood up. Balancing on one foot, then the other, she put on the man's dark sneakers. "Disgusting," she muttered.

"What?"

"Wearing his shoes. But at least they aren't gigantic." She squatted and tied the laces. Then she duckwalked away from the body and tugged a couple of thick, leafy weeds out of the ground.

"What're you doing?" Neal asked.

"I want to hide him."

"Shouldn't we just get out of here?"

She twisted sideways and tossed the weeds at the body. One landed on the chest, the other on the face. "If the cops were coming," she said, "they'd be here by now. Don't you think so?"

"I don't know. Depends on how busy they are, I guess."

"I think they'd show up fast for a report of shots being fired."

"Probably," Neal admitted. He pulled a handkerchief out of his pocket. As he wiped the pliers, he said, "I'd still like to get out of here."

"This won't take long." She pulled out more weeds.

Done wiping the pliers, Neal squatted beside the man. He placed the tool on the ground near the gloved hand.

"The longer he goes without being found," Elise said, "the better off we'll be. Don't you think?"

"Yeah," Neal said. "Things'll deteriorate. It won't be so easy for the cops to pinpoint when he died."

"And people might forget they saw us," Elise added.

"Let's hope nobody *does* see us."

"But if they do, it won't matter so much if the body doesn't get found for a while. If nobody knows for sure when anything happened . . ."

"Yeah. You're right."

"I wish we had a shovel."

"That'd be pushing it," Neal said. "The quicker we get out of here, the better."

"Maybe so."

"You go ahead with that," he told her. "I'll look for my brass."

"Your brass?"

"My cartridge casings. I want to find them if I can. We should try not to leave anything behind."

On hands and knees, he searched the ground to the right of where he had stood while firing. He quickly found two of the shells. The chances of finding all four were remote, but he figured there was no reason to quit. Not yet. Not while Elise continued to work at concealing the body.

She hurried about, pulling bunches of weeds and grass, and even uprooting a couple of small bushes.

Neal found the third casing. It must've flown six feet before landing on the ground beside an old beer can.

"That should about do it," Elise said.

Neal raised his head. The body had disappeared under a cover of foliage.

"I'm still missing one shell," Neal told her.

She came over. On hands and knees, she helped him search. "What happens if we don't find it?" she asked.

"The cops will."

"Does that matter?"

"It might. I'll have to get rid of the pistol, anyway. But the shell might have my prints on it. Partials. Maybe not, but I'd feel a lot . . ."

"Is this it?" Elise picked an object out of the weeds. She held it up between the tips of her thumb and forefinger.

"Let's see." Neal held out his hand. She dropped it into his palm. "That's it. Good going."

"The least I could do."

The four brass casings jingled in the pocket of his shorts as he got to his feet. Beside him, Elise stood up. She bent over and brushed off her bare knees.

"What about you?" he asked. "We can't leave anything of yours behind."

"Nothing here. He just brought me."

"You weren't wearing anything at all?"

"Nothing."

"How about jewelry? Earrings? Anything like that?"

"No."

"Okay, good. Did you touch anything around here?"

"Just the rope, I think."

"That's all right. I don't think they could lift any sort of decent prints off that. What about him? Did you touch him? His pants?"

"With my hands?"

"Yeah. They're leather. That goes for his gloves, too. Any chance your prints might be on them?"

"I doubt it."

"There wasn't any sort of struggle?" Neal asked.

"He got me from behind," she explained. "All of a sudden, I had this arm across my neck. It lifted me right off my feet. I didn't have a *chance* to struggle. Next thing I knew, I was in the back of his van with my hands tied behind me."

"Okay. Good."

"Good?"

"Just that we don't have to worry about his pants and gloves. Anyway, even if you did leave some prints, all that stuff we piled on him'll probably mess them up pretty good." He frowned down at the oblong, bushy mound.

"What?" Elise asked.

"I'm just wondering if we should go ahead and take them anyway, just to play it safe."

"Take what, his pants?"

"And gloves."

"Are you kidding?"

"You could wear his pants," Neal said.

"Not a chance. It's awful enough having his shoes on. If you think for one second . . . no way. Not his pants. Let's just go." She took hold of Neal's hand and pulled him along beside her.

"Are you sure you aren't leaving anything behind?" he asked.

"I'm sure.

"You didn't have a purse, or . . ."

"No purse. Some blood, that's all. I guess I'm leaving some of that behind. Along with some sweat and tears."

"Nobody can identify you from any of that."

"What about DNA and that sort of thing?"

"They might be able to match you to it, but first they'd have to know who you are. You'd basically have to be arrested and indicted before they'd ever run tests like that."

"You seem to know a lot about . . . crime things."

He shrugged. "Not that much. I see a lot of movies, read a lot of books. Watch some trials on TV. That's all."

Before stepping out of the trees, they stopped and scanned the field, the nearby streets, the sidewalks and yards. They saw no one. A couple porch lights. A few lights showing through windows. But no headlights.

Elise let go of Neal's hand and started to run. More of a quick jog than a dash. Neal guessed that she might be afraid to go all-out wearing the large shoes.

He rushed along beside her.

At first, he had almost objected to running. *We'll look too conspicuous.* But he realized it would be a silly argument. At this hour of night, coming through this no-man's-land, they were so out of place that running wasn't likely to draw any additional attention.

Better to hurry and reach the street as fast as possible. They'd be far less conspicuous there.

Except she's not wearing anything but my shirt.

And a dead man's shoes.

As he jogged by her side, he glanced all around. So far, so good. Still nobody in sight. Still no cars coming.

Doesn't mean we aren't being watched.

Doesn't matter, he told himself. In this light, somebody'd have to be right in our faces to get a good look.

A block to the left, the street suddenly brightened with the lights of a car approaching the intersection. "Watch out," Neal gasped. Moments later, the headlights appeared. No turn signal, but the car started to make a left-hand turn.

Elise dropped. Neal dropped.

They were both flat on the ground before the headlights swept by.

Neal kept his head down as the brightness washed over him and went away. Not moving, he listened to the car's engine. A steady, windy noise.

What if it's a cop car?

What if it stops and the cops get out?

The thoughts sickened him.

But the car kept on moving. As its engine sound began to diminish, Neal raised his head. Just a regular passenger car. Near the stop sign at the corner, its brake lights came on, doubling the red brightness of its rear end. Though no turn signal started to blink, the car turned right and headed for the underpass.

In front of Neal, Elise rose to her hands and knees.

The shirttail covered less than when she was standing. A lot less. Neal glimpsed the pale curves of her buttocks, the dark split between them, the backs of her legs. He turned away quickly, feeling guilty.

Looking over his shoulder, he saw the car disappear into the underpass.

When he faced forward, Elise was scurrying up. The shirttail slid down and covered her rump.

Neal scrambled to his feet and ran after her.

Watched her leap the railroad tracks. Watched her duck through the gap in the chain-link fence. Watched her crouch by the side of the van.

A few seconds later, he crouched facing her.

They both huffed for air. His heart was slamming.

"What'll we do . . . with his van?" Elise asked.

"What's in it? Anything of yours?"

"Blood, sweat, whatever."

"Clothes?"

"No."

"Jewelry? Purse?"

"Nothing."

"Fingerprints?"

"My hands were tied behind me. I was on a mattress."

"What's in there?"

"I don't know. It was dark. Should we drive it away? We could leave it a few miles from here, or something."

"We didn't bring the keys."

For a few moments, Elise didn't speak. Neal heard her quick breathing. Then she said, "One of us could go back for them."

"That'd be fun."

"Yeah. Any volunteers?"

Neal imagined himself running all the way back, entering the darkness of the trees, creeping over to the body, reaching into the bushy mound, feeling blindly, digging a hand into a pocket of the dead man's leather pants. All alone.

And what if he's not dead, after all?

And if he *is* dead—a corpse?

I'm all alone in the dark, digging into the pocket of a corpse.

And while I'm busy at that cheerful task, Elise is waiting for me here, all by herself. God only knows who might happen to come along . . .

Have her wait in my car.

Big improvement.

Neal was not about to let *her* go for the keys while he stayed behind. If it came to that, he would go instead.

"We could both go back," Elise suggested.

"Let's just leave the thing here. Even if we had the keys . . . The less we have to do with the van, the better. You never know. We try driving it someplace, we're just asking for trouble. Somebody might see us. We might get stopped by a cop. We'd have to worry about leaving prints inside—hair, blood. Let's not bother. It isn't all that conspicuous here, anyway. It could probably sit here for a week without anyone giving it a second thought."

"You're probably right about that."

"Besides," Neal said, "there might be something inside that'll incriminate the guy. Which would be good for us, in case we do end up getting caught."

"Okay. So we leave it here?"

"Might as well. I'll drive you home in my car. Wait here for a minute. I'll back it up to the rear of the van."

Leaving Elise crouched beside the van, Neal hurried to his car. He jerked open the door. The overhead light came on. He dropped behind the wheel and swung the door shut, quickly but silently. The car went dark.

He reached to the ceiling, removed the courtesy light's plastic cover, and popped the bulb out of its socket. After tossing the cover and bulb onto the passenger seat, he dug the keys out of his pocket. He fumbled in the darkness for the ignition key, found it, slid it in and gave it a twist. The engine started.

Keeping the headlights off, he backed slowly to the front of the van. He stopped and shifted. Brakes on, he called out the window, "Stay low and get into the backseat."

Eyes on the side mirror, he watched Elise rush forward. She squatted beside his car, reached up and opened the rear door. After climbing in, she pulled the door shut gently.

Neal drove forward.

He kept his headlights off.

Chapter Four

After turning right at the corner, Neal put his headlights on. "You okay back there?" he asked.

"Fine."

"Why don't you stay down for a few minutes? I'll go ahead and drop off the videos."

"What time is it?"

He glanced at the bright green numbers of the clock. "Twelve forty-five. Guess there'll be a late charge."

"I'll pay it."

"It's no problem. Let's just make sure nobody sees you."

A couple of minutes later, he steered into Video City's parking lot. Though brightly lighted, it was nearly deserted. A few cars remained on the lot, as if abandoned there. The store's interior was dimly illuminated. Nobody seemed to be inside. Nor was anyone roaming the lot—or loitering near the entrance.

More often than not, a filthy vagrant could be found in front, standing sentry at the video return slot. All set to snatch the videos out of your hand, drop them into the slot, and demand a fee for the service.

Neal had wondered what to do about the guy.

He didn't want to risk an encounter. Best to keep the videos and drive on by . . . return them tomorrow.

He was glad to find the post deserted.

"Coast is clear," he said, and swung into the space in front of the return slot. "Stay down, though. This place is really well-lighted."

He climbed out of the car and walked casually toward the slot, swinging the two videos by his side and keeping his back to Venice Boulevard. It had a fair amount of traffic. He knew he could be seen by anyone in the passing cars.

The night was somewhat cool. After such a hot day, however,

nobody was likely to find it peculiar that he didn't wear a shirt. He hoped Venice was too far away for anyone to notice his injuries, filth and blood.

He dropped the videos through the slot, one at a time, then turned around.

A cluster of cars approached on Venice, still crowded together after being released by a nearby traffic signal.

Neal raised his forearm and rubbed it across his face as if wiping sweat away. He kept his face hidden until after he'd turned toward his car. Quickly, he pulled open the door and climbed in.

"How'd it go?" Elise asked from behind him.

"No problem." He backed out of the space and steered toward one of the exits. "Where to?" he asked.

"Well, you said you'd take me home."

"To your place."

"That'd be perfect," she said. "Do you know how to get to Brentwood?"

"You live in *Brentwood?*"

"If it's too far away . . ."

"No, no. I'll drive you anywhere you want. Hell, I'd drive you to San Francisco if that's what you want."

She made a soft, laughing sound. "Brentwood will do fine."

"Venice runs into Bundy, doesn't it?" he asked.

"Centinela, I think. It turns into Bundy after a while."

He made a right-hand turn out of the parking lot and onto Venice Boulevard. "Where did that guy get you?" he asked.

"At home."

"In Brentwood?"

"Yeah."

"And he brought you all the way over here?"

"It's where we ended up."

"Weird. Maybe this was his home territory. That'd make sense, I guess. If he wanted to take you someplace familiar to him."

"I don't know," she said.

"Do you live in an apartment building?"

"A house."

"A house in Brentwood?" Smiling over his shoulder, he glimpsed Elise curled across the back seat. "You must be loaded."

"Pretty loaded."

"Great."

"You're not going to suddenly hate me, are you? Just because I'm well-off?"

"Nah."

He felt a certain disappointment, though.

"Hope not," she said. "Some people act as if it's a sin to have money."

"Not me," he said. "Do I look like a Commie?"

She laughed softly.

"Do you live alone?" he asked. "I mean, I'm just wondering why this jerk didn't . . . uh . . . why not do everything to you right there in your own house?"

"He wanted to get me screaming. Maybe that's why he took me away. One good scream at my house, and the cops would've gotten hit by so many 911 calls they'd think the Martians had landed. It's a *very* quiet neighborhood. And very nervous. All my neighbors know I live alone. And they know I've had some troubles with my ex-husband. I think they're all expecting him to drop in on me some night with a knife."

"This wasn't him, was it?"

"No. No, no. This guy was a complete stranger."

"Sent by your ex-husband?"

She didn't answer for a while. Then she said, "I doubt it. I think this guy just picked me at random. Maybe saw me out shopping today, or something, and followed me home. You know?"

"Maybe. But if he *was* hired by your ex-husband this might not be the end of it."

"All right if I sit up, now?" she asked.

"It might look funny, the front seat empty and you in the back."

"Pull over and I'll get in front. We'll look like a couple on our way home."

"I don't know. You're not exactly wearing any pants."

"Pull over someplace dark."

"Well . . . All right." He wished she would stay in back, out of sight. He didn't want to argue, though.

If I ever tell Marta about this, he thought, *Elise is going to be dressed from head to toe.*

Better not tell her anything.

I never left the apartment tonight.

Nice. Start lying to her.

He turned onto a narrow street with homes on both sides, found a blot of darkness and pulled over. He cut off his headlights. "Okay."

Before Elise opened the passenger door, Neal picked up the bulb and light cover that he'd tossed onto the seat. He put them into the console.

Elise sat down and shut her door.

Neal made a U-turn. On the way back toward Venice Boulevard, he put his headlights on.

"This is much better," Elise said. She fastened her seat belt. "I didn't like it back there. It was like being a prisoner all over again."

He turned onto the boulevard, and light filled the car. He kept his eyes on the road. "I've got maps in the glove compartment," he said.

"I know the way."

"No, I figured . . . you might want to use one."

"I'm not lost."

He looked at her. She was smiling, and Neal realized this was the first time he'd been able to see her in halfway decent light. She had dirt and blood on her face. And shadows still hid her eyes. But he saw, at once, that she was a beautiful woman.

Her beauty didn't seem austere or threatening. There was something warm about it. Soft and appealing.

"I thought you might want to take out a map and, uh . . . open it."

"Oh." She glanced down at herself. "Nothing shows, really."

Neal lowered his eyes. The front tails of the big, loose shirt were drawn together and tucked between Elise's legs. They formed a triangle that covered her groin but left her thighs almost entirely bare.

"If it makes you uncomfortable . . ."

"Doesn't matter to me," Neal said, and returned his eyes to the road.

"Well, there isn't much of me you haven't already seen."

It was dark then, he thought. He decided not to say it.

"That's all right," he said. "What did the guy do with your clothes, anyway?"

"Nothing. I didn't have any on."

"When he got you?"

"Right. I was in my pool."

"Ah."

"Actually, I was *out* of the pool when he grabbed me. I'd just climbed out, and was on my way over to the diving board. I used to be a diver. Guess I still am. I mean, I still do a lot of diving, but now it's just for fun."

"You used to compete?" Neal asked.

"Oh, yeah. Back in the Dark Ages. Anyway, he must've been hiding somewhere near the pool. I didn't even hear him coming. I was just walking toward the board, and all of a sudden he grabbed me around the neck. I think it must've been one of those holds that cuts off your circulation and makes you pass out."

"And you woke up in his van?"

"Yeah."

"You'd never seen the guy before?"

"I don't think so. But who knows what might've been under all that hair and beard?"

"You're sure it couldn't have been your ex-husband?"

"Vince? No. Not a chance."

"I just keep wondering if you were a random victim, or if maybe there was some other motive."

"I'd guess random victim. I think he was one of these nutcases you hear about. The kind of guy who gets his kicks out of things like torturing and killing people." Looking at Neal, she ran her hands up and down her thighs a few times as if trying to rub away goosebumps. "He didn't rape me, by the way. In case you're wondering. I don't think I'd be feeling quite so chipper . . . Why the hell *do* I feel so chipper? It's not as if I exactly got off unscathed."

"Maybe you're just glad to be alive."

"Something like that. Who knows? I got off light, that's for sure. Thanks to you. My God, if you hadn't come along with your trusty gun . . ." She shook her head and rubbed her legs some more. "I'd probably still be tied to that tree. And screaming for mercy."

"I'm just glad things worked out the way they did."

"You and me both, Neal. Especially me." She laughed softly. "Have you ever saved anyone before?"

"No. Not hardly."

"What do you suppose a customary reward might be for rescuing a person from . . . that sort of a situation?"

Neal blushed. He was sure Elise couldn't see it, though. "I don't want any reward," he said.

"Whether you want it or not, you're going to get it."

He looked at her. She was smiling.

"I'm not taking any money from you," he insisted.

"Why not? Are you rich?"

"Ha. That'll be the day."

"What do you do?" she asked.

"I'm a substitute high school teacher."

"And?"

"And?" he asked.

"What else? You're a sub and you live in Los Angeles. Therefore, you must be trying for a career in the movies. Not an actor, though. You're not the type. Screenwriter?"

He shook his head. "That's right."

"And you specialize in crime stories?"

"You must be psychic."

"I just pay attention," she said.

"What do *you* do?" he asked.

"When I'm not being abducted by psychos?"

"Right."

"Mostly, I drift. Have you had any luck at all with your scripts?"

"Nothing worth mentioning."

"And you sub. Are you sure you should go around turning down money?"

"I'm *not* going to take money for saving you. No way. Not a chance."

"Okay," she said.

"Good," he said.

"That's not what I'm planning to give you, tonight."

"Good, because I wouldn't take it."

"I'm going to give you something much more valuable than money."

"And what would that be?"

"You'll find out."

Chapter Five

He stopped his car at the gate of Elise's driveway. Through its wrought iron bars, he saw that the driveway led to a garage with a closed door.

"Wait here and I'll open the gate," Elise said.

"Okay."

She climbed out and walked around the front of the car. Neal watched her in his headlights. The shirttail over her buttocks shifted with each stride. Below it, her legs were long and slender. She still wore the shoes that she'd taken off the dead man. They looked huge on her, but she seemed to have no trouble walking in them.

At a post beside the gate, she tapped a few numbers on a keypad—her security code, Neal supposed.

She stepped through the gate as it swung open. Inside, she moved out of the way and waved Neal forward. He drove through. The moment he stopped the car, his passenger door opened and Elise leaned in.

"Come on into the house," she said.

"I really should be getting home," he told her.

The best way to avoid becoming more deeply involved with

this woman, he'd already decided, was simply to drop her off and leave. If he went into her house, no telling what might happen.

At the very least, she was bound to bring up the business of a reward.

"Just come in for a few minutes," Elise said. "I have something for you."

"I don't want anything. Really."

She smiled. "Shouldn't you wait and see what it is?"

"No, I don't think so."

"Well, then, come in and have a drink with me."

"I'd better be getting home," he said.

"Please?"

The way she said it, Neal realized she might be afraid to go into her house alone.

Should've known. After what she's gone through tonight . . .

He suddenly felt like a jerk. He should've *offered* to go in with her, check around, make sure it was safe.

"Okay," he said. "But just for a few minutes."

"Great. Thank you." She stepped away from the door and shut it.

Neal climbed out. They met in front of his car.

"I don't have my keys," she said. "We'll have to go around to the back."

She led the way, leaving the driveway and walking across the grass of the front lawn. Thick shrubbery and a brick wall stood between the narrow lawn and the road. But Neal glimpsed the road through a small, open gate.

"Is that how he came in?"

"I don't know," Elise said. "He might've jumped a wall, or something. It's probably the way he carried me out, though."

Neal went to the gate and shut it. Reaching over it, he tried the knob. It turned in his hand. "You don't keep this locked?"

"Not all the time."

"Maybe you should."

"Vince was the nut about security," she said. "The way I see it, if they're gonna get you, they're gonna get you."

"Tonight, they got you."

She turned to Neal. A corner of her mouth lifted. "Almost," she said.

From the gate, a walkway led to the front door. Above the door, a light was on.

"Have you got an alarm system?" Neal asked.

"Yep."

"I hope you use it."

She flashed another smile at him. "Sometimes." She resumed walking. Neal looked at the house as he followed her.

He was a little surprised to see how normal it appeared. He hadn't exactly known what to expect. Something more impressive, he supposed. But this looked pretty much like a typical Los Angeles home—or an old Spanish mission. A low, sprawling structure of stucco, red tiles, and arches. It looked fairly large. Certainly not a mansion, though.

Just priced like one, more than likely.

If she can afford a house like this, he thought, she could probably throw a hundred thousand at me without even blinking.

I don't want her money.

Besides, she probably got this place in her divorce settlement. She might not be . . . no, she admitted she was loaded.

Doesn't matter, he told himself. I'm not taking a penny from her.

He followed her around the corner. There, a small grove of fruit trees stood between the side of the house and the brick wall at the edge of the property. No light came from the windows of the house. When they entered the grove, darkness surrounded them.

Neal walked slowly, ducking beneath low limbs, keeping his eyes on Elise. She was a vague, moving blur.

At the rear of the house, they stepped out of the trees. No lights were on, but there were no trees to shade the area. It seemed bright after the walk through the grove.

Back here, the pool dominated everything. A large, rectangular swimming pool with two diving boards at the far end: a low board and a high dive. The pool was bordered by a broad, concrete apron. Neal could see a few places where the concrete appeared to be wet—probably where Elise had climbed out of the water earlier that night.

Just off the nearest corner of the pool was a hot tub. Close to the house were a couple of padded lounges. Farther off, but also near the house, Neal saw a barbecue grill, a table and a set of chairs.

As they walked past the lounges, Elise reached down and plucked a large towel off one of the pads. She flopped it over her shoulder.

"Why aren't there any lights on?" Neal asked.

"I didn't have them on." Elise turned and headed for the sliding glass door.

"You were diving in the dark?"

She glanced over her shoulder at him. "Makes it more interesting."

"I'll bet."

She rolled open the sliding door. "Actually, you can see pretty well by the full moon."

Neal followed her inside. A lamp came on. The brightness made his eyes ache. Squinting, he saw that he was standing in a large bedroom. It looked feminine, fresh and tidy.

Elise tossed her towel onto the king-size bed.

Heading for a doorway at the corner of her room, she glanced over her shoulder and said, "Why don't you come along? I'll show you the guest restroom. You want to clean up, don't you?"

"It can wait till I get home."

"There's no need for that. Just relax, all right?"

He followed her into a hallway.

After flicking on a light, she walked to the right. "If you'd like to take a shower," she said, "I'll find you something clean to wear."

"No, really. I'm fine."

She reached through a doorway and flipped a light switch, then turned toward him.

For the first time, he was able to get a look at her in good light. Her face was filthy, smudged with dirt and blood, and more beautiful than he had imagined. He had never seen such eyes.

They were shocking. A rich, blue-green color unlike any eyes he had ever seen before.

She had hair like a pixie. Short, golden, but wildly mussed.

Her shirt was unfastened partway down. It showed her throat, the curves of her collar bones, and a narrowing strip of tanned skin down the middle of her chest. The skin there looked shiny with sweat. A few inches below her throat was a smear of blood.

In several places, her blood had soaked through the shirt. Some of the blood, Neal realized, might be his own. The rips and dirt, and likely some of the blood, had probably been the result of his rough fall in the field.

Most of the blood, though, had to be Elise's.

Her legs looked as if someone had rubbed them, thigh to knee, with wet red hands.

"I'll have to find you something to wear," she said. "Your shirt's ruined."

"That's all right. I'll . . ."

"What *happened* to you, anyway?" she asked.

"Huh?"

"You're a wreck, too."

He looked down at himself. He was a little surprised to find that he was bare to the waist. He had a few scratches on his chest and belly. And some reddish areas that would soon become bruises. Nothing serious. His shorts were filthy in front, but not torn. Layers of skin had been scraped off both his knees. His elbows were probably as bad as his knees, but he didn't bother to look at them.

"I took a little fall," he explained.

"I didn't see it."

"On my way over to you."

"I'm sorry."

"Hey, it's nothing. Really. You're the one who got messed up."

She shrugged. "You really should take a shower," she said. "Wait here a second."

She hurried past him, disappeared briefly into her bedroom, and returned with a white terry cloth robe. She held it out to him. "You can put this on after you're done, and I'll run your things through the wash."

"It's really not necessary."

"You'll feel a lot better once you're all nice and clean."

"I don't . . ."

"Please."

He sighed. "Well . . . okay." He took the robe from her.

"Good. When you're finished, just make yourself at home. There's a bar in the den." She nodded down the hall. "Go ahead and make yourself a drink if I'm not out yet."

"Do you want me to look the place over, first? Make sure nobody's . . . you know, lurking around?"

"Don't bother. Unless you want to. I don't think there's anything to worry about. Two attackers in one night? What're the odds?"

"Not very great," Neal admitted. "Unless the guy had an accomplice."

"I didn't see one."

"People like him usually work alone. Not always, but usually."

"I'm not worried. If you're worried, though, feel free to look around. My house is your house. In the meantime, though, I have to get cleaned up." She turned away and headed for her bedroom. Not looking back, she raised a hand and said, "Later." Then she was gone.

Neal stood in the hallway, holding the robe, listening. When he heard the water start to run, he figured that Elise was safe: nobody, at least, had jumped her in the master bathroom.

He entered the guest bathroom, shut the door, and hung the robe on a hook.

The doorknob had a lock button.

He thumbed it down.

Just in case, he thought.

He looked at himself in the enormous mirror over the sink and counter, and shook his head.

You're nuts if you think she'll try to come in.

Am I? he wondered. I'm not such a bad-looking guy, we're about the same age, she obviously likes me, and I *did* save her life.

He started unloading his pockets onto the counter by the sink.

She won't come, he told himself. For one thing, I told her all about Marta in the car. For another, I'm not in her class. Financially *or* physically. Not even close. Gals like her don't get involved with guys like me.

She's awfully grateful, though. Who knows? Maybe my reward will be a visit while I'm showering.

Done emptying his pockets, he took off his shoes and socks, his shorts and briefs.

It seemed odd to be naked in a stranger's house.

We're not exactly strangers, he told himself. I did save her life.

He could hear the faint, rushy sound of water from the other bathroom.

She's naked, too, he thought. We both are.

Separated only by a few walls and doors.

He pictured her standing under the other shower, water cascading down her body, her skin agleam.

What would she do if I went to her?

He smirked and shook his head.

No way, he thought. And if she tries coming to me, she'll have to pick the lock.

Chapter Six

When Neal was done showering, he couldn't hear water from Elise's bathroom. He dried himself, keeping the towel away from the abrasions on his knees and elbows. He used toilet paper to pat those areas dry. The wounds seemed a little leaky, but not bad.

A gentle knocking on the door made him flinch.

"It's me," Elise said.

He snatched the robe off the hook.

"When you're done," Elise continued, "just leave your clothes in there, and I'll . . ."

Robe on, he said, "Just a second." He shut the robe and tied its cloth belt. "You can have them now." He opened the door.

Elise smiled. "Good timing," she said. She looked wonderfully fresh and clean. Her short hair, damp and shiny, was neatly combed. Her face was a little flushed from the shower. She wore blue satin pajamas. Here and there, small drops of moisture had seeped through the top. "What?" she asked.

He shrugged. "Nothing. You look . . . like nothing ever happened to you."

"You should see all the bandages under my pj's. Here, let me in and I'll pick up your stuff."

"I'll do it," he said.

"No, no. Go on to the bar and make yourself something. I already turned the lights on for you. Next room down the hall. You can't miss it. I'll be along in a couple of minutes. Make me a vodka and tonic, okay?"

"Well . . ." He wondered if there might be an inconspicuous way to rescue his briefs from the small heap of clothes on the bathroom floor. Sort of embarrassing to think of Elise picking them up.

"Chop-chop, move it or lose it."

"Let me get my socks and underwear," he muttered.

"They'll be safe with me. I promise. Out of my way, buddy."

Blushing, Neal smiled and shook his head and stepped past her. She entered the bathroom.

Okay, he told himself. No big deal. Forget it.

The next room down was lighted, just as she'd said. An L-shaped counter occupied a corner near the sliding doors to the pool. It had four padded stools in front of it.

Neal stepped down off the hallway and walked toward the bar. The carpet felt soft and thick under his bare feet.

Ahead of him, a wall of glass faced the pool area. He couldn't see the pool, though. He couldn't see much of anything out there. The glass, like a black mirror, reflected the living room and Neal walking in the white terry robe.

He looked a little transparent. So did everything else.

He didn't enjoy the view.

He wondered if someone might be on the side of the glass, staring in.

Turning away from the glass, he gave the den a casual scan. It had a long oak coffee table, a large sofa that looked very comfortable, several lamps and a few reclining chairs. Most of the wall space consisted of bookshelves. Across the floor from the sofa was a television with a screen that looked about four times larger than the screen of Neal's TV.

Man, he thought, what would it be like to watch some videos on *that* baby!

That's a reward I might be tempted to accept.

But I won't, he told himself. I won't accept anything. Wouldn't be right.

Before stepping behind the bar, he grabbed the handle of the sliding door and pulled. The door skidded sideways.

My God, he thought. Doesn't she lock anything? She's lucky she's lasted *this* long.

He shut the door and locked it.

Then he stepped around the bar. Behind it were shelves of drinking glasses and bottles, a sink, and a small refrigerator. He took down a couple of glasses. In the freezer compartment of the refrigerator, he found ice cubes.

What a setup, he thought. What a house. Must be incredible to live like this.

What the hey, he thought. You, too, might have a place like this someday. All it'll take is a little luck, a little hard work, a major miracle . . .

From somewhere near the other end of the house came a faint, low humming sound. The washing machine starting, he supposed.

He made a vodka and tonic for Elise, and the same for himself. He had just squeezed a wedge of lemon into each drink when she arrived.

"All set," she said, stepping down into the den. "Did you find everything you needed?"

He lifted both glasses.

"Great." She walked toward the bar, her bare feet silent on

the carpet. Neal saw the way her breasts were moving inside her satin pajama shirt, and looked away.

My God, he thought, if Marta ever found out about this. . . .

Not that I've done anything wrong.

Just that it would *seem* so bad.

Elise stopped at the other side of the bar. As she reached for one of the drinks, her sleeve slipped away from her wrist.

She wore a brilliant, gold bracelet.

It looked heavy and very expensive.

Though Neal only caught a glimpse of the bracelet, it appeared to have a reptile design—a slender body in the shape of a lizard, or maybe an alligator or snake.

"Thank you, sir," she said as she took the drink.

"Thank *you*. Your stuff."

"What's mine is yours."

"No. Huh-uh."

"Oh yes it is. Everything. From now on."

"I don't want anything of yours," he told her. "Really."

"You don't have to take anything you don't want," she told him. "But everything is yours."

He shook his head.

She smiled. "Anyway, don't worry about it. Why don't you come over here and sit down?"

Carrying his drink, he stepped around the bar. He followed Elise to the sofa. She sat on it, switched the glass to her other hand, and patted the cushion by her side. "Right here," she said.

Neal sat beside her, but a little farther away than she'd indicated.

She turned toward him, lifting her arm onto the back of the sofa and sliding her right leg onto the cushion. She bent her leg at the knee, and tucked its foot beneath her left knee.

She raised her glass. "A toast," she said. "To a fate worse than death, and the fellow who saved me from it."

"Well . . ."

She clinked her glass against his, then took a drink. "Mmmm. Very good."

Neal tasted some of his, then took a large swallow. He sighed. "Does hit the spot," he said.

"Now, down to business."

"There isn't any business, Elise. Really. I don't want a reward. I just happened to be at the right place at the right time, and things worked out. I'm really *glad* I saved you. I mean, I think you're . . . a very nice woman."

She grinned. "Nice?"

"Hell, you're terrific."

"Thank you."

"So, I mean, saving you was its own reward. You know what I mean?"

"I know. But I'm not going to let it go at that."

"You can't make me take anything."

"I'm not going to try. I already told you that. But everything is yours, when you want it. And I intend to write a will . . ."

"No, don't. My God."

"That's all right, I don't plan to die in the near future."

"You can't put me in your *will*."

"Sure I can. And I *will*. That's why they call it a 'will.' "

"No, jeez."

"Don't sweat it, I might even outlive you. How old are you, anyway?"

"Twenty-eight."

"I'm thirty-two, so . . ."

"You are?"

"I know, I'm well preserved."

"My God. I would've thought twenty-five."

"Thanks, I guess. Anyway, I don't have any family. You're the most important person in my life, Neal."

"The most . . . ? No. Come on. Maybe I seem that way tonight, but . . ."

"You *saved* me," she said with a sudden fierce urgency. "Don't you *get* it? I'd be toast right now . . . or maybe screaming my head off and *wishing* I was dead. He would've killed me, sooner or later. No question about it. I'd be dead. So this is the thing: I'd have *nothing* if it weren't for you. No house, no bank accounts, no jewelry, no future, nothing. No me. So it's all yours."

"But I don't want . . ."

"I know, I know. And I understand that, and I accept it. You don't have to take anything. But everything is yours, regardless. Everything."

His mouth suddenly felt awfully dry. He took another drink. "You don't mean . . ." He couldn't say it.

"Me?"

He nodded.

"Of course."

He heard himself moan.

Elise's smile returned. "Don't worry about it. If you're in love with Marta . . . just figure you've always got me in reserve, if you want me."

"You gotta be kidding," he mumbled.

"I think you know better than that."

"You don't even know me."

"I know enough," she said. "I'm yours—if and when you want me."

Elise took another drink, then leaned out toward the coffee table and set down her glass. "Everything that's mine is yours," she said. "Whenever you want it. But I *would* like you to have this tonight."

She slipped the gold bracelet off her hand, and held it toward him.

A snake—a single, thick coil of intricately detailed gold, the head swallowing the tail. The eyes of the snake were a pair of brilliant green gems. Emeralds?

Neal shook his head. "No, no. I can't take that."

"It's the most valuable thing I have."

"All the more reason."

"Put out your hand."

"Elise."

"Please. For me."

"What am I supposed to tell Marta, she sees me with a thing like this?"

"Just the truth. Or don't let her see it. That's up to you."

"I can't take it. Really."

"Just try it on for a minute."

He couldn't see any harm in that, so he switched the glass to his left hand and held his right toward Elise. She slipped the bracelet over his hand and around his wrist.

It was warm from being on Elise.

It felt heavy.

"Really beautiful," he said.

"It's a lot more than that."

"What do you mean?"

"It's not just beautiful, it's magical."

Smiling, he raised his eyes to Elise. "It does card tricks?" he asked.

"I'm serious."

"A magic bracelet?"

"That's right. It was a gift to me. I've had it since I was sixteen. It was a present from . . . a very wonderful man. A poet. His name was Jimmy O'Rourke. We fell quite madly in love. But he had to go back to Ireland."

"An Irishman?"

Elise nodded. "He was over here as a guest lecturer at UCLA."

"How old was he?" Neal asked.

"Oh, thirty-five."

"And you were sixteen?"

"I know. Awful. But I was smitten. He was lovely, and you should've heard him talk." She sighed. "Anyway, I met him when I was with some girlfriends over in Westwood Village. We were browsing through a bookstore, and . . . he started talking to me. He hardly had two words out of his mouth before I was head over heels. After that, we could hardly stay away from each other."

"What about your parents?"

"They didn't know anything about him. I made up stories about going over to a friend's house. Or to the mall. Or to the beach. But the friend was always Jimmy O'Rourke, and my folks never caught on. They would've been horrified, no doubt about it—their daughter going around with a man that age. Not that we . . . there was nothing at all sordid about it. We were so much in love."

Neal saw tears in her eyes.

"Then the end of summer came, and Jimmy's mother phoned

him from Shannon. His sister'd been in a car accident. She was in critical condition, and they didn't know whether she would make it." Sniffing, Elise wiped her eyes.

"Did she live?" Neal asked.

"I don't know. I never heard from Jimmy again, after he left. Before he went away, though, he gave me this." With the tips of her fingers, she patted the bracelet on Neal's wrist. "He called it a 'faerie bracelet.' Apparently, back when he was a student at Trinity, he was out on the town one night and happened across a burning building. He heard someone screaming, so he rushed in. He found a blind woman upstairs. She was hysterical, didn't know which way to go. So Jimmy picked her up and carried her outside. Saved her life. She was wearing this bracelet, and she gave it to him. She insisted that he take it. And she told him that he was free to give it away, whenever he pleased, if he should find someone deserving. So he gave it to me."

"Did you save his life?" Neal asked.

"No."

"Why did you deserve it?"

"He loved me." Tears again came to her eyes. "He told me that he had never loved anyone the way he loved me. And that I deserved to have a life full of wonders and strange delights." Again, she used the back of her hand to wipe her tears away. Then she sniffed. "So, that's that."

Neal's throat felt tight. He swallowed, then said, "You never heard from him again?"

"Never."

"Why? If he loved you so much . . ."

"I don't know."

"Did you ever try to get in touch with him?"

"I wrote him letters. Scads of letters. I never mailed any of them, though." She shrugged. "I was afraid . . . they might be returned to me. Maybe marked 'deceased,' or . . . I don't know, I just didn't have the courage. For all I really knew, he might've had a wife. He claimed that he didn't, but who knows? I didn't want to find out."

"Must've been awful for you."

"I was heartbroken. But I had the bracelet. I don't know if I could've survived without it. I might've done a triple back-flip off a freeway overpass. But the bracelet kept me going. It helped take my mind off Jimmy."

Neal slipped the bracelet off his hand. He held it out to her. "There's no way I can take this."

She shook her head. "I want you to have it."

"It means too much to you."

"It's yours, now. Use it for as long as you wish, then pass it on if you find someone you feel should have it."

He shook his head. "I don't know."

"Put it back on. Please." A corner of Elise's mouth tilted upward. "Take it, or else."

"Or else what?"

"You'll risk my wrath, which is indeed a terrible thing to behold."

Neal broke into a grin. "I bet," he said.

"Go ahead and put it back on. Please. We'll have a little demonstration. Once you find out what it does, I think you might have some second thoughts about turning it down."

He slid the bracelet onto his wrist again. "Okay. What does it do?"

Chapter Seven

Elise patted Neal's leg through the robe, then leaned forward and picked up her glass. "You should probably lie down," she said. "I'll get out of your way." She stood up and walked around to the other side of the table.

"Why do I want to lie down?" Neal asked.

Elise grinned. "Don't give me trouble. It's how it's done."

"Okay." He took another drink, then set his glass on the table. Holding the robe to keep it from falling open, he swung his legs onto the sofa and sank down onto his back. He rested his hands on his belly.

"Very good," Elise said. "Now, close your eyes."

"What's supposed to happen?"

"You'll see."

"Not if my eyes are shut."

"Are you going to be difficult?"

"No, no, not me." He closed his eyes.

"Now, kiss the serpent's head."

"You're kidding."

"Neal."

"How can I kneel when I'm lying down?"

"Very funny. Kiss the serpent's head."

"Okay." Keeping his eyes shut, he lifted his right hand to his face. Then he hesitated.

"Do you want to give me a hint?" he asked.

"There's nothing to be afraid of."

"If this thing does some kind of magic stuff, I really don't want to get involved."

"I'm surprised you believe in magic."

"I don't. But it scares me."

"You trust me, don't you?"

"I guess so. Sure, I do."

"Do you think I'd ask you to do something dangerous?"

"I guess not."

"There *are* a few dangers, but nothing you need to worry about. Not yet. This is just a trial run."

"What dangers?"

"Later, all right?"

"I think I'd rather find out that sort of thing *before* I take my trial run."

Elise laughed softly. He looked at her. She was smiling, shaking her head. "I'm still here, right?" she asked. "Still in one piece? Still sane?"

"You seem to be."

"Well, I've used the bracelet thousands of times."

"Thousands?"

"I've had it for sixteen years, Neal. I can't say that I've used it every single day—I went through periods without using it at all. Other times, though, I might've used it . . . I don't know, eight or ten times in one day."

"Well, I guess you survived it okay."

"I'm sure you will, too."

"This *guy* didn't have anything to do with the bracelet, did he?"

Her smile died. "I don't think so. I don't see how . . . no. Look, if you'd rather not do this . . . I'll tell you something, though. I've never much regretted anything that I've done in my life. What I regret are a few of the things I decided *not* to do. If you don't give the bracelet a try, Neal, you might look back on tonight, in years to come, and wonder what would've happened—and wish like hell that you'd taken the chance."

"Can't you just tell me what the thing is supposed to do?"

"It'll change your life."

"Maybe I like my life the way it is."

Her smile returned. "You'll *love* what the bracelet does. I promise."

"What *does* it do?"

"Try it and find out."

"Okay." He smirked at her. "Here goes nothing." He turned his face toward the ceiling, shut his eyes, and touched the bracelet to his mouth. He felt the emerald eyes against his lips. He felt the warm gold.

Soothing.

As he waited for the next instruction, he kept the bracelet to his mouth and thought of Elise's lips. She must've kissed it thousands of times. Her lips had touched it here, just where his lips were touching it now.

Feeling pleasantly light-headed, he pictured himself floating up from the sofa. Elise watched him. With the hand that didn't hold her drink, she gestured for him to approach. "Right this way," she said. "Come on in."

Don't mind if I do, he thought.

And suddenly he was inside her.

As if looking through Elise's eyes, he saw himself stretched out on the sofa, his hands again resting on his belly, his eyes shut. He appeared to be asleep.

I'm asleep, all right. Dreaming this whole bit.

Is he here yet? Must be. "Hello? Neal? Are you in me? Welcome aboard."

Jesus, he thought.

He could feel everything: Elise from head to toe, inside and out. She had numerous pains, but didn't seem especially bothered by them. She was a little trembly, nervous and excited—and thrilled to have him aboard.

Neal tried to speak, but couldn't: not from his own body on the sofa, not from Elise.

So he said in his mind, "I'm here, Elise. What's going on? Has to be a dream, right?"

Elise thought: "*Actually, I can't hear you. This is pretty much a one-way deal, Neal.*" *I'm a poet, but I don't know it. My feet show it. Longfellows. Stop that, he'll think I'm an idiot.* "*Neal? You can't communicate with me. I can't even tell whether or not you're in here, but I assume you are. So, how do you like it so far?*"

Incredible, he thought.

Let's see how he likes this.

She lifted the glass and drank.

Neal felt the cold rim of the glass on his lips—on *her* lips. He felt the liquid flood her mouth, chill her teeth. He felt the sizzle of the tonic, tasted the vodka and the tart lemon. Then she was swallowing. It was as if *Neal* were swallowing. He felt the drink slide down his gullet, grow warm in his belly.

All the while, Elise kept on thinking. Not as if talking to Neal, but going along on her own—talking to herself but also wondering and considering things on other levels, a level or two (maybe more) that seemed deep down and barely articulate.

A little like listening to a radio that was picking up a few different stations—some coming in more clearly than others, some nearly inaudible.

She lowered the glass.

Hope he's not freaking out in there. "How's it going Neal?" *Let's see what he thinks of this.*

She turned around and started walking across the den.

Neal felt every movement. Very much as if he were the person walking, but different because he had no control. He was merely a passenger along for the ride.

A passenger riding in Elise.

He felt her muscles work. He felt the carpet under her bare feet, and the satin of the pajamas sliding softly against her skin. He felt how her breasts, rather small and not very heavy, sprang up and down with each step. He felt the solid tightness of her flexing buttocks, and a curious absence of weight and movement at her groin.

This is what it's like to be her, he thought.

Fabulous.

Except for the pain.

The bastard had done real numbers on her. Neal felt where she had been cut by the knife, pinched by fingers, teeth or pliers—hurt in other ways. Where she wore bandages, he detected a slight stiffness on her skin.

Her face seemed fine. But the guy must've really worked on her breasts. They hurt all over, and Elise seemed to be wearing about seven bandages on them. Her nipples were very sore, but not bandaged. She wore a few bandages on her belly, and a couple on her left buttock. The lips of her vagina burned as if they'd been pinched or gnawed. Neal didn't feel bandages down there.

He found no pain deep inside her. She'd apparently told the truth about not being raped.

While Neal concentrated on the sensations of her body, Elise walked slowly about the room, holding her nearly empty glass. Though she was thinking nonstop, she didn't seem to be addressing Neal, so he paid little attention.

He was fascinated.

Is this what the bracelet does? It gives you a ride like this?

Incredible!

It's like I'm her!

"You all right?" Elise asked in her mind.

Fine, he thought.

"I've never done this before." It's kind of spooky having him in me. Seems like a great guy, though. But God, it's so intimate. Has he paid a visit to my pussy, yet? Oh shit, what if he heard that? Of course he heard it. Be grateful, at least you didn't call it . . . No no no no. "Hello there, Neal. Hey, look, time to vacate the premises, *okay? This was just to give you a little taste."* Must've been out of my mind. *Oh, great, now he's probably heard that, too. Probably, my ass. Ass. Terrific.* "Now that I don't have any dignity left, Neal. Anyway, you saved my life, so now you haven't got any illusions about who you saved." *Hey, I'm not that bad. Could've been a lot worse. Get him out of here!* "Neal? Hey! Time to go, okay? If you're still here. Are you? Anyway, you have to wish yourself back into your own body." *What if he won't leave? What if he likes it in here so much . . ."*

He was out.

No longer inside Elise, no longer feeling the weight and motion of her body, no longer seeing what she saw, feeling what she felt. No more eavesdropping on her mind.

At least the pain was gone. But it had been a small price to pay for the multitude of other sensations.

He felt sad and lost. He wanted to return to her.

Knew he shouldn't, though.

So he settled down into the body that was stretched out on the sofa as if asleep.

Home.

Nothing exciting or strange about this body. It felt familiar all over. His weight, his size, his muscles. All the same as when he'd left. Though he could feel several sore areas, he seemed remarkably free from pain, compared with Elise.

He opened his eyes and turned his head.

Elise, standing at the other side of the table, grimaced at him and blushed fiercely. She shrugged. "So," she said. "That's the magic bracelet."

"Wow," he said. He sat up and swung his legs off the sofa. Leaning forward, he picked up his glass. He took a few big swallows of his vodka and tonic.

Elise's had tasted better.

"Sorry I had to kick you out," she told him.

"That's all right."

"It was . . . it got embarrassing."

"Nothing to be embarrassed about."

"I should've known better. I mean, I've been in enough people to know you can't hide anything from a hitcher. The mere act of *trying* to hide something reveals it. Almost always. You have to think it to avoid it. The whole situation is impossible. Not to mention, the hitcher gets to feel every part of the person's body. Forget any kind of privacy."

"I thought it was great."

She made a face and shrugged her shoulders. "Great if you're the hitcher. But God, it's such an *invasion* of the people you're in."

"They don't know it's happening?" Neal asked.

"They haven't got a clue. So, in a sense, there's no damage done. They don't *know* that every corner of their being is getting explored by a secret intruder. Hell, *I* didn't know for sure. I just assumed you were in me."

"I was."

"Well, that's what I figured. I mean, that was the whole idea."

"I thought I was dreaming. At first, anyway."

"You weren't dreaming."

"I was 'hitching.' "

"That's it. Like hitching a ride. A *lot* like hitching a ride. This was a little different, tonight, because we know each other. Usually, you'll be taking your rides in strangers. I mean, that's where the real adventure comes in. You know little or nothing about them. You just jump aboard and ride them down the road for a while, see where they take you. When you've had enough—or if things get hairy—you bail out."

"Sounds simple enough," Neal said, then polished off his drink.

"It *is* simple. It can get nasty, though. My God, I've gone through some incredible things."

"Incredibly good or incredibly bad?"

"Both. You wouldn't believe it. Just wait and see for yourself. I'm getting another drink. Want one?"

"I'll make them," he offered, and quickly got to his feet.

Elise smiled over her shoulder at him as she walked toward the bar. "It's all right. I'm perfectly capable—"

"Maybe you should sit down and take it easy. I mean, I know you're in a lot of pain."

Her face went crimson. "Guess you know everything. It isn't

that bad, though. Give me your glass. I'll make these."

He surrendered his glass.

Elise stepped behind the bar. "Pull yourself up a stool," she said.

He hopped aboard one of the stools. Leaning forward, he put his elbows on the counter. And winced.

"I'd say we're both in some pain."

"Mine is nothing compared to yours," Neal said.

"I guess you're in a position to know. Women are tougher than guys, though."

"Is that so?"

"That's so. When it comes to pain. Believe me, I know." She started to make the drinks, and kept on talking. "I know damn near everything there *is* to know about people. You hitch enough rides, you find out . . ." She shook her head. "More than you want to know. But it's always fascinating. You're a writer, so this'll be like a godsend. You'll run into so many odd characters and weird stories you won't know what to do with them all. Your main problem will be pulling yourself away from the hitching . . . finding time to write. Finding time for *anything* else, as a matter of fact. Which is Warning Number One: don't let it run your life. If you're not really careful, you'll get addicted."

"Yeah, I can see how that might happen."

"It *will* happen. Just fight it like any other addiction. Abstain. Or at least cut back. You want it to be like a hobby, not an obsession."

"I usually have fairly good self-control."

"I hope so." Glasses full, she squeezed a wedge of lemon into each. Then she stirred with a red plastic swizzle stick and slid one of the drinks toward Neal.

They raised their glasses.

"Chug-a-lug," Elise said.

"Cheers," Neal said.

They drank. This one tasted stronger than those that Neal had made. He liked it better.

"Now," Elise said, "on to Warning Number Two: don't ride in anyone you know. You can take my word on that. I learned the hard way. Even with people who love you, you'll be shocked by what's going on in their minds. You *don't* want to know. Believe me."

"It'd be awfully tempting."

"It's terribly tempting. And I'm sure you'll end up doing it. But fight the temptation as hard as you can. Stick with strangers. They'll be shocking, too, but at least you won't have an emotional link with them. And you won't often find yourself as the subject of their thoughts."

"Well . . ."

"In other words, stay out of your family. And stay out of Marta."

"Boy, I don't know. I'd sure like to hop in Marta for a few minutes."

Elise smirked. "I warned you. But I'm not the bracelet police. Do whatever you want with it. If you go hitching in girlfriends or lovers, though, you might find yourself a very lonely boy."

"I'll have to think about it."

"Think long and hard."

"Any other warnings?"

"How long have you got?"

Chapter Eight

He laughed. "How long have I got? I thought you said it's safe."

"The trial run was safe. There are all sorts of dangers when you start hitching in the real world. Mostly psychological. But some physical risks, too."

"Can I get hurt when I'm in someone?"

"You feel their pain. Of course, you already know that."

"Yeah, sure do."

"The pain can't actually harm you, though."

"That's good to know."

"Other than whatever psychological or emotional damage it may do—going through someone else's suffering that way."

"What doesn't kill me, makes me stronger."

"Well, we're coming to that. Try not to be inside anyone at the time of his or her death."

"Wouldn't *want* to be."

"It might happen, though, if you aren't careful." She frowned, shook her head, and took a sip of her drink. "You hitch with a few thousand people, you'd be surprised what happens. A gunshot, a car crash, a heart attack. If anything like that starts going down, bail. Bail fast."

"Why? I mean, what happens if I don't, and the person dies?"

She gave him a very solemn look and said, "I don't know."

"You don't know?"

"That's the point."

"It never happened to you?"

"I made real sure it didn't."

"What do you *think* would happen?"

"I don't know. But I had this fear about it. I was afraid I might end up trapped."

"Trapped?"

"In the dead body." She shrugged. "I know it sounds crazy. But I had a few close calls, and it almost got to be a phobia with me. I reached the point where I was terrified, every time I hitched, that the person might keel over dead and there I'd be, stuck inside."

"Yuck."

"Yeah. Freaked me out. The fact is, I stopped using the bracelet a few years ago. Because of that. I was hitching in this guy during the '92 riot. He was a nutcase. Fascinating guy, but scary as hell. He was out to kill some cops. I stuck with him. Nothing I could do to stop him, anyway, so I figured to hang around for the action. About two seconds after he opens up on some LAPD guys with his AK-47, he catches a bullet in the brain." Elise suddenly flinched, gritting her teeth and squeezing her eyes shut. "Arh! Hurt like you wouldn't believe. And it scared the absolute shit out of me. I figured he'd had it, and I'd end up . . ." She shook her head. She blew out a long breath that puffed her cheeks out, then took a couple of swallows from her glass, and sighed. "Anyway, the shot didn't kill him right away, so I had time to get out. He actually lasted a couple of days on life support before he kicked the bucket. But it was too close. I never had the guts to hitch again, after that."

Neal stared at her. She looked frightened.

"Now I'm not so sure *I* want to use the thing," he said.

"It's up to you. You shouldn't put too much stock, though, in my obsession. I mean, maybe you *don't* get trapped if somebody dies. For all I really know, you might zoom out and return to your own body as if nothing is wrong. The bracelet didn't come with an instruction manual."

"What about Jimmy? What did he tell you?"

"Not a whole lot. Nothing at all about what happens if your ride goes toes up on you. Maybe he never found himself in that sort of situation. And back then, I didn't know enough to ask." She shrugged. "Jimmy only gave me one warning. This should be sort of obvious, but your own body is awfully vulnerable when you're off hitching. It can't do anything to protect itself. It might as well be in a coma. If something should happen to it, you wouldn't have a clue until you tried to return."

Neal bared his teeth. "That's terrific news. I could be off having a great time, I come back and find out my apartment house burned down—with me in it?"

"Or you might've been murdered. Or had some other fatal mishap."

He shook his head. "So then what?"

Elise grinned at him over the top of her glass. "Who knows? That's one more of those mysteries of the magic bracelet."

"And you went ahead and used it anyway?"

"I'm still here."

"But you quit . . . back in '92."

"The dangers aren't really all that great. Just don't get caught in a dead person, and watch where you leave your body when you go hitching. As for your body, use common sense. I mean, if you're in bed in your own apartment, not much is likely to happen to you. But play it safe. Act as if you're going away on a trip—because you are. Make sure the doors are locked, you aren't leaving the stove on, that sort of thing. Don't leave a candle burning. Don't go on a hitch with a cigarette in your mouth."

"I don't smoke."

"Good. Just try to take every precaution before you go off.
And don't stay away for hours at a time. If you're somewhere
iffy—the beach, for instance—make your hitches shorter. Ten
or fifteen minutes, maybe. Come back every once in a while to
check up on yourself."

"You did it on the beach?" he asked.

"Sure. It's a great place for hitching. So many people to
choose from."

"Couldn't you just do it from home?"

"Oh, sure. To a certain extent. The thing is, you're always
better off hitching in the general vicinity of your body. Makes
coming and going a lot easier and quicker."

"So, you just stretched out on your towel, or something, and
pretended to be sunbathing?"

"That's about it."

"Weren't you ever robbed?"

She shook her head. "The thing is, nobody knows you're basically dead to the world. For all they know, you might be completely awake with your eyes shut."

"But what if somebody *does* rob you?" Neal asked. "What if
you're off hitching and somebody takes the bracelet off your
body?"

"Ah. I've *had* the bracelet taken off. Vince did it once. What
happens is, you're sort of dragged out of your hitch and straight
back into your own body. Then you take the bracelet back."

"Did he know about it?"

"The bracelet?" Elise shook her head. "I told Vince it was a
graduation gift from my parents. He never had a clue that you
could travel with it. That's another thing: Don't let *anyone* know
what the bracelet does. I mean, that should be pretty obvious."

"It is."

"Can you imagine what would happen if people found about
it? Everybody'd want it. They'd want to borrow it, buy it from
you, steal it. Some people would probably even kill you to get
their hands on the thing."

"Are you the only person who knows what it can do?" Neal
asked.

"Far as I know. I mean, I've had it for sixteen years and I've never told a soul about its power. Not until you, tonight. The only reason I told you is because it's your bracelet, now."

"Are there any more of them?"

Elise shook her head. "Not to my knowledge. I've done loads of research work, and I've never been able to find any mention of a bracelet like this. As far as I know, it's one of a kind. And I've never found a record of *its* existence, either."

Neal lifted his arm and studied the bracelet. "My guess is it was probably forged by Merlin."

Elise laughed. "Or maybe Saint Patrick. In collaboration with a pack of leprechauns."

"I can't believe it really works."

"It works."

"I *know*. I just can't believe it. My God. I can . . . tune in on anybody I choose? Kiss the bracelet and wish myself into them?"

"That's basically it. You do have to locate your target, though. You can't simply think the person's name, for instance. You need to *go* to him. Or her. Like the way you went from the sofa to me. But I was right there. Sometimes, it might take a bit of hunting."

"You said it's better if they're nearby."

"Right. There's some travel time involved. The farther you have to go, the longer it takes. Both ways. And there seem to be some distance limits."

"How far?"

"All depends. You'll have to play it by ear. The farthest I ever got was about thirty miles. But I had to work up to it."

Shaking his head, Neal rubbed the bracelet. "My God, this is going to be incredible."

"Just remember to be careful."

"You're sure you want me to have this?"

"I'm absolutely sure."

"It will be great for my writing. Man oh man, I'll be able to get right *inside* people, really find out what makes them tick."

He heard a distant buzzer.

"That's the washing machine," Elise said. "I'll go throw your clothes in the dryer. Be right back."

She set her drink on the counter, stepped around the end of the bar and hurried across the room to the hallway. When she was gone, Neal sipped his drink. He stared at the bracelet.

What about now? he wondered. Pay Elise a surprise visit.

No. That'd be a crappy thing to do.

She'll never know, he thought.

She might suspect.

And what if I fall off the damn bar stool?

He supposed that he wouldn't fall if he slumped forward on the counter.

Forget it, he told himself. I'm not even going to try. It'd be a dirty trick. She *gave* me the thing. I can't go and use it to spy on her.

In a deeper part of his mind, he thought, Maybe someday.

Returning, Elise said, "They should take about half an hour in the dryer."

"Looks like you'll never get rid of me."

"I'm in no hurry," she said, stepping behind the bar. "This isn't a night when I'm exactly looking forward to being alone."

"Well . . ."

"Don't worry, I'm not going to force you to stay. It's been a long night. For both of us."

"Is there anything else I need to know about the bracelet?"

She shrugged. "I think we've covered the main stuff. I'd hate to tell you everything I know, and ruin all the surprises for you."

"No other warnings?"

She took a drink, and sighed. "Well . . . not really."

"What if I have some questions? Will it be all right if I call?"

"Questions or no questions. Call me, come over for a visit . . . move in, if you're ever so inclined. I wasn't joking when I said that everything is yours. I meant it."

"Well . . . I've got a place. And a girlfriend. So . . . I don't know."

"Maybe you'd like to bring Marta over for a visit. Does she like to swim?"

"Sure."

"Come over for a swim, and we'll have a barbecue . . . make a day of it."

"Sounds nice. Though I'm not sure she'd be thrilled to know I've got a friend like you. You're a little too . . . attractive, if you know what I mean."

"Marta the jealous type?"

"Well, I don't know. But she's a woman. I can't imagine she'd be pleased to find out I have a friend who looks like you. I was actually planning to keep everything quiet. Not tell her anything. I *did* kill a guy. I don't think we should tell anyone about that. Especially now that we've tried to cover it up."

"No. Obviously."

"So how would I explain about *you?*"

"Make up something," she suggested. "Tell her I'm your sister."

He laughed. "Right."

"Don't worry about it. If you decide you want to bring her over, we'll work out some sort of cover story. I'd better give you my number, though." She sidestepped toward the end of the counter. Next to the telephone was a scratch pad. She scribbled on it, tore off the page, and returned. She handed the paper to Neal.

"I'm unlisted," she said, and took a drink. "Lose it, you'll have to come over if you want to get in touch."

"You didn't put your name on here."

"Do you want Marta to see it and wonder who Elise is? Anyway, you know who I am."

"Not your last name."

She looked slightly surprised and amused. "I think you're right. Weird. I feel like we're old friends, but . . . I don't know your name, either, do I?"

"Not unless you read my mind."

Maybe she did, he suddenly thought. What if she's used the bracelet on me?

"I'll tell you mine," she said, "if you'll tell me yours."

He felt a hot blush flood his skin.

"Darden," he muttered. "Neal Darden."

She reached her hand across the counter. "Pleased to meet you, Neal Darden. I'm Elise Waters."

He shook her hand. It felt slightly cool from her glass.

She held on. "Are you okay? What's wrong?"

"Nothing."

"Come on. Hey. You can tell me. Can't you? After everything we've been through?"

Neal grimaced. He felt awfully warm and squirmy. "I . . . it just suddenly . . . it's okay if you *did*. I mean, I was in you, so it'd only be fair."

"You're not making much sense."

"I just suddenly got embarrassed," he explained, already guessing that she hadn't paid him a secret visit. Too late to turn back, though. "It crossed my mind that maybe you used the bracelet on me."

Smiling, she raised her eyebrows. "When would I have done that?"

"While I was showering, maybe. But . . ."

"Ah. I see. No wonder your face is red."

"You didn't, though, did you." Not really a question.

"I didn't."

He tried to laugh. "Well, that's sure a relief."

He felt relieved, all right. But also embarrassed that he'd brought the subject up.

And something else.

Elise still held his hand. "Now what's wrong?" she asked.

"I don't know. I guess . . . in a way, maybe I sort of wish you *had* done it."

Her hand tightened. She stared for a long time into his eyes. "If that's what you want," she finally said, "I'll do it."

In the shower? he wondered.

What if I'm in the shower, all naked, and I know she's in me and I start thinking about her and I get a hard-on?

Under the robe, his penis began to grow and rise.

"You'd better think about it, though," Elise said. "Are you sure you want me inside? You were in me, so you know how it is. I'd be aware of *everything* that's going on in you."

Everything.

He smiled in a way that he knew must look sickly. "Well, maybe it wouldn't be such a hot idea, after all."

Chapter Nine

Neal waited beside Elise while she squatted in front of the dryer, reached in, and removed the clothes. Out came his shorts, a sock, his shirt, his other sock, and his underwear. With the clothes clutched to her chest, she stood up.

"I can take this stuff," Neal said. Reaching out, he took them from her. He tried not to touch her, but the back of his right hand accidentally slid against her pajama shirt, and he felt her skin beneath the satin. "Sorry," he mumbled.

"No problem." She shrugged. "I'm all yours, remember? You're free to touch or look to your heart's content."

"Jeez. Don't tempt me."

"Just remember. If you ever split up with Marta . . ."

"I don't think I'm likely to forget."

"Anyway," she said, "your shirt is pretty much ruined. I'd be glad to give you one of mine."

"The shirt off your back?" he asked, and found himself blushing again.

"Whatever you want. But I don't think this would fit you very well. I do have some nice, large shirts, though."

"I can wear mine home," he told her. "It won't be any problem."

"Up to you," she said.

"I'm sure it'll be fine."

In the bathroom, Neal hung the robe on the back of the door and hurried into his clothes. After putting on his belt, he filled the pockets of his shorts with the wallet, pistol, shell casings, car keys and handkerchief that he'd removed before his shower. Then he stepped into his shoes and tied them. In a pocket of the robe, he found the note with Elise's phone number. He folded it, slipped it into his wallet, and stepped into the hallway.

He found Elise in the kitchen, rinsing out their glasses.

When she turned around, he spread his arms. "Shirt's fine."

"Other than the bloodstains that didn't come out. And the rips."

"No big deal. It did look a lot better on you, though."

"A matter of opinion." She dried her hands.

"So," he said. "Guess it's about time for me to hit the road."

She came toward him. "You have my number?"

Neal patted his rear pocket.

She stepped up to him and put her hands on his shoulders. "Stay in touch, okay?"

"I will."

"And speaking of wills, I meant it about mine."

"You shouldn't do that."

"I do need your address and number. Do you have a card?"

"Oh, yeah."

"Thought you might."

As he pulled the wallet out, Elise dropped her hands and stepped back. She watched him pluck a business card out of its slot. He handed it to her, and she read it. Then she looked up at him. "No cute little typewriter or ink bottle?"

"Are you kidding?"

"How do I know you're really a writer?"

"You don't."

Grinning, she slipped the card into the pocket over her left breast.

"Well," he said. "Guess I'd better go."

"This time, you can use the front door."

They walked side by side to the front door. She opened it for Neal, and stepped outside with him. "Will you be able to find your way home from here okay?" she asked.

"I think so." He nodded to the left. "San Vicente's that way, right?"

"Left."

"Exactly." He faced Elise. The porch light was on. She looked beautiful in its mellow glow.

I must be nuts to leave, he thought.

Yeah, and what would Marta have to say about that?

Who cares?

I do. Obviously. Or I wouldn't be leaving.

He sighed. "Well. Thank you for the bracelet."

"Use it in good health. And thank *you* for saving my life."

"We were just lucky, I guess. But, you know what? I sort of feel as if my life is going to be downhill from here."

"Oh, very nice."

"No, I don't mean it that way. Just that . . . I'll probably never do anything as important as saving you. So it's bound to be an anticlimax."

Smiling, Elise shook her head. "Don't count on it."

"Well . . ."

"How about a kiss?" she asked.

"Oh, I don't know."

"Don't worry, I'm not trying to seduce you."

"Maybe not. But I might get carried away."

"You don't want the temptation?"

"That's about it."

"That Marta of yours, she's a lucky gal."

"Oh, I don't know."

"Has herself a loyal fellow like you. And a hero, to boot."

"I'm no hero."

"Sure you are." With a smile, she said, "So you're going to leave me standing here, kissless?"

"I'd *like* to kiss you. It's just . . . like I said."

"We'll compromise, then. A friendly kiss. A chaste kiss."

"Without any hugging," he added.

"Gonna leave me kissed but hugless."

Neal laughed softly.

"Okay," she said. "I'll take what I can get." She stepped closer to him, but stopped before their bodies met. Then she turned her head sideways, offering her cheek.

He leaned forward to kiss it.

Her head turned quickly.

An old trick. An ancient trick. He nearly laughed, but his urge to laugh was shut down fast by the feel of her lips.

As he drove away, he thought about the kiss. He smiled, remembering the trick she'd pulled on him. Then he sighed, remembering the feel of her lips.

He'd put his hands on her sides, ready to pull her against him, but she'd lifted them away and stepped back, saying "Ah-ah. No hugging allowed."

Good thing she stopped me, he thought.

It had hurt, though. He'd wanted so badly to hold her, to embrace her hard and feel the whole length of her body pressing against him.

I could go back.

Yeah, right. And that'd be the end of me and Marta. You don't dump someone like her just because you run into the most gorgeous gal in the world . . . who also happens to be intelligent and sensitive and funny, who is also rich, who also happens to be eternally grateful to you for saving her life.

Not even if you've fallen in love with her?

How can I be in love with her? he asked himself. We just met. I hardly even know her.

But he felt as if he'd known her for a long, long time.

How does she *really* feel about me, he wondered. Is it only that she's so grateful?

It had seemed like more than that.

Could it be possible, he wondered, that she might actually love *me*?

An easy way to find out.

Neal's hands were near the top of the steering wheel. The gold bracelet hung heavily on his right forearm, a couple of inches below his wrist.

One kiss . . .

And I crash and burn.

I'd have to pull over, he thought.

That'd be real safe. Pull off to the side of the road at this hour.

Deep in thought, he hadn't been paying much attention to his route. Now he found that he was heading east on Venice Boulevard.

He must've simply backtracked.

A mistake. Long before reaching Venice, he should've turned onto Pico. This route had taken him two or three miles farther south than he needed to go.

That's what I get for daydreaming, he thought.

He kept on driving.

I'll be home in fifteen minutes, he told himself. I can wait that long.

He knew that he shouldn't pay Elise a visit, though.

What good is the bracelet if I don't use it?

I shouldn't use it on her. Anyone but her. She hated it, having me inside knowing everything. Embarrassed the hell out of her.

Besides, he thought, Brentwood's awfully far to travel. Especially for my first solo.

Eight or ten miles?

It'd be crazy to try that sort of distance right off the bat. What I need is to try a few things closer to home, first. Work my way up.

But not so I can go to Elise's house.

I've got to *never* use the bracelet on her. Never again.

While I'm busy making pledges, Neal thought, I should promise never to use the bracelet on Marta, either.

He didn't feel quite ready for such a pledge; if he made the promise and broke it, he would feel ashamed of himself.

We'll see, he thought.

But it's definite about Elise. If I want to find out how she feels or thinks, I'll do it the right way. By going to her, by being with her, by talking to her.

How about tomorrow?

No.

I've got to stay away from Elise unless things go wrong with Marta.

I don't *want* things to go wrong with Marta. I love her.

You can't love them both.

What a mess, he thought.

A nice sort of mess, though. A lot better to be crazy about two women than none at all.

Probably.

Neal saw the sign for Video City. Suddenly remembering the man he'd shot, he felt a plunging sensation as if the car had suddenly dropped out from under him.

Though he'd never completely forgotten about the man, his strange, amazing experiences with Elise and her bracelet had occupied most of his thoughts for the past couple of hours. He'd been given a temporary reprieve.

But now it all came slamming back through him.

Memories of the terror. Worries about getting caught.

What if the cops get me for it?

How could they? he asked himself.

Easy. All it would take is one person who saw a bit of what was going on, got suspicious, and wrote down Neal's license plate number.

Other than that?

If nobody got the license number, he was home free.

Unless he or Elise should make the mistake of telling someone about the incident.

Not likely.

If it ever *does* come out, he told himself, we shouldn't have much trouble convincing the cops that it was self-defense.

So why did we cover it up?

"Seemed like a good idea at the time," he muttered.

And then he turned left at the first street after Video City. He drove past the parking lot entrance.

Am I nuts? he wondered.

Still time to turn around.

No. He needed to take a look down the next street to see if the area was crawling with cops.

Suppose it is? he thought. If they stop and search me, they'll find the gun in my pocket.

They'd need probable cause for anything like that. Can't just search a guy for no good reason, and they've got no reason to suspect me of anything.

All I have to do is act normal.

Besides, Neal would be turning onto the road more than a block past the area where the cops would likely be—if they'd arrived, at all. He could simply hang a left before reaching the crime scene and return to Venice Boulevard.

Easy.

As he approached the dead-end, his headlights pushed twin,

pale beams into the field, lighting the old railroad tracks, junk and rocky ground, weeds, and the strip of woods below the freeway embankment.

He slowed, signaled a left, and made the turn.

His headlights swept sideways.

No lights among the trees or on the road. No people wandering about. No street barricade. No police cars.

And no van.

The van's gone!

Neal felt as if his wind had gotten kicked out.

"Oh, shit," he muttered.

Heart slamming, mouth parched, he drove slowly toward the place where the van had been parked.

It was gone, all right. No question about it.

He swung to the side, stopped his car on the dirt shoulder, and killed the headlights.

What the hell is going on?

He gazed across the dark field.

Nothing at all seemed to be going on.

But where's the van?

Neal realized he was gasping for air as if he'd just finished a race.

Calm down, he told himself. No reason to panic.

Like hell. Somebody drove the bastard's van away!

Best-case scenario: a thief came along and stole it.

A possibility.

But what if the guy had climbed back into his own van and driven off?

He was dead!

Maybe not.

Neal had fired four shots. He'd seen the man go down. But he'd never examined the wounds. Never checked vital signs.

I hit him. I know I hit him.

Three in the body and one in the head.

One or two of the body shots might have been misses, but he doubted it. And he was sure that the head shot had been on target.

Doing research for various scripts, however, Neal had encountered stories of men surviving multiple gunshot wounds. Cole Younger, the western outlaw, had supposedly caught about twenty rounds from the posse that ambushed him and his gang. He'd recovered.

And what about Rasputin?

This jerk even looked like Rasputin.

That crazy old Russian monk had been damn near impossible to kill. He'd survived being poisoned, stabbed and shot. They'd finally managed to drown him.

Those were oddities, though.

This guy didn't get up and walk all the way over here and drive away.

Probably.

If he did come over, there should be lots of blood on the ground.

Neal put on his headlights, leaped out of the car and hurried to the front. Standing in the brightness of the beams, he scanned the shoulder of the road. He saw tire tracks in the dry dirt— plenty of them. He also saw a few patches of grass and clumps of weed, a smashed beer can, glittery shards of broken glass, candy and cigarette wrappers, an old dark sock, the flattened ruin of a small paper sack.

No blood.

I might be in the wrong place.

The van had been parked *near* here, but Neal hadn't made a point of noting its precise location. He might be too far forward, or too far back. He even might've parked his own car in the very spot where the van had been.

What should I do, drive back and forth a few times?

Nothing conspicuous about that.

He looked toward the wooded area where he'd left the body.

Quit screwing around, he told himself. *Run over and see if it's still there.*

He didn't want to.

The idea of returning to look for the body gave him a sick, scared feeling in the pit of his stomach.

Besides, it would take forever to run all the way there and back. And somebody might see him.

The bracelet!

Of course!

A few seconds later, in the driver's seat, he eased his door shut and killed the headlights. He locked the doors. After taking a quick look around to make sure nobody was nearby, he raised his right wrist toward his mouth.

Wait a second, he thought. I'd better stop and think about this. What if the creep *is* there? And I zip into his body?

Can't, not if he's dead.

Probably can't, he corrected himself. Elise hadn't mentioned anything about entering dead people, just that you don't want to be in someone at the moment of death.

Which could happen.

The man might be teetering on the brink, might take the fall while Neal was inside.

I'll get out quick, he told himself.

If the guy's even there.

He closed his eyes and kissed the gold bracelet. Even as his lips touched the warm gold, he felt himself rise weightless out of his body. He feared for a moment that the car roof might stop him, but he drifted through it. He hovered above his car.

Amazing, he thought.

This really *must* be a dream.

Analyze it some other time. Check on Rasputin.

Eyes on the dark section of trees below the freeway slope, Neal flew over the field. In what seemed like a few seconds, he found himself in the dark clearing. He saw the tree where Elise had been tortured. Veering away from it, he darted to the place where they'd left the body.

The burial pile of weeds and bushes was thrown apart, scattered.

Let's get!

He sped out of the clearing, across the field and down through the roof of his car. The solid mass of his body seemed to overwhelm him. He felt his weight, his tiredness, his aches and pains.

Quickly, he glanced about.

Nobody coming.

Okay, he thought. Now what? The body's gone. Rasputin has

risen from the grave. I didn't kill the bastard, after all.

Unless someone came and got him.

That didn't seem very likely, though.

He imagined the mound of foliage falling away from the rising body, saw the gawky man struggle to his feet and hobble across the field, bleeding and groaning, watched him climb in behind the driver's seat of the van, crank up the engine and drive away.

Going where? he wondered.

Better be on his way to a hospital.

But what if he headed for Elise's house?

Chapter Ten

Neal felt a rush of hot panic.

The guy could be at her house right now. He might already have her. She might already be his prisoner again—or dead.

On the other hand, maybe he was still on his way over.

Or just arriving.

Or not going to Elise's house, at all.

Gotta figure he's after her, Neal told himself.

What'll I do?

Save her. Somehow.

Okay, how?

Send the police? They could be at her house in a few minutes—but only if they get a call.

Neal had no car phone.

He was at least a five-minute drive from his own apartment. He supposed there must be a public phone closer than that— maybe over near Video City, somewhere.

The houses across the road probably had telephones.

He glanced at the dashboard clock: ten till three.

How do you get someone to answer the door at this hour?

At best, he figured it'd take him five minutes to reach a phone and put a call through to the police. At best, the cops might reach Elise's house three to five minutes after that.

Too long!

Forget the cops—call Elise. Warn her. Tell her to get out.

Right, he thought. And waste five minutes getting to a phone?

He kissed the bracelet.

Lifted out of his body, left the car below him, and raced northward climbing fast.

Don't go *too* high, he warned himself. Waste of time.

He crossed the Santa Monica Freeway at an altitude of about fifty feet. Cars and trucks sped along the lanes below him. He was vaguely aware of having an incredible experience, but he couldn't appreciate it.

He was too scared for Elise.

The flight meant only one thing to him: the fastest way to reach Brentwood.

He hoped.

It was eerie, though. He could see and hear everything clearly, as if airborne in his own body. He was able to think clearly. He could even *feel* many things: his fear and hope and maybe an odd sort of excitement.

He couldn't feel the speed, though. He felt no momentum or velocity or drag. He felt no rush of wind against his face as he raced through the night.

His awareness of speed depended entirely on his view of the buildings and streetlights, trees and billboards, parked cars and roads rushing along beneath him.

He flashed past Pico Boulevard. Considered following it west to Bundy, but found that he was already above Olympic.

Take Wilshire to Bundy, he told himself.

Seconds later, he swung left and raced westward through the heart of Beverly Hills, some fifty to sixty feet above the broad pavement of Wilshire Boulevard.

Not much moving around down there.

He willed himself to pour on the speed, but didn't seem to go any faster. Probably already at the maximum, he realized.

As he passed above the San Diego Freeway, he began to bog down.

What's happening?

You're slowing down, that's what.

Shit!

He felt almost as if he were attached to an elastic cord—a cord that reached all the way back to his body inside the parked car. Like a rubber band, it had run out of slack. Now, it was stretching, allowing him to continue, but resisting.

Elise had said there were distance limits.

Now, Neal knew what she'd meant.

But she'd made thirty miles, hadn't she?

That was after lots of practice, he reminded himself. That was her record distance.

If she can make thirty, I can make eight or ten.

Already, San Vicente was below him; he recognized its wide center island.

He turned west off Bundy and descended. Speeding just above the pavement of San Vicente, he watched for narrow roads to the right. And spotted Elise's road, Greenhaven. And shot around the corner. Following the narrow lane, he didn't spot the van.

Maybe this is a false alarm, he thought.

He veered away from the road. Heading for Elise's house, he passed through bushes and trees—but didn't feel them. They felt no different from the air.

What am I, a ghost?

He sped through the walls of Elise's house.

Found her standing at the mirror in a bathroom he hadn't seen before. The master bathroom, he guessed. Where she'd taken her shower. Now, she was brushing her teeth.

He entered her.

Yes!

Relieved to find her safe, Neal was amused to find her stewed. She must've had another vodka and tonic—or more—after he'd left.

There was a vagueness in her mind. And the pains from her numerous injuries didn't hurt very much, anymore.

Mouth full of minty-flavored froth, she worked the brush over her teeth and gums. She seemed to be enjoying herself.

Do-de-do-do, dum-de-dum. What shall we do with the drunken sailor? Oh boy oh boy oh boy, I'm gonna have me a doozy tomorrow.

She took the brush out of her mouth, grinned at herself in the mirror, and let the white froth flow over her lip and down her chin. Large dollops of it fell into the sink—splot, splot, splot. Then she spat out the rest, ran her brush under the faucet, and started scrubbing her teeth with the clean, dripping brush.

Better take me some aspirin. Gonna be headache city in the morning. Should've stopped after one or two. Yeah, well, what the hell. Not every night you get yourself kidnapped and tortured and damn near killed. Thank God for Neal.

How nice, Neal thought.

Hope he doesn't get himself jammed up with the bracelet. Maybe I shouldn't have given him . . . Ah, he'll be fine. Fine and dandy. Wish he'd stayed. Sweet guy. Ah, well. Win a few, lose a few. Anyway, he'll be back. He knows a good thing when he sees one.

Shaking her head, she laughed a bit.

Yeah, I'm a prize, all right. Drunk out of my gourd. Blotto city. Wonder what that Marta's like.

Wonder if he'll try and pull another hitch on me? Never gonna know. Less he tells. Wouldn't mind if he did, anyhow. Wonder if he's in here, now? "Hello, hello, wherever you are. Neal? You in here?"

Sure am, he thought.

Didn't think so. Alas.

She spit into the sink again, rinsed her brush and resumed scrubbing her teeth.

Alas, alas, he ain't in the lass.

Unless he is.

Neal noticed how the quick motions of her arm made her breasts jiggle. He felt her nipples slide against the inside of her pajama shirt. Elise didn't seem interested in any of that.

Of course not, Neal thought. *They're hers. She's used to them.*

He tuned in on her thoughts again as she rinsed her brush and put it away.

Alka-Seltzer or aspirin? How about both? Some for the ol' hangover and some for my multiple contusions, abrasions and lacerations.

That's me, a cut above the rest.

Ho ho ho.

How could that bastard do those things to me? Godsake. Biting me.

Neal felt a hollow chill in her groin. She pressed her thighs together, and he felt stinging sensations.

Should I go to a doctor? Yeah, sure. Wouldn't that be cute? What's your problem, dear? Oh, nothing, had a little run-in with a sadistic . . .

She took a foil pack of Alka-Seltzer out of a box in the medicine cabinet, then glanced around, looking for her glass.

Ah, yeah. In the dishwasher. Took it there this morning. Yesterday morning. Right. Fooey-kablooey.

In a lower part of her mind, she imagined herself dropping Alka-Seltzer tablets into water cupped in her hand. And she supposed they would make her hand tingle.

Not quite smashed enough to pull that stunt. Some other time. Maybe. Fat chance.

She dropped the packet into her shirt pocket. Neal felt its stiffness against her nipple.

She took a plastic bottle of aspirin off one of the shelves, popped its lid, and shook two capsules into her palm. Then she returned the bottle to the medicine cabinet and swung the door shut.

She walked out of the bathroom, across the soft carpet of her bedroom, and out to the hallway.

On her way to find a drinking glass, Neal figured.

In front of Elise, the lights were off.

He felt a small tremor of fear slide through her.

Since when are you afraid of the dark? Forget it, the bastard's dead. Kaput. Finito. Gone with the wind. Toes up. His ticket canceled, his farm bought.

You're wrong! Neal thought.

And then he thought, My God, I've got to warn her!

That's why I came here, he reminded himself. *Can't take all night about it, either. My damn body's sitting by itself in the car. No telling what might happen to it . . .*

What if I'm afraid to go out after dark?

Elise stepped down from the hallway and walked through the

den. On her way to the bar, Neal supposed. Plenty of glasses there. Closer than the kitchen.

Pit city. What I oughta do, I oughta step out there right now, do a few laps, make a few dives.

He could feel her excitement as she approached the sliding glass door, her eyes on the dim shape of the moonlit swimming pool.

Not a smart move. Screw up all my bandages. Sides, might get busted for drunk diving.

She laughed.

Instead of reaching for the door handle, she stepped behind the bar. She flicked a light switch, and a bulb came on above the sink. As she reached high to open a cupboard door, Neal felt the adhesive strip of a bandage pull loose from the underside of her right breast.

Shoot.

She studied the rows of glasses, reached up and pulled down a fair-sized tumbler. She set it on the counter. Then she reached under the hanging front of her pajama shirt, determined to fix the bandage.

Won't stay stuck, anyway. Why in heaven's name can't they make bandages that stay where you put them?

She fingered the dangling strip. Its lower end still clung to her ribcage.

Should've tried putting it on sideways, not up and down like this.

With a wordless thought process similar to what had gone on when she wondered about drinking Alka-Seltzer from the palm of her hand, Elise considered removing the bandage completely and putting it on crosswise. But she seemed to think that the removal would do further damage to the adhesive, so she decided against it.

Pressing the lower end to her ribcage, she used the side of her forefinger to lift the fallen part of the bandage. She touched her wound through the thin pad, and Neal felt a sting of pain. Then she rubbed the upper adhesive strip against the bottom of her breast.

Her breast felt soft, springy.

Oh, man, Neal thought.

She rubbed her finger up the bandage again.

Now stay stuck.

Somebody seemed to be aroused.

Didn't seem to be Elise.

How can *I* be? Neal wondered. I'm just a . . . a nothing. I can't be getting turned on.

Sure felt that way, though.

He wished Elise's finger would slide upward past the top of the bandage so he could feel her bare skin. But her hand lowered, came out from under the shirt, and took hold of the drinking glass.

With the hand that held the aspirin, she turned the water on. She filled her glass halfway, popped the two capsules into her mouth, then raised the glass to her mouth and drank. The capsules went down with her first swallow.

Drinking no more, she checked the water level inside the glass. A few inches remained.

Ought to be enough.

She set down the glass.

Okay, Neal thought. I'd better get on with it. Didn't come here for a good time. Gotta tell her about Rasputin—even if he isn't here.

Right. How?

Must be a way.

"*Elise!*" he shouted in his mind. "*Elise!*"

He shouted into her head, "*It's Neal! I'm in! The guy's not dead! Do you hear me? He's not dead! He might be coming after you!*"

He focused on her thoughts.

Probably have to get up and pee in the middle of the night. Who am I kidding—it's already the middle of the night.

Damn!

There *must* be a way to communicate!

With her right hand, Elise reached into the pocket of her pajama shirt. She pinched the top edge of the Alka-Seltzer packet and lifted it out.

Looking at it, she found herself staring at Neal's business card. She'd pinched it together with the Alka-Seltzer.

"Ah," she said.

Hope he made it home all right. He only had a couple. Why don't I give him a call? No no no. Might wake him up. Anyway, he's got that Marta. Don't want him to think I'm trying to butt in.

She slipped the card back into her pocket, then tore the foil pouch, spread it, upended it and dumped the two white tablets into her water glass. They started to fizz.

Maybe I can make her do something, Neal thought. *If I could force her hand to move . . . might get her to write a warning.*

As Elise watched the water in her glass grow white and fuzzy with bubbles from the dissolving tablets, her hands were busy folding the empty foil packet, making it into a tiny hard square.

Neal put all his energy into her right hand.

Make it let go, he thought.

It tossed the tiny square onto the counter, and picked up the glass.

This one's busy, he thought. *Try her left hand; it isn't doing anything.*

Make it tap on the counter.

It hung by her side and lightly stroked her thigh while she gulped down the fizzing water.

This isn't working, Neal thought.

He suddenly felt as if he were being smothered. He struggled to breathe. Couldn't. His lungs ached.

What the . . . ?

Elise came up for air.

Thank God, he thought.

After a few quick breaths, she resumed drinking. Not much left, now. A few more swallows, no problems, and the glass was empty except for a white, powdery residue.

Elise rinsed the glass and set it down by the sink. Then she took a deep, deep breath. The air felt great, filling her lungs. But her expanding chest popped the same bandage loose.

Phooey. Ah, well, least the others are holding.

She flicked the light off, then walked around the end of the bar and headed for the hallway.

Neal was aware of a decision, below word level, not to fool again with the bandage, leave it as-is until morning.

The decision seemed to trouble her, though.

Don't want to bleed on my jammies. Take them off? Good idea, then I'll bleed on my sheets.

I'm probably done bleeding, all nicely coagulated . . .

Don't count on it. Bound to be some dribbling ooze of some sort, this many wounds.

Walking up the hallway toward her lighted bedroom, she considered changing the bandage, after all.

Just take a minute or two.

What am I going to do? Neal wondered. I came here to warn her, but . . . What the hell was I thinking, anyway? Did I think I could change the rules just because I wanted to? She can't pick up my thoughts. Doesn't have a clue I'm even in her. I can't make her lift a damn finger . . .

He realized that he'd made a big mistake.

He'd gotten here fast, all right. But so what? He might as well have stayed in his car.

I *did* stay in my car, he thought.

And what I'd better do now is get back to it. Drive to the nearest phone and call her. Which is what I should've done in the first place, if I'd had an ounce of sense.

Thank God it was a false alarm, he thought.

Just as he was about to will himself back to his own body, Elise walked past the doorway to the guest bathroom and a dark shape leaped at her out of the darkness.

Chapter Eleven

Elise glimpsed the quick dark motion. She gasped, "Ah!"

Oh God, who is it? No!

Hit hard from the side, she was hurled across the hallway. Her shoulder crashed against the wall.

Shit! No! Oh, God! Who is it? What's going on?

Him? Is it him?

He slammed her back to the wall.

Wild hair and beard.

Him, all right. Neal hadn't doubted it for an instant.

No! You're dead! Why aren't you dead!

Gotta do something! Neal thought. Gotta help her!

If I scream . . . !

The attacker suddenly pistoned fists into her belly, blasting her air out. She folded with the pain and dropped to her knees.

Inside, she felt as if her stomach had caved in, as if her lungs had been squeezed empty.

Neal was suffocating. Like with the Alka-Seltzer, but ten times worse.

Oh God, he's gonna kill me. Can't be happening. How am I gonna get out of this? Has to be a way!

I have to help her, Neal thought. Leave now? Get to my car and race back over here and blow this fucking bastard's head off.

Never make it in time.

Why the hell didn't I drive back in the first place? I might be here by now!

It'll all be over by the time I can get back!

Maybe not, maybe not.

Elise was getting some breath, now. She was on her knees, hunched over, hugging her belly, head down as she wheezed. She kept thinking, *What'm I gonna do? Gotta stop him. He's gonna kill me. What'm I gonna do? Has to be a way. Can't let him kill me. Can't.*

Below those thoughts, she seemed certain that she wouldn't survive. And she wondered how much pain there would be. And she wondered what she would miss the most, being dead. And she was glad her parents weren't alive to find out that their daughter had been murdered.

Hope on the surface, despair below.

I can't save her if I stay! Neal shouted at himself.

But he hated to abandon her.

But he couldn't stand to stay, either, and go through any more of this.

"Get up, bitch."

Neal thought, I'll be back, Elise. Hold on. Please!

But he knew she couldn't hear him. She had no idea he was even inside her, much less trying to communicate.

The attacker grabbed Elise by the hair on top of her head, and pulled. She gasped with pain. Neal felt the burning hurt of her scalp as she tried to stand up.

Gotta fight him. It's the only way. He's shot up. Isn't he? Has to be. Can't be all that strong.

Below, she knew he was still strong enough to overpower her. Knew she didn't stand much chance.

At least I'll go down fighting.

I'm out of here!

And he was.

The moment Neal willed himself to leave, he was torn out of Elise's body and flung up through the roof of her house. He had no control. As he shot through the treetops and gained speed, he felt as if he were being sucked through the night by the gravity of his own body.

Not falling to earth, but hurtling across the miles to the place where he'd left himself.

The city beneath him raced by in a blur. The streetlights were long, jagged streaks.

Suddenly, he found himself inside his own body. Even before he opened his eyes, he realized that he was a wreck: gasping for air, sobbing, tears running down his face.

He opened his eyes. Knuckled the tears away. Then reached out and twisted the ignition key. As the engine kicked to life, he put on the headlights. He shifted and hit the gas. The car took off.

Oh God, he thought, let me be quick enough.

Let the bastard take his time.

Work on her slowly.

Let her be alive!

Neal drove faster than he'd ever driven before on city streets. He didn't stop for traffic signals. He swerved past slower cars. His tires screamed on the turns. He had a hard time breathing. The steering wheel was slick in his hands, but he held on tight—except when he had to let go, one hand at a time, to wipe the tears from his eyes.

I'll never make it in time, he thought.

Please, God, save her. Don't let him kill her. Please!

Lower in his mind, he figured that God probably didn't have much to do with it.

Maybe, he thought. You never know.

I already saved her once, tonight. What are the odds I can do it again? It'd be a miracle.

Let's have a miracle! Please!

The real miracles, he realized, seemed to be working for the other side. That *was* the same guy. He *had* been shot at least twice—once in the head. But he'd still been able to get up and drive over to Elise's house and jump her.

No bulletproof vest, either. That's movie stuff. That's cop stuff. Maybe some nutcases *do* wear vests, but not this guy. Neal had noticed, way back at the start, how he'd been able to see the shape of the guy's cadaverous torso through the skintight shirt.

I hit the bastard, Neal thought. Hit him good.

Not good enough.

Maybe he's close to the end of his rope.

But those punches Elise caught in the guts hadn't felt like they'd come from a guy on the verge of collapse. They'd been damn hard. And the way he'd picked her up by the hair . . .

But who knows?

He can't keep going and going forever.

Maybe she'll be able to take him. Hurt him enough to get away. Or enough to slow him down.

Neal had the green at Olympic Boulevard. Not that it mattered. Red, amber or green, he wouldn't have stopped. He'd been blowing through intersections against the red all down Venice Boulevard, Centinela, and now Bundy. Hoping not to end the race with a crash. Hoping a cop might see him and give chase.

Tonight, the cops must be somewhere else.

Soon, he shot across Santa Monica Boulevard.

Almost there, he thought. A few more minutes.

Fight him, Elise! Hang on.

What if they're gone?

Last time, the bastard hadn't worked on her in the house; he'd driven her away.

Maybe he'll do that again, carry her out to the van and head for somewhere else.

Maybe he's too hurt to carry her.

Find out soon.

At the corner of Bundy and San Vicente, the traffic light was red. The intersection looked clear. Knowing he would probably flip over if he took the turn at full speed, he slowed down slightly. He swung left. He skidded, tires squealing. Came out of the skid, and stepped on the gas.

Greenhaven coming up.

Nothing in the rearview.

Bearing down on Greenhaven, he hit the brakes. Slowed abruptly and almost came to a stop before making his turn onto the narrow lane.

As he raced the final stretch to Elise's house, he knew he'd made good time.

Must've averaged sixty.

Doubted he could've gone faster.

But the guy'd had at least ten minutes with Elise. More like fifteen.

No sign of the van.

Was it just around the bend? Or gone? Gone with Elise inside?

As Neal swung into her driveway, his headlights reached past the open iron gate and lit the rear of a black van parked in front of Elise's garage.

The sight of the van struck him like a kick to the heart.

Still here, he thought. Oh, God.

He killed his lights, shut off the engine, pulled the ignition key and switched the key case to his left hand. With his right, he flipped open the console and dug for the bottom.

Come on, come on, where is it!

He found the spare ammo magazine.

Snatched it up.

Flung open his door and leaped out.

Running toward the van, he pocketed the keys. He clamped

the steel magazine between his teeth, reached deep into his right pocket and drew out the pistol.

The van was dark and quiet.

Engine not running.

Not yet.

You're not going anywhere, bastard, he thought.

Ducking as he rushed past the rear, he shoved his pistol toward the tire and fired. The blast stunned his ears. The gun bucked in his hand. He didn't stop to check the effect, but hurried on to the front right tire and shot it, too.

Then he glanced through the side window.

Nobody in the front seats.

He thought about making a quick search of the van. He doubted anyone was in it, though. And he didn't want to waste time opening the door and climbing in.

A few lost seconds might make all the difference to Elise.

So he kept on running.

As he raced toward the corner of the house, he changed magazines and jacked a fresh round into the chamber. On his way through the grove at the side, he dropped his used magazine into a pocket. He dodged his way through the fruit trees, ducking under low limbs. Suddenly, the trees ended. He rushed out onto the concrete apron of the pool.

Light spilled out from the sliding glass door of Elise's bedroom.

Neal ran toward it.

Open.

I was the last one in, he thought.

Elise had picked up the towel she'd left on the lounge and stepped into her bedroom, and Neal had followed her through the sliding door.

He couldn't remember locking it.

Did I lock it? he wondered. Did I even *shut* it?

Must be how *he* got in.

Fuck!

Doesn't matter now, Neal told himself.

And charged through the open door.

Elise's bedroom looked almost the same as when he'd last seen it. The big blue towel was gone, that's all. She'd thrown it onto her bed, but someone had taken it away.

On the other side of the room, the door to the master bathroom was ajar.

Light showed through the crack.

Neal jumped onto the bed and ran across it, the mattress bouncy under his feet. At the other side, he leaped down. He ran at the bathroom door.

"Hey!" he yelled. No answer.

He kicked the door open. It slammed the wall behind it, bounced and swung back.

In the moments it was wide open, Neal glimpsed a small heap of shiny blue cloth on the floor. Elise's pajamas?

He didn't see her, though.

Or the attacker.

So he kneed the door wide open, gently so it wouldn't fly back.

This was much larger than the guest bathroom. Over to the right, it had a long counter with twin sinks, cupboards underneath. A mirror ran the length of the wall. Down at the far end was a toilet.

From where Neal stood, just inside the doorway, he couldn't see the tub.

But there seemed to be a large, recessed area to the left, just beyond the small heap of Elise's pajamas.

He walked toward it.

They aren't here, he thought. I'm wasting time.

What about her pajamas?

Then he saw Elise.

Saw her reflection in the mirror to his right.

It wrenched out a moan.

He told himself that maybe it wasn't as bad as it looked. Mirrors distort things.

He turned his face away from the mirror and hurried on and stepped over Elise's pajamas and found her. Not a reflection. Not a distortion.

The bath was a sunken tub, rectangular and tiled like a miniature swimming pool, a ledge around it.

She sat on the ledge at the far side, her feet in the tub.

Her arms were stretched out to her right and left, her wrists bound with tape to chrome fixtures that appeared to be hand-holds. The way she leaned forward, the fixtures seemed to be bearing most of her weight. Her head hung down so Neal couldn't see her face.

There was no water in the tub.

Its tile bottom was puddled and spattered with blood.

The towel from the bed lay in a heap near her feet. It looked sodden. It wasn't very blue anymore.

Neal stepped down into the tub.

He had to see her face.

Maybe it *isn't* Elise, he thought. Maybe it's a trick to make me think she's dead, and this is some other woman.

This *can't* be her, he told himself. Not this slaughtered, mutilated ruin.

"No," Neal muttered. "No, no. Huh-uh."

The tiles were slippery.

He crouched in front of her and looked up at her face. Coils of hair clung to her bloody forehead. Her eyes were wide open, bulging. A thick bar of pink soap was jammed into her mouth.

He looked away quickly and stood up.

He suddenly went dizzy. His vision darkened. Blinking, he saw electric blue auras. He heard ringing in his ears.

God, I'm gonna faint!

He staggered backward and sat on the edge of the tub. Bending at the waist, he lowered his head. He gazed down between his knees. Down at the tile steps.

As his head cleared, he noticed there was no blood on the steps.

He looked to his left. No blood, anywhere, on the bathroom floor.

Maybe that's what the guy did with the towel, he thought. Used it to clean up after himself, then tossed it into the tub.

Neal kept his head turned away so he wouldn't see Elise again, and climbed backward up the steps. He turned and backed away from the tub.

Leaving bloody shoeprints.

They're gonna think I did this.

The crime scene investigators would find *his* shoe prints in Elise's blood, his fingerprints all over the place . . . his hair in the drain of the guest bathroom's tub, even traces of his blood on the tissues he'd used for drying his abrasions after the shower.

Other evidence, too.

The task of cleaning up after himself to make all the traces disappear seemed overwhelming. And even if he spent hours, he couldn't possibly eliminate every print, stain, hair . . .

Forget it, he thought.

"Who cares," he muttered.

He felt sick, confused, tired, scared.

Where's the bastard who killed her? That's what I want to know. Gotta get my hands on him. He has to be around here someplace.

Van isn't going anywhere.

He wondered if the cops would be arriving soon.

Only if someone reported my shots, he thought.

If Elise had been right about the neighbors, the cops should've gotten a dozen calls by now.

So where are they?

He suddenly felt an odd sensation of having drifted into an alien land—an unreal, twisted copy of Los Angeles where nothing quite worked out the way it should.

A place where madmen don't die when you shoot them.

A place where damsels in distress can't really be saved, after all.

A place where magic bracelets let you inhabit people but won't allow you to help them.

A place where no cops come.

He wondered if he should call the police, himself.

Maybe they could surround the place and catch the killer.

They'll think I did it.

Where is he? Neal wondered. Turning around, he found himself standing above Elise's pajamas. He gazed at them.

My card.

He crouched. Keeping his head up and the pistol ready in his right hand, he used his left hand to separate the pajama shirt from the pants. He turned the shirt until he found its pocket.

As he dug his fingers into the pocket, he remembered Elise slipping the Alka-Seltzer packet in—the feel of the stiff foil against her nipple.

Where's that nipple now?

In the bastard's belly?

The thoughts made Neal want to scream and crash his head against a wall.

None of this happened! Not really.

Then what was that in the tub?

I'm asleep and dreaming . . .

Neal knew he was awake.

His fingers were delving inside an empty pocket.

My card!

His first thought was that the killer had taken it. Then he realized it might've simply fallen out of Elise's pocket during the struggles, or when the man stripped her.

He picked up her pajamas and checked the floor.

No card.

Worry about it later, he told himself. The killer's still around here, someplace.

Probably.

He let the pajamas drift from his fingers. As he stood up, he scanned the bathroom floor.

No sign of his card.

If the cops find it . . . Least of my worries. What if he has it?

He'll know where to find me.

"Good!" Neal blurted.

The sound of his voice shocked him. He didn't dare speak again.

But he thought, Come and get me.

Chapter Twelve

Neal searched the house.

He worked his way carefully from room to room, looking for the killer.

And looking for his business card.

He felt oddly calm.

The worst had already happened.

He sort of hoped the police wouldn't show up and catch him here, but he didn't actually care that much, one way or the other. If they showed up, they might shoot him. LAPD cops weren't trigger-happy cowboys, though. That was movie crap. He'd be fine if he put his gun down.

They would almost certainly arrest him, but so what?

He could live with that.

He would prefer to avoid the mess, but it didn't seem like much of a big deal.

Elise dead, that was a big deal.

So was finding her killer.

Empty my pistol into his face.

As Neal searched, he found small amounts of blood on the carpet of Elise's bedroom, and in the hallway. Not much. A few drops and smears here and there.

But he found a pattern of spots on the rug just inside the doorway of the guest bathroom.

The rat-fuck's blood.

This was where he'd waited before jumping her.

At least I didn't just imagine hitting him, Neal thought.

There was hardly more blood, however, than might come from a small cut on the finger.

He bandaged himself, Neal realized.

Probably bled like a stuck pig when I nailed him. Probably out cold. Woke up after we left. By then, a lot of the bleeding must've already stopped. He made it back to his van, crawled in and patched himself.

Bastard carries a toolbox, why not a first-aid kit, too?

More likely, he put together makeshift bandages from whatever odds and ends he could find in his van. He was bound to have something. An old shirt, a towel, a sheet. Elise had mentioned a mattress; there might've been a pillow case, a blanket.

One way or another, he'd stopped most of the bleeding.

Not all of it, though.

If only I'd been a better shot!

Should've killed him.

Should've finished him off. Stuck my gun in his mouth when he was down on the ground in the trees, and blown his fucking head off.

Elise wouldn't be dead now.

Whirling away from the bathroom door, he shouted, "Where are you!"

No answer came.

He finished searching the house.

He didn't find the killer.

He had no luck finding the business card, either.

The bastard's got it, all right.

Neal left the house without entering Elise's bathroom again. He knew that he wouldn't be able to stand another look at her.

He also left without making any attempt to clean up after himself.

If the cops came after him, so be it.

Outside, he checked around the pool. Then he went to the front of the house.

After seeing that the van and his own car were still parked in the driveway, he walked completely around the outside of the house, listening and watching, hoping the killer might leap out at him.

But nothing happened.

At the driveway again, he opened the driver's door of the van. No light came on. He climbed in. Kneeling on the seat, he peered into the back. He couldn't see much. A few dim shapes, that's all: the gray rectangle of the mattress, several scattered objects too small for anyone to hide behind.

The killer wasn't there.

Must've taken off on foot, Neal thought.

Unless he's still somewhere in the house.

Might be anywhere, Neal told himself. Not here in the van, though.

Quickly, he switched the pistol to his left hand, leaned to the right and popped open the glove compartment. Its light came on.

Empty.

As empty as Elise's pocket when he'd felt inside for his card.

The registration papers should've been in the glove compartment—with the killer's name and address.

Van's probably stolen, anyway.

Neal imagined the killer returning, climbing in and driving it away in spite of the two flat tires. He could see it moving down the street, lopsided. He could hear the loud thumping of the flats.

So he leaped out. Crouching in the V of the open door, he reached under the dashboard. He found wires, grabbed them and jerked them loose.

At the front of the van, he smashed both headlights with the butt of his pistol.

At the rear, he smashed the taillights.

He considered shooting the other two tires, but decided it would be pointless. If the guy could drive away with two flats, why not with four?

Besides, any more shooting and the cops probably *would* show up.

Yeah, right. There aren't any cops, remember?

Everything is topsy-turvy, all fucked up.

Don't count on it.

Let them come, he thought.

And stepped to the front of the van.

He put a line of four shots across the grill, the gun jumping with each blast. In the quiet that followed, his ears rang and the car hissed. He heard the tinkly sound of a rolling brass shell. Then came the sounds of coolant splashing onto the driveway.

Bastard's not going far in this van.

Neal thought about his brass. Firing at the grill had sent four casings spitting out the side of his pistol. The cops were sure to find them.

So what? he thought. I've left so much else behind. Doesn't matter, anymore.

As he walked to his car, he hoped the killer might be hiding inside.

He looked through the windows, gun ready.

Nobody there.

Nobody anywhere as he backed out of the driveway and drove slowly down Greenhaven with his headlights off.

Before turning onto San Vicente, he put them on.

He checked his rearview mirror many times during the long drive back to his apartment.

Nobody seemed to be following him.

He spotted a total of five police cars. A couple seemed to be on routine patrol, one raced by at a high speed, one had a biker pulled over, and another was stopped in the parking lot of McDonald's. Each sighting gave Neal a horrible rush of terror.

He realized he'd been kidding himself: he *did* care about getting arrested and being charged with the murder of Elise. Just imagining it, he got a sickish feeling in his stomach.

They could never make it stick, he told himself.

But they would sure have plenty of evidence putting him at the scene of the crime. He'd be arrested, for sure. Thrown in jail. And maybe indicted, maybe put on trial.

If it went that far, he might spend months in county jail. Even a year or more. He would probably be acquitted, eventually, but maybe not. Maybe found guilty.

It was torture murder, a "special circumstances" crime. He could get the death penalty.

Death by lethal injection.

It'll never come to that, he told himself. Too much reasonable doubt. They probably wouldn't even prosecute him.

But *anything* might happen. He might be tried and found guilty.

Tonight had taught him many things.

Its biggest lesson: The worst *does* happen.

As Neal parked in his own space behind the apartment building, he took a deep breath, sighed, and muttered, "Made it."

Then he sat for a while in his car, trying to calm down.

Trying to stop shaking.

Monday morning was gray with the approach of dawn when Neal finally climbed out of his car. He stuffed the pistol into his pocket and walked to the rear gate. Elise's gold bracelet felt heavy on his wrist.

Maybe I can use it to find the bastard.

Too tired.

Anyway, he'll find me. Knows right where to look, if he has the card.

Let him come.

Neal shut the gate carefully so it wouldn't clank and wake people up.

The only lights came from above the doors of several apartments that surrounded the courtyard. And from the curtained window of his own living room on the second floor. He had left a lamp on, figuring to be back from the video store in a few minutes. It had been on all night. Every other window facing the courtyard was dark.

As Neal climbed the outside stairs, he looked at the swimming pool. It occupied the center of the courtyard. The reflections of a few lights streaked its surface.

It looked very calm and peaceful.

He thought about Elise's pool.

Imagined her naked on the high-dive, leaping, twirling, flipping, maybe touching her toes in midair before knifing down through the darkness and into the cool water.

She'll never get to dive again.

His throat tightened.

How could this happen?

He followed the balcony to the door of his apartment. He unlocked the door, entered, shut it and closed the dead bolt.

Then he removed the pistol from his pocket.

Keeping it ready, he started to walk through his rooms.

He told himself there was no reason to worry. The killer couldn't be hiding here, no transportation.

That I know of, he reminded himself.

But who knows? The guy might've had a spare car waiting for him nearby, just in case. Or maybe he stole a car from one of Elise's neighbors.

Or took Elise's car?

While searching her house, Neal had checked inside the garage. A two-car garage. A white Mercedes had been there. He'd supposed, at the time, that it was the only vehicle she owned.

What if there was another? he asked himself. The killer might've taken it before I showed up. Or he might've waited, hiding, and stolen the Mercedes after I left.

Wasn't the van blocking the driveway, though?

Not completely, Neal thought. Probably enough space for a car to slip by.

The bastard might be anywhere.

Not here, though. Not in Neal's small living room, eating area, or kitchen. He had already checked those places, but now he found himself afraid to enter the bathroom and turn on its light.

He's not in there, Neal told himself.

It's not him I'm afraid of.

Who will it be? he wondered.

Marta?

Naked and bloody, ripped and chewed, bound with her arms outstretched as if asking for a last embrace?

"She's at work," Neal muttered. "Nobody's in here. Nobody."

Gritting his teeth, holding his breath, he stepped into the bathroom and flicked the light switch.

The tub was white and clean and empty.

Nobody was in the bathroom except him.

He turned toward the mirror. He saw his own face, but it didn't look a way that he had ever seen it before. Haggard, dazed, shocked. The sort of face he might expect to see on the last survivor after a stroll through the wasteland.

He turned away from the mirror and left the bathroom.

He didn't hesitate at the door to his bedroom, but stepped in and turned on the light. Fine. Nothing appeared to be out of place. But he checked inside the closet and underneath the bed, just to be safe.

Then he removed a box of ammunition from a top drawer of his dresser. Standing at the dresser, he reloaded both his pistol magazines. He put one of the full magazines up the Sig's handle, and shoved it home with the heel of his hand. He jacked a round into the chamber. After decocking, he set the pistol down while he took off his clothes.

He dropped the clothes onto the floor near his feet. He didn't want to deal with them now.

He still wore the bracelet.

No more hitching, he thought. Not tonight.

He liked wearing the bracelet. It let him feel as if he still had a connection with Elise.

He didn't want to have it on, however, if Marta should show up. She would be getting off work at eight, and might stop by instead of going home to her own apartment.

She sometimes came over without notice, and she had a key.

So Neal removed the bracelet. He put it into the dresser drawer and tucked it under some socks.

Then he picked up the pistol and carried it with him into the living room. He turned off the lamp there, and then switched off the lights in the kitchen. In the bathroom again, he placed the pistol on the counter where it would be within easy reach.

He washed, brushed his teeth, and used the toilet.

After retrieving the pistol, he turned off the bathroom light and went to his bedroom.

He turned off his bedroom light.

He crossed the room with the pistol in his hand, and took the pistol with him into bed.

The sheets felt cool and good against his bare skin.

The pistol thumped quietly against the wood of his headboard shelf when he set it down beside his clock radio.

The green digital numbers on the clock read 5:42.

Jesus, he thought.

Which reminded him to say a prayer.

A prayer was routine for Neal at bedtime. Usually a quick run-through of the Lord's Prayer in his head. Usually without giving it much thought. Just something he'd done since childhood.

God might be out there someplace.

If He was, however, Neal rather doubted that He paid much attention to prayers. And doubted strongly that a prayer, if heard, was likely to change God's mind about anything at all, or alter the course of events.

But you never know.

Tonight, Neal's mental recitation didn't stop at "for thine is the kingdom and the power and the glory forever." He went on from there. "And dear God, please watch over Elise. I don't know why you let something like that happen to her. You probably didn't have much to do with it, I don't know. Shit. Sorry. Anyway, I guess her number was up, or whatever. Anyway, be good to her in heaven, if there is such a place, because she sure got fucked down here. Sorry about that. It's how I feel. And if You're listening, I'd appreciate it, too, if You'd not let that scumbag sneak in here and nail me while I'm asleep. Thank you. Amen."

Chapter Thirteen

Neal slept fitfully, troubled by nightmares and strange dreams, disturbed every so often by sounds from outside his windows as other tenants started their day. Throughout the morning and afternoon, noises intruded on his sleep: banging doors and gates, voices, footsteps, laughter, splashes in the pool, distant lawnmowers and leaf blowers and sirens, an occasional faraway bam that might be a gunshot, a backfire, a board being dropped onto concrete, who knows?

The noises lifted him toward consciousness. Few of them woke him completely, though. The times that he did wake up, he was too confused to focus on what had happened last night, and slipped back into his uneasy sleep.

When Neal finally did wake up, he found himself sprawled on his back, naked and sweaty in the afternoon heat, his sheet kicked off.

He used his pillow to mop his face dry. Then he rolled onto his side and looked at his clock radio.

4:23

He'd slept about ten hours.

He glanced at his pistol on the shelf beside the clock.

With the weight of memory caving down on him, he wished he'd gone on sleeping.

Nice not to wake up at all.

He wondered if he might be able to fall back asleep.

Impossible. He was wide awake, now. Not just awake, but sick with fear and guilt and revulsion and sorrow.

Move it, he told himself. Won't be as bad if I'm up and around.

He scurried off his bed. Though he moaned at the stiffness and aches from his injuries, he didn't pause. He rushed into the bathroom, remembered his pistol, trotted back to his bedroom and grabbed it off the headboard, then returned with it to the bathroom.

He locked the bathroom door, but didn't take the pistol with him into the shower.

Didn't want to get it wet.

Besides, taking it into the shower would've been going a bit too far.

I'm not *that* paranoid, Neal told himself as he showered. If the bastard hasn't shown up for the past ten hours, it's not likely he'll try to make his kill at four-thirty in the afternoon.

What kept him, anyway?

Maybe he had trouble finding the place. Or trouble finding transporation.

He might still be in Brentwood.

Might be in police custody.

Might even be dead.

Wishful thinking, Neal told himself. A guy doesn't get up

after being shot two or three or four times, then drive all the way to Brentwood, beat up Elise and drag her all the way from the hall to the master bathroom, tie her in the tub and *do* all that to her, *then* go off somewhere and drop dead from his gunshot wounds.

Maybe the bastard's just resting up.

That seemed a lot more likely.

All the work on Elise had probably worn him out, so he went to ground.

Not to a hospital. He wouldn't be that stupid. The cops would nail him for sure if he checked in for a little treatment of his gunshot wounds. They'd put two and two together—blood at the scene, .380 caliber brass at the scene, and he's got .380 size holes in his body. They'd be sure to connect him with Elise's murder.

No, no hospital for Rasputin. He'd go home, patch himself up the best he could, and hit the sack.

He'll probably come for me tonight, Neal thought. But not until after dark.

This was July, daylight saving time, so darkness wouldn't come until well after eight o'clock.

Neal figured he was probably safe until then, at least.

Done in the shower, he quickly dried himself, being careful to avoid the abrasions on his knees and elbow. Scabs were starting to form, but the wounds still felt raw and sore. He patted them dry with a tissue. The white tissue came away wet, but not discolored. He tossed it into the wastebasket.

And thought about the tissue in Elise's wastebasket.

It had been pink with his blood and puss.

Evidence that could put him at the scene of the crime.

He should've flushed it down the toilet—then gone around Elise's house and wiped away every trace of his fingerprints and shoe prints.

He'd been too messed up, at the time.

Too scared and outraged and confused.

It had seemed like too big a job, an overwhelming and impossible task, and not an important thing to do. Finding the killer had been the important thing. Not trying to cover up for himself.

If he had it to do over again, though . . .

You can't go back, he told himself.

Unless the body hasn't been found yet.

He draped his towel over the bar to dry, rolled deodorant onto his armpits, then picked up his pistol and opened the door. After the steamy heat of the bathroom, the hallway felt cool. So did his bedroom.

He took a pair of faded blue gym shorts out of his dresser drawer, and put them on.

He started to shut the drawer. Then stopped and reached inside. He slipped his hand underneath the socks, and touched the bracelet.

Leave it, he told himself. Don't want to have it on if Marta shows up.

So he shut the drawer, picked up his pistol and walked into the living room. The clock on the VCR showed 4:57. In three minutes, local news should be starting.

He hurried into the kitchen, took a can of Budweiser out of the refrigerator, returned to the living room and picked up the television remote. He thumbed the TV on. Seated on the sofa, he popped open the can. He took a swallow of beer, then made sure he was on one of the three channels that carried local news at five.

Elise was the top story.

They found her.

Neal had a sudden urge to turn off the TV. He didn't want to see this, didn't want to know.

I *need* to watch, he told himself.

A photo of Elise appeared behind the anchorwoman. A photograph from the past. She was hardly more than a teenager, and dressed in a swimsuit. Her hair was wet. She looked beautiful. Neal groaned.

"The affluent west-side community of Brentwood has once again been shocked by a brutal slaying in its midst. Elise Waters, former Olympic diving great and wife of actor Vince Conrad was found murdered in their home on Greenhaven Lane this morning. Jody Bain is live at the scene."

The reporter seemed to be standing somewhere on the road near the front of Elise's house. "The grim discovery," she said, "was made at approximately nine o'clock this morning when the victim's housekeeper, Maria Martinez, arrived for . . ."

Neal flinched as someone knocked on his door.

Then he recognized the quick, light rhythm of the rapping.

Marta.

"Thank God," he muttered, and shut off the television.

"You in there? It's me."

He hid the pistol underneath one of the sofa's pillows, then stood up. "Just a second," he said. He considered hurrying to his bedroom and putting on enough clothes to hide his injuries. But she was bound to see them, sooner or later.

So he stepped over to the door, unbolted it and swung it open.

Seeing Marta, he felt some of his pain slide away. She looked so fresh and cheerful and alive.

And familiar.

Nothing about her had changed since last night, except her outfit. When he'd last seen her, she'd been wearing her airline clothes: blue blazer, silk scarf, white blouse, blue slacks and black leather shoes. Now, she wore a big, loose T-shirt, denim shorts, and sandals.

So familiar and so normal.

As if nothing had happened.

Since seeing her last night, Neal had shot a man, saved a woman's life, fallen suddenly in love, taken trips with a magic bracelet, and let the wonderful new woman get destroyed. But Marta looked as if everything had gone along in a normal, fine fashion, nothing out of the ordinary happening since her last visit.

She was smiling when Neal opened the door. Moments later, however, she frowned. "What happened?" she asked.

"A long story," he said.

"Are you all right?"

"Yeah, I'm okay."

She stepped inside and swung the door shut. "Come here," she said. "I'll make you feel better."

When he moved closer, she put out her hands to stop him. She leaned forward, kissed him on the mouth, then worked her way slowly down his body, squatting lower and lower as she gently touched her lips to every scratch and scrape and bruise on his chest and belly.

By the time she faced his shorts, they were jutting out.

"Glad to see you're feeling better," she said.

Neal pushed his fingers through her thick, soft hair.

She slipped her fingertips under the elastic waistband at the front of his shorts. "What've we got in here?" she asked. She drew the band toward her and down. "Well, now," she said.

The shorts came to rest around Neal's feet.

Marta kissed the tip of his penis. She licked him. Her tongue was slick. Then her lips were a slick, tight circle sliding down while her hands clutched his buttocks and urged him closer.

Neal was astonished.

She had never done anything like this before.

It was almost as if she'd sensed a need in him—a need to be surprised, shocked, delighted.

Or maybe the need was hers.

For a while, he forgot about everything except Marta and her mouth.

When it was over, she quit sucking and swallowing, but kept him inside, holding him softly with her lips.

Neal felt weak and shaky.

She pulled her mouth away, lifted his shorts to their usual place, then tilted back her head and looked up at him. Her lips were shiny. "How was that?" she asked.

"Are you kidding?"

She stood and leaned forward against him and put her arms around his back. She was breathing hard. Her breasts pushed at his chest. "Did I do it right?" she asked.

"It was great."

"I wasn't so sure about the swallowing."

"I think it's optional."

She laughed. "Would've made a mess if I hadn't." She kissed

him gently on the mouth, then eased her face away so that she could look into his eyes.

Her eyes switched from side to side. After a while, she asked, "Something's the matter, isn't it?"

"Everything's fine," Neal said, and saw a change in her eyes. They stayed the same pale blue color, but somehow they seemed to darken. She knew he'd lied.

"Is it something I did?" she asked.

"No. No. Are you kidding?"

"Are you sure?"

"Positive."

"Then, is there anything I can do to help?"

"You just did."

"Ho ho."

"I mean it."

"I know. But I hate to see you this way. Do you want to tell me about it?"

"I don't know," he said.

"Do you want to get me a beer?"

"Sure."

Leaving Marta, he hurried into the kitchen. He took a Budweiser out of the refrigerator, a glass mug out of the cupboard. He had nearly filled the mug when Marta stepped into the eating area.

Neal had never eaten there. The table held his word processor, printer, scattered pens and notepads and a few stacks of books.

Marta glanced at the blank screen of his monitor, then looked at Neal and raised her eyebrows. "Writer's block?" she asked.

"Worse than that."

"What could be worse than that?"

He shook his head. "Plenty."

He saw that she was already holding a can of beer. She raised it to her mouth, and drank.

"That's mine," he said.

"Do you mind? I saw it on the table in there. Couldn't help myself."

"Don't you want a glass for it?"

"Fine this way," Marta said. With her free hand, she pulled the straight-backed chair out from under the table. She turned it around and sat down, then tipped it back on its rear legs.

"You're gonna fall and break your head open."

It was what Neal always said when she did that. She did it a lot. Teetering on the back legs of his kitchen chair seemed to be one of her favorite pastimes.

"I'll take my chances," she told him. It was what she always answered. Smiling, she took a drink of beer. Then she said, "How did you get banged up like that?"

"Taking the videos back," he said.

"Fall down?"

"Yeah." He lifted the mug and took a few swallows of beer. Then he leaned back against the counter. Legs out in front of him, he gazed down at the dark scabs on his knees. "Nothing very serious," he added.

"What *is* serious, then?" Marta asked.

"What do you mean?"

"I don't know." Frowning, she shook her head. "Are your parents okay? Did something happen to . . . ?"

"No, no. It's nothing like that."

"Are you going to make me guess?"

"I really don't want to talk about it."

"Okay." She shrugged. "I'm just concerned, that's all. When you're hurting, it hurts me."

Her words gave him a tight feeling in the throat.

"Maybe it shouldn't be that way," she said. She lowered the chair so its front legs touched the floor. "I mean, we aren't even married or anything. But I love you. I can't help it. And you're getting me awfully damned worried, here. You aren't sick, are you? You don't have something . . . drastic?"

"I got involved in something last night," he said. "That's all. I'm not sick. I tried to stop a crime, but everything went haywire and the woman ended up getting killed. She was nice. I couldn't save her, though. This . . . this *bastard* . . . he decimated her, and I couldn't stop him."

"My God," Marta muttered.

"Not only did she get destroyed, but the cops might end up

thinking *I'm* the guy who did it. And the guy who *did* do it knows who I am. I think he got away, and I think he has the business card I gave to Elise, so he knows where I live, so he might come over and . . ."

"*Elise Waters?*"

"Yeah."

"You were *there?*"

"Yeah."

"My God!"

"What?"

"The woman in Brentwood? Elise Waters? The Olympic diver?"

"Yeah."

"Holy jeez. It's all over the news. You were there? When it happened?"

He drank some more beer, then shook his head. "Sort of. Maybe I'd better start at the beginning."

"Wait," Marta said.

"Wait?"

"Don't start yet." She stood up. "Let's get it on videotape."

"What?"

"We'll record your whole statement, and take it to the cops."

"I'm not going to the cops."

Marta sat down again, rather hard. Her mouth drooped open for a moment. Then she said, "Why not?"

"I used my gun. I *shot* the guy."

"Shot who?"

"The killer."

"*You shot the killer? Holy shit!*"

"Don't get too excited, I didn't kill him. He's still out there, as far as I know. But if the cops find out what I did, I can be arrested for carrying a loaded firearm, discharging it . . . And they might even think I'm the one who murdered Elise. I was in her house. Right there at the scene of the crime, and I must've left fingerprints, at the very least."

Scowling, Marta was silent for a while. Then she said, "Okay. It's your call. If you think it's best to stay away from the cops . . . But I definitely think we should tape your story. I'll do the taping, and you tell me everything, every little detail. It'll be great evidence in case you *do* end up getting busted."

"I don't have a camcorder," Neal reminded her.

"I do."

"I know."

"So let's go over to my place," Marta said.

"I was about to suggest that, anyway. I don't like you being here. The guy's probably gonna pay me a visit. When he does, I sure don't want him to get his hands on you."

Chapter Fourteen

Marta waited in the kitchen while Neal went into his bedroom to get dressed. He wanted to look fairly respectable for the videotape, so he put on his best short-sleeved shirt and gray dockers.

He thought about dropping the bracelet into his pocket, taking it with him, showing it to Marta and explaining its magic.

Don't, he warned himself. Are you nuts? Whatever you tell her, keep the bracelet out of it.

He left the bracelet hidden under the socks, and shut the drawer.

He slipped the spare ammo magazine into a front pocket of his trousers.

"All set," he announced, returning to the kitchen.

Marta, tilted backward on the chair, tossed her empty beer can at the recycling bin beside the doorway. It flew past Neal and dropped in. "Bingo," she said.

"Good shot."

"I'm a whizz."

Neal polished off the beer in his mug, tossed his can into the bin, and gave the mug a quick rinse under the faucet. Marta led the way into the living room.

As she headed for the door, Neal stepped over to the sofa.

He pulled the pistol out from under the pillow, and showed it to her. "Okay?" he asked.

"Just don't shoot *me* with it."

He eased it down into the right front pocket of his Dockers.

Hand on the doorknob, Marta frowned over her shoulder at him. "You know, I was thinking. Do you want to bring something for overnight? Your toothbrush? Pajamas?"

"I thought that wasn't allowed. No overnights. Isn't that one of your rules?"

"This can be an exception. You shouldn't be staying here. Besides, I work tonight so I won't be there, anyway. You can use my bed."

"Well, I guess I can grab a few things. If you're sure about this."

"I sure don't want you staying here if the killer might show up."

"Okay. Hang on." He hurried to the bathroom and dug his toilet kit out of a cupboard. He checked inside to make sure it still contained his travel gear: spare toothbrush, toothpaste, shampoo, razor and shaving cream, soap and deodorant, along with an assortment of pills and bandages. Everything seemed to be in place, so he closed the zipper.

In his bedroom closet, he found a nylon overnight bag. He carried it over to the dresser, unzipped it, stuffed the toilet kit inside, then opened his drawer again. He tossed in a pair of clean socks and underwear for tomorrow.

He tossed in the bracelet, too.

If I'm staying all night, he thought, I might want to use it.

He had no pajamas or nightshirt, so he tossed his gym shorts into the bag. He could wear them to bed, if necessary.

After zipping the bag shut, he carried it into the living room. Marta was leaning backward, her rump against the door.

"Anything else I might need?" he asked.

She gave her head a quick shake, then shoved off from the door. Neal opened it for her. He stepped out after her, shut the door and made sure it was locked.

Walking with her along the balcony, he looked around.

No sign of Rasputin.

No sign of anyone except for the woman he had dubbed Miss Universe. She could often be seen sunbathing by the pool in the skimpiest of bikinis, her body brown and oily. But now the sun was too low, the courtyard and pool in shadow. Wearing a white T-shirt and carrying a basket of clothes, she was striding alongside the pool in the direction of the laundry room.

Marta bumped against Neal. "I could look like that," she told him.

"Ah," Neal said.

"You believe in reincarnation?"

He laughed. "How would I recognize you?"

"Oh, thanks a heap."

"I didn't mean it that way."

"Oh, sure."

They started down the stairs. "Anyway," Neal said, "how could you possibly be improved upon?"

"You're right, you know. How right you are!"

Neal, laughing softly, stroked her back.

How strange, he thought, to feel so fine at a time like this.

The thought sent his good feelings crashing down.

"Where'd you park?" he asked at the bottom of the stairs. "In front?"

She nodded.

"I might as well take my own car," he said.

"Okay. Meet you at my place."

They split up. As they headed for opposite ends of the courtyard, Neal looked over his shoulder at her. She walked quickly, her sandals smacking the concrete. The back of her T-shirt hung crooked across the seat of her shorts. Her blond hair, long and loose, blew slightly away from the sides of her head.

What if the bastard gets her, does what he did to Elise?

Neal turned away quickly and walked fast.

Not gonna happen, he told himself.

Might.

No! I won't let it!

On his way to the rear gate, he passed the open door to the laundry room. He heard Miss Universe drop a coin into a washing machine, but he hurried on by without looking in.

Outside the gate, he checked the alley.

No Rasputin.

He's probably in bed somewhere, Neal told himself. Maybe even in a morgue.

No dark van, either.

Why even look for the van? he thought. Not a chance in hell that it could be up and running, by now. The thing's probably in police custody.

Neal climbed into his car, swung his bag onto the passenger seat, then backed out of the parking space and headed for Marta's apartment.

It was less than a mile away, an easy walk. He wanted to have his car available tonight, however, just in case. Nice that Marta hadn't made a fuss about it.

One of her better traits: she didn't try to run his life.

He turned on the car radio, hoping to find some news about the killing. As he drove, he changed to several different stations.

But he found only traffic reports, music, and call-in talk shows. He liked John and Ken's show, so he listened for a while.

Soon, he reached Marta's street. As he turned onto it, he saw her green Jeep Wrangler pull into her reserved space at the front of the building. He parked at the curb, grabbed his bag and climbed out.

They met at the walkway.

Neal scanned the area, checking the nearby buildings, driveways and sidewalks as they headed for the front gate.

No Rasputin.

Don't even bother looking for the van, he told himself.

But he looked, anyway.

Just because I shot the thing doesn't mean it's dead.

No sign of it, though.

He spotted a black-and-white police car halfway down the block, however, and felt a sudden sickening rush of fear.

They don't know anything, he told himself. Calm down.

Marta unlocked the gate. They entered the courtyard. It was very similar to the courtyard of Neal's building, but larger. The pool was larger, and so was the concrete apron surrounding it. More apartments faced it, too.

Her building had a hot tub near one end of the pool.

And better apartments. Neal had only been inside Marta's, but it was much larger and newer than his.

It also cost nearly twice as much per month.

He was looking forward to spending a night in it—even if Marta wouldn't be there after 11:15 or so.

He followed her up the outside stairs. Her leather purse swung by her side. The backs of her legs looked slender and lightly tanned. The seat of her denim shorts pulled taut against her buttocks as she climbed.

At the top, she moved out of the way and waited for him. Then they walked together along the balcony to her door. She unlocked it, and they stepped inside.

The apartment seemed very dark.

Marta took the overnight bag from Neal, set it aside, and stepped into his arms. Her skin and clothes felt hot against him, as if she'd brought the heat of the afternoon sunlight into the room with her.

They kissed.

"Do I get the whole treatment again?" he asked, still holding her.

She grinned. "Wouldn't want to spoil you. Let's go in the kitchen, I'll make us something to drink." On their way to the kitchen, she asked, "How does vodka and tonic sound?"

"Fine," he said. But there must've been something wrong with the way he said it.

"What's the matter?"

He shrugged.

He already felt guilty about his plan to keep the bracelet a secret. He didn't want to start lying outright, so he decided on the truth. "It's what *we* drank last night. Elise and I. Vodka and tonics."

Marta lifted her eyebrows. She looked curious, maybe a little disappointed. "Have a party with her?"

"We were . . . sort of trying to recover, I think. After we got away from the guy." He met her eyes, and knew she could probably see the misery in his. "We thought we'd made it," he said, "that I'd saved her and everything would be all right."

"I'm sorry," Marta murmured.

"Anyway." He shrugged. "That's what we had. Vodka and tonics."

"Would you rather have something different?" Marta asked.

"Well . . ."

"How about margaritas?"

"Okay. Good idea."

Before starting to make the drinks, she took out a package of tortilla chips. She opened the bag and handed it to Neal. "Help yourself. This may take a while."

She crouched down, opened a cupboard, and lifted out an electric blender.

"So," Neal said. "What have you heard? I was asleep all day. I didn't get a chance to watch the news, and you showed up just at five . . ."

"Well, if they're after you, they haven't announced it."

"That's good," Neal said. He popped a tortilla chip into his mouth. It was crisp and salty, and tasted good, so he ate a few more.

Marta set the blender onto the counter and plugged it in. Then she took out a couple drinking glasses. "Last I heard," she said, "they don't have any suspects at all. They haven't really said very much." She crossed the kitchen, opened another cupboard, and took out bottles of tequila and triple sec. "Just that the victim was a woman named Elise Waters, and she used to be a diving champion. Won a silver medal in the Olympics."

He was surprised. Elise had told him about being a diver, but he'd never suspected she might've been *that* good. He usually followed the Olympic Games on TV.

Had he actually *watched* Elise dive, admired her beauty, studied how the swimsuit revealed her body, cheered her on, seen her on the podium when they awarded her the silver medal?

Probably.

If so, however, he had no memory of it.

"What year?" he asked.

Marta shrugged. "Don't ask me. I think they might've said, but I don't remember." She brought the bottles over to the blender.

"What else did they say on the news?" he asked.

"Well, that she's married to some guy who was out of the country when it happened. And how it was very brutal, the way she was killed. She was—"

"That's her *ex*-husband?" Neal interrupted.

"They didn't say *ex*." Elise set down the bottles.

"She told me that she was divorced from him. A guy named Vince?"

"I think so. Vince something. He's supposed to be an actor, but I didn't catch his last name. I don't think it's Waters, though."

"But they're *not* divorced?" Neal asked.

"Not on the news I heard. You know how they get it wrong, though." She took out a measuring cup. "Elise told you she was divorced from the guy?"

"Yeah, she sure did." So much for the will, he thought. Not that he'd wanted anything . . . Funny for her to make such a grand offer, though, if she still had a husband.

"Maybe the divorce wasn't final, yet," Marta suggested. "Isn't there a six-month waiting period, or something?"

"I think so."

She stepped past Neal, opened the freezer compartment of the refrigerator, and took out a plastic bin full of ice cubes. "Well, maybe it's just that the waiting period hadn't ended. Some people might consider themselves divorced even if they've still got a few months to go."

"I suppose."

Back at the counter, Marta tossed a dozen ice cubes into the blender.

"I'll take it," Neal said.

She handed the bin to him, and he returned it to the freezer. "Would you grab me a couple of limes while you're over there?" she asked.

"Sure." He opened the refrigerator, spotted a plastic bag of limes, and took out two.

"Anyway," Marta said, "it looks like hubby didn't do it. From what I heard, he was in Hawaii at the time of the killing. He'd been there for about a week. In Honolulu, I think they said."

"I know *he* didn't do it. But who did, that's what I want to know?"

"They don't know. Or if they do, they aren't saying."

Neal watched her fill the measuring cup with tequila and empty it into the blender. As she filled it again, he said, "The bastard is all shot up. How hard can he be to find?"

"I don't know." Marta dumped in another cupful of tequila, then a third. Then she picked up the bottle of triple sec.

"Not to mention," Neal said, "I shot up his van."

"It was a stolen van, I *do* know that."

"So they found it?"

"In the driveway of the house. You shot it up, huh?"

"Sure did."

Marta looked over her shoulder at him. "You killed an innocent van."

"Didn't want the bastard to get away in it."

She added a cupful of triple sec to the tequila and ice inside the blender. "A car was stolen from a house down the street sometime during the night. They think that's how he got away."

"I bet they're wondering who disabled his van. I mean, I only put about six bullets into it."

Marta took out a knife. As she split the limes in half, she shook her head and said, "There was no mention of any bullet holes. Not that I heard, and I caught the whole story on the four o'clock news."

Neal supposed the police must've decided to keep quiet about someone shooting up the van. There were often details that the investigators kept from the press—or tried to: so there would be secrets known only by themselves and the suspects.

"Did anybody hear my gunshots?" he asked.

"I don't know. You can go in and turn on the news, if you'd like."

The suggestion alarmed him. He shrugged and shook his head. "Maybe later. I want to find out what's going on, but . . . It can wait."

She looked at him.

Can't I hide anything from her?

"Might be easier to take," he explained, "after a margarita or two."

"Most things are," Marta said. She held one of the lime halves over the blender, and squeezed. Its juice spilled out of her fist. "I forgot the margarita salt. Do you want to grab it for me?" She nodded toward the liquor cupboard. "It's in a little white plastic tub."

"Sure." He crossed the kitchen, crouched, and opened the cupboard door. The tub was in front. "Got it."

As he returned, Marta said, "We should probably go ahead and tape your statement before we sit down to watch the news. And before you get too polluted."

"I won't get polluted," he told her.

"And I can't. Not on a work night."

As Neal opened the salt container and set it on the counter, Marta finished squeezing the last section of lime. Instead of tossing that one into the sink, she used it to rub the rims of the glasses. Then she set it aside, turned one of the glasses upside down and pressed it into the tub of salt. When she lifted it, the sticky rim was thick with white, clinging salt.

"Go easy on that for mine," Neal said.

"Health nut."

"I'm just not a salt nut."

"Would you rather have none?"

"I guess so."

Without dipping his rim in the salt, she placed the two glasses side by side. Then she put the lid on the blender. "Here we go." She thumbed the switch.

Neal cringed at the sudden noise.

The clear, greenish mixture seemed to lurch. The ice cubes leaped and whirled. An instant later, the blender was full of froth. White froth with a hint of green hue.

The machine went silent.

Marta peeled off the rubber lid, lifted the container off its base, and poured the concoction into the glasses. It plopped into them almost as thick as a milkshake. After the pouring was done, Neal heard the quiet fizzy sound of the bubbles breaking up. Murky green fluid, clear of froth, rose from the bottom of each glass until only a head of white foam remained.

Before drinking, they clinked their glasses together. A few crumbs of salt fell off Marta's rim.

"Here's to the future," she said.

"For those of us who have one," Neal added.

When he saw how sadness filled her eyes, he wished he hadn't said it.

"I'm sorry," he told her.

"Don't be sorry," she said. "I know you're hurting."

They both drank. Neal's margarita felt cold and soft in his mouth. It was sweet and tart. As it went down, it spread a soothing warmth through him.

Marta lowered her glass. She had pale froth on her lips. She wiped it away with the back of her hand. Watching Neal's eyes, she said, "Did you . . . fall in love with her?"

"I don't know. In a way, maybe."

In a big way, he thought.

"I only knew her for a couple hours," he explained. "It was all so strange. I mean, I saved her life. She was beautiful and . . . very nice. She was a lot like you, I think. Maybe that's why . . . I guess I sort of fell in love with her, there for a while."

"Yeah, that's what I thought."

"You would've liked her. Really. And you probably would've met her, too, if . . . things hadn't gone bad. She asked us to come over for a barbecue, and to swim in her pool."

Marta looked surprised, a little relieved, but wary. "You told her about me?"

"Sure. You were the reason I didn't stay the night with her."

"She asked you to spend the night?"

"Yeah. But I wouldn't."

"Because of me?"

He nodded.

She stared at him, frowning slightly, slowly shaking her head. Finally, she spoke again. Softly, almost as if talking to herself. "My God," she said. "Elise might still be alive if you'd stayed. Or *you* might've gotten killed. But you didn't stay. Because of me?"

"None of it is your fault," Neal said.

"But I'm sure part of it."

"Sort of, I guess. If you want to look at it that way. But—"

"Funny. I don't even know her, but I had a hand in getting her killed."

"No. Not really. Things just happened."

"Man, oh man." She shook her head, then tilted up her glass and took several swallows. When she lowered the glass, her lips were frothy again. "Let's do that videotape."

Chapter Fifteen

Marta refilled their glasses. Then they went into the living room. While Neal waited on the sofa, she brought in the bag of tortilla chips. Then she disappeared for several minutes. She returned with a VCR camcorder in one hand, a tripod in the other.

"I'll have this set up in a jiffy," she said. "You'll need to move, though. We don't want all that light behind you. Maybe bring in a chair from the dining room."

He did as she suggested, and placed the chair off to the side so he wouldn't have the window to his back.

When the camcorder was fixed atop its tripod, Marta sat on a chair behind it. "The tape'll show the date and time," she said as she leaned toward the viewfinder. "So we'll have proof as to when we did this."

"We won't be turning it in, though. Right?"

"You might *want* to, at some point. You know, if you need to clear yourself."

Neal finished his margarita, then peered at the camera's lens. "That isn't going yet, is it?"

"Nope."

"How's this supposed to clear me of stuff I *did?*"

"You didn't kill Elise."

"No, I know that. *Boy*, do I know that." He tried to laugh. "But I carried a concealed weapon. A *loaded* weapon. Which is a felony, and which is the main reason why Elise and I decided to stay away from the cops in the first place, last night. So I wouldn't get busted for carrying. Isn't that a laugh? They do that, you know? You use your gun to save yourself, next thing you know, you're behind bars." He tried to take another drink, but found nothing left except a patch of foam at the bottom of his glass. "I mean, I have a Constitutional right to bear arms. Or I *had* one. Back in the good old days when we *had* a U.S. Constitution. So I use my gun to save Elise from this asshole, but then we can't even go to the cops about it . . . suddenly *we're* the criminals . . . so we sneak off and he gets up and comes after her and finishes the job. Isn't *that* wonderful? Isn't *that* beautiful?"

He started crying.

"Oh, shit," he muttered.

Marta hurried over to him. She took the glass out of his hand. Then she was pulling his head forward, murmuring, "It's all right."

He snuggled his face against her belly.

"It's all right, honey," she said, gently stroking his hair. "It's all right."

The front of her T-shirt felt soft. Her skin beneath it felt warm and smooth. He wrapped his arms around the backs of her thighs.

"I'm sorry," he said against her T-shirt.

"Don't be sorry."

He tried to stop crying. "I thought I'd . . . saved her. That's what . . . it's *hard*."

"I know. I know."

"I let her down."

"No, you didn't."

"We . . . *should've* gone to the cops. If only we'd gone to the cops . . . right then and there, right after I got her free. Or *phoned* them. They would've come and taken the guy. Elise, she'd still be alive."

"Maybe."

"I didn't even make sure he was *dead*. God! If only I'd checked!"

"The if-onlys can kill you," Marta said.

"She'd still be alive."

"She might be. Or maybe not. Maybe her number was up, no matter what you did." Marta's hand moved slowly and gently down the back of his head.

He nodded, rubbing his face against her belly. "Shit happens," he muttered.

"And we can't always duck in time."

He laughed and sobbed and almost choked. "Shit," he said. Then he eased his face away from her soft warmth. "I drenched your shirt."

"It'll dry," Marta said. Her curled hand stroked him over and behind the ears.

He tilted back his head. She was staring down at him. Her eyes were wet and shiny. "Why don't I fix us something to eat?" she suggested. "Then we'll try again."

He nodded.

"How about tacos?"

"That'd be appropriate."

"My name is Neal Darden," he said, looking into the lens of the camcorder. Then he gave his address and telephone number. He spoke carefully, though he no longer felt particulary high.

An hour had gone by since his first attempt at the tape—and his breakdown. During that time, he'd consumed a Pepsi, lots of tortilla chips and salsa, and four beef tacos. No beer, and no more margaritas.

"I'm making this videotape," he said, "as a record of what happened to me on the night of Sunday, July 9, 1995. And in the early morning of the tenth.

"I left my apartment at about 11:30 Sunday night to return a couple of tapes to Video City, over on Venice Boulevard. I wanted to get them in before midnight. It was warm out, so my window was down. Otherwise, I probably wouldn't have heard the screams."

He went on, talking at the camera. Though aware that the tape might someday be viewed by strangers, Marta was his true audience. He wanted her to know every detail—*almost* every detail—because in some ways it was her story, too.

He wouldn't have been out last night, returning the videos at such a late hour, if he hadn't rented them in the first place. He had rented them because he wanted Marta to sit beside him and watch a couple of his favorite films.

And then, instead of leaving by ten to return to her own place and get ready for work, she had stayed. They had made love right there on his sofa. Then she had gone down to her car and returned with her work clothes in a bag. "I brought them along in case things got late," she'd explained. After vanishing into the bathroom, she'd come out dressed in her sharp airline outfit, her makeup on, her hair neatly brushed.

It had been wonderful.

And it had put Neal exactly where he needed to be at the time of Elise's screams.

So this was Marta's story, too. Neal felt as if he were filling her in on part of her own life—an important part that had occurred in her absence.

He'd always figured he would end up telling her *something*. After all, she was bound to see his injuries. But he was surprised to find himself telling her so much—giving her details that he'd expected to keep secret.

He had even told about Elise being tied to the tree naked. He'd intended to leave out the naked part, but he found himself speaking the truth, regardless.

He did manage to keep silent about his arousal. He'd already admitted to falling in love with Elise; Marta sure didn't need a history of his erections.

Or how he'd struggled against the temptations to have sex with Elise.

The less said about such things, the better.

He didn't attempt to hide his feelings of love for Elise (a bit too late for that), but he tried to make it seem like innocent affection. He spoke of her as if she had been his sister or a wonderful, old friend.

And realized he *did* feel that way about her.

Mostly.

And mostly because of Marta. His loyalty to Marta had kept him out of Elise's bed, prevented him from becoming her lover.

Now she's gone, he thought. Dead and gone, so it will always be innocent between us.

He found himself weeping again.

Several times, he wept as he told his story. Each time, he paused for a while to regain control, and Marta kept the camcorder running.

"Can't you turn it off?" he'd asked, the first time.

"It'll be better if we don't. Let's keep this a continuous shot so they'll be able to see we didn't make any cuts."

So she kept it running, no matter what.

Sometimes, Neal heard sniffles from behind the camera. Sometimes, groans. Rarely did Marta speak. Once in a while, she asked questions when Neal didn't seem to be making himself clear or when he left out details that she thought might be important. She almost never made comments, though.

Until he described Elise's body in the bathtub.

"Oh, dear God," she'd said.

Neal wished he hadn't told her so much. It would've been easy to leave out the worst of it. But he felt that she deserved the truth.

The truth about almost everything except the bracelet.

Elise's private gift to him.

Telling Marta about the bracelet would be like breaking Elise's trust, so he kept it to himself.

He simply omitted it from the story.

In the story he told, he was never given the bracelet or any other reward for saving Elise's life. He never tried it out on her, there in the den. Nor did he use it, after leaving her house, to take a quick look at where they'd left the man's body, or to rush back and try to warn her that the bastard might not be dead, after all—only to find himself helpless inside her body when she was jumped in the hallway.

For Marta and the videotape, none of those things had ever happened.

The way Neal told the story, curiosity had gotten the best of him while he was driving home from Elise's house. Instead of taking the shortest route, he'd chosen a detour that would take him past the place by the freeway where he'd rescued her.

Only to discover that the van was gone.

He'd run across the field.

The man's body was missing.

Fearing the worst, he'd dashed back to his car.

Back to the truth, he'd told of his race to Elise's house, breaking every traffic rule but never able to speed as fast as he wished—fast enough to save her from torture and death at the hands of the madman who should've been dead.

Finally, he said, "That's about it, I guess."

"Okay," Elise said from behind the camcorder. "Now, let me ask a few questions."

"Sure."

"You already described the guy pretty well, but about how tall do you think he is?"

"Maybe six feet, six-one. An inch or two taller than me."

"Weight?"

"I don't know. He was skinny. Skin and bones. Cadaverous. I could see his ribs through his shirt. That's why I'm so sure he wasn't wearing a bulletproof vest."

"Age?"

"That's like weight. Who knows? I never got much of a look at his face. All that hair and beard. I didn't see any gray hair, though. And he was quick and strong. Just a guess, I'd say he was in his twenties or thirties."

"That's a *real* help." Her face was mostly hidden behind the camera, but she sounded amused.

"I'm not good on ages," Neal explained.

"That's for sure." After a pause, she asked, "Could you identify the man if you ever saw him again?"

He had to think about it. After a few moments, he answered, "Probably not. I wouldn't be able to tell him from any other skinny guy with a big black beard and wild hair. And if he paid a visit to a barber, I wouldn't know him from Adam."

"Or if the hair and beard were fake?" Marta suggested.

"A disguise?"

"Yeah."

"They might've been, huh? Great. I had the impression they were real, but . . . who knows? The thing is, I don't have the slightest idea what he might look like without the beard and hair."

"He'd be the skinny guy with the gunshot wounds," Marta pointed out.

"That's about it. At least I'm *pretty* sure he's wounded."

"Okay. Next. Other than giving the police a description of the man and telling that he's been shot, do you have any information that might help them solve the crime?"

"I don't think so. And I did what I could last night. Searched for him, disabled his van. I'm surprised he got away. Hell, I'm surprised he didn't die when I shot him back by the freeway. I *know* I didn't miss. I mean, he went down. And he bled in Elise's house."

"Anything else you want to add?" Marta asked.

"That's about it, I guess. Any other questions?"

Marta shrugged, shut off the camcorder, and scooted her chair out from behind it.

"Now what?" Neal asked.

"Should we go ahead and turn the tape over to the police?"

"No. Are you kidding? I confessed stuff that could get me fined and jailed. Not to mention, I'd probably end up with a criminal record. I hadn't even thought about *that*, till now. My teaching credentials might get revoked. I could lose my job."

"Could they fire you over something like this?"

"I'm not sure, but I'd hate to find out the hard way."

"You *ought* to be given a medal."

"They don't hand out medals for shooting bad guys. Not unless you're a cop . . . and around here, even a *cop* is likely to get prosecuted for it."

"So, we don't turn over the tape," Marta said.

"I don't see what good it would do, anyway. It'd clear up a bunch of confusion for them, maybe, over things *I* did at Elise's house, but it won't tell them who did the killing. And it might give them the idea that I'm the best candidate."

"Okay," Marta said. "You're probably right."

"If I *do* get pulled into it, that's when we'll think about turning over the tape. It should help get me off the hook for the murder, at least."

"Fine. That's what we'll do." She reached over to the camcorder, opened it and removed the tape cassette. She tossed it to Neal. "All yours. But I have one suggestion."

To: Investigating Officers
    Elise Waters case
Date: July 10, 1995
Sirs:

I have firsthand information regarding the identity of the man who murdered Elise Waters on the night of July 9, 1995.

He is a male Caucasian, approximately six feet tall, and thin to the point of emaciation. On the night of the crime, he had very long, unruly black hair and a full beard. His age is unknown, but he is probably in the twenty to forty range.

He was a stranger to the victim.

On the night of the crime, he may have suffered gunshot wounds to his head and torso. One head wound, one to three body wounds. All inflicted by .380 caliber bullets.

Fingers still resting on the typewriter keys, Neal looked over his shoulder at Marta. "How's that?"

"Looks fine." She smiled. "They'll go ape when they see this. I just hope they believe it."

"They'll believe it, all right," Neal said. "The bastard bled in her house. And I left my brass behind after I shot up the van. It's .380. They'll believe."

He turned the platen knob of the old Royal portable.

Marta, wearing rubber dishwashing gloves, plucked the paper from the roller. She folded it and slipped it into an envelope that they had already stamped and addressed.

The address was typed:

LOS ANGELES POLICE DEPARTMENT
West Los Angeles Station
1663 Butler Avenue
Los Angeles, CA 90066

Marta sealed the note inside the envelope.

"When do you think they'll get it?" Neal asked.

"I'll mail it on my way to the airport. Maybe in Inglewood. So it'll probably go out tomorrow morning. The cops should have it on Wednesday."

"Good enough," Neal said.

Chapter Sixteen

Shortly after eleven o'clock that night, Marta left for work with the envelope in her purse.

After walking her down to her car, Neal returned to her apartment and let himself in with the key she'd given him. He sat down on the sofa. He felt shaky, and his heart beat fast.

Okay, he told himself. She's gone.

What'll I do?

He had two choices: either return to his own apartment in the flesh or go there with the help of the bracelet.

If he went over in person, he would wait in the darkness, maybe sitting in a corner of the living room, the pistol in his hand. Sometime during the night, the killer might show up.

He *will* show up, Neal told himself. For all he knows, I can identify him. Besides, he'll want to pay me back for shooting him. He'll want to kill me.

Torture me first?

Strip me and tie me up, stick a bar of soap in my mouth so I can't scream?

Do me the way he did Elise?

Going cold inside, Neal told himself that the guy probably wouldn't work on him the way he'd worked on Elise. That had been a sex thing. Elise had been a beautiful woman.

It won't get him off, doing that stuff to me.

Don't count on it, Neal thought. What if he isn't particular— goes both ways? Or maybe he'll torture me just for the hell of it. For revenge. I hurt him; he'll hurt me worse.

Have to get me first.

I'll empty my gun into the bastard, Neal thought. Won't matter how much he wants to torture me, if he's sprawled out dead with six slugs in his face.

Neal knew, however, that something could always go wrong. He might get taken by surprise—jumped from behind. What if he drifted off to sleep while waiting for the killer to arrive? What if something went wrong with his pistol?

What if I empty it into him and he keeps on coming?

The idea seemed ridiculous, but sent tiny cold fingers scurrying up Neal's spine. The nape of his neck went prickly with gooseflesh. His scalp crawled.

What if he isn't human? Something immortal. A vampire, or something.

That's crazy, Neal told himself. Of course he's human. He bled, didn't he? Vampires don't bleed.

"Shit," he muttered. "The bastard isn't any vampire."

Didn't drink her blood, he thought.

How do you know? He bit her. He bit off pieces. God knows what kind of monster he is.

"A man," Neal said.

A Dahmer sort of guy, he thought. Mad as a hatter, but die-able.

"Imminently die-able," Neal said. He smiled. He liked the sound of it.

Maybe use it in a script sometime, he thought.

"Imminently die-able," he repeated. "Bullet-resistant, but die-able."

Diabolical.

Rasputin, Neal thought. But give him a shave and he'll look like Nosferatu.

I'm not going over there, he decided.

Neal carried his overnight bag into Marta's bedroom and set it on top of her dresser. He took out only the bracelet.

In the lamplight, the gold gleamed with a deep, rich lustre. The emerald eyes of the snake sparkled brilliant green. He turned the bracelet, inspecting it closely. The details were intricate.

A gorgeous piece of jewelry, he thought. Too bad it has to be a snake.

Snakes bite.

He shook his head.

He supposed that the snake design was probably symbolic of something.

How about the serpent in the Garden of Eden? Which was Satan, right?

It had been quite a few years since Neal had studied *Paradise Lost,* and probably even longer since he'd read Genesis in the Bible. But it seemed to him that the serpent had led Adam and Eve "down the garden path" by offering them forbidden fruit from the tree of knowledge—knowledge of good and evil.

Which is pretty much what the bracelet does, he thought.

Probably no accident that it was made in the form of a serpent.

A warning? A promise of forbidden knowledge?

He wondered if the bracelet, itself, might be evil.

No. That didn't make sense. From what he'd seen of Elise, she had been a wonderful person—not a hint of meanness, dishonesty, or cruelty about her. She wouldn't have used the bracelet, time and time again, if there'd been anything sinister about it.

Besides, Neal had already used it three times. He'd noticed nothing evil about the bracelet or its effects.

He only wished it had a different design, something less ominous than a snake.

Don't worry about it, he told himself.

And slipped it onto his wrist.

Leaving the lamp on, he stepped over to Marta's bed. He sat on the edge of the mattress and pulled off his shoes. Then he stretched out. He removed the pistol from his pocket, and placed it near his right hip.

As he raised his arm, he shut his eyes and tried to imagine Elise kissing the bracelet.

But he pictured her dead on the edge of the bathtub, naked

and bloody and mutilated, her arms out, the bar of soap in her mouth. He could almost taste the soap.

Groaning, he kissed the gold head of the serpent.

My place, he thought as if giving directions to a cabby.

He felt himself rise out of his body, leaving behind its weight and aches. A moment later, he was outside the bedroom window. He glimpsed the balcony below him. Then he was above the dark swimming pool. He passed the far side of the apartment building as he climbed into the night. The moon was full, and very bright.

Suddenly too high for a good view of landmarks, he willed himself to descend. At treetop height, he prowled above the streets until he was able to orient himself. Then he headed straight for his own building.

He approached it from the front and swooped in through the wrought iron bars of the closed gate. As he made a pass above the swimming pool, he scanned the area. Nobody in the pool. Nobody wandering outside, either on ground level or on the balcony. Many of the apartment windows were dark, but some glowed with light from lamps or televisions on the other side of their curtains.

Maybe it's still too early, Neal thought. Not even 11:30 yet. The bastard might not make his try till two or three in the morning, just to make sure nobody'll be up and around.

Neal wondered if he would be able to remain that long.

He had no idea.

Gotta just play it by ear, he told himself.

And glided through the picture window and curtains of his living room.

The lights were off. He went to a wall switch and reached for it. No arm, however, appeared in his vision. He let out a small laugh, but didn't hear it.

Who needs light, anyway? he thought. It's not as if I'm going to crash into the furniture and hurt myself.

This is so damn odd!

Ought to be used to it by now, he told himself.

But the first trip last night, from the sofa to Elise and back, had started and ended very quickly. During the two trips that followed, he'd been preoccupied with worries about the killer and Elise, and hadn't focused much attention on the wild, fabulous magic of his flying.

Now, he suddenly found himself marveling at it.

He could hardly believe that he was actually floating through his apartment five feet above the floor—actually able to see the dim shapes of everything, actually able to hear various sounds such as the motor of his refrigerator—though he had no eyes or ears. He had no body at all. He *shouldn't* have any sensations at all.

For that matter, he shouldn't even *be* here.

None of this should be happening. Every bit of common sense told him that he was in the midst of an impossible experience. You can't leave your body behind and go on a flying trip like an odd patchwork of Peter Pan, the Invisible Man, and Casper the Friendly Ghost. It defied reality.

Only one way to accomplish such a feat—by dreaming it.

Maybe I'm asleep back at Marta's place, he thought, and this is nothing but a dream. I had to be dreaming last night, too, when I thought I was taking those bracelet trips.

I *imagined* going into Elise? Hearing her thoughts? Feeling everything she felt?

We talked about it later.

Had he imagined that, too? Where does it all stop? When did the dream begin? Did he ever really meet Elise? Maybe he crashed on the way to Video City, and he's been in a coma ever since.

Or dead.

"Bullshit," he muttered.

I'm alive, he told himself. Alive and awake. This is not a dream.

Whatever's going on, it's happening. Who knows why? Just accept it.

For now.

While pondering the strangeness of the situation, Neal had somehow roamed out of his apartment. He found himself drifting over the pool, moving toward the front gate.

As if being pulled by a subtle force.

He supposed it must be the same force that he'd experienced so strongly last night—the imaginary elastic strip connecting him to his body. Tonight, he hadn't noticed it until now. Its pull felt very weak, barely noticable.

Let's check the alley, he thought.

He willed himself toward the rear gate.

The pull didn't hold him back. He couldn't even feel it as he jetted in silence past the end of the pool, past the laundry room and out the gate to the alley.

I'll just make a quick run in both directions, he thought, then go back and wait in my—

Off to his right, far down the alley, a dark figure shambled toward him. He felt a quick lurch of fear.

Is it him?

Neal couldn't tell. The stranger's head was out of sight beneath a slouch-brimmed hat. A long, dark coat concealed the shape of his body.

Might even be a woman, Neal thought.

Or it might be the bastard coming for me.

One way to find out.

Even as he began to consider approaching for a closer look, he found himself suddenly rushing over the pavement, heading straight toward the stranger.

Who wore a cape, not a coat.

A cape?

Nobody wears a cape! What's going on?

Neal gazed into the darkness under the slouch hat.

Is it him?

The gray of a narrow, beardless face.

I don't know, Neal thought. Could've shaved, or . . .

Uh-oh!

Neal was suddenly inside the stranger.

No wounds.

The man seemed young and healthy and excited. He was sweaty inside the cape, but he kept it shut in spite of the warm night. The lining, where it rubbed him, felt like satin. He seemed to be wearing shorts, but no other clothes. From the calves down, he was encased in hot leather. The boots felt slimy inside, and his feet slid around in them as he limped through the alley.

A fake limp, Neal realized.

While taking a quick inventory of the body, he'd ignored the man's mind. Now, he tuned in on it.

"Yes yes yes. I am the creeper, creep-creep-creeping. All those who see me piss their pants. Where is everyone? Come out, come out, wherever you are. Here comes the creeper, creep-creep-creeping. Nightmare man. Who knows what evil lurks in my heart?"

Neal felt his glee, his anticipation.

What sort of nut is this guy? he wondered.

Not my nut.

"Yes, yes, yes. Here I come, creeping down the alley. Come one, come all. Behold the creeper. I am the black heart of the night. I'm coming for you."

Jesus H. Christ, Neal thought.

This is the sort of guy you find roaming down the alleys at night?

This and worse, he supposed. This guy is playing some sort of game.

While the weird monologue continued, another level of Creeper's mind seemed to be amazed and thrilled by his oddball behavior. He seemed to have a fantasy about revealing his midnight strolls to friends. They wouldn't find it cool, though, if he had to *tell* them about it. They'd need to find out by accident.

The fantasy—vague meanderings of thought when Neal first noticed it—became more and more focused. Soon, it broke into his monologue.

"I creep this way and that through the alleys of the night, bringing terror to all who see me." Maybe I should say this stuff out loud. That'd be cool. Nobody around to hear me, though. So what? Who cares?

"I am the creeper," he said, trying to make his voice a low, spooky groan. "Ho ho ho."

Knock off the ho ho ho, I'm not Santa Claus.

"I am the creeper," he tried again. "I own the night. I'm gathering souls. I eat them and laugh."

*What's the good of all this if there's nobody around? Need to have
an audience.*

*I've got it! Find a security camera! Yes! Go to a 7-Eleven. They're
open all night, and they've got cameras.*

Sound?

Doesn't matter, I can say my stuff to the clerk.

Creeper seemed to be more frightened than thrilled by the
idea of taking his show into a store. There would be so much
light. And maybe customers.

All fine and dandy, but what if I run into hooligans?

Neal laughed. He wondered if, blocks away, his body was
laughing on Marta's bed.

The passing thought was interrupted when a movie-like scene
started running through Creeper's mind. The guy was imagining
himself inside a brightly lighted 7-Eleven store, face-to-face with
a gang of sneering, vicious teenaged thugs. Seeing him, they
mutter among themselves. Then they start pointing at him and
laughing. He runs from the store. They chase him, hooting,
shouting, "Fag!"

The scene made the Creeper feel hot with humiliation.

It's a stupid, silly outfit!

He had a sudden urge to fling off the slouch hat and cape
and shove them into the nearest garbage container.

But he pictured himself walking home, dressed in nothing
except his swimming trunks and boots.

Neal saw the same mental image. A rear view of a young
man, probably no older than eighteen, quite tall but skinny and
weak, hurrying down an alley. Head shaved. Big ears sticking
out. Skin so white it almost glowed. A skimpy little bikini-style
swimming suit clinging to his skinny ass. Big old leather cowboy
boots clumping along as if he were wearing buckets on his feet.

A pretty sorry picture, Neal thought.

Creeper thought so, too. He decided to stay in his slouch hat
and cape.

Good idea, Neal thought.

Still hot and squirmy with embarrassment, Creeper was trying
to recover.

Nobody laughs at the Creeper. "See me and scream. I am the demon of the night, a vulture and you're my carrion. I peck your eyes out and swallow them whole." *Shit.*

The mood was gone.

This is no good. I should've stayed home. Must've been nuts. What if I run into someone I know? And they laugh at me? Who am I gonna scare in this getup, anyway? I look like a refugee from a bad Halloween party.

Creeper turned around and started walking the other way. He no longer tried to look spooky, hunching himself over and limping. Afraid of being seen, he glanced over his shoulder every few seconds.

Ready to bolt and find a hiding place in case a car might come along.

Fun's over, Neal thought. *Time to go back to my apartment and wait for Rasputin.*

No, no. Let's stick with Creeper for a while longer. See if I can find out where he lives.

Though Neal didn't care where Creeper might live, it would be a good experiment. If he could hitch his way to someone's home, he'd be able to return there, later, in the flesh.

He might need to do that with Rasputin.

Find the bastard first, of course . . .

Let's just see how it works.

Creeper reached the end of the alley. He checked both ways. No cars were coming, so he broke into a run and raced for the other side of the street. It was tough, running with boots on. Especially the way his sockless feet slid around in them. He couldn't pump his arms, either; they were busy keeping the cape shut. But he made it across the street all right, and ran on into the alley.

Entering a stretch that had no lights, he flung open his cape and ran on, arms wide. The night air rushed against his sweaty body. The cape fluttered behind him.

Hey, nice.

Next time, ditch the boots. Run free.

He wanted the hat off so he could feel the fresh air on his scalp. But as he clamped a hand on the edge of its brim, a gate swung open a few yards in front of him. Someone barged out into the alley.

Sudden fright blasted through Creeper.

He yelped with alarm.

The woman, coming to an abrupt halt just outside the gate, turned her head toward him. Behind her, the iron gate banged shut. She dropped her garbage bag.

Creeper was scared, confused.

The woman didn't move.

Creeper watched her as he ran closer.

She appeared to be in her early twenties, plump, with round glasses and a bowl-shaped haircut. She wore a tank top, as if proud to show off her thick arms, her breast tops, and the gorge of her cleavage. She also wore white shorts and white moccasins.

What a bowwow.

Swell guy, Neal thought.

She flung her hands up to the sides of her face and screamed.

Oh, shit! Now look what I've done!

Creeper considered stopping to apologize. But glee suddenly surged through him.

He ran straight at the woman, reaching for her.

"No!" she squealed.

She whirled around and grabbed the gate. But she was too slow. Before she could open it, Creeper clamped a hand on her shoulder. She screamed again. It was shrill, ear-splitting.

"I am the creeper," the guy said in the spookiest voice he could muster. "The night belongs to me, and so do you."

As if unhinged by fear, the woman sank against the shut gate, cowering and whining.

Wow!

Creeper took a step backward, trembling. He could hardly believe that he had done such a thing to a person—scared the hell out of her, turned her into a cringing heap of mindless terror.

He felt disgusted at himself.

And elated.

She's at my mercy! Why don't I do more?

In the distance somewhere beyond the gate, a door banged shut. Creeper heard footsteps on a stairway.

He whirled around and ran down the alley, boots clumping, cape afly. Afraid he might soon find himself pursued by the gal's husband or boyfriend, he glanced back.

Clear, so far.

He dodged into the nearest carport—a doorless structure with stalls for half a dozen vehicles. Every space was full. He slipped into the dark, narrow gap between a couple of parked cars.

Don't touch 'em. Set off an alarm, and you're screwed.

He made his way forward, then to the left. Midway between the headlights of a midsize car, he squatted down.

They won't find me here.

After a while, he was able to control his breathing. He continued to tremble, though.

Scared that someone might come along and find him.

Thrilled by the memory of how he'd scared the woman.

He realized his teeth were chattering.

What a rush!

"I am the creeper. Creep-creep-creeping through the alleys of the night. I'm coming for you, sweeties. I'll make you scream and piss your pants."

He wondered if the woman had wet her pants.

He pictured her cowering at the gate in her white shorts and tank top. Imagined himself shoving his hand against her crotch, feeling the hot and soggy cloth.

The thoughts were giving Creeper an erection.

In his mind, he grabbed the woman by the ankles and dragged her away from the gate. He ripped open the waist of her shorts. He tugged the shorts down her legs, tore away her dripping panties and . . .

Enough of this sick puppy, Neal thought. I'm out of here.

A moment later, he was free.

Clear of the parked cars, he found himself speeding up the alley. He glimpsed the gate. The woman was gone. Nobody there at all, but her overturned trash bag lay on the pavement. Nothing had fallen out of its tied mouth.

Neal wondered if Creeper would sneak back to see if she'd left a puddle.

Fucking weirdo.

But not *my* weirdo, Neal thought.

With no effort at all, he sped to the end of the alley and over the street, then on into the next alley. He swept through the rear gate of his apartment complex. He soared up to the balcony, heading straight for his own front door.

Approaching his door, he tried to slow down.

Couldn't.

He barged through the shut door and tried to stop. He wanted to sit down and wait for Rasputin. Or hover and wait. But he couldn't even decelerate, much less stop. He blew through furniture and walls that had no more substance than air, and suddenly found himself outside again, speeding above the pool on his way toward the front of the building.

What's going on?

It's taking me back, he realized. Won't let me stay.

Let's just see about that.

Though unable to slow down, he found that he still had some control over his direction of travel. Not much, but some.

Scanning the streets below him, Neal spotted a man wandering along the sidewalk behind a leashed dog.

Try this guy out.

Neal dived toward him.

Hope this isn't another weirdo.

Entered and exited, fast as an arrow, and kept on going.

Shit! I can't stop!

Chapter Seventeen

But he did stop, and very soon.

He stopped when he reached Marta's apartment, her bedroom, her bed, his own body.

What was *that* all about? he wondered.

The answer seemed obvious: there were a couple of rules to bracelet travel that Elise hadn't mentioned. For one, you can't linger around very long, disembodied. For another, no people-switching.

Try again?

Not just yet.

He folded his hands beneath his head.

Let's think about this for a minute. Gotta figure out a few of the rules.

For starters, they give you a while to scout around.

They? he wondered.

The bracelet police, of course.

Right.

There might be limits to the scouting time allowed, he thought, but at least they allow a while to search for someone interesting to ride.

You need to be careful, or you might end up inside someone by accident.

Me and Creeper boy, Neal thought.

Neal had not really intended to enter that guy. He would've preferred to avoid him and keep moving, but he'd approached closer and closer, hoping to get a look under the hat brim, and suddenly found himself sucked in, part of the guy.

From now on, he warned himself, keep your distance. And don't even *think* about getting into somebody unless you're ready to go ahead with it.

Never point your gun at anyone you don't intend to shoot.

And then there's the biggie—you can't switch people in the middle of a trip. They just won't let you hop from one to another. Once you leave the body you've been riding, you make a beeline back to your own body. Whether you want to or not.

What a drag, Neal thought. Puts some real limits on things.

If you want to switch people, you apparently need to start all over again. Return to your own body, kiss the bracelet and go looking . . .

Neal wondered what other rules there might be.

What if Elise had left something *really* important out of her instructions and warnings?

The possibility made him uneasy.

I've got to trust her, he thought. She *must've* told me every-thing that worried her about the bracelet—gave me all kinds of warnings.

Don't get addicted to it.

Don't ride in people you know.

Bail out quick, if someone's dying.

Be careful where you leave your body.

Where you leave your body . . .

Neal opened his eyes, sat up in Marta's bed, and glanced around. The pistol was still by his hip. Everything looked fine.

He picked up the pistol, then made a trip through the rooms just to be sure that nothing had gone wrong while he'd been away.

No problems.

He used the toilet, then returned to Marta's bedroom. Her clock on the headboard showed 11:55.

He certainly didn't feel sleepy.

Give it another try?

As he stretched out on the bed, he realized that he didn't *want* to make another trip to his own apartment. Rasputin hadn't been there five minutes ago; he wasn't likely to be there now. And having learned some more rules of bracelet travel, Neal figured it wouldn't be possible to hang around and wait for the killer's arrival.

Why bother making the trip? It was sure to be a waste of time.

Maybe give it a try in half an hour or so.

Neal thought about getting up, returning to the living room and turning on the TV. He might find some local news. Maybe Rasputin had been apprehended by now, or . . .

He didn't *want* to watch the news.

There would be photos of Elise, tales of what had been done to her . . .

They would hurt.

Let's take a trip, Neal thought, and kissed the bracelet.

* * *

He headed for his apartment building, even though he felt certain that Rasputin wouldn't be there yet.

I'll just take a quick look, then pay someone a visit.

Try not to pick a weirdo, this time.

The best way to avoid weirdos, he decided, was probably to stay away from people in alleys. And on streets. And in cars. Excluding cops and a few other types with night jobs, nine out of ten people roaming Los Angeles at this hour were probably oddballs, creeps and criminals. Most normal people would be locked inside their apartments and homes.

Maybe I'll try one of my neighbors, he thought.

As he approached the front gate of his apartment building, he realized he didn't *have* to use the gate. He wished himself high. In moments, he was well above the complex. He moved slowly, gazing down into the courtyard.

Few lights seemed to be on. The balcony was deserted. He saw nobody in or near the pool. Most of the tenants, he supposed, were probably asleep by now.

Gliding past the rear of the building, he looked up and down the alley. He scanned the puddles of light, the patches of gloom, the black places where no light reached.

From this height, he could see a great many black places.

Where someone might be lurking.

Nobody can touch me, he told himself. I'm invisible, invincible.

Can't *do* shit, but at least I'm safe.

Hearing a faint rattly-clattery-rolly sound, he peered to his left. A shopping cart had just entered the far end of the alley. Undoubtedly stolen from a local grocery store, it was now loaded with treasured junk and being pushed along by a squat person dressed in a knit cap and overcoat. Maybe a man, maybe a woman.

Not Rasputin, he told himself. Unless the bastard's not only bullet-resistent, but also a shape-changer—magically alters himself from tall and skinny to short and dumpy.

In a world where a bracelet like this really works . . .

Neal didn't want to pursue that line of thought; it could lead into very dark, disturbing places.

I have to go along as if everything's normal, he told himself. Everything except me. Right. The only supernatural stuff going on is me and my bracelet.

Sure as hell hope so.

What if that is Rasputin?

Tempted to check, he found himself racing toward the scavenger.

No!

He banked hard to the left, a panic turn that sent him through a stucco wall and into someone's kitchen. Nobody there, but light came in through an archway to other rooms. Curious, he slowed down and headed for the light.

In the living room, he found a woman seated at the end of a sofa, reading a paperback book under the bright yellow glow of a lamp. She seemed to be the only person in the room.

She looked reasonably young and normal.

In her early twenties, Neal guessed. Her soft brown hair looked clean and neatly brushed. She wore glasses. She had a pleasant face, pretty but not strikingly beautiful. She wore a big, loose T-shirt with a neck so wide that it hung off one of her shoulders. The shoulder was bare.

Give her a try? Neal wondered.

Why not? I could do worse.

Just pay her a little visit, find out what's . . .

He was in.

And reading.

The woman's eyes rushed across the lines of her paperback, so Neal tried to read with her. The words, being read in unison, seemed oddly doubled. He heard the woman's mental voice, but also his own. It sounded like a duet recitation.

Though the words matched, the images they called up in the woman's mind were different from those Neal was experiencing.

Her images seemed a lot more vivid than his.

They ought to, Neal thought. I'm just jumping in. She's halfway through the book. She knows what's going on, what the characters are supposed to look like . . .

He noticed something odd.

The female in the scene, whose name was Nora, looked very much like the woman reading the book.

He read on.

According to the writer's words, Nora was supposed to be a redhead.

But not in this gal's mind, she wasn't.

Ignoring the writer's description, the reader had given Nora brown hair the same as her own.

This gal's really into it, Neal thought.

Fascinated, he tried to keep on reading. The conflicting images were too confusing, though. Nothing looked quite the same in the woman's mind as in his. She saw the same words as Neal, but it was as if she were watching a movie of the book—a film with the same script as Neal's version, but with a different director and cast.

He gave up on the words, and turned his attention to the woman.

That, in itself, was confusing.

She seemed to have a split life. She existed simultaneously as two women in separate places, doing different things but joined and flowing together in strange ways.

The reading woman sat motionless on her sofa, leaning back comfortably in its soft cushions, one leg crossed and tucked beneath the other. Though deeply involved in the story, she was also aware of herself. She felt safe, cozy, and mildly aroused.

Neal found it quite pleasant, being in her.

He wondered what her name was.

No way of finding out, at least not yet.

She's Reader, he decided.

Reader and Nora.

Reader sat on the sofa, book in her hands, while Nora now sat astride a black stallion that trotted along a beach. Clear blue water rolled in calmly against the sand. The day was lovely, cloudless and warm. A sea breeze blew in softly, tossing Nora's hair so it flowed out behind her like a gleaming brown banner. She wore a loose, white nightshirt—the sort of garment Neal had seen men wearing in illustrated editions of Dickens novels.

He had no idea why she might be wearing such a thing for

her horseback ride on the beach. Obviously, she'd acquired it before his arrival in Reader.

She seemed to be naked under the garment. At least in the mind of Reader, she was. Reader felt the horse, hot and powerful between Nora's bare legs, pounding up against her, writhing and rubbing her. As it trotted, her breasts leaped about wildly inside the nightshirt.

Naked under her T-shirt, Reader felt it all. Not just the horse but the sunlight, the sea breeze, and Nora's breathless excitement. She took a deep, trembling breath. She squirmed a little. The front of her T-shirt stirred against her nipples, caressing them. Neal could feel their hardness. They felt so sensitive that the soft brush of the T-shirt sent a thrill of pleasure rushing through her.

Nora suddenly spotted a man in the distance. He was on foot, walking toward her along the water's edge. Too far away to recognize, but . . .

Tyrone?

Reader seemed very familiar with Tyrone. Along with Nora, she felt a surge of excitement. Nora urged the stallion to a gallop. She and Reader raced along the beach, hunched low on the horse and clutching its mane, the wind in their faces, hair blowing behind them, horse throbbing under them.

Is it my Tyrone? Nora wondered.

Of course it's him, Reader thought.

And she was right. When they were near enough, they recognized him.

In Reader's mind, Tyrone was slim and strong, dressed like a swashbuckler. His floppy white shirt, wide open to his waist, revealed a smooth and tawny chest. He wore a colorful sash instead of a belt. The sash held a dagger at one side, some sort of old-fashioned pistol at the other. He wore tight-fitting leather pants, and shiny black boots that reached up past his knees. His hair was long, dark, and flowing in the breeze.

Though Reader and Nora had already settled their doubts about the man's identity, Neal couldn't quite make out his face. Not that the distance or the jolting of the horse caused a problem: He could *see* Tyrone's face just fine.

It seemed, however, somewhat vague in Reader's mind. Almost as if the face kept undergoing subtle changes. One moment, Tyrone appeared to be the spitting image of Clark Gable's Rhett Butler. Another moment, he looked like Tom Selleck as Magnum. Then, Pierce Brosnan. Then Selleck again. Then Brosnan. As if Reader couldn't make up her mind which image she preferred.

"My love!" Nora suddenly cried out. The horse hadn't even stopped running before she leaped from its back. She stumbled over the sand toward Tyrone—who currently looked like Brosnan.

Reader wondered how he'd escaped, but she was in no mood for an explanation. Right now, she needed Nora to throw herself into Tyrone's arms.

Which Nora did.

Tyrone embraced her and Reader. Nora hugged him hard, mashing her breasts against his powerful chest. "Oh, my love!" she gasped. "I feared I should never see you again."

"Come on, knock off the chatter," Reader told her.

"How ever did you escape from the stockade?" Nora asked.

Reader thought, Oh, crap, here we go. Do we need this? Do we really? Give me a break. Make love to the guy, don't interrogate him.

Frustrated, she turned the page.

New chapter.

Reader scanned the first few lines, and realized this was going to be a flashback. Tyrone's daring escape from the stockade.

"Phooey," Reader muttered.

"Not me, pals. Lost me, there."

Feeling mildly annoyed, she reached down by her side and picked up a bookmark—a glossy triangle that looked like a corner torn from a magazine page. She tucked it in and shut the book.

That was enough for now, anyway. Tune in tomorrow, folks, and find out everything you always wanted to know about Tyrone's fabulous escape.

Then maybe we can get back to the beach, where the good stuff's going on.

Reader began thinking about herself on a beach. As her mind roamed, her eyes happened to be gazing at the book's cover. *The Wild Buccaneer*, Neal read, by Amanda Burns. Gotta be a pseudonym, he thought.

The guy on the cover wore a costume similar to Tyrone's, but he bore little resemblance to Reader's image of him. With a long and somewhat equine face, shoulder-length blond hair and bulging brown pecs, he could never be mistaken for Gable, Selleck or Brosnan: He looked like a bulked-up chorus line dancer.

The gal on the cover, cradled in Tyrone's bulging arms, had russet hair and bosoms bulging over the top of her bodice. Her soft, innocent face appeared hopeful and twenty years old.

She looked nothing at all like Nora—who looked exactly like Reader.

Attention on the cover, Neal was taken by surprise when Reader twisted sideways and dropped the book onto the lamp table.

She stood up. Her left leg felt a little stiff; she must've had it tucked up underneath her other leg for quite a while. She didn't give it much thought, though. She was mostly thinking about making a trip to Venice Beach next weekend.

Call up Trudy, see if she wants to go. Do I really want to go with her? She's always on the make, she'll get herself picked up by some guy and that'll be the last I see of her and I'll be stuck at the beach alone. Might as well go alone in the first place, save myself the aggravation.

While thinking those thoughts, she wondered (vaguely, less distinctly) if she had remembered to lock the front door. She took a few steps toward the door and saw that it was locked.

I oughta go by myself. Not Venice Beach, that'd be too yucky. What a freak show. And now they've got gangs over there shooting at each other every weekend. Don't wanna get myself shot. What about Santa Monica beach? Probably just as bad. Malibu? That might be okay.

Pleased by the idea of an adventure at Malibu beach, she reached up and turned off the lamp. The room went dark except for the murky haze coming in through the curtains.

Might meet a nice guy. Who knows? Miracles do happen.

As she stepped carefully through the near-darkness, she imagined herself walking along the beach, slim and tanned and wearing a white bikini. And along comes the cutest dog she has ever seen. She squats in front of it, says *"Hi, ya, fella,"* and rubs its neck. Then a voice says, *"His name's Growler."* She looks up, and there stands a gorgeous, tanned man in white swimming trunks. He looks a lot like Pierce Brosnan. *"And I'm Tom,"* he says. Reader stands up, smiling and flustered. *"I'm Karen,"* she says.

Ah-ha! Neal thought. Karen! She *must* be Karen. Nobody'd go around giving herself a fake name in her own fantasies.

"Hello, Karen," Neal said into her mind, though he knew she couldn't hear him. "My name's Neal. Nice to meet you."

Fat lousy chance, Karen thought, startling him.

Did she hear me?

No, she was still involved with Tom, but her fantasy had gone a bit sour with the intrusion of a cynical part of her mind. *Never gonna meet a guy like that. If he's that handsome, he's already taken, or he's gay. Or he's a total jerk who thinks he's God's gift to the universe. Or else he is perfect, in which case he won't give me a second glance.*

She stepped through a doorway, flicked a light switch, and squinted in the sudden brightness. She had entered her bedroom. Turning around, she shut the door. On its back was a full-length mirror. She stopped and looked at her reflection.

Not too bad.

Not bad at all, Neal thought. This was the best view he'd had of Karen, so far. She was prettier than he recalled. She wasn't as heavy, either. No skinny super-model type, but still a long way from chunky. She had fairly broad shoulders, and . . .

Neal's view of Karen disappeared. For a few moments, all he could see was the white of her T-shirt.

When the shirt no longer blocked his view, Karen was twisting sideways to toss it underhand toward her bed.

She wore nothing at all.

Holy smoking Toledo! Neal thought.

She looked at herself in the mirror, and shook her head.

Spectacular! Neal thought.

Could be worse, thought Karen, and wondered how many pounds she might be able to lose before next weekend.

She turned away from the mirror.

Shit! Neal thought. *"Don't go away! Gimme a break! Please!"*

His disappointment quickly faded. Though he could no longer see Karen in the mirror, he enjoyed the feel of the air on her bare skin, and the moving weight of her breasts as she walked across her room. She stopped in front of her dresser.

If none of these fit, I'm gonna just kill myself.

The words in her mind were an exaggeration.

She knew that she'd gained weight since last summer, but she had also been working out. Her swimsuits might or might not fit, but she felt fairly confident that she would look better than usual on the beach this year.

She almost hoped they *would* be too small for her. That way, she'd have a good reason to go shopping.

Crouching a bit, she bent over at the waist and reached for the handles of the bottom drawer. Her breasts pulled downward, swaying slightly.

Neal moaned, but heard nothing.

This is so fantastic, he thought.

Karen wasn't overly impressed by her naked body, but she did like the feel of the air on her skin, especially where it felt cool in the heat under her arms and between her legs.

In the drawer were several swimsuits. She wanted nothing to do with most of them. Pushing a couple aside, she spotted her white bikini. She took it out and stood up. Leaving the drawer open, she turned around and walked toward the mirror.

Neal watched Karen approach her reflection, watching herself.

Her arms swung by her sides, the bikini clamped in her right hand. Her breasts jiggled and bounced a bit. Her nipples stuck out. Neal could feel the air on them. He wished he could put his mouth on them.

But he could only look.

Stopping a few paces from the mirror, Karen separated the two pieces of her bikini. Eyes on the skimpy pants, she bent over and spread the elastic waist band. Then she raised her head.

Yes! Neal thought.

Head up, she watched her mirror image. It showed her bent low at the waist, gazing at herself. Her nose was wrinkled to keep her glasses high. A sweep of shiny brown hair draped her brow. Her arms were stretched straight down, breasts suspended between them.

She raised one foot and stepped into the bikini pants, then raised the other.

She was concerned. *Not only too fat, but I've got no damn tan at all. It's July already! The ninth? Tenth? And look at me. I can't go to the beach like this.*

As she unbent to pull up her pants, Neal could see all the way up her legs, to where they joined. He glimpsed a thatch of brown curls, and lips like the puffy edges of a gash. Then the wispy nylon came in underneath her, snug against her crotch and buttocks. When she let go, the elastic hugged her like a soft cord.

Karen looked down at herself.

Could be worse. Have to remember to shave, though. Good Lord—if I ever get one any smaller, there won't be any point.

She raised her head. The front of the pants appeared even smaller in the mirror. From the corners of the patch, elastic strips stetched upward over her hip bones. Turning, she looked over her shoulder. The strips slanted down behind her, where they kept the seat of her pants stretched taut against her buttocks. The sides of her cheeks were bare.

She wiggled her rear end, watched it shimmy, and wished it was firm with hollow cheeks.

Ah, well. Can't have everything. Not bad, as buns go.

"Lovely, as buns go." Neal told her with his mind, though he knew she couldn't hear him. "*Not to mention, you've got fabulous tits.*"

Neal suddenly felt ashamed of himself for the tit remark.

Nice going, he thought. Very nice.

What's the big deal? he asked himself. She doesn't know what I'm thinking. Hasn't got a clue.

That makes it okay?

What am I doing in here? he wondered. I'm no better than

a peeping Tom. *Worse* than a peeping Tom. *I get to spy on her thoughts, too. And her feelings.*

The bikini top still dangling from her right hand, Karen arched her back and sucked in her belly. She gazed at her profile.

Still got great boobs. A shame nobody gets to see them but me. I oughta find a nude beach somewhere.

Yeah, right.

Like I want a bunch of strange men drooling over me. Bet they'd really be strange, too, at a place like that. Perverts. A bunch of lechers hanging around with their whangs in the breeze.

She saw the scene in her mind.

To Neal, the nudist lechers looked like they'd just escaped from a home for scrawny lunatics.

Then the crowd dispersed, and only one man remained. He was especially cadaverous and ugly. Neal realized this was how Rasputin might look, beardless and naked.

Whose fantasy is this? he wondered.

Has to be Karen's.

She felt sick inside as he strolled toward her. Grinning, he grabbed his limp member, lifted it, and waved it at her like a snake. "Say hi to Monty," he said.

Karen grimaced at herself in the mirror.

Monty? Where on earth did I dig up a name like that? Never even known a guy named Monty. Much less a dick.

She shook her head and laughed. The horrible images faded, but she still felt a little uneasy because of them.

"Monty the dick," she said aloud, but softly. Neal liked her voice. "I'd better find me a guy fast, I'm losing my marbles. And now I'm talking to myself. Talking to myself and daydreaming about . . ."

"*Penises*," she finished the thought in silence. "*Too long since I've been around any.*"

A memory suddenly filled Karen's mind. She was on a bed in a sunlit room, stretched out on her back, a man on all fours above her. His name was Darren. She knew that, though she couldn't see his face. She could only see his belly, and sometimes his penis. His *thing*, that's what she always called it. Mostly, his thing was out of sight, hidden between her breasts. It felt enormous, hot and very hard.

Darren loved her breasts, so she was giving him a special treat. First, she had instructed him to rub oil on them. When they were slippery, she'd rolled onto her back and guided Darren onto her. Then she'd used both hands to push her breasts together and trap his thing.

Facing the mirror, Karen shook her fingers. The bikini top fell from them, brushed the side of her calf and dropped silently against the carpet.

She took hold of her breasts and pushed them together. Rubbed them against each other.

They felt a little slippery with sweat.

Not as slippery as they'd felt with Darren, though.

Concentrating, she tried to feel his thing.

Thick and long, sliding in and out of the crevice between her breasts. Rubbing up and down, sometimes plunging downward so deep it nudged her sternum. Other times sliding forward until its glistening head came squeezing out, inches from her mouth, like a wiener popping out of its bun.

"Next time, we'll use mustard."

She'd actually said that to Darren. But there hadn't been a next time.

Karen suddenly parted her breasts, clutched them by the front and squeezed, digging in her fingernails. Hard enough to hurt.

But the pain from her breasts was nothing compared to the agony crushing her heart.

She dropped to her knees, sobbing wildly.

Oh my God! Neal thought. What's going on? What's *the matter* with her?

He fled.

Chapter Eighteen

In his own body again, Neal found himself squirming on his back, breathless and sweaty. He swung his legs off the mattress. Sitting on the edge of the bed, he tried to calm down.

Horrible to see Karen go crazy like that, he thought. What the hell had gone wrong? She'd lost Darren, obviously. Lost him in a way that had done major damage to her. Did he get himself killed, or just dump her?

Go back and find out?

No thanks, he told himself.

Maybe she's over the tantrum, by now.

Neal didn't want to take the chance.

Poor gal, he thought. Jeez.

Being inside her had been wonderful for a while, though.

Wonderful? Spectacular!

My God, she stripped right in front of me!

He gazed at the bracelet on his wrist.

No wonder Elise warned me about getting hooked on it. I can go to anyone I want, get inside, watch her undress, take a bath, make love. But I don't just get to *look*, I get to *feel* everything she feels.

Incredible, Neal thought. Literally unbelievable. Way too good to be true.

He *couldn't* believe it was true, but neither could he find a way to deny it. The bracelet didn't bestow vivid dreams or fantasies, it allowed you to enter actual people. Which he knew to be impossible.

Impossible. But he was absolutely certain that, if he ran down to his car and drove to his own neighborhood and located Karen's apartment, he would be able to meet her in the flesh.

I must be out of my mind, he thought as he drove. He'd been thinking that, every so often, ever since the idea had popped into his head.

He knew he shouldn't do it.

Karen was not likely to appreciate a surprise visit from a stranger in the middle of the night.

And Neal felt as if he were cheating on Marta.

Not that he expected or wanted anything romantic to happen with Karen. He'd be lucky if she even opened her door for him, and the odds of being allowed into her apartment were slim to none.

So why am I doing this? he wondered.

Just to see. Just to see what I can find. See how reality matches up. If I can at least get a glimpse of her . . .

I don't need a glimpse. I know how reality will match up. Perfectly, that's how. This is bullshit.

But I want to do it.

I *am* doing it.

I must be out of my mind.

A few minutes after driving away from the curb in front of Marta's building, he drove past his own building. He turned the corner, then entered the alley. He drove slowly. The area ahead looked clear: nobody skulking about. Nobody that he could see, anyway. No scavenger creeping along behind a shopping cart, no Creeper sneaking through the shadows in his slouch hat and cape. No Rasputin.

He wondered where Rasputin might be.

As he drove by his own parking space at the rear of his building, he slowed and almost stopped.

I could just run up and check, he thought. If the bastard's there, I can blow him away . . .

Maybe later.

Maybe never.

I've gotta get him before he gets me, Neal told himself.

Yeah, but this isn't the time to try it. He's not there, anyway.

Make a run-through with the bracelet?

I didn't come here for that. I came to check on Karen.

He kept on driving, but felt guilty about it. He knew that he ought to visit his own place. If he stayed away from it, how could he ever hope to get the jump on Rasputin?

I'll try it later, he told himself. But first things first. Make this reality check on the bracelet, and then I'll know for sure.

I already know for sure.

No, I don't. Not a hundred percent. This will be the final proof. Then I'll never doubt it again.

He drove on past another building. The next was probably Karen's. Its parking spaces were full. He pulled forward so he wouldn't block them, swung close to the edge of the alley, then stopped. He killed the headlights and shut off the engine.

Then he climbed out of his car and walked to the other side of the alley. From there, he looked up at the stucco wall.

Is that it? he wondered.

He'd gone through Karen's wall by accident, really, after an emergency swerve to avoid plunging into the bum.

This looked like the wall.

Glancing from side to side, he tried to judge the distance back to his apartment building, then from where he now stood to the place where he'd seen the bum with the shopping cart.

The distances seemed about right.

And Karen's apartment was definitely not in the next building down. That place had balconies above the alley. There'd been no balcony on the wall he'd entered.

This has to be it, he decided.

Walking toward the rear gate of the building, he felt a strong mixture of dread and excitement. He had come on purpose, planning to pay a visit to Karen. But he was shocked, anyway, to find himself here. A strange but somewhat familiar sensation. He knew it from . . .

Amusement parks. Disneyland, Knott's Berry Farm, Magic Mountain, Funland, the Santa Cruz Boardwalk. It had happened to Neal in all those places, at one time or another.

You get into line for a thrill ride—one of the scary kind that takes you way too high and drops you way too fast. You stand in the line on purpose, planning to take the ride. Wanting to take the ride. But suddenly, there is no more line in front of you. You're next. And you suddenly realize the time is now and you've made a very large mistake.

You get a tightness in your chest and you want to cry out, *"What am I doing here? Let me outta here!"*

That was exactly the way Neal felt as he opened the rear gate, stepped through it, and shut it so gently that it didn't make a sound.

Why don't I just turn back? he told himself. This is nuts. What if she shoots me or something?

He never turned back from the roller coasters, either. Or from the huge and terrifying Ferris wheels. Not since being a grown-up. There was excitement along with the fear, and he always stepped aboard.

He glanced about as he made his way toward the stairs. This courtyard had no pool. A parklike area, instead: a lawn with bushes and trees, walkways, quaint lampposts, and even a few picnic tables. It seemed rather old-fashioned and peaceful.

He saw no one.

He climbed the stairs slowly, quietly.

His legs were shaking.

It'll be all right, he thought. I'm not doing anything wrong.

I know that. The cops won't know that, though. Nobody who sees me sneaking around will know that. I oughta get out of here before something happens.

Try not to look suspicious, he told himself.

At this hour? Fat chance.

Walk straight to her door as if you belong here.

The door nearest the top of the stairs was numbered 26. Neal realized that he didn't know Karen's apartment number, but 26 seemed to be located in the proper place—the northeast corner of the building, its rear wall facing the alley.

Off to the right of the door was a large picture window. No light came through it. Neal remembered Karen turning off the living room lamp before heading for her bedroom in the rear.

He wondered if she was still in her bedroom. Still kneeling on the floor in nothing but her bikini pants, hurting herself and crying her head off?

Who knows?

Not all that much time had gone by since Neal had left her there. Five minutes? Maybe a little more than that. Fewer than ten, though.

Halting in front of the door, he took a deep breath.

Oh, man, he thought. Gotta be out of my mind.

He rapped the door gently with his knuckles. A quick, furtive series of five taps, hopefully loud enough to be heard by Karen but not so loud as to alarm any of her neighbors.

At this hour, he thought, *any* knock is alarming.

He waited. No sound came from her apartment.

Had she heard him? Was she cowering on her bedroom floor, listening, fear spreading through her?

Give it one more try. Make it sound nice and friendly.

He rapped on the door again, five times and gently like before. Then he waited again.

She's not coming, he decided. Either couldn't hear me, or she's scared and hoping I'll go away. Or maybe she's calling the cops.

I oughta blow it outta here.

One last shot, then I'll go.

He spoke one word softly to the door. "Karen?"

A moment later, her voice came. Little more than a whisper, it sounded as if she assumed he must be a friend. "Who is it?"

"My name's Neal. I'm an old friend of Darren's. He used to talk about you. All the time. I always wanted to meet you, Karen, and . . . I know it's horrible to drop in on you like this. I mean, this late. But he said you're sort of a night owl, anyway, and . . . I'm driving down from San Francisco. I have to be in San Diego in the morning. I just thought I'd stop by for a minute, since I was sort of passing through the area, anyway."

A light suddenly came on above the door. "Hang on a second," Karen said. The door opened until the guard chain stopped it. Through the four-inch gap, Karen peered out at him.

That's Karen, all right.

His earlier visit hadn't been a dream. This was Reader, Karen. No doubt about it.

Behind her glasses, her eyes looked puffy and red from crying. She wore the big, white T-shirt. Neal wondered if she'd put it on quickly after hearing the knocks.

"Have we ever met?" she asked.

He blushed. "I don't think so."

"Are you sure? You seem . . . I don't know . . . a little familiar."

"So do you, actually." He smiled, still flustered, but feeling a little amused that he'd been able to speak the truth. She looked familiar, all right.

"Your name's Neal?" she asked.

"Right. Neal Darden."

My God, I told her my real name! Am I nuts?

"Anyway," he said, "I just thought I'd drop by. I've always wanted to meet you, so I figured I'd give it a shot since I was passing through. Nothing ventured, nothing gained."

Staring at him, she sniffed.

"Well," he said, "I'd better get going, now. I just wanted to stop by and say hi . . ."

"No, wait." She shut the door. Neal heard the chain rattle. Then the door swung open wide. Karen stepped backward, saying, "Come on in."

He hesitated. "I shouldn't. It's late, and . . ."

"No, please." She hurried over to the lamp and turned it on. Neal stepped into the lighted living room.

The living room.

"I guess I can stay a minute," he said, and shut the door.

On the lamp table was the paperback, *The Wild Buccaneer*, exactly where Karen had put it before going to her bedroom.

"What can I get you?" she asked. "A Pepsi? Or I could brew up some coffee . . ." She shrugged. She seemed nervous and figity, but pleased to have him as a guest.

"Oh, no thank you."

"You sure?" She waved her arms. She was almost *bubbly*.

This is so odd, Neal thought.

Being in Karen's actual presence confirmed the truth about the bracelet, but seemed very strange.

Not long ago, he'd been inside her. He'd read the book with her. He'd seen everything she saw, felt everything she felt, even viewed the scenes running through her imagination. He'd watched her strip naked to try on her white bikini. He'd even been a secret audience to her memories of Darren's *thing* plunging between her oiled breasts.

And there they are, he thought.

He could see the shape of them through her T-shirt. He turned his head away.

"Are you okay?" Karen asked.

He shrugged. "I think I've got a little fever."

"Could I get you some aspirin?"

"I'd better just get going."

"No, sit down and rest a while." She gestured toward the sofa.

"Well . . ." Neal walked over to it and sat down.

"Let me at least get you a Pepsi."

"All right."

She hurried away. Neal sighed, relieved to have her out of sight.

What the hell am I doing here? he wondered. I found out she's real. That's all I came for.

Get out now. Make a run for it.

No, no, I can't do that to her.

Would it be any worse than staying? he asked himself.

He had already invaded her privacy—*demolished* her privacy. In a way, staying would be like toying with her. If he fled, however, she would be hurt, puzzled, maybe even frightened.

I've got a lose-lose situation here, he thought.

Not necessarily.

Be nice to her, polite, play it out, try to leave her pleased by your visit.

And don't let her find out you're a fraud!

Chapter Nineteen

Moments later, Karen came into the living room with a glass of Pepsi in each hand. She walked carefully. Her breasts, between the glasses, wobbled and bounced a little. The ice cubes in the glasses made tinkly sounds.

Her T-shirt, though very large, didn't reach down past the middle of her thighs.

Neal forced himself to look up at her face.

She was blushing; she must've noticed the way he was checking her out.

"I guess I probably woke you up," Neal said, trying to give himself an excuse for staring at her T-shirt.

It seemed to work. She smiled and tilted her head a bit. "No. You got me just in time." Stopping in front of him, she held out one of the glasses.

Neal said, "Thank you," and took it.

"I'm not really used to having visitors at this hour," she told him.

"I'm not used to being one."

She made a quick, high laugh. "Well," she said. She glanced at the other end of the sofa, seemed to consider sitting there, then turned away and crossed over to a leather hassock. She lowered herself onto it, smiling a little nervously and pressing the T-shirt down between her thighs. Her knees were higher than her waist. She quickly lowered them, stretching her legs across the floor toward Neal.

He smiled and took a drink. "Ah, good," he said.

"Good." She took a sip. "So," she said. "How did you find me?"

If she's unlisted, I'm screwed.

"I stopped at a pay phone. Checked the directory."

"Ah." She nodded, apparently satisfied.

Thank God!

"And you were a friend of Darren's?" she asked.

Oh boy, oh boy, oh boy.

"Yeah," he said. "We were classmates."

Everybody has gone to school, right?

But he saw a look of confusion on Karen's face. "That's funny," she said. "You look a *little* familiar, but gosh . . . I knew all his friends at SC . . ."

"Oh! Not SC. University of Southern California? No. Not there. We were *high school* friends."

What if he's not my age?

"Ah. That explains it."

Thank God, Neal thought.

If she keeps on asking questions, though . . .

He suddenly had a brainstorm—a way to avoid further traps.

"I actually haven't heard from Darren in quite a while," he said. "I've tried calling him a few times, but . . ." He shook his head. "Has he moved, or . . . ?" He shrugged, stared at Karen, and waited.

She gazed at him.

"Do you have his new address, maybe?"

Pain came into her eyes.

Shouldn't have asked! She's gonna throw another fit! The guy probably kicked the bucket. New address, plot such-and-so at Friendly Hills Memorial Park or some damn place.

But her voice sounded fairly calm when she said, "I have it. Sure." She took a drink of Pepsi, then reached out and set her glass on a nearby table. "I'll get it for you." She drew up her knees.

"Oh, that's all right. Don't get up and get it. Unless . . . you know. If you're ready for me to go . . ."

"No. I just thought you wanted it."

"I didn't really come here for his address. I just wanted to meet you. He always . . . said such nice things about you."

"He did?" She lowered her knees again, stretching her legs out.

"Oh, yeah. Talked about how beautiful you are. He was right about that, too."

She blushed and smiled and shook her head. "It's very nice of you to say so, but . . ."

"He told me he'd stopped seeing you." *Careful. You're pushing it.* "I really couldn't understand that." *Watch out.* "You sounded like such a great couple." *She's starting to look funny.* "I was awfully sorry to hear it hadn't worked out."

She looked as if, before her very eyes, Neal had turned into an odd but not unattractive brown chimp. "What are you talking about?" she said.

"You and Darren."

"What about us?"

"Well, you know. He told me that you'd broken up."

"Broken up what?"

"Your . . . you know, your relationship."

She smiled in a frantic way, and her blush darkened to purple. "We never . . ." She shook her head. "Nothing's broken up. Just because he got married doesn't . . . I mean, he'll always be my brother."

Neal felt as if he'd been clubbed on the head.

He lifted the glass to his mouth, and drank, and tried not to choke.

There's gotta be some mistake!

Lowering his glass, he said, "The other Darren. Not your brother. The *other* Darren. He must be the one I know."

"I don't think I know any other Darren."

I didn't really think so.

"Sure you do," Neal insisted. "You must. The one I went to high school with. You don't remember me, right?"

"Not really. You look a little familiar, though. We might've met. Did you ever come over to the house? See, I didn't go to Hamilton. Mom and Dad sent me to Saint Joan's. That's a parochial school downtown. They, you know, wanted to protect their little girl from all the big, bad teenaged boys."

Neal struggled to smile. "That explains it, then. The Darren I know went to Santa Monica High School. We both did. Samohi."

"Weird," Karen said.

"Yeah. That his name should just happen to be Darren and he'd have a girlfriend named Karen . . ." Neal tried to recall Karen's last name.

I don't know it! Never did!

Oh shit!

She watched him, her eyebrows rising above the rims of her glasses.

A few seconds passed. Then she asked in a quiet, wary voice, "Karen what?"

"You know."

"I know. Don't you?"

"This is really embarrassing," he said. "I guess I've drawn one of those blanks. You know how sometimes a name just suddenly slips your mind for no reason at all?"

"You just looked *mine* up in the phone book, didn't you?"

"Yeah. Sure, I did. But haven't you ever had a name slip your mind?"

"What's going on?" she asked.

Neal shook his head, shrugged, and tried to look innocent. "Maybe I'd better just leave now. I'm sorry I can't remember your name." He laughed. "Half the time, I can't remember my own."

"Neal Darden," she told him.

Splendid. Great. Spectacular. She remembers.

"If it's even your real name."

"I'm sorry," he said. "I'll just leave, okay?" He twisted sideways and set down his glass on the lamp table.

As he stood up, so did Karen.

As he stepped toward the front door, so did she.

She got there first, and put her back against it.

"I just want to leave," he told her.

She stared into his eyes. "First tell me what's going on. Only this time, how about the truth? You didn't look me up in the phone book, did you? You don't even *know* my last name, do you?"

"Sure, I do."

"Stop lying, okay? Look, you seem like a decent person. I'm not going to call the police, or anything. I just want to know what you're doing here."

"Okay," he said, and wondered what to tell her. Not the truth, that's for sure. She wouldn't believe the truth. Besides, Neal was not about to tell *anyone* about the bracelet.

"You're right," he said. "I don't know you. I've seen you around the neighborhood, and I . . . sort of followed you home, one day." He smiled, trying to look sheepish.

"Why?"

"I wanted to know where you live."

"Why?"

"Uh . . . I thought I might like to meet you. I know, that probably sounds kind of creepy. Like I'm a stalker, or something."

"A little bit," she said. But she seemed more intrigued than wary. "How did you find out my name?"

The mailbox? Neal wondered.

No! If her building was like most, her mailbox label wouldn't show her first name. Probably just a K.

Followed by her full last name.

I should've looked there! I'd still be going along fine if I'd just taken the trouble to learn her last name!

Karen hoisted an eyebrow. "Trying to think of a good answer?"

I asked someone?

Sure. Who?

Saw her name somewhere? On her car registration?

Great idea. Give her the idea I searched inside her car. That'd *really* make me look like a jerk.

"I'm just a little embarrassed," he said.

"I bet you are."

I saw her name on her driver's license? How on earth would I get a look at her driver's license?

Yes!

"You'll think I'm a real snoop," he said, "but at this stage of things . . ." He grimaced. "I stood behind you in a checkout line at the grocery store, and sort of . . . I watched you filling out a check. All I could catch was your first name. I glimpsed the Karen, and then . . . I followed your car when you drove home."

Please don't ask any more questions!

She gazed at him. Frowning slightly, but not in an angry way. "You're kidding," she said.

"No. That's basically it. Tonight, I just . . . I couldn't wait any longer. I just had to come over and try to really meet you. I know it's crazy. Coming at an hour like this. But ever since I found out where you live, I've been . . . I haven't been able to think straight. So anyway. That's that."

"Why?" she asked.

"What do you mean, why?"

"Why me?"

"I just . . . there's something about you. The first time I saw you, I got this feeling. As if we'd known each other for a long time, or something."

Her frown vanished. "I sort of . . . feel that way, too."

"I know this wasn't the right way to go about meeting you. I mean, you probably think I'm some kind of lunatic . . ."

"I don't know." She shrugged. "Not really."

"That's good. Anyway, now that we've met, I'd better get out of here so you can get some sleep. Maybe we could meet again tomorrow, or . . ."

"That'd be great!"

"Great," Neal said, trying to match her enthusiasm. "Dinner?"

"Sure."

"Why don't I pick you up? Say, around six?"

"Six? Fine."

"Terrific."

But she still blocked the door.

Neal gave her a big smile. "Are you going to let me out?"

She smiled back. "Maybe, maybe not."

Oh, man. Now what?

"Before I let you go," she said, "you've got to tell me one thing."

No more questions! Damn!

"Any second now," he warned, "I'm gonna turn into a pumpkin."

"Then I'll make a pie," she said.

He didn't like how she looked, saying that. He tried to keep smiling, but it wasn't easy.

"What do you want to know?" he asked.

"How did you know about Darren?"

Neal felt a sinking sensation.

The very question he didn't want to hear.

"How did I know *what* about Darren?" he asked, trying to stall.

"You said you were a friend of his," Karen explained. "That's how you got me to let you in. So, if I'm just a stranger you . . . fell for and followed home, how do you know anything about Darren?"

"Oh, I picked his name at random."

"Darren?"

"Sure. Everybody knows a Darren."

She didn't seem amused. "Try again."

Neal hesistated, then said, "You don't really want to know."

"Yes, I do."

"You're going to keep me here till I tell you?"

"I'm not moving."

"I could move you."

"If you try, you'll be sorry."

"I thought you wanted to go *out* with me."

"Maybe I do," she said. "You seem . . . I think you're someone I might like very much. But I have to be able to trust you. There has to be honesty. And there hasn't been much of that, so far. You got me to open the door under false pretenses, by *lying* to me. That's no way to start a relationship."

"I know. But I just didn't figure you'd open the door if I told you I was some Joe Schmo off the streets."

She nodded as if she understood and agreed. But then she asked, "So how did you know about Darren?"

What the hell.

"From you," he said.

She frowned. "What're you talking about?"

"This is gonna sound crazy, and you'll think it's another lie. But it's the truth. Honest to God. I have this gift, this ability . . . Sometimes, I can tell what someone's thinking. I can read minds."

Karen's face went crimson. "Oh, yes," she said. "Every day, and twice on Sunday."

"When I came to your door? I concentrated on you. And I found Darren's name in your mind."

She stared at him. "No. No, you didn't."

"I did."

Her head jerked a couple of times quickly from side to side. "That's impossible. Nobody can read minds."

"I can."

"No."

"I had no idea he was your brother," Neal explained.

And wished, right away, that he could call the words back.

Karen's lips moved, but no words came out. She was breathing hard.

Why didn't I keep my mouth shut!

"It's all right," he told her. "I'll never tell anyone."

She looked horrified. "Tell what?"

"About you and Darren. The things you've done together."

"You . . . you *know?*"

"I'm sorry."

"Oh, God!" Her hands flew to her face. She dug her fingertips into her cheeks and blurted, "Oh, God, no!"

"It's all right," Neal said again.

"No!" she cried out.

"Shhh. I'll just leave. Okay? If you'll move out of the way? You'll never see me again. I'll never tell anyone."

"Bastard!"

She threw herself at him, squealing, reaching for him with hooked fingers.

Neal lurched backward. "No!" he gasped. "Jeez!"

"Bastard!"

He flung his arms up to protect his face. She raked his forearms. "Ow!" He shoved her away and glanced at the raw furrows on his arms. "Look what you did to me! Jeez!"

She came charging at him again. She was sobbing. Tears poured down her face.

"No!" he snapped.

She kept on coming, hands up, fingers ready for clawing.

Neal said, "Shit!" Then he braced himself, rammed his left arm up to block her, and drove his right fist into her belly. She was soft there. His fist pounded deep. Her breath exploded out and she folded over his hand.

As she went down, he caught her under the armpits. He lowered her gently to her knees. When he pulled his hands free, she slumped over and pressed her forehead to the floor. She made noisy sucking sounds, trying to breathe.

Neal crouched in front of her head. "Are you okay?" he asked.

She kept on gasping.

"I'm sorry I had to do that, Karen. I shouldn't have come here. I'm sorry. But as far as I'm concerned, this is the end of it. It was all a big mistake, and I'm sorry I found out about your . . . your thing with Darren. But I'll never tell anyone, I promise. Your secret's safe with me. Okay? Just don't call the cops on me. I'm going. I'm going right now. You'll never see me again."

I hope, he thought.

Then he stood up, stepped around her, and hurried to the door. As he grabbed the knob, he looked back at her. She was still on her knees, her head to the floor. Neal expected her white bikini pants to show, but she didn't have them on anymore. He glimpsed pale buttocks, a shadowy cleft, a glistening slit, hair. Looking away quickly, he jerked the door open.

He shut it gently, silently.

Then trotted down the stairs and ran for the rear gate of the courtyard.

Chapter Twenty

In Marta's bathroom, Neal used toilet paper and water to clean the bloody scratches on his forearms.

Everything just keeps on getting worse, he thought.

How could he explain to Marta about the scratches? She was bound to notice them. He couldn't make them go away. Nor could he hide them by wearing long sleeves, not every minute he was in Marta's presence, not in July.

How does a guy get his arms scratched in the middle of the night?

He needed an explanation that didn't involve leaving Marta's apartment and having a fight.

Tell her I went back to my own place and tangled with Rasputin?

No!

He'd had enough of lying. Lies had gotten him into this mess. Lies, and curiosity.

Never should've gone to see Karen, he thought.

That had been his first mistake. He made a second mistake when he stepped through her door. By then, he'd already seen her and confirmed the reality of his earlier visit. There'd been no need to enter her apartment.

So why did I do it? he wondered.

He wanted to think that he'd gone in because he felt sorry for her and hoped to distract her from her loneliness. That had been part of it, at least. But he'd also been attracted to her. He'd liked her mind, while inside it, and he'd liked her looks.

Hoping to get lucky?

No, he told himself. It wasn't like that. I don't cheat on Marta. Hell, I proved that, didn't I? If I was going to fool around with anyone, I would've done it with Elise. She was much better looking than Karen. And willing. But I refused.

So why *did* I go into Karen's apartment, if it wasn't to mess with her?

Just to see what might happen?

Yeah, right. You wanted to see her in that T-shirt. And maybe without it. And maybe you'd get to fool around with her through no fault of your own.

He had gone in knowing that she was terribly lonely.

Figured you might at least get to hug her.

Maybe cop a little feel along the way, all innocent.

Never thought she'd attack.

He remembered punching her. He'd been scared at the time. He'd only hit her to defend himself, and he felt a little sick at the memory of it.

But the punch . . . feeling his fist drive into her soft belly . . . and grabbing her so she wouldn't fall hard . . . knowing she was naked under the T-shirt . . .

He'd caught her beneath the arms, but he could've easily grabbed her breasts. Grabbed them, and told himself later that he'd done it by accident . . . just trying to help.

I didn't, he reminded himself. I didn't take any sort of advantage of her.

All I did was look . . . a glance back on my way to the door. Nothing wrong with that. Not my fault she'd taken off her pants. Besides, I didn't *really* look. It's not like I stopped and crouched down and *inspected* her. I *left*.

Remembering it, he felt aroused and guilty.

And I'm trying to tell myself I didn't mess with her?

I messed with her, all right. Didn't make love with her, but I sure as hell *fucked* her.

And she fucked me, he thought, looking at his ripped arms.

The scratches stung. She'd raked away strips of skin from both his forearms: three scratches on one, four on the other. Some were insignificant. On each arm, however, were two deep furrows that still leaked blood.

Her middle and ring fingers had done the main damage.

The wounds looked like exactly what they were. Nobody was likely to mistake them for scatches from thorns, a cat, or anything other than human fingernails.

Marta sees these, Neal thought, and she'll start thinking maybe I *am* the guy who killed Elise.

He opened her medicine cabinet to look for an antiseptic.

And he realized that he'd never been inside this cabinet before. Its shelves were lined with Marta's private things: her toothbrush, dental floss, toothpaste, little plastic bottles of aspirin, Tylenol and prescription drugs, cotton balls, tubes of ointments and creams, a dispenser of birth control pills.

Talk about invading someone's privacy . . .

He didn't want to know what she kept in here.

This is almost as bad as riding someone, he thought.

As good as.

Embarrassed, he tried to ignore the labels. And he listened, afraid Marta might arrive home early for some reason and catch him looking at these things.

When he found a tube of antiseptic ointment, he turned his back to the cabinet, twisted off the tube's cap, and squeezed some goop onto a finger.

As he spread it onto his wounds, he wondered how to deal with the *real* problem: not the injuries themselves, but how to prevent Marta from finding out about them.

He could think of only one solution.

Leave.

Disappear, and not come back until they're healed.

My God, he thought, that might take a couple weeks.

It seemed like an awfully extreme way to solve the problem. But also an attractive way.

As he finished applying the ointment to his injuries, he thought of some very good reasons to disappear. Mainly, it would save him from Marta's curiosity about the scratches. Also, however, it would take him away from his apartment: the place where he was most in danger from Rasputin.

If I'm not there, he thought, the bastard won't have a chance of finding me.

Neither will the police. In case they should come looking.

And the same with Karen. Neal was probably the *last* person she ever wanted to see again. But she knew his real name. If she looked him up in the phone directory, she would find that he's her neighbor. For one reason or another, she might come looking for him.

Nice not to be there, if she does.

He capped the ointment, put it away, then cleaned his fingertips with toilet paper. He flushed all the toilet paper that he'd used on his wounds.

Then he headed for the bedroom.

To pack.

Is there any reason *not* to take off? he wondered.

Wouldn't miss any subbing jobs, since this was summer break. As far as he could remember, he had no appointments set for the next couple of weeks. Though he had a few screen projects in various stages of development, no deadlines or meetings were coming up in the near future. He'd planned to spend all his time fooling around with some new ideas for screenplays.

Money shouldn't be a problem, either. He still had more than five thousand dollars in his checking account—money left over from the payment he'd received for the first draft of *Dead Babes*. And another good chunk was due in September, when primary filming was scheduled to begin on *Depth of Night*.

Assuming they don't blow it, he thought.

Can't ever count on a damn thing with these film jerks.

Yeah, you can count on something—that one way or another the whole deal will be blown out of the water so they never get to the primary filming of anything.

September doesn't matter, he told himself. I've got the money for my getaway.

Two weeks, probably.

Or until my arms heal. Or until I figure a great excuse for the scratches.

Before Neal had driven over to Karen's apartment, he'd put the videotape of his statement, along with the bracelet and pistol, into the bottom of his overnight bag. He'd hidden them beneath his toilet kit, gym shorts, socks and underwear.

They were still there.

He left the videotape where it was, but took out the bracelet and gun. He slipped the bracelet onto his wrist. He stuffed the pistol into the right front pocket of his trousers.

Then he took his bag into the living room. Leaving it near the door, he entered the kitchen. Marta's old Royal portable typewriter was still on the table. Neal rolled a sheet of paper into it, and typed.

Dear Marta,

You've probably noticed that I'm gone. I decided to take the proverbial "powder."

Don't be alarmed, okay?

Everything is fine, really.

It just seems like a good idea to pull a disappearing act for a while.

For one thing, I don't like getting you involved in all this. It might be dangerous. After all, I *am* the only living witness to Elise's murder. Not that I actually saw it happen—but as good as. Also, I shot the guy and hurt him. He would probably like to kill me if at all possible.

If he makes a try for me, I don't want you to be anywhere nearby.

I don't want him to even *suspect* that you are a person who has anything to do with me.

I don't want him to know that you exist.

I hate to think what he would do to you.

Anyway, there's less chance of Raspy coming after you if I take a leave of absence.

Also, I don't want to get you in trouble with the police.

At this point, I don't know where I'll be heading. Somewhere out of town, where I can relax and not have to worry about either the police or Rasp.

I probably won't get in touch with you. The less you know, the better.

I'm awfully sorry for dragging you into my mess. I would've kept it all to myself, but I cared too much for you, and couldn't lie.

I love you, Marta. I'll be thinking about you, and missing you. Again, please don't worry. I'll be a lot safer, hiding out. And I won't stay away any longer than I have to.

Adios for now.

All my love,

After signing the letter, Neal slipped its bottom edge into the rear of the typewriter's roller so that the sheet stood upright.

Then he picked up his bag, turned off the lights in Marta's apartment, and left. He went out to his car. He needed to return to his own apartment and pack a few things before taking off for anywhere.

Where *should* I go? he wondered as he started to drive.

To a motel or hotel. Outside of Los Angeles, since he didn't want to run a risk of bumping into anyone he knew. Outside Southern California, for that matter. Why take chances? It's a small world. Try hanging out at the Disneyland Hotel, for instance, and he very well might run into someone he knew. San Diego seemed a little risky, too.

Too bad Disneyland isn't a few hundred miles from here, he thought.

There's always Disney World.

But that seemed *too* far away. Besides, he'd heard that Florida could be awful in summer: terrible heat, humidity so bad that you're never dry, and mosquitoes.

He liked the idea of going somewhere with an amusement park, though. If he had to run off and hide somewhere, why not make the best of it? Treat it as a holiday.

He *liked* amusement parks.

Couldn't get enough of them.

Disneyland and Disney World were great places; friendly and

pleasant and fun and nonthreatening, and full of cuteness.

Knott's Berry Farm had some reality going for it. In addition to having plenty of rides and nifty shops, there were real horses, real museums full of Old West artifacts, and live performers doing gunfights in the streets.

Magic Mountain didn't have much to offer except thrill rides. It was also a favorite hangout for gang types. Neal wouldn't like to spend much time there.

Besides, Disneyland, Knott's and Magic Mountain were all too close to home.

He needed to go at least a couple of hundred miles.

The Santa Cruz Boardwalk was a possibility. Neal had been born too late for such grand old parks as the Long Beach Pike and Pacific Ocean Park in Venice, but the Santa Cruz Boardwalk still survived. It was one of Neal's favorite places. He'd been there five times, over the years.

How about it? he wondered.

Not a good idea. He'd taken Marta there.

That'll be the first place she thinks of, if she tries to figure out where I've gone.

So how about Funland? he wondered.

Funland, in Boleta Bay, was a lot like Santa Cruz. A boardwalk amusement park on the beach—old, tacky, creepy.

Maybe too creepy.

A few years ago, a bunch of people had gotten killed there. Something to do with an abandoned funhouse. Indigents had gotten into it and turned it into some sort of torture chamber, or obstacle course. Grabbed people off the beach and sent them through. That sort of thing.

Neal had been to Funland *before* all that. And he'd found it too spooky for his taste, even then. Take the Santa Cruz Boardwalk, age it and run it down, fill it with carny types who looked like they might want to cut your throat, load the crowd with outlaw bikers and loving couples like Starkweather and Fugate, and there you've got Funland.

Not to mention the freak show.

Not actually a freak show, he reminded himself. Weird stuff. *Jasper's Oddities*. That's it.

"Shit," he muttered.

He *still* sometimes had nightmares about what he'd seen in there.

"Forget Funland," he said.

What's left? he wondered.

He'd heard of a place called The Fort, over in Nevada. It was supposed to be an amusement park with an Old West theme. He'd never been there, he didn't think he'd ever talked to Marta about it, and it was probably four or five hundred miles from Los Angeles. Just about the right distance. Though near enough to reach with a full day of driving, it probably didn't draw huge crowds from southern California.

From what he'd heard, The Fort didn't draw huge crowds from anywhere.

It had opened a few years ago with a lot of fanfare. But it hadn't caught on.

Hope it hasn't shut down, he thought.

Last he'd heard, it had still been up and running.

Give the place a try, he decided.

Chapter Twenty-one

Neal felt excited about the trip. But he grew nervous as he turned into the alley that ran behind his apartment building—and Karen's.

No cop cars, thank God.

Karen probably hadn't called the police, fearing that Neal might tell them about her relationship with Darren.

Must be terrified somebody'll find out.

Though the alley looked all right, Neal drove slowly, searching the area beyond his headlights.

He saw nobody. No Creeper, no bums, no Rasputin.

No Karen.

I'm gonna have to move, he told himself. Can't go on living here.

But a final decision about that could wait. For now, he just wanted to put some miles behind him.

He swung into his parking space and shut down his car, then wondered if he should use the bracelet for a quick scouting expedition through his apartment.

And what, leave my body here?

Not a great idea, he thought.

He could feel the weight of the pistol against his thigh.

Hope the bastard is up there waiting for me.

Sure I do.

Nervous, he climbed out of his car and walked quickly. He looked all around as he hurried through the rear gate and up the stairs to the balcony. Everything looked okay. In front of his own door, he took the pistol out of his pocket. He held it ready in his right hand, finger against the trigger guard, while he used his left hand to unlock and open the door.

Inside, he flicked a light switch. A lamp came on. The living room looked okay, so he shut the door.

Then he walked through every room, gun in hand.

Nobody.

We're in business.

It took Neal half an hour to pack, and another ten minutes to study road maps. After figuring out how to reach The Fort, he tucked his maps under one arm and carried a single, heavy suitcase down to his car. He tossed the suitcase into the trunk, climbed into the driver's seat, and took off.

He drove through backstreets, taking much the same route he'd used Sunday night on his way to Video City. Robertson would've been faster, but the boulevard seemed more dangerous to Neal than the hidden roads that twisted through this quiet residential neighborhood.

He didn't want to encounter a car full of trigger-happy gangsters.

And he wanted to know if he was being followed.

No headlights showed in his rearview mirror. But he supposed Rasputin might be tailing him without headlights, so he made several random turns. A few times, he even swung over to the curb, shut off his lights and engine, and waited.

Nothing went by.

At last, he sped up the on-ramp to the Santa Monica Freeway, fairly certain that he wasn't being followed. He headed west for only a couple of minutes before starting north on the 405 Freeway. The traffic was light and there would be no more turns for about half an hour, so he took a deep breath and tried to relax.

He felt as if he were starting off on a holiday trip—but also as if he were a fugitive on his way to a hideout.

Which is it? he wondered.

Both?

The two feelings seemed to conflict with each other, yet they each held a place in him.

He'd seen such things in the people he'd entered with the bracelet: They were packed with contradictions.

Maybe we all are, he thought.

Maybe not.

Neal himself seemed to have conflicting emotions and thoughts about nearly everything.

At least about the big stuff, he told himself. Like making this trip.

Leaving Marta . . .

He *really* hated to leave Marta behind.

On the other hand, there was a certain sense of freedom in the prospect of being far away from her.

He found himself daydreaming about their reunion.

He imagined entering her apartment after being gone for a week or two. She is wearing a T-shirt and nothing else—the same as Karen. She rushes into his arms and embraces him. "*Oh, God, Neal, I was so worried about you.*" And he says, "*I missed you so much, Marta.*" And he slips his hands under the hanging back of her shirt and curls his hands over her buttocks. He feels their cool smoothness.

This is one of those mind-movies, he realized. Just like Karen had about Darren.

He supposed he'd always experienced such things.

The mind-movies, various internal conversations, the vague

and wordless notions floating around in his head, plus a constant general awareness of his physical sensations and surroundings—they'd been part of his life all along, but he'd never paid any particular attention to them. They'd simply been the mixture of thoughts and feelings that lived inside him. He'd taken them for granted, never analyzed them.

Not until the bracelet came along.

He sure hoped his new awareness of the processes wouldn't end up intruding too much on his own mind.

Like the way it just screwed up my nice little reunion with Marta . . .

He focused on where he'd left off in the fantasy.

They'd been embracing, relieved and happy about being together again, and he'd been going up underneath the back of her T-shirt, exploring her smooth bare skin.

He was there again, thinking about it as he drove north through the San Fernando Valley.

The back of her T-shirt lifted as his hands roamed higher. Soon, her buttocks were bare. In front, the shirt climbed above her waist.

He caressed the tops of her shoulders, then slipped a hand down her back and around her hip and down to the moist, warm cleft between her legs. He slipped a finger into her. She gasped and stiffened, the way she did in real life when he touched her that way.

Must feel awfully good for her, he thought.

Easy to find out. Just pay her a little visit with the bracelet sometime.

No way, he told himself. Tough to look her in the face again if I'd snuck inside and spied on her.

Besides, I couldn't do it to her, even if I wanted to. I can't be in her *and* touching her.

He wondered, though. There were probably ways . . .

Don't even think about it.

All else aside, Neal realized that he might find out things that he didn't want to know. Elise had been clear in her warnings about that: Stay out of relatives, close friends and lovers.

An awfully good way to find out where you stand, though, he

thought. If there's a problem, better to find out about it before you get any more committed to her.

It'd be such a dirty trick.

He was opposed to doing it, but excited by the idea.

Bad enough, invading a total stranger like that.

He planned to invade plenty of those, as soon as he reached The Fort.

He could hardly wait.

You'll have to wait, he told himself. No way to go bracelet-hitching on the freeway.

Unless I pull over.

Which didn't seem like a great idea.

Just hold your horses, he thought. Wait till you're inside a nice, safe hotel room.

Just after dawn, with the sun in his eyes, Neal stopped for breakfast at Sunny's Café in the town of Mojave. Before leaving his car, he removed the pistol from his pocket and slipped off the bracelet. He stashed the gun in the glove compartment. He shoved the bracelet into the right front pocket of his trousers. Then he climbed out, stretched, and walked across the gravel parking lot to the restaurant entrance.

He was told by a middle-aged woman at the cash register to sit anywhere, so he picked a corner booth. It was large enough for four people. The place wasn't crowded, though, so he felt okay about sitting there.

A waitress came along. A cute blond gum-snapper who was probably not much older than eighteen. The name tag above her left breast indicated that her name was Sue.

"You all there is?" she asked.

"Just me."

"Coffee?"

"Yeah, please."

"Ya got it." She filled the mug, then handed him a plastic menu. "Back in a jiff." She swaggered away with her coffeepot. Her thick ponytail swished from side to side. So did her rump.

She wore a very short skirt.

How'd you like to ride her?

Shaking his head, Neal turned his attention to the menu. After a quick study of it, he decided on the Sunny Combo #1. It consisted of two eggs, bacon or sausage links, hash browns or home fries, and a choice of toast, an English muffin, or a bagel.

When Sue returned, he said, "I'll have the number one combo."

She jotted something down on a small pad. "How'd ya like yer eggs?"

"Over easy."

She jotted. "Ya got it."

"And I'll have the sausage, the hash browns, and toast."

Her pencil twitched. Neal could hear its point making quiet scratchy sounds on the paper. When her pencil stopped, she said, "Right, ya got it. What kinda toast? We got yer white, yer wheat, yer rye, yer raisin, or yer sourdough."

"Sourdough."

She marked on the pad, gave her gum a couple of chews, and said, "What'd ya do to yer arms?"

"What?" Neal asked, and felt the hot surge of a blush.

"Yer arms. Yer girl get ya?"

He glanced down at the scratches. "Yeah, she sure did." He quickly added, "She fell backward and tried to grab me. We were out on a boat yesterday and she lost her balance."

"She okay?" Sue asked. "Didn't drown or nothin?"

"She got a little wet, that's all. But I got myself torn apart by her lousy fingernails."

He glanced at Sue's hands. Her fingernails were chewed down to the quick.

Sue winced. "Musta hurt like shit."

"Yeah."

"Oops!" She pursed her lips and pressed the pencil against them. "We ain't supposed to curse. Against the rules."

"Well, I won't tell."

She cast him a wink. "Yer a sweetie." She tapped him on top of the head a couple of times with the eraser end of her pencil, then twirled around and swaggered toward the counter.

Neal found himself grinning as he watched her.

Maybe I *should* try giving her a ride, he thought. Must be pretty strange territory inside a mind like that.

Not necessarily *enjoyable* territory, but strange. And probably interesting.

Ought to do it, he told himself—if only for research.

He wondered about the logistics.

Try it right now?

He pictured his abandoned body at the table, tilting slightly, tilting a bit more, then toppling sideways onto the seat cushion and rolling onto the floor under the table.

That'd be *real* neat, he thought. Forget it.

He drank some coffee and looked around. In a booth across the room from him sat a couple of Highway Patrol officers.

He felt a kick of alarm.

They were facing each other, one eating and nodding while the other talked. Neal couldn't hear what was being said. Must've been fairly amusing, though.

Afraid they might notice him staring, he looked away and drank some more coffee.

He wondered if he was a suspect yet.

Was there an APB out on him?

An all points bulletin would probably describe him and his car and give his license plate number. But he doubted it would include a photo of him. These officers, if they saw his face, weren't likely to gasp and go for their guns.

I'd better check the news, he thought.

He didn't *want* to hear about Elise's murder, but he knew that he should at least turn on the car radio and find out what was being said about suspects.

Maybe they already got Rasputin.

I'll do it, he decided. Soon as I'm done with breakfast.

When his breakfast arrived, he saw that the egg whites were runny.

"Ya all set?" Sue asked.

"Fine," he said.

"Get ya anything else?"

"That's about it."

"Ya got it, then." She winked at him, and spun away.

He lifted some egg white on the tines of his fork. The substance came up, clear and slimy, dangling like mucous. His appetite dwindled.

Good thing I'm by myself, he thought. If Mom was here, she'd make me send it back. Marta probably would, too.

He didn't like to make trouble, though.

Especially not about a matter like this. In some places, "over easy" got you fried eggs with runny yolks and firm, white whites—the way he liked them. In other places, though, "over easy" got you a runny yolk and a white like snot.

This wasn't the cook's fault, or Sue's. Neal should've ordered "over medium."

He went ahead and ate his meal. All except the egg whites.

Sue came by, now and again, to fill his coffee mug and to ask if everything was okay.

"Real good," he told her.

Finally, he stopped her from giving him another refill. "Better not," he said. "I've got a long drive ahead."

"Where ya goin?"

"The Fort."

"Yeah? The Fort?"

"Have you heard of it?"

"Sure! Never been there, though. What they say, they got a rolly coaster'll knock ya outta yer shorts. The Pony Express, that's what they call it. The rolly coaster. Sure'd like to try it. I *like* rolly coasters." She grinned and chomped her gum.

"So do I."

"Say what, how about lettin me come with ya?"

"Come with me?"

"Sure!" She bobbed her head up and down. "How about it?"

"Are you kidding?"

"Hey, no. Me? What do ya say?"

"What about your job?"

"No biggie. Sunny'll get ol' Marge to fill in for me. I never been to The Fort. This'll be *so* cool!"

This is crazy, Neal thought. Gotta talk her out of it.

"I might not be coming back this way," he explained. "I mean, how'll you get back?"

"Easy. I'll juss get me a ride. I get me rides all the time. Ain't no one ever says no, not less he's got his wife with him. So, how about it?"

"Well . . ." He couldn't think of a good excuse.

He didn't want Sue to ride with him. He didn't want *any* companion. He wanted to be alone. Besides, he found her a bit strange and scary. She seemed a little wild and unpredictable.

He also liked her, though. She seemed sweet. Even in her wildness, there was a certain innocence.

It's asking for trouble, he told himself.

Just say no.

Yeah, sure. Easier said than done. I'd need to give her a reason, or she'll just think I'm some sort of jerk.

Sue slung her hip to one side. "If ya don't want me, just say so. I ain't one to go where I ain't wanted."

"No, no. It's just sort of surprising, that's all."

"Tell ya what, I'll take care of yer meal." She plucked his bill from a pocket of her apron. "Meet ya at yer car. What's it look like?"

"It's the blue Ford."

"Catch ya in a jiff," she said. With a wink, she said, "Save yer tip." Then she swaggered toward the cashier.

"Holy Moses," Neal murmured.

Chapter Twenty-two

This is about as safe as picking up a hitchhiker, Neal thought as he hunted for the men's rest room. I don't know a *thing* about her. For all I know, she might be some sort of a lunatic.

Inviting herself to join his trip to The Fort was certainly not the act of a normal, rational young woman.

Should be interesting.

What if she's a scam artist, or something? Even a thief? Her real plan might be to steal my car. Maybe she's got confederates who'll tail us for a few miles, then . . .

Neal found the men's rest room. As he pushed the door open, the sight of his bare wrist reminded him of the bracelet.

Of course!

He was glad to see that this was a one-at-a-time toilet: only a single set of facilities, and a lock on the door.

He locked the door. Then he used the urinal.

After washing his hands, he put the bracelet on. He glanced at the toilet seat. It looked reasonably clean, but he was afraid he might fall off.

They should come with safety belts . . .

The only safe place was the floor, which looked a little grubby, but not disgusting. He pulled out a paper towel and placed it on the floor. Then he sat on it, leaned back against the door, brought his knees up and spread his legs, planting his feet on the floor to brace himself.

He felt like a bit of a fool.

"Okay," he muttered, "let's pay Sue a little visit." Then he kissed the bracelet.

He drifted up out of his body. No longer felt the hard floor under his rump or the door against his back or the stiff scabs on his knees and elbow or the soreness of his scratched arms. He felt as light as air.

Let's go find her, he thought.

And zipped through the rest room door and straight into the body of a Highway Patrol officer.

And stuck.

The cop was slim and fit, but felt swollen and heavy in the bowels. He obviously needed a toilet—fast.

Shit! Neal thought.

Almost . . . the cop was thinking. Almost. Just hang on, old pardner, almost there. What the hell did I eat? Couldn't be the break-fast. Just ate it, for Pete's sake. Must be the onions in the chili last night.

Charming, Neal thought.

The cop reached out, grabbed the knob of the men's room door, and tried to turn it.

It didn't turn.

Oh, no. Great. Now what'm I gonna do? Gonna shit my pants.

Go to the gals' john? Why not? Any port in a storm.

Hurrying toward the door to the women's rest room, the officer pictured himself rushing in and finding himself face-to-face with a shocked female. She screams.

He suddenly imagined himself facing a board of inquiry.

"You entered the LADIES' room, Mr. Jones. In uniform, no less."

"I'm aware of that, sir. But I had no choice. It was an extreme emergency, sir."

Mr. Jones grabbed the knob of the ladies' rest room door and tried to turn it. The knob rattled. Frozen, locked.

Jones made a slight whimpering sound.

He quickly returned to the men's room.

Gonna kick the fucker down.

No! Neal thought.

Outta here!

Neal crashed out of the cop's body, through the door and into himself. He leaned forward fast and scooted away from the door, expecting it to explode open at any moment.

As he scampered to his feet, he heard a firm but calm knocking on the door. "Excuse me," the officer called. "I'm having a little problem out here. If you could speed things up for me, I'd sure . . ."

Neal unlocked the door and jerked it open.

Mr. Jones, looking pale and sick, forced a smile. "Ah, thank you. You're a lifesaver."

"Sorry I kept you waiting."

As they stepped past each other, the cop said, "No problem. Thanks a million. Must've been the onions."

"Chili?"

"Watch out for the stuff," Jones said in a tight, strained voice, and shut the door.

Neal headed for the café's exit.

Lord, he thought. That was sure a close one. For both of us. I'm lucky Jones showed some retraint.

Outside, he found Sue in the parking lot. She stood by his car, leaning back against it, her rump to the passenger door. Beside her feet was a large paper bag, folded down at the top.

She grinned when she saw him. "Hey, there ya are," she called.

"Yep." He suddenly realized he was still wearing the bracelet. *Damn!*

Too late to do anything about it. Sue couldn't have avoided noticing the thick coil of gold around his wrist. If he tried to slip it into his pocket, at this point, she would only wonder why he wanted to hide it.

For now, she didn't appear interested in his jewelry. She picked up her bag and stepped out of his way.

"Are you sure you want to do this?" Neal asked as he unlocked the door for her.

"Sure. Hey, what sorta name ya got?"

"Neal."

A corner of her mouth slipped high. "Just like in church, huh?"

"It's N-e-a-l." He opened the door for her, and stepped back.

"Well, I'm Sue, but I reckon ya know that." With the tip of her forefinger, she tapped the name tag on her chest. "That's me. Sue. It ain't the name of my boob, in case yer wondering."

Astonished, he shook his head.

"I just say that on account of these guys, they get to thinkin' how smart they are and go and ask me what I call my other one."

"I've never done that."

"Well, I reckon yer a gentleman."

"Wouldn't go that far."

She ducked into the car, sat down, and placed the bag on her lap. Neal shut the door.

He went around to his own side and climbed in. "Do you want to . . . stop by your place before we go?"

"Nah."

"You don't want to pack, or . . . ?"

"Got all I need." She patted the bag.

Neal started the car and steered toward the road. "You travel light," he said.

"That's me. All I need's my jeans and stuff. Generally, I'll change in Sunny's john. Don't wanna go round town lookin'

like a waitress, do I? First thing ya know, folks start pesterin' ya
to bring 'em burgers and shakes."

Neal laughed. "Wouldn't want that." He stopped at the edge
of the road. "Anybody you need to see before we go?"

"Nope."

"Your parents, or . . . ?"

"Good luck findin 'em."

"Oh. Okay. So you're on your own?"

"Only just the three of us. Me, myself, and I."

"Okay." He turned onto the road, and headed for the freeway
on-ramp.

"Who you got?" Sue asked.

"Same three."

"No folks?"

"Yeah, but they live in San Francisco. I live in L.A., by the
way."

"Married?"

"My parents?"

"Haw! You! Smarty!" She reached out and poked the side of
his head with her forefinger. "*You* married?"

"Nope."

"Me either. You got a *girl*friend?"

"Yep."

"What's her name?"

"Marta."

"She the gal fell in the lake?"

Fell in the lake? What the hell is she . . . ?

He suddenly remembered the lie he'd made up to explain the
scratches on his arms. "Yeah, that was Marta."

"How come she ain't here?"

"She has a job."

Sue's left shoulder made a quick hop. "Me too, but I ain't
gonna let it stop me, not when I got me a ride to The Fort."

"You sure are eager to go to this place. How come you waited
till now?"

"Needed me a ride."

"You said you can *always* get rides from guys."

"Just so they ain't got no gals with 'em. Gals, they never let a guy give me no rides. They're generally an onry lot. Ya ever happen to notice how onry gals are, in a general sense?" She looked at him and lifted her eyebrows high.

Neal noticed how golden her eyebrows were. And he saw innocence and amusement and wonder in the blue of her wide eyes.

"You mean, ornery?" he asked.

"Yeah. Onry."

"Well," he said. "I don't know."

"Most fellas, they're all easygoing and friendly. Seems like, anyways. That's how come I like guys. They ain't a bunch of bitches."

"I'd say there are plenty of bad men around," Neal told her. "I've sure run into a few. And I've known some very nice women."

"Name two," she said.

"You and Marta."

"Haw! Me? Thank ya very much! So how come ya think I'm nice?"

"Oh, I can just tell."

"Well, I got ya fooled! I'm a shit! Ask anyone!"

He looked at her and burst out laughing.

It's not *that* funny, he thought. But he couldn't help it. And he couldn't stop. Tears filled his eyes, streamed down his cheeks.

Calm down, he told himself.

He took deep breaths. He wiped his eyes. He was beginning to settle down when his mind replayed Sue blurting out, *"Well, I got ya fooled! I'm a shit!"*

And he exploded with laughter again, fresh tears flooding his eyes.

"Ya okay?" Sue asked after a while. "It weren't all that funny, ya ask me."

"Well . . . I'm sorry."

"Ya ain't some sorta moron . . . ?"

Neal squealed. He was laughing and crying so hard that he could barely see the road.

So he pulled over and stopped on the shoulder. "I'm sorry," he gasped. "Can't . . . help it." He took deep breaths. "I'll be . . .

all right. Just a minute." He wiped his eyes. After he'd calmed down, he said, "Don't know what's wrong with me."

"Ya okay?" She looked concerned.

He nodded. After drying his eyes again, he checked the traffic. He waited for a truck to pass. Then the road was clear, so he steered onto the pavement and accelerated.

"Cool bracelet," Sue said.

The words sobered Neal fast.

Here we go, he thought. Just act as if everything's normal. "Thanks," he said.

"Where'd ya get it?"

"Marta gave it to me. It was a birthday present."

"What'd she wanna give ya a *bracelet* for? It's girl stuff, y'know?"

Neal shrugged. He smiled at her. "This is a *guy* bracelet. It's actually a replica of an ancient Egyptian artifact. I'm sort of an amateur Egyptologist."

Shoveling it now, he thought. Why not? She doesn't know any better.

Sue, gazing at the bracelet, wrinkled her nose. "*What* is it?"

"A replica of an ancient Egyptian bracelet found in the tomb of King Tut. It was supposed to protect the young king against snakes in the afterlife."

"No kiddin'?"

"Nope."

"They got snakes in the afterlife?"

"The ancient Egyptians thought so. They were worried about asps. That's how Cleopatra died, you know. An asp bit her on the ass."

Sue laughed. "Now I *know* yer kiddin' me."

Neal let go of the steering wheel and jiggled his hand. "I haven't gotten snake-bit since I started wearing this thing."

"Let's see it."

"See?"

When she reached for it, he pulled his hand back and clutched the wheel.

"C'mon, let me *see*. I ain't gonna *run off* with it. Cripes."

"I've let you see it."

"C'mon." She tapped the bracelet with a knuckle. "Let's *see* it."

What could it hurt? he wondered. As long as she doesn't kiss it.

I can't warn her not to kiss it.

"Just be careful," he said. He released his grip on the steering wheel and stretched his arm toward Sue.

"Thanks." She slipped the bracelet off Neal's wrist. "Ooo, heavy. This thing made outta solid gold?"

"Nah," he said. "It's just gold-plated."

"Looks like the real stuff to me." She put it onto her own wrist and turned it slowly, gazing at it. "It's sure a snake, all right. And look at them eyes. Look at them *jewels*. They're just as green as can be. Ya think they're emeralds?"

"Just green glass."

"I don't know, buddy. Ya ask me, this ain't fake. How much she pay for it?"

"It was a gift. People don't tell how much they paid."

"Ya don't know? Bet it was plenty." Sue raised the bracelet toward the sunlit windshield. She pursed her lips and shook her head. "Man, look at how shiny it is!"

"Pretty shiny," Neal agreed.

"That Marta, she sure must love you."

He blushed a little. "I guess so," he said. He figured that Marta probably *did* love him, but that wasn't the reason for his embarrassment. He felt ashamed of himself for telling such a string of lies to Sue, who seemed so trusting and sincere.

Still holding the bracelet near the windshield, she stroked it with the back of her left forefinger. She made no comment. Neal tried to keep his eyes on the road, but he couldn't stop himself from glancing over at her.

She brought the bracelet toward her face.

"Hey!" Neal snapped.

She flinched. "What?"

"What're you doing?"

"Nothin. I just wanta feel it." Giving him an injured frown, she gently rubbed the bracelet against her cheek. "Feels good."

She closed her eyes and continued caressing herself with the bracelet.

"Maybe you'd better give it back to me, now," Neal said.

"Okay."

But she didn't stop.

"Sue?"

"Okay, okay. Gee, it's just the smoothest thing . . ." She brushed it softly against her lips.

Chapter Twenty-three

"No!" Neal yelled and tried to snatch the bracelet away.

Too late.

An instant after her lips brushed against the bracelet, Sue went limp in the passenger seat and her arm dropped, taking the bracelet down onto the cushion by her right thigh.

Neal tried to reach it. His seat belt stopped him. So did his other hand on the left side of the steering wheel. For the moment, he could only stretch far enough to touch the top of Sue's thigh.

He went for the buckle of his seat belt.

Oh, God, he thought. *She's done it. She's out. Where'd she go? In me? What if she's in me!!!*

Maybe she isn't. She could've gone anywhere.

I'm nearest.

Buckle unclasped, he jerked the belt out of his way. As he moved his left hand to the top of the steering wheel, he checked the nearby freeway lanes. No traffic close enough to worry about.

She'd better not be in me! Better not be! Damn it! Never should've let her touch the bracelet! My God, I knew better!

He leaned and reached across Sue's lap.

And, leaning, bumped her with his shoulder.

Not much of a bump, but enough to change her balance. As Neal reached, she shifted in her seat and slumped sideways until her right shoulder met the door. Her head thumped the window.

And her hand tumbled over the seat edge, into the gap between the seat and the door.

Neal could no longer see her hand or the bracelet.

"*Fall off!*" he commanded the bracelet in his mind. He knew it was too large for Sue; it ought to slide down her hand and drop to the floor.

She remained limp.

According to Elise, you return to your own body immediately if you break contact with the bracelet.

She'd be back by now.

Obviously, it hadn't dropped off.

Gotta pull over, get it off her quick. My God, my God. "You in me, Sue? Get out!" Damn it! This is what I get for being nice to someone! "Get out!"

Foot off the gas pedal, he saw a wide section of shoulder ahead. He checked his rearview mirror. Nothing on his tail.

Sue still didn't move.

"*You'd better not be in me! Get the hell out!*"

Neal stepped on the brake pedal. As his car slowed, he eased it onto the hard dirt shoulder of the road. Pebbles flew up, clattering against the undercarriage. In the mirror, a cloud of yellow dust rose into the air.

The car skidded, stopped.

Foot clamped to the brake pedal, Neal let go of the steering wheel, threw himself across Sue and reached down into the gap for her hidden hand. He knew he might be hurting her: digging his left elbow into her leg, shoving at her belly, mashing her breasts with his right upper arm. But he didn't much care.

Serves her right, he thought, not caring that she was probably in his mind and well aware of the thought.

All he cared about was getting the bracelet away from her.

Get it before I think about the murder!

Oh God, I just did.

At that moment, he wrapped his right hand around Sue's wrist. He hooked a finger underneath the heavy coil and jerked it forward.

Sue's hand came up out of the crevice. It hovered beside her leg, supported by the bracelet. It jumped and shook as Neal tugged at the solid hoop. When the bracelet flew clear, her hand fell and slapped her thigh.

Neal pushed at Sue, trying to shove himself off her.

"Ow!" she gasped. She twitched and squirmed. "Get off me! Ouch!"

A moment later, Neal was sitting upright. He slipped the bracelet onto his left hand, where it would be safe from a sudden grab by Sue. Trying to catch his breath, he shook his head. "Sorry," he said.

"Like fun ya are." Scowling at him, Sue rubbed her leg. "Ya didn't have to get so rough. Cripes, I was *gonna* give it back to ya."

"I didn't mean to hurt you."

"Like I believe *that*." She rubbed her left breast. Just above it, the red plastic name-plate tilted and wobbled like a raft on a stormy lake. "Damn near creamed my tit," she pouted.

"Uh . . ."

"Ya don't gotta *stare*."

He turned to the windshield.

What's going on? he wondered. Sue was acting like a girl who'd gotten roughed up, not like someone who'd just taken a magic ride to weirdsville.

"We just gonna sit here all day?" she asked.

"I don't know," Neal said. He faced her. "Are you okay?"

"I'll live," she said. An odd look suddenly came into her eyes. She turned her head away. "C'mon, let's go."

"Are you sure?"

"Sure I'm sure."

"I could let you out right here, if that's what you want."

"Why'd I want that?"

"You aren't frightened?"

"Of what?"

"Me."

"I ain't scared of you." She looked him in the eyes. "Anyhow, Sunny *knows* I gone off with ya. She took down yer license plate. Somethin' happens to me, and yer gonna be in a whole heap of trouble."

"I wouldn't do anything to you."

"Okay, then. We gonna get a move on?"

Nodding, he waited for some traffic to pass. Then he pulled onto the highway again and poured on the speed.

She must not realize what happened to her with the bracelet, Neal thought. Maybe she figured she was hallucinating.

Should he come right out and ask her about it?

Better not.

She *had* given him that funny look after saying, "I'll live." As if she knew he'd already murdered someone else and might be tempted to do away with her, too.

If she thinks I'm a killer, she's acting pretty cool about it.

She doesn't believe any of it happened, he told himself. Or, at the very least, she's so confused about it that she doesn't know what to think.

Nobody would immediately assume the truth.

She'd slipped out of her own body and taken a detour into Neal?

That would be about the *last* thing she would figure for the truth.

So if I don't confirm it for her . . .

"Sure wish I had *me* a bracelet like that," Sue said.

Neal felt a sinking sensation.

"S'pose to ward off snakes?"

"That's the story."

"How come ya went nuts and grabbed it back? Got a rattler under yer seat, or somethin?"

"No. I was just worried."

Go for it!

"The thing is," he said, "you passed out. Right after you put it to your mouth. I was afraid you might've been poisoned."

"Huh?"

"Marta warned me . . . I thought she must be joking about it, but . . . well, she told me that part of the bracelet's magic comes from snake poison. That's what the guy told her at the gift shop where she found it. That it had been dipped in asp venom. Which is supposed to keep the snakes away. She said he seemed pretty serious about it. He warned against getting the thing near your mouth."

"Sounds like a crock to me."

"Well, apparently it's not supposed to be enough to kill someone. When I saw you pass out, though . . ." Neal shook his head. "You're feeling okay now?"

He looked at her. She was frowning as if deep in thought.

"One other thing," he said, "asp venom is supposed to be hallucinogenic."

"Huh?"

"In small doses, it makes you see and hear things that aren't there. You know, hallucinate. Like LSD, or something. Hippies used to use it, but it fell out of favor after a while. Just a little too much, and you're a dead duck."

"Really?"

"Really," he said, though he'd never heard such a thing. For all he knew, the asp that nailed Cleopatra might've been the last of its species.

Maybe it isn't a species at all, he thought. *Asp might be nothing but a synonym for snake.*

Whatever it is, I'm getting plenty of mileage out of it.

Have to look it up sometime . . .

He forced himself to smile. "Did you have any interesting hallucinations from the venom?" he asked.

She was giving him a funny stare again.

"Maybe," she said.

"You don't have to tell me if you don't want to. I mean, hallucinations are sort of like dreams. They're mostly just an expression of your own worries, obsessions, fantasies. Stuff you might want to keep private."

"Yer handin' me a load," she said.

"No, I'm not."

"Ya know darn well I wasn't havin' no hallucination. I was in yer head, and you know it."

"No, I . . ."

"Shoot, ya kept on yelling at me to get out."

He tried to look amused. "Really? *I* was in your fantasy? I'm flattered."

"Weren't no fantasy. I got in ya 'cause of the bracelet, I

reckon. That's how come ya was in such a hot rush to get it off me and break the spell."

"There wasn't any spell," he said. "I was afraid you'd been poisoned."

"Bull-roar. You figured I was in ya, and you didn't like it one whit. Kept yelling at me with yer thoughts. Said stuff like, 'Damn it, Sue, get the hell outta here!' Which I figure is 'cause ya didn't want me findin out how yer a murderer."

"I'm not a murderer," he said.

"Who'd ya kill?"

"Nobody!"

"C'mon, fess up." Sue smiled. Was she actually *amused* to find herself riding with a murderer? "I been in yer brain," she said. "So c'mon, who'd ya kill? Marta? Did ya kill her to get yer hands on her bracelet?"

"No!"

"Bet she scratched up yer arms while ya was murderin her."

"No! That's ridiculous. Marta's perfectly fine."

"Don't worry, I ain't gonna tell on ya."

He gaped at her, hardly able to believe he'd heard her correctly. "No? Not tell on me?" He was amazed, shocked. "Why the hell not?"

"Yer my ride."

"Aren't you afraid of me?"

"Ya got no call to kill me. Anyhow, like I said, Sunny got yer license number."

"Oh, that's right."

"So we oughta just keep on goin' to The Fort like nothin' happened. How's that suit ya?"

"Suits me fine," Neal muttered.

"Good."

"Anyway," he said, "I never killed anyone. I might be in some trouble because of a murder that happened a couple days ago, that's the thing. I actually *shot* the guy who did the killing, but it seems that he got away. So there's a chance I might end up being a suspect, even though I'm completely innocent. And the *real* killer is probably after me. Unless he died, or something. So that's why I've got murder on my mind, not because I did someone in. And that's why I'm going to The Fort, just to stay out of L.A. and let things blow over for a while."

The way Sue looked at Neal, he might've been a dog that had just performed a wonderful trick. "Yer the guy," she said, "that musta killed that diver champ. Alice Waters?"

Chapter Twenty-four

"Elise," Neal said. "Her name was Elise, not Alice. And I didn't kill her. I saved her life."

"Oh, no ya didn't. She's deader than hell."

"I know. I know, all right. You don't have to tell *me* she's dead. She got murdered *after* I'd saved her. The fact is, *she's* the one who gave me the bracelet. Marta never gave it to me, Elise did. Just before she was killed. She gave it to me as a reward because I'd saved her life."

Sue raised her eyebrows. "Really?"

"That's right. Cross my heart and hope to die." With his right hand, he let go of the steering wheel and marked an X on his chest.

Sue reached out and knuckled his upper arm as if it were a door. "Gimme back the bracelet."

"You've got to be kidding."

"I wanna try it again. C'mon. Wanna see if yer still lyin' to me."

"No way."

"C'mon." She rapped on his arm again. "Give it over."

Ridiculous. Let her at me again? Not a chance.

But in another part of his mind, he thought, *Why not? She's already figured out what the bracelet does, and she already knows about Elise. What harm can it do, now?*

If it'll convince her I'm innocent . . .

"All right," he said. Holding the wheel steady with his right hand, he swung his left arm across his body.

Sue reached out and removed the bracelet from his wrist. She slipped it over her own left hand. "How do ya make it work? Rub it on yer face, or . . . ?"

"Your lips. Kiss it."

"Oh. Okay." She raised the bracelet, looked at it, then frowned at Neal. "This time, don't go ape and start jumpin' all over me, okay?"

"All right. Before you do it, though, I'd better warn you about a few things. It can be dangerous. Don't go anywhere but into me, and . . ."

"Fine, okay." She kissed the bracelet.

"Hey! I'm not . . ."

She sagged limp in the passenger seat, hand and bracelet flopping onto her left thigh.

"I wasn't done with the warnings," he said, knowing she could hear him—not with her own ears, but through himself.

If she's in here, he thought.

She probably is. So weird, though, not being able to tell. "Hello in there, Sue. Are you in? Never mind. Don't try to answer. There's no two-way communication. You can't get in touch with me while you're in there. Not even if it's a matter of life and death. You can't tell me anything, can't make me do anything. You're just a passenger along for the ride. We can discuss it later."

What's she doing in there? he wondered. *Exploring around? This could be awfully embarrassing. Better watch what I think about.*

No, no no. Don't go down that road or you'll start thinking about exactly what you don't *want to think about.*

He looked over at Sue's body, and his eyes settled on the rise of her white blouse beneath the name tag. He could see her white bra through the fabric. And the roundness of her breast filling the bra. *No! Stop it!*

He jerked his gaze forward.

Don't think about her!

(Damn good thing I didn't try to take a peek up her skirt.)

Even as he thought the thought, he imagined the shadowy view he might obtain by peering between her knees.

Shit! She's gonna think I'm a pervert!

THINK ABOUT SOMETHING ELSE!!!

Elise. Think about Elise. That's why Sue's doing this, right? To find out what happened. To find out if I'm the guy who killed her.

"Hey in there, sorry about thinking the nasty stuff. These things happen you know? They can't necessarily be helped. Anyway, I'll try to make myself have memories of what happened on the night of the murder. Okay? I'll, like, imagine it the way it happened. You just sit tight. By the time I'm done, you'll know everything."

Everything, all right. Including the size of my cock.

OH, MY GOD! I CAN'T BELIEVE I THOUGHT THAT!!!

"Sue," he said aloud, "I think I'll try talking to you. You can just sit back and monitor my thought processes, or whatever. You'll see that I'm not lying. Okay? Here goes.

"It all started on Sunday night. Marta was over at my place, and we watched a couple of videos. They were rentals. So after Marta left for her job—she works at LAX, the airport—I decided to return the videos. You know, to avoid paying a late charge?"

Why don't I just show her the tape we made?

Yeah? How? Where do we get our hands on a VCR?

Besides, the tape doesn't prove anything. I could be lying on the tape. This way, she can tell . . .

"It was about eleven-thirty," Neal said, "when I got in my car and headed for the video store . . ."

He told his story in much the same way that he'd told it last night to Marta and her camcorder. As he spoke, he found himself reliving it all in his mind. He was there again, going through it all.

He supposed that Sue was probably viewing it like a film.

A film noir with a voice-over: a running commentary, but not by Marlowe or Mike Hammer or Sam Spade . . . by me, Neal Darden.

All we need's the lonely growl of a saxophone in the background.

Though Neal had continued the verbal narration, he realized that his thoughts had interrupted the memories—and must've put a halt to Sue's movie as if the projector had broken down.

And now she's picking up this.

This? Everything.

Terrific.

"Hello in there. Sorry about that. Where'd we leave off?"

"I didn't want a reward," Neal said. "When a dame's getting

carved, a reward's not why you go in. You go in because you have to, because a dame's getting carved and a man's got to stop it."

A fair imitation of Bogart's voice.

But then he felt ashamed of his performance.

This isn't some damn movie, it's Elise and the bastard that killed her.

Into his mind slammed a picture of Elise in the bathtub. A close-in color photo, the blood so bright red it seemed like a mocking exaggeration.

Sue, in the seat beside him, gasped. Then she was panting hard for air.

Neal looked at her. She sat rigid and trembling, her mouth wide open, her eyes shut.

A moment later, her eyes jerked open.

She stared at him. She had droplets of sweat under her eyes, a shiny mustache of sweat speckles above her mouth. She breathed hard.

"Sorry about that," Neal said.

With the back of a hand, she wiped the sweat from her upper lip. Grimacing at Neal, she said, "That was *her?* Elise?"

"Yeah. That's how she looked after . . ."

"Judas H. Priest."

"But I didn't do it."

She nodded. She seemed worn out. "I know." She held up her wrist as if to show him the bracelet. "It works."

"I know."

Shaking her head, she lowered her arm and pulled the bracelet off. "Here, take the thing."

She gave it to Neal, and he put it onto his wrist.

"Reckon ya ain't no killer, after all."

"I wish I'd at least killed Rasputin."

"Well, it ain't like ya didn't try. Ya musta hurt him pretty bad, though."

"Not nearly bad enough. He was still in good enough shape to do that to Elise."

Sue made a face as if the memory of it hurt her. A few moments later, she said, "Yer gonna have to finish the job ya started."

"What do you mean?"

"Ya gotta kill him."

"I'm hoping maybe he'll just go ahead and die on his own, but . . ."

"What in hell are ya goin to The Fort for, when ya got a guy like him that needs killin'? That's what I wanna know."

"Maybe I'd better tell you the rest of it."

"How about ya just *tell* me, this time. I ain't inclined ta jump in ya again right now. Not that it weren't an eye-opener."

Neal blushed. "Well . . ."

"Ya got yerself a dirty mind, Neal Darden."

He winced.

Sue grinned and shook her head. "Not that I ain't flattered," she said.

"I'm sorry. Really."

"I *got* panties on, by the way. They're white. And, yeah, I got me a good idea just how big yer *thing* is."

He felt as if his face might erupt in flame. "Wonderful," he muttered.

"Well, I wouldn't go *that* far." After a pause, she said, "Do ya know it got sorta funny and stiff when ya started checkin' out my tits?"

"Did not."

Had it?

Wouldn't surprise me.

"Sure did." Sue beamed at him. "Reckon I turn ya on, huh?"

"Oh, man."

"Aw, don't fret. I like ya. I like ya even more, now I been inside ya. It's mighty exhaustin', though. So why don't I just sit back and listen? I wanna hear the resta yer story, only from the outside, this time."

So he told her, picking up his story at the time he'd first entered Elise's house.

He told her about receiving the bracelet as a reward for saving Elise from Rasputin by the freeway embankment. He recounted a bit of the bracelet's history—as much as he'd been able to learn from Elise. He explained the warnings. And then he told Sue about his trial run, when he'd kissed the bracelet and gone into Elise.

None of this was on the videotape he'd made for Marta.

He'd kept the story of the bracelet to himself—and therefore hadn't been able to tell the whole truth about what had happened the night of the killing.

To Sue, he was able to tell the story as it had truly occurred.

How, after leaving Elise's house, he'd returned to look for Rasputin's body.

How he'd used the bracelet, first in a futile attempt to locate the body, then to make a long flight back to Elise's house, fearing she might be in danger.

How he'd been inside her.

Unable to warn her.

Powerless to help when she was attacked.

How he'd escaped from her body, returned to his own, then raced back to her house in a panic, only to arrive too late and find her dead in the tub.

Sue listened, watching him, often making faces, sometimes commenting or asking a question. She seemed very interested in all that he had to say. Almost as if *she* were going through the experiences.

Neal felt that he'd found a real companion.

Someone he could truly confide in.

As he spoke to Sue, he wondered why he hadn't been able to confide this way in Marta.

Easier to tell secrets to a stranger, he supposed. He'd always heard that. Maybe it was true.

No particular consequences, telling things to a stranger—someone you probably won't have to face an hour later, or the next day, or for years to come.

Like writing your tale in sand.

Say anything; it'll soon be gone without a trace.

He had a feeling, however, that Sue might *not* be gone very soon.

He was certain to be stuck with her for the next few hours. At least until they reached The Fort. And he doubted that he would have an easy time getting rid of her then.

Maybe I don't want to get rid of her.

What is this? You get smitten by every gal you meet? Control yourself. She's sort of nifty, but she's not someone you want to get involved with. Too young. Too goofy. The only reason you're pouring out your life story is because she accidentally latched onto the truth about the bracelet.

That, he realized, was probably true. He shouldn't be making such a big deal of the fact that he was confiding in her; he would've told the whole truth to Marta, if Marta had stumbled onto the secret of the bracelet.

He wished he *had* confided in Marta.

But how can you tell someone you've got a magic bracelet that lets you climb into other people as if they were carnival rides?

He never would've told Sue: She'd found out on her own.

He never would've told anyone.

He was glad Sue knew about it, though. Glad to have someone to whom he could speak the truth.

So he kept talking, not stopping with the murder, but going on about what happened afterward.

How he hadn't been able to find the business card he'd given to Elise, and assumed the killer must have it.

How he'd returned to his own apartment, figuring that he might be the next victim. How he'd kept his gun handy, frightened but also *hoping* Rasputin might show up—so he'd have a chance to kill the bastard.

When he told of Marta's arrival the next day, he was glad Sue was no longer inside him; she would've gotten a chance to watch Marta sucking him, and she'd be feeling how the memory aroused him.

He didn't tell Sue about that episode. But he told her the rest of it: how he'd explained his situation to Marta, explained the danger he was in—from Rasputin and maybe from the police—and how she'd insisted that he spend the night at her apartment, where nobody should be able to find him.

He told about the videotape they'd made together.

A tape tarnished by lies because he'd been unwilling to speak of the bracelet.

Finally, he told Sue about his letter to the police. "Marta took it with her when she left for work. She was going to mail it on the way. I guess the cops'll probably get it tomorrow. Maybe even today."

"That how come ya hit the road? Scared they'd be after ya?"

He shook his head. "The letter was anonymous. We were careful not to touch it, too. I don't think there's any way for them to find out who it came from."

"So how come ya took off, then?"

"Because of the scratches." He nodded toward his right arm.

Sue stared at his forearm. "These the ones ya *didn't* get when yer girlfriend was fallin' off a boat?"

"These are the ones."

"Who *was* it scratched ya?"

"A woman named Karen."

"Ya saw a gal name of Karen last night? After Marta went off to work? Cripes, I'm gonna need me a scorecard, you and all these gals. Marta, Elise, now this Karen . . . and me."

Neal shook his head. "Karen's no big deal. You can forget about her. She's just someone I visited with the bracelet. Things got weird, so I paid her a visit in person and she ended up scratching me. That's all there is to it."

"What'd she wanna scratch ya for?"

"Doesn't matter. We had a little misunderstanding, that's all."

"Ya didn't attack 'r or . . . ?"

"No. Well, not exactly. I had to defend myself. I didn't hurt her, though. Not seriously. The thing is, I didn't know how to explain the scratches to Marta. I mean, they weren't there when she left for work. And I couldn't tell her the truth. Not without telling her about the bracelet. So I left her the note, and took off. I figured I'd stay away until they've had a chance to heal."

"That's gonna take a *week* or two. Jeezle-peezle. Ain't you a *writer?*"

He frowned. "Did I tell you that?"

"I was jammed inside ya for five, ten minutes. Found out plenty."

"Did I *think* about my job?"

She shrugged. "Not sure. Anyways, it's somethin' I picked up. You *are* a writer, what I'm gettin' at—so ya shoulda been able to come up with a good lie."

"Maybe so. I didn't want to lie to her again, though. And I guess . . . I figured it'd be better for both of us if I just vanished for a while."

"Now ya got me, ya can *un*vanish any time ya want."

"What do you mean?" he asked.

"Well, I'll let on as how *I'm* the gal that scratched yer arms for ya. Then ya can just leave out Karen. We'll tell Marta how we both just happened to be at The Fort, and how ya saved my life when I almost fell outta the rolly coaster. That'd make a pretty good story, huh?"

"Only one problem," Neal said. "Look at your fingernails."

She raised both hands in front of her, palms out, like a mime pushing at an invisible wall. "I could scratch ya with 'em."

"They're awfully short."

"Well, they're bound to grow. Give 'em a few days. What I'll do, I'll lay off bitin' 'em while we're at The Fort. Then they'll be all ready for when we show 'em to Marta."

"Ah," Neal said.

He tried to smile.

What's she planning to do, move in with me?

Chapter Twenty-five

When Neal stopped for gas, Sue said, "I'm gonna see a feller about a dog."

"Huh?" he asked.

"Gonna go and take a *pee.* Ain't you s'pose to be a writer? Don't ya know what it means when someone's goin' to see about a dog?"

"I guess not."

"I don't wanna be castin' no dispersions on yer intelligence, or nothin, but *jeezle!*" She reached down between her knees to pick up her sack. "See ya in a shake," she said as she opened the door. She climbed out of the car and headed for the gas station's minimart, swinging the sack by her side.

Neal, still behind the wheel, slipped the bracelet off his wrist and put it into a pocket of his trousers. Then he reached out to turn off the ignition.

He suddenly imagined himself driving off. Right now. Without Sue. By the time she realized what was happening, he'd be gone.

Why would I want to do that? he wondered.

Because she knows about the bracelet.

But she also knows about my involvement in the murder, he reminded himself. And she knows who I am, and where I'm going.

The bracelet's going to be a real problem. She'll be wanting to use it all the time. Maybe she'll even try to steal it.

He never should've let her touch it.

I could ditch her right now. She might not know my last name. I could change my destination . . .

"Yeah, right," he muttered, and pulled the key and climbed out of the car.

No matter how much trouble might be saved by ditching Sue now, Neal knew he wasn't capable of such a thing.

Leave her stranded at a gas station in the middle of nowhere?

He supposed that Sue would probably get along just fine. Probably be stranded for all of five minutes before finding a ride with someone else. But he couldn't do it.

He studied the gas pumps, trying to find a sign that might tell him to pay before pumping. He didn't see one. Not unusual. Away from places like Los Angeles, gas stations often let you pay *after* filling your tank. They trusted people more, out in the boonies. Not as much experience dealing with barbarians.

Pleased, Neal took down a nozzle and started to pump.

Maybe I should just let Sue use the bracelet as much as she wants, as long as she's with me. Take her back to Mojave in a few days and drop her off at Sunny's. After that, I'll have the bracelet all to myself again.

Unless she steals it.

Might even want to kill me for it.

No, he told himself. Not Sue.

Though she apparently found the bracelet interesting—and a useful tool for getting to the truth—she didn't act *enthralled* by it. Considering the magic of the thing, which she'd experienced twice, she seemed quite nonchalant.

Might be an act, Neal thought.

I need to get into her head with it.

Sue hadn't returned by the time the nozzle clicked off. Neal hooked up the nozzle, made sure to put the cap on his gas tank, checked the pump number and price, and headed for the mini-mart.

After paying at the counter, he went into the men's room. As he locked the door, he realized he was alone.

He could use the bracelet, pay a visit to Sue.

"Yeah," he muttered. "It went so well, last time."

If he hadn't tried to use the bracelet in the rest room at Sunny's, it would've been in his pocket when he went back out to his car and Sue wouldn't have seen it.

He left the bracelet in his pocket.

When he was done urinating, he washed his hands and studied himself in the mirror. He looked okay except for his mussed hair. He ran a dry comb through it, then left.

Stepping out of the minimart, he saw Sue in his car. Not in the passenger seat, though. In the driver's seat.

He opened the passenger door and peered in.

Instead of the white, short-sleeved blouse of her waitress costume, she now wore a blue chambray work shirt. It was faded and its sleeves had been taken off at the shoulders. It wasn't tucked in. It hung down past the waist of her skirt. The skirt looked like black leather. It was tight and very short. Her white socks and sneakers were all that remained of her waitress outfit.

She watched Neal stare at her. After a few moments, she said, "Want me to drive for a while? Ya been at it a long time."

"Sure. Okay. Thanks." He climbed in, being careful not to step on her big paper sack—which now, he assumed, held her waitress costume. "I see that you changed."

"Yup."

He shut the door and fastened his seat belt. "You do have a driver's license and everything, don't you?"

"Don't know about *everything*, but I got me a license. Wanna see it, just open up the bag and look in my purse."

He looked down at the paper sack.

Maybe I should, he thought.

"Do you mind?" he asked.

"Help yerself. I got nothin' to hide."

As Sue drove away from the pumps, Neal picked up the bag. He opened it on his lap and looked down into it. Except for the denim strap, her purse was out of sight under the clothes. Reaching in, he pushed aside Sue's skirt and blouse. And her bra.

Don't think about it, he told himself.

Oh, man, she took her bra off when she changed.

Who cares, he told himself. No big deal. I'm not interested.

Good thing she isn't in me now.

Taking a deep breath, he pulled out Sue's purse and set the sack on the floor. The zipper across the top of the purse was shut. "You're sure it's all right for me to look?"

"Snoop all ya want."

He looked at her. She grinned at him.

He unzipped the purse. Spreading it open, he glimpsed a folded wallet, a hair brush, a couple of tampons, an emery board, packs of gum and mints, lipstick . . .

He took out her wallet, then quickly zipped her purse shut.

God knows what else she's got in there.

Neal didn't want to know. He felt as if he'd invaded a private place—like Marta's bathroom medicine cabinet—and he was blushing.

He considered putting her wallet away.

"Go on," Sue told him.

A very thick wallet, red leather, worn at the corners.

"What've you *got* in here?"

"All kinds of stuff."

Neal opened it.

"There's my license." Sue reached over with her right hand and tapped it.

The license was encased in a cloudy, gray plastic cardholder. She tapped the photo. "That's me."

"Appears to be."

"It *is* me. Who else'd it be?"

"Says it's Barbra Sue Babcock."

"I don't let nobody call me Barbra. I think it stinks. But I reckon I'm stuck with it, so I just been goin' by Sue."

"Ah," Neal said.

The license gave a Mojave address for her.

After making sure the license hadn't expired yet, he glanced at her date of birth.

"You're only eighteen."

"Gonna be nineteen this time next month."

"Jeez."

"So ya got a problem with that?"

"You're just . . . so young."

"So what're you, ninety?"

"Pretty near."

She laughed.

"Anyway," Neal said, "I guess you're a legal driver."

"What'd I tell ya?"

He shut her wallet and unzipped her purse.

"Don't ya wanna look through the whole thing?"

"No, that's okay. I just wanted to make sure about the license." He slipped the wallet into her purse and quickly shut the zipper again. Then he lowered the purse into her brown paper bag on the floor, and folded down the bag's crumpled top.

She smiled at him. "I'm a good driver, too. Ya noticed?"

"Well, I noticed you haven't crashed yet."

"I aim to get me a brand-new car all my own, one of these days. I been savin' up. Gonna get me one of them Jeep Cherokees with the four-wheel drive, and go all over the whole country in it. On all the back roads, much as I can. Can't see nothin' on these dang freeways. Gonna try out all the back roads, and stop in and visit folks."

"Relatives?"

"No! Gonna drop in on folks I don't know. Just to say howdy and see what they're like. Chat with 'em, ya know? Then I'll just move on, and they'll watch me drive off and say, 'That was a nice girl. Wish she coulda stayed.' "

Neal stared at her.

She frowned at him. "*Well?* What's wrong with that?"

"Nothing." He shook his head. "Nothing at all."

She stared forward for a while. Then she sighed. "That's if I ain't a broken-down ol' cripple by the time I scrape up enough to buy me that Jeep."

"I guess you don't make much at Sunny's."

"Nope." She looked at him and knitted her eyebrows. "I been considerin' a life of crime."

He laughed.

"You think I'm kiddin'?"

"I *hope* you're kidding."

"Well, I am," she said, as if annoyed at herself. "I ain't no Bonnie and Clyde. Ya ever see that movie?"

"Yeah."

"Ya see how ol' Bonnie 'n Clyde got perferated, there at the end?"

"Yeah. In slow motion."

"It's *always* slow motion, ya ever notice that? Same goes with ol' Thelma and Louise when they went off the Grand Canyon. Slow motion. Always slow motion. Anyhow, I don't aim to end up like none of them. Ya get into the life of crime, yer just as likely to get yerself killed, and where are ya then? Dead. What's the gooda havin' a four-wheel drive Jeep Cherokee if yer dead?"

"Not much," Neal said.

"Anyhow, who'm I gonna rob? Where'm I gonna find someone to rob, that I ain't gonna end up feelin' sorry for? 'Cause it'd really be *their* money, ya know? I got no right to it. It'd just make me feel bad."

"If you feel that way," Neal said, "you might as well forget about a life of crime."

"I know. It's disgustin'."

"You're a good, decent person, that's all. Nothing to regret."

"Well, can I regret I ain't likely to land my hands on a four-wheel drive Jeep Cherokee till I'm older than Methuselah?"

"Yeah, I guess."

After that, Sue stopped talking for a while. Lips pursed, she moved her head and shoulders slightly as if she had a tune in her head.

Neal was about to reach for the radio, but she suddenly spoke up again. "Ya know that bracelet?" she asked. "I'll bet there's a whole lotta money ya might make off somethin' like that."

"I'm not really planning to sell it," Neal told her.

"No, I don't mean sell it. I mean . . . it'll getcha into people's *heads*, ya know? Ya thoughta that?"

"What do you mean?"

"Gotta be a *hundred* ways to make money outta that. Ya know? We're gonna be in Nevada. They got gamblin' there. What if we can figure a way so we can win at somethin'? Ya know? By being in somebody's head."

"Are you serious?"

She cast him a look as if she questioned his sanity, and made a loud *pfffff!* sound with her lips.

"You are serious," Neal said, as if translating.

"You betcha."

"If we *could* figure a way, wouldn't that be theft?"

"It'd just be winnin'."

"But cheating."

"Well . . ." She shrugged.

"Besides," Neal said, "I'm not sure there's even a way to do it. You couldn't have any effect on things like the slots. Not on roulette or craps, either . . . nothing that relies completely on chance, or machines. I don't even know how *keno* works, but I doubt if being able to read someone's mind would make you able to win at it. The only . . . card games. Blackjack, poker, that kind of thing. You might be able to win at some of those with the bracelet. It'd still be cheating, though."

"I don't mind cheatin'. It ain't the same as robbin' people."

"You draw fine distinctions."

"How 'bout you?"

"Basically, I'm opposed to anything like that."

"You don't never cheat?"

He shook his head. "No. Not really. I *have* cheated on a few things—like on my French homework back in college—but I felt so rotten about it . . . I always try to play by the rules, now."

"How 'bout helpin' *me* cheat?"

"With the gambling?"

"Yeah. Wouldn't be the same as doin' it for yerself."

He looked at her. She grinned at him. He hated to refuse her.

I'd look like a self-righteous stick-in-the-mud.

"The thing is," he said, "I don't think there's a *way* to win at something with the bracelet. I mean, it might be possible in theory . . . if we knew which cards were being held by the dealer, or something . . . The problem is, one of us would have to be physically present at the table, *playing* the game. That'd have to be me, since you're underage. So you'd have to be in the dealer's mind, with your body somewhere else. You wouldn't be able to affect what he does. All you could possibly do is communicate stuff to *me* . . . which cards he's holding. To do that, you'd have to leave him, return to your own body, and . . . signal me, or something."

"Sounds good to me."

"It would never work. You'd need to be someplace where I could see you, for one thing. You'd have to jump back and forth between the dealer and yourself. And there's *surveillance*. These casinos have security cameras all over the place. You'd be caught in about two minutes if you tried to signal me from across the floor."

"Ya sure 'bout all that?"

"Pretty sure."

"That ain't a good way to try, then."

"No, it isn't"

"Gotta be a way, though. Ya know?"

"Gambling?"

"Well . . . by gettin' in a head."

"I'm not sure there is, not if you exclude out-and-out theft. If you didn't have scruples, I suppose you could use the bracelet to get your hands on certain information. The combination to a safe, for instance."

"Yeah!"

"Or where a person might have some valuables stashed. You

know, like cash or jewels they've hidden in their house. That sort of thing. But then you'd have to *steal* the stuff."

"Yeah, well, don't wanna do that. But cripes, there's gotta be *some* way to make a fortune off this thing. A way where ya ain't gotta rob nobody."

Sue scowled out the windshield, apparently hunting for a solution.

A solution already known by Neal.

He wondered if he should mention it to her.

Probably not.

"S'pose we *charge* folks?" Sue blurted. "Let 'em use the bracelet for maybe half an hour? How much ya s'pose they'd pay? Fifty bucks? A hundred?" She turned her face toward Neal, her eyes and mouth wide open like someone struck with astonishment. "Just thinka that! We get us ten people to try it, a hundred bucks apiece, we'll make us a thousand smackaroos!"

"How much is that Jeep you want?" Neal asked.

"Well, all depends. Say 'round twenty-five grand."

"Then we'd need to get two hundred and fifty people to try the bracelet at a hundred dollars a pop."

"Maybe all I need's enough for the down payment."

Neal shook his head. "It's a fine idea, but it'll never work. For one thing, nobody would pay us a dime to ride the bracelet without proof of what it does. And if people actually find out that it works, they'll try to take it from us. *Nobody's* supposed to know what the bracelet does. Nobody except the person who *has* it. *You're* not supposed to know. You just found out by accident. We can't go around and tell *anyone* what it does. Some people would probably be happy to kill us for the thing."

Sue stuck out her lower lip and blew. The gust of air lifted her bangs off her forehead. "Don't see why they'd wanta kill for some bracelet when ya can't even make no money off it."

Just let her go on thinking that, Neal told himself. Better if she doesn't have a clue.

She resumed frowning. After a while, she said, "*Gotta* be a way. Something like this, gotta be a way to make yerself a fortune."

"If you think of it," Neal said, "let me know."

Then he reached out and touched the radio's on button. Static hissed and crackled through the speakers. He touched the search button. The radio began to hunt for a strong signal, and soon found a station playing the golden oldie, "I Fall to Pieces."

"I just love ol' Patsy Cline," Sue said.

"Me, too," Neal said.

He looked at Sue. She mouthed the words to the song in silence, a sad and wistful look on her face.

God, she's so young.

Young and cute and sweet and vulnerable, full of odd notions and simple dreams.

A tightness came to Neal's throat.

And he thought that maybe he should help Sue get the money for the four-wheel drive Jeep Cherokee.

Chapter Twenty-six

At the top of the hour, the music was interrupted by a news update.

The third story dealt with Elise.

"Though police are so far without suspects in the murder of former Olympic diving great, Elise Waters, her husband, actor Vince Conrad, held an early morning news conference today to announce a reward of fifty thousand dollars for information leading to the arrest and conviction of her killer, or killers. Conrad, who returned yesterday from Hawaii upon the news of his wife's death, told the press . . ." In a sound bite from the actor's news conference, Conrad said, "The world lost a rare treasure when Elise was slain. But I have every confidence that . . ." His voice broke, and Neal's eyes suddenly brimmed with tears. "I just hope that the animal who did this to her is caught and . . . brought to justice."

The newscaster's voice returned. "In other news . . ."

Sue turned the radio off. "Reckon they ain't after you. Not yet, anyhow."

"You never know," Neal said. "The police keep a lot of stuff to themselves."

"S'pose they'd hand over the reward to me if I turned ya in?"

"Maybe," he admitted, feeling a little sick. "They'd have to convict me, though. And I didn't do it."

"Well, don't worry 'bout it, I ain't gonna blow the whistle on ya."

"Thanks." He wondered if she was telling the truth.

" 'Sides," Sue said, "I think her husband done the dirty deed."

Neal gave her a look.

"Yup," she said, and bobbed her head.

"I know who did it, and it wasn't Vince Conrad. It was the guy I shot. Rasputin."

"So who's to say Conrad didn't like *hire* yer Rasputin to do it?"

"There's no reason to think he did," Neal told her.

"Ya hear how he talked?"

"He sounded upset."

"Well, he's an *actor*. Guy like that, I betcha he can turn it on and off like a faucet. Anyways, I thought he sounded real phoney. Ya know? Like he was *too* sad."

"She was his wife."

"Yeah, but they was separated, right? Gonna get divorced?"

"Apparently."

"Well, there ya go." She gave Neal a quick, decisive nod, as if she'd just proven her case.

"People get divorced all the time," Neal pointed out.

"Only sometimes they just go and slit their wife's throat, instead."

"That's fairly rare," Neal said. "Even in Brentwood."

"Sure's convenient, ol' Vince just *happenin'* to be in Hawaii when she got herself murdered. I mean, ya can't find yerself much of a better alibi than that."

"Doesn't prove anything."

"Ya ever see him in the movies?"

"Conrad? Sure."

"Makes my skin crawl." As if to prove her point, she grimaced and writhed.

Neal saw goosebumps rise on the back of her right forearm. And as he looked, he noticed the mellow tan of her arm, and how it had a fine layer of golden, downy hair.

Sue let go of the steering wheel with one hand, and rubbed the arm as if trying to make the bumps go away.

"Ya ever see him in that *Dead Eyes* movie?" she asked.

"Yeah."

"Didn't he just give ya the *worst* kinda creeps?"

"He was supposed to. He's an actor. It was just a role he was playing. Look at all the creeps Karloff played, but everyone says he was the greatest guy . . . a real gentleman, sensitive, kind . . ."

"Well, Conrad ain't no Karloff. He's just a weird creep, ya ask me."

"Which doesn't make him a killer," Neal said.

"How come *yer* stickin up for him?"

"I just don't see any reason to think he had a hand in it. You should *see* this Rasputin character. I mean, I hope to God you never do, but . . . he sure didn't seem like someone who'd been hired. He's a sadistic degenerate."

"Now that there's a reward, we *gotta* get him."

Neal stared at her.

"Ya know?" Letting go of the wheel with her right hand, she reached out and gently rapped Neal on the upper arm. "How 'bout it? We can split the reward fifty-fifty."

"Twenty-five thousand each," Neal said.

"That's a brand-new four-wheel drive Jeep Cherokee for me. How 'bout you? What'll ya get yerself?"

Neal shrugged. "I don't know. I'd probably put it in the bank, save it for a down payment on a house."

"There ya go! A nice, big ol' house fer you and Marta. Ya gonna marry her?"

"Eventually, I guess."

"Whatcha waitin' on?"

"My career to take off, I guess. I can't marry someone when she's making more money than I am. I'd have to be able to support her."

"Well, first ya get the reward for this Rasputin guy, then ya write up a movie about it, and yer gonna be rollin' in dough."

"It's a thought," he admitted.

"How 'bout we turn this buggy 'round right now, and head on back to Los Angeles . . . ?"

"What about The Fort?" Neal asked.

"If we wanna get that reward, we gotta act quick 'fore somebody else beats us to the punch."

"I don't know how we'd go about finding him, anyway."

"Well, he's gonna come after *you* ain't he? Ya said how he's got yer address. What we gotta do is be there, all set to catch him when he shows up."

"There's no telling *when* he might decide to come after me," Neal pointed out. "Since he didn't do it right away . . . My guess is, he's probably laying low somewhere, too badly hurt to worry about me. So it might be . . . who knows? A few days . . . even weeks . . . before he drops in on my place."

"Well, we wanna be there when he does."

"Right now," Neal said, "we're only a two- or three-hour drive from The Fort. It'd take us *six* if we went back to L.A. So why don't we just go on ahead? I mean, I want to see The Fort. Don't you?"

"Well, sure."

"We can *do* the place, find a motel or something and spend the night, then worry about all this other stuff tomorrow. How does that sound?"

"Well, okay."

"Good." He yawned. "Now let me get a little rest. I'll take over the driving in a while."

"Okeydoke."

He settled down in his seat, shut his eyes, and yawned again. He felt as if he'd been worn out by so much talking to Sue.

It's going to be a long day, he thought.

Everything's gotten so complicated.

All he'd wanted to do was get away from Los Angeles and his problems about the murder—go off and hide from the police and Rasputin . . . even from Marta.

A few days, a week maybe. Solitude and quiet so he would have a chance not only to recover from his wounds, but to figure out what he should do next.

A chance to play with the bracelet, too.

So much for all that, he thought.

Maybe we should go back and try to nail Rasputin.

Tomorrow, he told himself. Or the day after. No big hurry.

In a vague and tired way, he wondered if he should try to get separate rooms for the night.

Better, he thought. Stay in the same room, what'll I tell Marta?

Even if we don't sleep together . . .

Neal fell asleep.

He woke up suddenly when the brakes screamed and he was thrown against his safety harness.

He couldn't see what the trouble was.

"Sorry 'bout that," Sue said.

"Jeez! What happened?"

"Some ol' kitty cat run out. Thank God I missed him." She glowered at the rearview mirror.

"Scared the hell out of me," Neal said. His heart was still slamming.

"Well, I'da hated to just squish the thing. I *like* kitties."

Neal inhaled deeply and tried to calm down. "I didn't know what was going on."

"Anyway, I was wantin' to wake ya up. I'm starvin', and we're coming to a town pretty soon. Wanna stop and get us some lunch, maybe?"

"Sure, I guess so. How long was I asleep?"

"Oh, I reckon maybe ten minutes." She grinned at him. "Do ya feel refreshed?"

He laughed. "I'm wide awake, that's for sure."

A few minutes later, they stopped at a place called Yosemite Slim's Café in the town of Lee Vining. Neal wasn't terribly hungry, so he ordered a plate of hot wings. He wanted a beer to go with it. He figured he would soon be driving, though, so he went for a Pepsi, instead. Sue asked for a bacon-cheeseburger, chili fries, and a Pepsi.

Their drinks were brought right away. While they sipped and waited for the food, Sue glanced around at the other customers.

"Ya got the bracelet on ya?"

"In my pocket. But we're not going to use it here, if that's what you're thinking."

"Just for a second, okay? Kid over there's got himself a milk-shake. I wanta see how it tastes."

"You could've ordered one."

"Ya got any notion the *calories* in a shake?"

"Y'got any notion the calories in a bacon-cheeseburger and chili fries?"

Sue laughed. "Well, ya gotta draw the line someplace, or ya turn out fat as a blimp. C'mon. Reach it to me under the table."

Again, Neal hated to seem like a stodgy old stick-in-the-mud. If they were sitting in chairs . . . but they weren't; they sat across from each other in a booth.

Neal couldn't think of a good reason to refuse her request.

If she wants to do it, why not let her?

"Okay," he said. As he took the bracelet out of his pocket, he told her to lean against the wall and brace herself. "You don't want to fall under the table."

He reached out beneath the table, and felt Sue pluck the bracelet from his fingers.

"Thanks," she whispered. Grinning, she wiggled her eyebrows at him. She scooted sideways a bit, and leaned to the left until her upper arm met the wall.

"Here goes," she whispered.

Neal felt like a conspirator, a partner in crime. His heartbeat quickened as Sue lowered her head.

"Coast clear?" she asked.

Neal glanced around. Nobody seemed to be approaching or watching. "Yep."

Sue raised her right arm. She was wearing the bracelet. She brushed her wrist across her lips and suddenly went limp. Her arm dropped out of sight.

She looked as if she'd fallen asleep.

Trying to appear casual, Neal sipped some Pepsi up through his straw.

Sue started to sink.

Oh, my God!

Though she still leaned against the wall and seat cushion, she was going down—her rump sliding forward, slipping out from under her.

Neal flung his right leg sideways and blocked her knees.

She stopped sliding.

But she was already dangerously slumped. Her breasts were level with the table's edge. Neal supposed that half her rump must be off the seat. The pressure against his leg seemed to be increasing.

Turning his head, he spotted the kid with the milkshake. The boy sat at a table with his family, his right side toward Neal.

No way to catch the boy's eye.

Never should've let her do this.

Get back here! he shouted in his mind.

The kid took a big bite out of a hot dog.

Is that even where she went? Maybe she decided on someone else. Maybe she's in me. "Sue? You in here? Hello? If you're in here, get the hell out. Right now! You're falling under the damn table!"

Neal's leg, all that held her up, was starting to tremble from the awkward position and the strain of her weight.

He coughed loudly.

Several people glanced at him. Even the kid's mother. Not the kid, though; he was blithely stretching his mouth open wide for another bite of the wiener.

Neal wondered if there might be a way to pull the bracelet off Sue's wrist.

No. Her right arm hung at her side. Though he couldn't see the bracelet, it was obviously down beside her hip—the table in the way. No way to reach it without drawing all sorts of attention.

Get back here. Sue!

Damn it!

The kid was now picking up his milkshake.

The mother noticed Neal glaring at the boy.

He smiled at her and looked away fast.

This is what I get!

Sue!

He jerked his leg upward, freeing it from the push of her knees.

She slid fast.

Too fast.

Neal tried to stop her, but couldn't.

He blurted, "Watch out!"

The edge of the table clipped Sue's chin so hard that the table shook, the silverware rattled, and ice cubes clinked inside their Pepsi glasses. The blow knocked her head backward. A moment later, she vanished under the table.

Everybody looked.

Including the kid.

Ducking, Neal peered under the table. Sue was scrunched in the narrow space, her back against the booth, one knee up, her other leg shoved sideways at an awkward angle as if she'd fallen in the act of trying to kick Neal in the shin.

Her panties were white.

Her throat was red with blood.

Chapter Twenty-seven

Neal opened the car door for Sue.

She muttered, "Thanks," and climbed in. He shut the door.

As he strapped himself into the driver's seat, he looked at her. She met his eyes with a hurt, accusing stare.

She wore a bandage on her chin.

The blue of her chambray shirt was still dark in front with moisture from the washing she'd given it in the rest room. With the help of the waitress, she'd apparently been able to get out most of the blood.

"I'm really sorry," Neal told her.

He'd already said it a dozen times during their meal—and been answered by a stare. Though they'd both eaten, Neal hadn't been able to enjoy the taste of his hot wings; he'd felt too sick with guilt.

"I thought ya was s'pose to be a *nice* guy," Sue said.

"I usually am," he told her through the tightness in his throat.

Shaking his head, he started the car. As he drove out of the parking lot, he said, "I don't know why I did that to you. I was angry, and . . . I didn't mean for you to get hurt."

"Well, I *did*."

"I know." His eyes stung. Not for the first time since letting her fall. "I just wish there was some way to take it back."

"There never is. I been hurt by guys before, and they're always *so* sorry later on. But that don't make it go away."

"It wasn't like I beat you up," he protested, annoyed at finding himself lumped in with others. "I just got tired of holding you up. It was your own fault just as much as mine. You were only supposed to be gone for a minute. If I hadn't been so quick to act, you would've fallen under the table right away."

"Yer real good at savin' gals fer a *little* while."

"Oh, thank you. Very nice."

She turned her head and looked out the passenger window.

Down the hillside from the road was Mono Lake, California's version of the Great Salt Lake. Neal had seen it many years ago, but didn't remember it being so large.

"That's Mono Lake," he told Sue, hoping to take her mind off the incident at the restaurant.

"I know."

"Pretty, isn't it?"

"No. It's spooky lookin'. Like it oughta be someplace on the moon."

"Would you like to go down for a closer look? I think there's an access road just ahead."

"No."

"It's salt water, you know. It's so salty that it won't let you sink."

"I ain't aiming to swim in the thing. If I *was* aiming to swim, I wouldn't wanna go in, anyhow, 'cause of my cut chin."

"I sure wish I could remember what Mark Twain wrote about it."

"What, my chin?"

"Mono Lake. He wrote all sorts of stuff about it in *Roughing It*. I read the book a couple of years ago, but . . ."

"I shouldn't of said it," she interrupted, turning to face him.

"Shouldn't have said what?"

"That about . . . not savin' gals. It was a low-down, dirty crack. I'm sorry."

"Well, thank you."

"Anyhow, reckon I *did* stay in that kid too long. Sorry 'bout that, too."

She's trying to make up. This is great!

"How was the milkshake?" Neal asked.

A corner of her mouth lifted. "Never got more than a sip. The dang thing was so thick, the poor little snot couldn't hardly get it up his straw. Thought he was gonna suck his eyeballs in. It sure was a tasty hot dog, though. Flame-broiled, ya know, so its skin was all crispy. Mmmm."

"Glad you enjoyed it."

"Not sure it was worth gettin' my chin split open."

Neal took a deep breath. "We both need to be a lot more careful about when we use the bracelet."

She grinned. "We sure raised some commotion, though, huh?"

"God almighty," Neal muttered, shaking his head. "That fat guy was bound and determined to call the paramedics."

"How 'bout that little girl started bawlin' her head off?"

"You think that's funny?"

"Didn't amuse me at the time," she said, and laughed.

"In retrospect, however," Neal pointed out, "there's not much that's funnier than making a little girl cry."

Sue laughed harder. Then she winced and cupped a hand against her chin. It seemed to take a few moments for the pain to subside. Then she said, "Ya know what the *really* bad part was? Bein down there kinda trapped like that, and everybody gawping down at my drawers."

"Your *drawers?*"

"My undies. My panties."

"I know what drawers are. I'm just surprised you do. Only not very. Where'd you pick up a word like that?"

"It's what my pappy called 'em."

"Ah."

"Anyhow, ya don't exactly feel like the Queen of the Hop

when yer down on yer back like that showin' off yer skivvies to every dink in ten counties."

"They looked fine," Neal said.

Blushing, Sue said, "Well, thank ya very much."

Ahead was the turnoff that led to the shore of Mono Lake, so Neal said, "Are you sure you don't want to go over to the water? We have plenty of time. As it is, we'll probably reach The Fort before two o'clock. You usually can't check in to a motel or anything before three."

Sue lifted her eyebrows and the corners of her mouth. "Ya gonna tell 'em I'm yer wife?" she asked.

"We don't have rings."

"Well, that didn't stop ya back at Yosemite Slim's."

"I had to tell them something. They were starting to think I'd kidnapped you."

"We could get us rings at a souvenir shop," Sue said. "Or we could tell 'em I'm yer sister."

Neal suddenly thought about Karen and Darren.

"Lord, no," he said. "The *last* thing I'd want is to have people think I'm shacking up with my sister."

"Well then, I'll just go ahead and be yer wife."

"That'd be better. Or we could get separate rooms."

"No! I don't wanna stay all by myself at some ol' motel. I'd *hate* it. Anyhow, it'd cost twice as much. Thanks but no thanks. I'll be yer wife, thanks all the same. Nobody's gonna care, anyhow, if we ain't got rings. Shoot, ain't nobody gonna care if we're even married or not."

"You never know about that. If we have to check in with some prudish old hag . . ."

"We'll stay someplace else. Hey, I've spent nights in cars. We can always do that, ya know."

"Well, let's hope it doesn't come to that."

"There went the road to the lake," Sue pointed out.

Neal glimpsed it in the rearview mirror. "I could turn around."

"Don't do that. Let's just go on and get where we're goin."

Reaching The Fort was going to take longer than Neal had expected; he hadn't known that they would be spending the last fifty miles on a narrow, curvy mountain road instead of a highway. The road cut their speed in half. It would add an hour to their arrival time—if it didn't prevent them from arriving at all.

One wrong turn . . .

He felt a little giddy and sick every time he glanced past the side of the road.

A long, long way down.

Now and again, they drove past crosses planted in the dirt.

"Reckon that's where someone kicked it," Sue said at the sight of the first cross.

"No wonder The Fort never hit the big time," Neal said. "All the potential customers bit the dust trying to reach it."

"Why *is* it way up here?" Sue asked.

"There used to be a mining town. After the mines played out, they tried to make a go of the place as a ghost town, but nobody came. Probably because it was too close to Virginia City. So they figured to bring in tourists by turning it into The Fort."

"It weren't never a real fort?" Sue asked.

"Nope. It's just somebody's grand idea for a theme park."

Soon, they began to come upon colorful, wooden signs that stood at the roadside, intermixed with several more white crosses.

THE FORT
Fun! Souvenirs! Rides!
Authentic Western Relics
Great Eats!
twenty miles dead ahead

HOTEL CASINO
Slots! Video Poker! Blackjack!
And much, much more!
Top Payoffs!
THE APACHE INN!
(a short block from The Fort)

RIDE THE PONY EXPRESS!
Death-Defying High-Speed Roller Coaster

THE THRILL OF A LIFETIME!
AT THE FORT!
ten miles up the road

FOOD, LODGING, GAMBLING!
Satellite TV in every room.
Swimming pool and sauna!
Low prices! Clean rooms!
THE APACHE INN

!!! Yum Yum Scrumptious !!!
EAT AT WILLY'S
Best vittles in Nevada!
—a tomahawk throw from Apache Inn—

AUTHENTIC WESTERN ARMY STOCKADE
Museums! Memorabilia! Food! Crafts!
Rides Galore! Daily Shootouts!
THE FORT!
six miles

CLIMB ABOARD THE "STAGECOACH"
WORLD-FAMOUS FERRIS WHEEL
Fun for the whole family!
WHERE IS IT?
AT THE FORT!
just round the next bend

THIRSTY?
WE GOT MARGARITAS!
!ICE COLD!
STRAWBERRY! BANANA! REGULAR!
!!DRINK 'EM UP BY THE PITCHER!!
DON'T MISS OUR WORLD-FAMOUS
GOLDEN MARGARITA AT
PUNCHO VIVA!
(just before the fort)

"I could go for one of those," Neal said.

"Same here," said Sue.

"Too bad you're underage."

"Oh? Well, ya didn't see my *other* license."

"You've got a false ID?"

"I got *lotsa* stuff."

Moments later, they rounded a bend and came upon a small settlement: a gas station and minimart; a drive-in restaurant, a souvenir shop, a motel called The Wigwam that appeared to have gone out of business; Willy's Eatery; the Puncho Viva bar; and the Apache Inn.

"They got a vacancy," Sue pointed out.

"We're in luck," Neal said.

As he drove toward the three-story brick casino, he said, "Looks like it's left over from the old mining town."

"Hope it don't fall over on us."

"It's been standing *this* long."

"Reckon they ain't got earthquakes in Nevada."

"They're few and far between."

"Where'd everybody *come* from?" she said.

Neal shook his head. Until rounding the bend, they'd only seen two or three cars for the past fifty miles. Here, however, there was actual traffic on the street. Cars, pickup trucks, vans and RVs were parked in every available space. Along with all sorts of four-wheel drive trucks: Cherokees, Broncos, Range Rovers, Land Cruisers . . .

"There's one of them four-wheel drive Jeep Cherokees, right there!" Sue pointed at a red one.

"Wouldn't you rather get a Range Rover?"

"Cost too much," Sue said.

"That's 'cause they're better," Neal told her.

"I'll get me a Range Rover if *you'll* throw in another ten grand outta *yer* end of the reward loot."

"Ah. Well. Hmm." Neal doubted that either of them would ever see any reward money, but he didn't want to dash Sue's hopes so he kept the opinion to himself.

A short distance beyond the Apache Inn, both sides of the road appeared to be parking lots for The Fort. They were far from full: more vehicles, it seemed to Neal, were parked along the main road through town.

The Fort looked wonderful, though.

Its huge stockade fence had guard towers at both the front corners. Its main gate was flanked by a couple of howitzers. Neal glimpsed the tops of several rides in the distance. Then he turned and drove into the Apache Inn's parking lot.

"I think we'll go ahead and check in first," he said.

"I'm gonna be yer wife?"

"I guess so." He stopped the car, shut off its engine and removed the key. "In fact," he said, "why don't you just wait here while I register?"

"You say so." She reached out and rapped on his arm. "Let me use the bracelet."

"What for?"

"Why not? C'mon. I ain't gonna lose it. Anyhow, it'll help take my mind off all the pain." She tilted back her head to show him the bandage on her chin.

"Yeah, okay." Neal handed the bracelet to her. "Just stay out of me. And don't go anywhere. I'll be back in a few minutes."

"Take yer time."

Chapter Twenty-eight

Checking into the Apache Inn, Neal found that he needn't have worried about whether to identify Sue as his wife. The desk clerk asked how many were in his party, then gave him a choice of rooms: He could have either a queen-size bed, or a queen and a double. He chose a room with two beds.

The registration form requested no information about traveling companions. After filling it out, he slid it across the counter and handed a credit card to the clerk.

As he signed the credit card slip, he wondered if he should've gotten a separate room for Sue.

I'll have a lot of explaining to do, he thought, if Marta ever finds out.

I did get the room with two beds.

He imagined Marta smirking and shaking her head and saying, "Oh, well, in *that* case. Whew! I'm so relieved."

Then he was trying to defend himself. "We didn't *do* anything, Marta."

"How many room keys would you like, Mr. Darden?" the clerk asked, interrupting his daydream.

"Two, I guess."

She passed the keys to him, told him the room's location, then asked if he would need help with his luggage. Neal shook his head. "Thanks, but we'll be able to handle it." He frowned. "I *would* like to make a call before I go up to the room. Is there a public phone?"

She pointed. "Just past the end of the bar, near the rest rooms."

"Thanks."

Heading in the direction she'd pointed, he entered the hotel's casino area. This was very different from the big casinos he'd seen in such places as Las Vegas, Lake Tahoe, Reno and Laughlin. This looked more like a saloon from an old cowboy movie: dimly lit, smoky, with a low wooden ceiling and chandeliers.

It sounded like every casino he'd ever been in, though: a quiet chaos of jingling and clattering coins, slot machines getting cranked, voices, bells going off because someone was hitting a jackpot.

It smelled of cigarettes, perfume and booze.

The bar stretched along the wall to the right. With only a few customers sitting at its stools, Neal could see several painted panels along the front: a rugged, snow-capped mountain peak; a brook curling its way through shadowy woods; surf smashing itself to froth on the rocks of a desolate seashore.

The bar was a work of art. Neal wondered if, like so many other relics of the Old West that had found their way into boomtown bars, it might been created in Europe and shipped 'round the Horn to San Francisco.

A panel near the end showed a pudgy, pink-nippled nude admiring herself in a looking glass.

As Neal walked by it, he glanced at her groin.

Not much to see there. Just a hint of pale hair.

But it triggered a memory of Karen: seeing her from behind, down on her knees after he'd punched her. The hair. The fleshy, glistening slit.

Too bad Sue had her "drawers" on when she fell under the table. Would've had a great view . . .

What if she's in my head!

He suddenly felt hot and sick with embarrassment.

Shouldn't have let her have the bracelet. Stupid!

For some reason, at the time she'd asked for it, Neal had assumed she wouldn't use it on him.

She probably isn't, he told himself.

No way to be sure.

When he found the bank of pay phones, he considered hurrying out to the car and taking the bracelet from her.

But then what?

The hell with it.

"If you're in me, Sue, get out. I don't want you listening in on my call to Marta. I'll consider it a major invasion of my privacy, and I'll never let you use the bracelet again. Got it?"

"And don't think I won't know," he added.

Yeah, right. She's too smart to fall for that one.

Shaking his head, he took out his wallet. He found his telephone calling card, stepped up to one of the phones, and read the instructions for making a long-distance call. Then he dialed.

He knew Marta's number by heart.

When he heard ringing, he grimaced and glanced at his wristwatch. A quarter to four.

Her phone rang twice, three times.

Probably waking her up.

This seemed like the best time to call, though—while Sue thought he was busy checking them into the hotel.

Unless . . .

"Hello?" Marta asked. Her voice sounded huskier than usual.

"Hey," Neal said. "It's me. Did I wake you up?"

"It's all right." A pause. Neal heard a sound like a quiet yawn. "I didn't think I'd hear from you," she told him.

"Well . . . I missed you."

"Some fugitive you are. Can't even be away for a day without calling in."

"Yeah."

"Wish you were here."

"Same here," Neal said.

"I suppose you don't want to tell me where you are."

"I'd better not."

"I mailed the letter, by the way. The cops'll probably get it tomorrow."

"Anything going on?" Neal asked.

"Have you been listening to your radio?"

"Not much.

"Elise's husband offered a big reward."

"I did hear that."

"Fifty thousand bucks."

"Yeah."

"That's a lot of money."

"Gonna turn me in?"

Marta laughed softly. "Just might, babe."

"Have to find me, first."

"You know, *you* probably stand a better chance than anyone of actually cashing in on that reward. I mean, you were there. You've seen the killer. Hell, you even *shot* him. Maybe you should think about dumping the Dr. Kimble routine and coming back to look for the killer."

Where've I heard that before?

"Maybe I should," he admitted. "I don't know. Anyway, I've already got a room for tonight, so . . ."

"In a Nevada casino."

"What makes you think so?"

"Just call me Sherlock."

"The sounds of the slot machines?"

"I'll never tell."

"So much for hiding out," he said.

"I still don't know what town you're in."

"I *could* be in Atlantic City."

"Not likely. You would've had to fly, and I don't think you'd want to risk running into me or one of my friends at the airport."

"Could've flown out of Burbank or Orange County."

"Nope. You get *lost* every time you try to drive in those places."

"You sure know a lot about me."

"More than you'll ever know," she said, her voice teasing.

"That sounds ominous."

"Why should it?" she asked. Neal could imagine the smile on her face. "You feeling guilty about something?"

"No." When he heard the sound of his "No," he wished he could take it back. It had sounded all wrong.

"What is it?" Marta asked. She wouldn't be smiling, now. Neal could imagine her big, blue eyes studying him.

He didn't want to lie to her. Not again. He'd already told her far too many lies.

I can't tell her about Sue. No way.

But if I don't, and she finds out later . . .

Neal realized that she was almost certain to find out about Sue. The girl seemed determined to stay with him, intending to accompany him back to Los Angeles and be his partner in the hunt for Rasputin.

Marta obviously planned to be his partner in the same quest.

This might get sticky.

Unless he could figure out a way to ditch Sue . . .

He didn't want to ditch her, though. He liked her. He wanted to help her.

Better cut my losses right now. Let her know I'm not trying to hide anything.

"I don't want you taking this the wrong way . . ." he started, and realized immediately that it was a lousy choice of starts.

"Oh, boy," Marta said.

"There's this girl with me. She wanted a ride."

"So, naturally, you obliged her."

"Yeah. Well, she's a nice kid. Anyway, one thing led to an-other, and . . ."

Any way I put it, this is gonna end up looking bad.

"Don't stop now," Marta told him. She sounded as if she were still trying to keep it light, but having difficulty.

"It's just that she knows all about Sunday night. About me and Elise and the murder. And about you, too. The thing is, we heard about the reward, so now she has this idea in her head that we should try to collect it."

"We?"

"She wants to split it with me, fifty-fifty."

"You picked up this *total stranger*, told her your life story—including your involvement in a murder—and agreed to go in halvsies on the reward for Rasputin?"

Neal grimaced. "I guess it *sounds* kind of funny."

When Marta spoke again, all traces of humor were gone from her voice. "Well," she said. "Hey. It's your life." After a long pause, she asked, "So, how do I fit into all this? Or don't I?"

"Of course you do."

"Have you fallen in love with her yet?"

"No!"

"You sure about that? You fell in love with Elise Waters in about two minutes . . ."

Never should've told her . . .

"And you've been with *this* girl how long?"

"Most of today, I guess. But we're not . . . I'm *not* in love with her. She's just a twerp. She's an eighteen-year-old gum-snapper with hardly a brain in her head. My God, you should hear her talk—it's like she strayed off the set of the *Beverly Hillbillies*."

"And where's *she* going to spend the night?"

"I got her a separate room."

So much for telling the truth.

"Well," Marta said. "Whatever. Like I said, it's your life."

"I love *you*, Marta. I don't care at all about this girl. She's a good kid, though. I can't just dump her by the side of the road."

"Doesn't she have a home?"

"No. Not really."

"What *are* you going to do with her?"

"Nothing!"

"That's not what I meant. Of course, maybe it's none of my business."

"Of course it's your business. I don't know what I'm going to do with her. Maybe bring her back to Los Angeles. That's what she wants."

"Cool."

Neal groaned. "Look," he said, "I'll try to get rid of her. I might not be able to, though. I mean, she's *really* pushy. But I'll do what I can. You've got no idea what a pain in the ass she's been. I'd like nothing *more* than to get rid of her. But I feel sorry for her, too. I mean, she's got no one."

"She's got you," Marta said.

"In a way. But not . . ."

"I have to go."

Neal grimaced. "Oh, man," he muttered.

"I'm sorry. I'd like to be big and understanding about everything, but—" Her voice broke. "I've gotta go. Have fun. Bye." She hung up.

Shit!

Neal hung up, and stared at the phone.

She thinks I'm having a fling with Sue! Damn it! Didn't she listen? It isn't fair!

He picked up the phone again and called Marta back.

He listened to the ringing.

Come on, I know you're there. Pick up. Damn it!

"Okay," he muttered as the ringing continued.

She wants to play games, she can play them without me.

He hung up.

He was breathing hard, his heart pounding. He hurt inside. He felt as if he'd lost her.

Lost her, but for no real reason.

Just for being nice to a person.

He realized that his fists were clenched. He wanted to slug the telephone.

Or Marta.

He opened his hands and shook them by his sides.

It'll be all right, he told himself. She just doesn't get it.

What makes you think she'll ever get it?

"Who cares," he muttered.

Let her think what she wants. If she isn't gonna listen to the truth, anyway, the hell with her.

He turned away from the telephone and started walking back through the casino. He'd been away from Sue too long.

What'll she think? he wondered. *Maybe she'll figure I've been in the backroom boffing the desk clerk.*

Women!

Never should've told Marta about her. That was the big mistake. Trusting her to understand.

Just because she'd been okay about Elise . . .

Who says she was okay about Elise?

Maybe that had been an act.

Besides, by the time I made that bonehead confession about falling for Elise, she was dead. Hardly in any position to steal me away from Marta.

Whereas Sue is alive and well and a threat.

Striding across the hotel's parking lot, he could see her through the rear window of his car. She seemed to be slumped sideways against the passenger door.

Neal went to the opposite side. As he climbed in behind the steering wheel, she sat up. She looked at him. Though she smiled, her eyes were wet and red, and she had tear streaks down both sides of her face.

"So," she said, "we all set?" She wiped her eyes with the back of her hand. "Ya git us a room?"

He stared at her.

He knew why she'd been crying.

Shaking his head, he muttered, "Great. Terrific."

"Huh?"

"You were in me, weren't you?" he asked. "The whole time."

Chapter Twenty-nine

Without being asked, Sue slipped the bracelet off her wrist and gave it back to Neal. "I'm awful sorry," she said.

"How could you *do* that to me?"

She lowered her head. "I'm a shit."

"You're damn right you're a shit! I trusted you!"

"I know."

"Damn it!"

"I aimed to lie and let on I'd gone off in someone else, but then . . . I ain't never lied to ya, Neal. Didn't seem like a good time to start, right after ya got yerself in such a jam by tellin' the truth to Marta."

Recalling things he'd said about Sue, he felt a sickening rush of shame. "It wasn't all the truth," he told her.

"Ya mean like how I'm a teenage lame-brain gum-chompin' hillbilly?"

He grimaced. "I was . . . exaggerating."

Sue raised her head and gave him a crooked smile. "I know that, pal. I was in yer *head*, remember? In the resta ya, too. I got me a purty good notion *exactly* what ya thinka me. How ya *feel* 'bout me, too."

"You think so?"

"I know so." With that, she clapped him on the thigh. "C'mon, let's get up to the room."

Sue had only her paper sack for luggage, so she helped Neal by carrying his overnight bag while he hurried along with his suitcase.

He knew that he ought to be furious with her. Bad enough that she'd snuck into him with the bracelet, but she hadn't *gotten out* when he told her to.

Knew everything . . .

But it was hard to be furious with someone, knowing that she was aware of all those terrible things he'd said about her.

Especially when she'd seen beyond the words and recognized the truth: that he hadn't really meant them, that he'd said them to mislead Marta about his true feeling for her.

They must've hurt her, anyway.

She'd been in tears.

In his own limited experiences with the bracelet, Neal had discovered that his body had reacted in certain ways, even though abandoned—apparently responding to things that happened on the "ride." He'd returned to find it sweaty, breathless, agitated . . . even aroused.

What had he thought, or said, to make Sue cry?

The insults? Something else?

Ask her.

Maybe some other time.

Following him through the dim and smoky casino, Sue said, "There's that nudie gal."

He glanced at the painted panel near the end of the bar, and blushed.

"She looks sorta lumpy to me."

"Yeah," he said, and wished she would drop the subject.

"She ain't gotta you-know-what, either." Sue flashed a grin at him. "But I reckon ya already noticed."

"Very funny."

The elevator was just beyond the pay phones. Sue pushed the button. As they waited for the elevator to arrive, she said, "Hasn't."

"Hasn't what?"

"*Hasn't* gotta you-know-what."

The doors slid open. They stepped inside. As the doors shut, Sue said, "It's room four-twenty?" She hadn't yet seen either of the keys; she apparently knew the room number because she'd been in Neal at the front desk.

"Yeah," he said.

She set her bags on the floor and pushed the button for the fourth floor. The elevator started upward.

"Hey, look at us!" she blurted.

Looking around, Neal realized there were mirrors on three

sides of the elevator, and on its ceiling. The glass was flecked with gold. "Fancy," he said.

In the mirror to his left, he gazed at the reflection of Sue standing beside him. She was leaning forward slightly, studying the same images, a look of amused curiosity on her face.

They could not only see themselves in the mirror, but also its reflection of the mirror to their right, which showed them and the mirror to their left, which showed them again and . . .

"We just keep on goin' and goin'," Sue whispered.

Neal saw her frown at herself, saw the back of her head with its thick blond ponytail, then her frowning face deeper in the mirror, then her ponytail again, then her frown again, still smaller and farther away. "S'pose we go on back like that forever?" Sue asked.

"More than likely," Neal said.

She laughed and bumped her shoulder against him, and Sue's bumped Neals deep into the mirrors.

The elevator stopped and its doors slowly slid open. Neal and Sue picked up their bags and stepped out. The corridor was deserted.

Sue hurried on ahead of him. When she found the door to their room, she leaned back against the wall and crossed her ankles. "Ya gonna take all day?" she asked.

"What's the big hurry?"

"Wanna see what we got."

In front of the door, Neal set down his suitcase. He dug into a pocket and took out the two keys. "You want one?" he asked.

"Sure," she said. Her hands were full. She bared her teeth and clicked them together.

"I'm not putting a key in your mouth. It's probably filthy."

"My mouth or the key?"

"I was speaking of the key, but . . ."

"Well, good. I try and not swear any more than I have to." She grinned. "Ya gonna let us in, or ain't ya? *Aren't* you."

Neal looked at her, amazed. So *that's* what she'd meant by the "hasn't" downstairs: she'd been correcting herself. Unlocking the door, he said, "You don't need to improve your language on my account."

"Well, it isn't exactly flattering to go around and get yerself called an ignerunt twerp."

"I just said it so Marta wouldn't . . . I didn't mean it. You know that. You were in me."

"Well, ya meant it, all right. Only thing is, ya still like me anyhow. Spite-a how . . . *in spite of* the way I talk like a dope."

"You're fine the way you are," he said, and opened the door.

Sue stepped into the room. "Look at this!"

Neal scanned the room. He'd been in plenty of motel rooms, and the rooms of several good hotels. Never in one this large, though. And never in one this old-fashioned. The wallpaper, the paintings, the dresser, the lamps and chairs, the rugs spread here and there on the dark and glossy hardwood floor—all looked like real antiques. Even the four-poster beds looked as if they might've been around in the days of the gold rush.

Sue dropped her bags onto the smaller of the two beds, then hurried into the bathroom. Standing in the doorway, she said, "Get a loada this." She sounded more wary than impressed.

Neal put down his suitcase and joined her.

"What'n tar is *that*?" Sue asked, nodding at the toilet.

The white porcelain water tank was up near the ceiling above the toilet, not down behind the seat. A chain with a wooden handle dangled from the bottom of the tank.

"I guess they wanted to keep things authentic," Neal said.

"Ya think it works?"

"I imagine. There'd probably be a mess if it didn't."

Sue nudged him with her elbow.

"Besides," he said, "it looks like new piping."

"Hmm." She wandered past the sink and mirror, past a full-length wall mirror that was flecked with gold like those in the elevator, and halted near the side of the tub.

The large, claw-footed boat of a bathtub stood away from the walls. A shower curtain hung behind it on a curtain rod that curved around, just below the ceiling, like a suspended racetrack. "How ya s'pose to use it?" Sue asked.

"For a shower?"

She frowned over her shoulder at Neal. "Yeah."

"Just pull the curtain around on the rod. Make sure it hangs *inside* the tub."

"Looks mighty all-fired queer to me. It'd likely get *on* ya. Maybe I'll just have me a bath, 'stead . . . *instead* of a shower."

"*Now?*"

"Sure. It'll perk me up."

"What about The Fort?"

"Don't ya wanna rest up awhile 'fore . . . *before* we go over there?"

"Wouldn't be a bad idea. I'm pretty tired. I could use a little nap."

"Good. So you take yerself a nap, and I'll take me a bath. Then we'll head on over to The Fort in maybe like an hour?"

"Sounds good to me."

"Ya better *go* first."

He raised his eyebrows.

Sue nodded toward the toilet. "I know ya gotta."

He grimaced, and she laughed.

A few minutes later, lying on the bed with his shoes off, Neal heard the water start to run. Quickly, he pulled the bracelet out of his pocket. He slipped it onto his wrist.

Why not? Turnabout's fair play. She did it to me . . .

When Neal heard the door open, he lifted his head off the pillow. Sue stepped out of the bathroom. She was barefoot but wearing her black leather skirt and her sleeveless blue shirt. Both her hands were busy rubbing her hair with a towel.

Her gaze flicked to the bracelet on Neal's wrist. A corner of her mouth curved up. "Where *you* been?" she asked.

Neal sat up on the mattress, and crossed his legs. "Just sleeping," he said. He gave her a smile that he hoped looked good and smirky.

Standing near the foot of the bed, Sue continued to rub her hair with the towel as she stared into his eyes. "So ya slept, huh?"

"Yep."

She smiled as if she knew better. "I know good an' well ya was in me. *Were* in me. And you know I know."

"How would I know that?"

"You know how."

"Tell me."

"I told ya in my head, and ya know it," Sue said. "We had us a fine, long talk."

"Must've been rather one-sided."

"Ya know dang well . . . !"

He shook his head.

Somehow managing to frown and smile at the same time, Sue draped the towel over her shoulders and crawled onto the mattress. On hands and knees, she stared into Neal's eyes. "Admit it. C'mon."

"No."

"Come *on*. It ain't no big deal."

"Isn't," he said.

Sue rolled her eyes upward. "I *knew* ya were gonna do it. I *planned* on ya doin it. That was the whole idea. Ya know? Cause I owed ya. And I wanted ya to know how I feel . . . about you. From the inside."

She gazed into his eyes.

"Ya know all that," she muttered. "Ya were in me, so ya know everything."

He shook his head.

"Like all 'bout the grand tour."

He smiled. "Grand tour? of what?"

"Ya know dang well."

"Of *you?*"

Her mouth dropped open again. She gaped at him.

"Damn! I missed it."

Shaking her head slowly from side to side, Sue muttered, "Judas H. Priest on a rubber crutch."

"I slept," Neal said.

"Ya slept."

"Honest to God. The fact is, I *almost* paid you a visit. I put the bracelet on. I sure *wanted* to jump inside you and . . . I mean, my God, everything else aside, you were taking a *bath*."

"Ya better believe it."

"I just figured . . . you know, there's Marta."

"Ya were't aimin' to *tell* her?"

"Even if she never found out about it," he said, "*I'd* know. It would've been like cheating on her."

"Ya aren't married to her."

"No, but . . . It wasn't just because of Marta. I didn't want to use you that way. Invade your privacy. Spy on you. It seemed wrong. Besides, it's against the rules to use the bracelet on someone you . . . care about. That was Elise's first warning. You might find out things you shouldn't."

Sue, still on her hands and knees in front of him, still gazing into his eyes, was now slowly moving her head up and down. "You'd of found out plenty," she said.

"Well . . ." Neal shrugged.

Sue raised her right hand off the mattress and pointed her forefinger at him. "Ya got no idea what ya missed, buddy," she said. Smiling gently, she pressed her fingertip against the end of his nose.

He tried to smile.

"But ya sure win points for honor." She put her hand down and crawled backward. As she lowered her legs off the end of the mattress, she said, "Betcha was a Boy Scout."

He blushed. "Yep. A Baptist, too. But that was all a long time ago."

"Well, some stuff sticks."

"It's pure hell, being virtuous."

Laughing, Sue tugged the towel off her shoulders. "Ya got yerself a long ways to go before they start puttin' ya up fer sainthood. Ya got that honor, but ya also got a dirty mind and a mean temper."

The words shocked him.

"Temper? What temper?"

"Ya let me fall and hit the table on purpose, back at lunch. I also happen to know all 'bout how ya slugged that Karen gal in the belly last night."

"I had to do that."

"Didn't have to *like* it."

He started to protest, but realized it would be pointless. Why try to deny it? Sue had been inside his head when he saw the nude painting on the bar and remembered punching Karen. She knew the truth.

Hot with shame, he muttered, "I'm not perfect."

"Nope. But y'ain't too bad, taken all-round."

"Thanks. You ain't, either."

"Aren't." She grinned.

Chapter Thirty

As Neal put his shoes back on, Sue said, "We could save us some money if only just one of us goes in The Fort."

"Save even more if *neither* of us goes in," he told her.

"How I meant is like, I go in normal, and *you* go in by the bracelet. Ya know? Ridin me? That way, we get in for half the price."

He looked at her, and was tempted.

But the temptation had been far greater when she'd been taking her bath. He'd resisted that; he could resist this blatant offer.

"You sure are eager to get me in you," he pointed out.

She shrugged. "I got nothin' to hide."

"So it would seem."

"Anyhow, ya know?" She wiggled her shoulders and hips, moving her hands slightly up and down in front of her like a juggler. "I'd be like yer host, ya know? It'd be my job to show you a good time. I'd go on all the rides, and chow down on snacks, and just do *everything*. It'd be great, ya know? You just stay here in the room, and I gain all the weight, and if the Pony Express crashes or somethin' when I'm on it, I'm the one that cashes in her chips, and yer home free."

"That's a pleasant thought."

"Well, I . . . I'm not lookin' to get killed. Only if it *did* happen, you could just bail and stay all nice and safe."

"Very thoughtful of you."

"Well, it'd save us the money, too."

"Why do we want to save money? Before you know it, we'll have fifty thousand dollars."

"Well, that's still sort of iffy, ya know?"

Neal got to his feet and said, "Let's both go over to The Fort. I came all this way; I'm not about to stay in the room and try to get all my fun from in *you*."

"It'd be *more* fun from in me."

"Maybe."

"Ya don't know what yer missing."

"Oh, I can imagine. But I need to go myself. For one thing, I'm hungry. Getting to enjoy *your* snacks won't quite do the trick."

"Okeydoke," she said. "Just thought I'd make the offer."

"You ready to go?"

"Almost." She returned to the bathroom and shut the door.

While she was gone, Neal wondered what to do with the bracelet. He thought about putting it into his overnight bag with the pistol, but was afraid that it might get stolen if he left it in the room. So he took it off his wrist and stuffed it into a front pocket of his trousers.

Sue came out of the bathroom with her denim purse swinging by her hip. She was wearing her white socks and sneakers. The towel no longer draped her shoulders, but it had left dark patches of moisture on the blue of her shirt. Her hair, still damp, had been combed or brushed backward. It swept behind her ears and hung like a thick yellow banner down her back. She looked pale and fresh and wonderful.

"Do I look okay?" she asked.

"Great. Ready to go?"

She peered down at herself, then stepped over to a mirror and studied her reflection. "I look great to me, too," she finally said, and laughed.

Able to see her front and back simultaneously, Neal was struck by the bareness of her arms and legs. No sleeves at all, hardly enough skirt to mention . . .

"You aren't afraid you might get cold?" he asked.

"What am I gonna do? This is all I got, less ya want me goin' over there lookin like a waitress."

"I have some extra clothes in my suitcase."

"I'll be fine," she said. Then she came over to him, took hold of his arm, and led him to the door.

They passed nobody in the corridor. After a brief wait, the elevator arrived. It was empty, the same as last time. They stepped inside.

Again, Sue seemed fascinated by the mirrors. "It's like yer disappearin' in 'em," she said. "Ya keep on gettin tinier and tinier, and then it's like yer just *gone*." She grimaced. "Kinda gives me the creeps." Her hand tightened its grip on Neal's arm.

"They need to have a mirror on the floor," he said.

"You!" Without letting go, she bumped him with her shoulder.

"I just said that to cure you of the creeps."

"You'd just *love* to have a mirror down there, and then ya could look up my skirt."

"Nah," Neal said.

The elevator stopped for no one else. They stepped out at the casino level, walked through the smoke and odors of booze and perfume and noises of clanking coins and ringing jackpot bells, walked past the registration area and out a door into a late afternoon of sunlight and quiet, and a fresh, warm wind.

"Ooh, this is niiiice," Sue said. Hurrying ahead, she raised her arms as if she wanted to embrace the sunlight or wind. After a few strides, she whirled around. As she turned, Neal glimpsed the pale skin of her armpit and side through the gaping hole where her sleeve had been removed. Then she was walking backward, smiling at him, her arms still high. The wind, coming from behind, blew her hair forward past the sides of her face.

My God, look at her.

Neal felt a sudden sharp sadness and longing and joy.

He shook his head.

I can't be falling for her, he told himself. *She's a kid.*

An airhead. A nuisance. A nitwit.

An angel.

Knock it off! Remember Marta.

Sue lowered her arms, but kept on walking backward. "What's the matter?" she asked.

"Nothing."

"Ya look like ya got a pain."

"Just you."

"Ain't *you* sweet," she said, then laughed, came back to walk beside him, and took his hand.

With the town behind them and nothing except The Fort ahead, they left the sidewalk and strolled up the middle of the street. Soon, the pavement ended. A smooth, yellow dirt lane led between the twin fieldpieces to the stockade entrance. Just beyond the main gate, they came to a row of ticket booths. Of the dozen cubicles, only one was open. Seven or eight people waited in front of it, standing in line to buy tickets.

The admission price, announced on large signs above every booth, was twenty dollars per adult.

Closing time was midnight on Fridays and Saturdays, but 10:00 P.M. every other night.

This was a Tuesday.

"Holy cripes!" Sue blurted.

"What?"

"Twenty bucks! That's gonna be *forty!* Told ya we oughta use the bracelet."

"Still cheaper than Disneyland," Neal pointed out.

"We ain't gonna pay all that!"

"I'm paying," Neal said. "It's fine. It's on me. Don't worry about it."

"Forty bucks!"

"Take it easy."

She shook her head. "It's robbery."

"A drop in the bucket," Neal told her. "We'll have that fifty thousand in a few days."

"Oh, sure thing."

In spite of Sue's protests, they remained in line. The admission price didn't bother Neal, but he *didn't* want to use up that much cash, so he decided to pay with a credit card. The card would create a plastic trail. That shouldn't matter, though; he didn't think the cops were after him.

How could they be?

They might've found his business card in Elise's house, but

he doubted it. He was nearly certain that Rasputin had taken the card.

And Rasputin apparently hadn't paid him a visit at the apartment, so it hardly seemed likely that the guy would try hunting him down by checking on his credit card purchases.

A guy like that might not even have the capability.

But suppose he does? Suppose he's feeling better now, and figures it's time to pay me back, shut me up . . .

Neal slipped the MasterCard back into his wallet, reached for some cash, and suddenly remembered that he'd already used the credit card to pay for their room at the Apache Inn.

The damage is already done.

There probably isn't any damage, he told himself. It had been a mistake, though, using the credit card for the hotel. At the time, he hadn't even considered that Rasputin might be able to locate him from it.

Don't worry about it. Even if he's one of those guys who knows how to find out everything about you on that information superhighway, he'd still have to deal with the concrete highways. Take him eight or nine hours to get here.

Neal did some mental arithmetic, counting hours from the time they'd checked into the Apache Inn.

The bastard could be here by midnight!

But he won't be, Neal told himself. Not unless he magically recovered from his gunshot wounds. Nobody would put himself through the torture of driving a car five hundred miles when he has two or three bullet holes in him.

If he's not nuts—or dead—he won't do anything for the next couple of weeks except stay in bed.

Neal went ahead and used the MasterCard to pay for their admission tickets. Which he soon handed to a fellow dressed in a blue calvary uniform, who tore them in half. Stubs in hand, Neal led the way through a turnstile.

On the other side of the turnstile, Sue took hold of his hand. They stood side by side, looking around.

In front of them was a broad, open area that appeared to be The Fort's parade ground. A pretty good crowd had gathered, up ahead. The spectators seemed to be watching some sort of performance by a squad of mounted soldiers. The soldiers had their sabers drawn.

The parade ground was surrounded by log buildings that appeared to house a variety of shops and restaurants. All the rides, and whatever else The Fort had to offer, seemed to be located beyond the far end of the grounds. People were wandering through a broad opening at the rear of the stockade fence. Neal could see the tops of the rides in the distance.

"Where do you want to start?" he asked.

Sue shrugged. "Don't wanna miss noth—anything. Wanta start over there, and work our way 'round?"

"The time-honored counterclockwise method of amusement park perusal."

She contorted her face at him. *"What?"*

"This way," he said, and pointed.

They crossed the dusty parade grounds, walked behind a couple of horses at a hitching post, then climbed onto an elevated wooden walkway and entered the first shop.

It specialized in western wear. They wandered around for a while, admiring the cowboy hats, boots, fancy shirts, blue jeans, leather vests, buckskin jackets, silver belt buckles and bolo ties. "If you see anything you want," Neal said, "just let me know."

Sue made a face, shrugged, and shook her head.

"I love that stuff," Neal confessed after leaving the shop. "Only problem is, you go around dressed like a cowboy in L.A., and somebody's likely to beat you up. Or shoot you."

"Ya oughta move."

"I don't know."

"Why not hit the roads with me? We'll go off in my four-wheel drive Jeep Cherokee, and see the country. Ya can wear the whole nine yards—chaps and a ten-gallon hat and spurs that jingle. I won't even beat ya up or shoot ya."

Neal knew that she was joking around.

But he also suspected that she meant it.

As they roamed from shop to shop, Neal thought about how it might be, traveling the country with Sue. It seemed like a fantasy, not a real possibility. He had a living to earn, his career to build. And what about Marta? He couldn't just dump her.

Hell, he didn't *want* to dump Marta. He loved her. He'd supposed that, before long, he would probably ask her to marry him.

He probably *still* wanted to marry her.

But now there was Sue.

What if it turns out that she loves me and she really wants me with her?

Then you've got a problem, buddy. You'll have to choose between the two of them.

How ironic that would be, he thought. Suddenly having to make a choice between two women, when he'd gone so long without any. Before Marta, there'd been about ten years of nothing.

A girlfriend now and then, but nothing serious.

He'd gotten serious about a few of them, but they hadn't shared his enthusiasm. Most of them seemed to be looking for "the big kill"—a guy who was already rich, or well on his way toward major bucks.

Neal never quite filled that bill.

He had made his first and only marriage proposal at the age of twenty-one to Judy Fain, a classmate at U.S.C. She'd responded, "I dearly love you, Neal. You're so sweet. But I'm afraid that you'd never be able to support me in the manner to which I intend to become accustomed."

The money issue had never come up with his first love, Sammi Wyatt. But she'd moved back East when they were both seventeen. They'd kept in touch for about nine months, but then she'd told him on the phone about a guy named Keith . . .

It had all been downhill after that, in the woman department. Until Marta.

She didn't seem to mind that he wasn't on the road to riches. *Loves me for myself.*

By the time he'd met Marta, however, he'd already sold one screenplay and had a few other projects in various stages of development.

I wasn't a complete loser anymore.

"Are you starvin'?" Sue asked, interrupting his thoughts.

"Sure am," he said, and found himself standing with her at the door to the Mess o' Ribs Mess Hall.

Sue tipped back her head. Eyes half shut, she breathed in deeply through her nostrils. "Sure smells fine," she said.

The air coming through the doorway was rich with aromas of wood fires, sizzling meat and barbecue sauces.

"Let's go in," Neal said.

"Might cost an arm and a leg. Maybe only just one of us oughta really eat, and . . ."

"Don't worry about it. Get on in there."

She hesitated.

Neal swatted her gently on the rump. He meant it only to encourage her to move, so he was surprised by the way he noticed the soft warmth of her leather skirt and the firm, bouncy feel of her buttock.

Seated across from each other in a booth near the back of the Mess o' Ribs Mess Hall, they both ordered margaritas.

The waiter asked to see Sue's ID. Smiling pleasantly, she took out her wallet, searched through its fat bill compartment, and came up with a driver's license.

The waiter studied it for a moment, then said, "Thank you, Miss Taylor."

After he left, Neal said, "Isn't your name suposed to be Babcock? Barbra Sue Babcock?"

She grinned. "My drinkin' name's Elaine Taylor."

"You're a criminal."

"Yup."

"What else do you do?"

"Not much." Leaning forward and looking him in the eyes, she said, "Is it breakin the law if ya go and sit in a rib joint without yer drawers on?"

Neal gaped at her. "You're kidding," he muttered.

Grinning, she sat up straight, wiggled a bit, and said, "Nope."

"What're you trying to do?" Neal asked.

She shrugged.

"I'm . . . involved with Marta."

"I know. But that don't mean I gotta wear drawers. *Doesn't*."

The waiter arrived with their drinks. When he was gone, Sue

lifted her cloth napkin off the table, shook it open, and spread it across her lap.

Neal opened his napkin, too.

"Make sure ya don't drop that on the floor," Sue told him. "The way yer lookin, ya wouldn't never have the guts to bend down and pick it up."

Neal laughed, and some of the tension eased out of him. He calmed down more while they talked, sipped their margaritas, joked around, and studied the menus.

They both ordered dinners of honey-glazed barbecued pork ribs, corn on the cob, and french fries. When the waiter was about to leave, Neal asked for another round of margaritas.

"So," Sue said, "are ya fixin to marry Marta?"

"Maybe. Not necessarily."

"She seemed real nice, from what I heard."

Neal frowned for a moment, confused. *How did Sue . . . ?* "Oh, that's right."

"Forgot I was in ya?"

"It had slipped my mind."

"I don't wanna go and butt in on yer business, but . . ."

"But you're going to do it?"

"Well . . ." She frowned. "Thing of it is, seems like ya sorta *scared* of Marta. Ya know? I saw that without ever usin' the bracelet. Ya never told her 'bout the bracelet, for one thing. For another, ya ran off just cause-a them . . . *the* scratches on yer arms. See what I mean? Then on the phone, only reason why ya told her 'bout me was 'cause ya figured she'd find out sooner or later, anyhow. Ya figured it'd go easier if ya fessed up at the start."

He stared at Sue. He took a deep breath.

This is what I get for letting her use the bracelet. Is there anything she doesn't know?

"So?" he asked.

"I'm not sayin ya oughta dump her or nothin' . . ."

"Or anything."

"Right. I'm not sayin' that."

"Well, good."

"I'm not sayin' there's somethin' *wrong* with her, either. I'm *only* sayin' ya ain't even married yet, but she's already got ya towin' the line and scared ya might do somethin' to piss her off."

"I love her," Neal said.

And felt as if he'd spoken the words too easily.

"If you say so," Sue said. "Only thing is, I figure ya love *me* more than ya do her."

"You're nuts. I hardly even know you."

"Don't forget, I been in yer head." Enunciating each word carefully as if venturing forward with a new language, she repeated, "I've been . . . in . . . your head."

Chapter Thirty-one

Done eating, Neal paid the bill with his credit card. As they walked out of the restaurant, he checked his wristwatch.

Ten till seven.

"Late for a date?" Sue asked.

"The park closes at ten," he said.

"What we oughta do," she suggested, "is maybe hurry right on over to the rides and leave the resta the shops and stuff for later. Think so?"

"I think so," he said.

"I think so, too." Smiling, Sue took hold of his hand. "Thanks for the dinner. It sure hit the spot. Those ribs, they were slip-smackin' good."

"They were good, all right," he said.

"Did I say that okay?"

"You said it fine."

"Catch how I didn't call 'em *them* ribs?"

"I noticed."

"They sure were delicious," she said, speaking with care.

"Yes, they were."

Neal, at dinner, had noticed only vaguely how sweet and tangy the ribs tasted. For the most part, he hadn't been able to focus on the food. His mind had been spinning—not so much from the margaritas as from Sue. His heart had gone thumping along too fast. He'd had an achy, tight feeling in his throat and, throughout the meal, an erection of varying stiffness in his pants.

It hadn't helped at all, being told she was drawerless.

Nor had it helped, watching the way she licked and sucked the sticky barbecue sauce off her fingers, sometimes moaning with pleasure and rolling her eyes.

This is what *did* help.

Shortly before the food's arrival, Sue had turned the conversation into a direction that had nothing to do with women or drawers. "It isn't that I *don't* know sorta how to talk right. Just that I never done it much. Never had no call to. How 'bout ya point out where I'm goin' wrong?"

"Are you sure you want to be bothered with it?"

"Sure. I don't wanta go 'round being an embarrassment to ya, soundin' like Jed Clampett. Shoot, you're a big ol' movie writer."

Neal laughed. "Not that big. Maybe someday."

"Anyhow, I gotta learn me how to talk right." The way she grinned, saying that, she'd known it was a doozy.

"Well," Neal said, "let's start with double negatives. They're not no good."

Sue grinned.

After that, when they weren't drinking margaritas, chewing food or trying to lick sauce off their fingers, they were talking about how Sue might improve her verbal skills.

Being Sue's teacher had helped Neal. He'd been able to focus on language, and nothing else, for moments at a time.

But he'd never been able to free himself from the knowledge that Sue was aware of how he felt about her.

She knows I've fallen for her.

She's got no panties on.

By the time they walked out of the Mess o' Ribs Mess Hall, he felt exhausted. He looked at his wristwatch. The park would close in three hours.

"Late for a date?" Sue asked.

*   *   *

Neal and Sue walked hand in hand toward the opening at the rear of the stockade fence.

The sun had just gone down behind the mountains to the west. The ridge blocking it was edged with blinding gold, which vanished as they passed beneath the rustic branch sign that read, UNTAMED TERRITORIES.

"Well, now," Neal said.

Sue squeezed his hand and grinned at him.

"This is the real thing," he told her.

"Real what?" she asked.

"Carnival."

Though the sun had barely gone down, all the lights in the Untamed Territories burned brightly, filling the dusk with reds and greens and yellows. Dozens of brilliant colors, it seemed to Neal.

And *noise*.

Carny noise.

The tooting tune of a calliope, somewhere a strumming banjo, the clatter and roar of a roller coaster, shouts and squeals, the spiel of a barker, the *bam bam bam* from a shooting gallery, bells clanging . . . other sounds, too many for Neal to separate or identify.

Carny noise.

And the carny smells of cigar smoke, cotton candy, popcorn, booze, perfume and suntan lotion . . .

And the people.

Not the mobs that would normally be found at Disneyland, Magic Mountain or Knotts Berry Farm, but a great many more people than Neal expected to find at a place like The Fort. They couldn't all be locals. Neal supposed that some must come from Reno, Sparks, Truckee, Lake Tahoe . . .

They looked like cowboys, truckers, carpenters, waitresses, students, mountain hikers taking a break from the wilds, school-teachers, middle-aged hippies, and spritely retired folks. There were young married couples. Babies in strollers and backpacks. Little kids running around shouting. Clusters of teenage guys trying to look cool and tough. Clusters of teenage girls snapping gum, smirking, whispering and giggling. And teenaged couples roaming around hand in hand, looking enthralled by each other.

Not a gangsta in sight, Neal noticed.

He saw cowboy hats, tight jeans and boots. No baggy trousers hanging at half-mast, no bulky shirts or overcoats worn to hide the bulges of a 9 mm semi-auto, a sawed-off shotgun or an Uzi.

"Well, Toto, we ain't in L.A. anymore," Neal muttered.

"Aren't," Sue told him. "And *I* never *have* been. In L.A. But yer gonna take me there tomorrow, right?"

He smiled and shrugged. "I don't know. I just might want to stay here where it's nice and safe."

"S'pose it's safe on the Pony Express?"

"I doubt it," Neal said.

The enormous, white framework of the roller coaster loomed above all the other rides and attractions at the far end of the midway. It looked like a railroad bridge built by a madman, the tracks climbing into the dusky sky then swooping down, steep as a cliffside, banking into hairpin turns and climbing again.

All of it festooned with lights like a Christmas tree.

As Neal stared at the distant structure, a train of half a dozen cars crested its highest summit and plunged straight down. He saw many of the riders raise their arms high as if surrendering. He heard faint, faraway screams of terror and delight.

"Lordy," he said.

"Still wanna go on it, don't ya?"

"We owe God a death."

"Nobody's gonna die." They started walking toward the distant ride. "If yer scared," Sue said, "ya can always stay behind on a bench, or somethin, kiss yer bracelet and go along on the ride with me."

"I'm not scared."

"Liar, liar, pants on fire."

"At least I'm *wearing* pants."

She bumped him gently. "Ya don't have to tell the whole world."

"You there!"

Neal turned his head.

A guy in a cowboy hat and a red apron, standing behind the

knee-high counter of a game booth, held up a softball. He seemed to be staring straight at Neal.

"Yeah, you! Step right over here! Win the little lady a fabulous prize! One ball for a dollar! Knock over all three bottles, and win! Step right up, duke! Show her what you've got!"

Neal smiled sheepishly, shook his head, and kept on walking.

"Don't ya wanna show me what you've got?" Sue asked, grinning.

"I'm not much good at games like that. Would *you* like to try it?" he asked.

"Me? I wanna go on the Pony Express."

So they kept on walking down the dusty lane between game booths, snack shops, souvenir stands, a variety of rides and funhouses—looking but not stopping. With every step Neal took, the Pony Express seemed to grow higher.

By the time they reached the far end of the midway, it towered above them—a colossus of rickety, white-painted beams strung with colored lights.

They took their place at the rear of the line.

Sue tilted back her head, shook it from side to side, and said, "She sure is a *big* booger."

"There's no law that says we *have* to ride it."

"Sure there is. Sue's Law. 'Don't worry 'bout it, just do it.' "

"That law could get a person into loads of trouble."

"I've done okay by it."

"Well, I imagine we'll probably survive."

As the line became shorter, however, Neal started to imagine otherwise. He pictured a whole string of cars leaping off a high stretch of tracks and flying out over the park—himself and Sue in the front car.

Plunging through the night, crashing through trees . . .

It's not going to happen, he told himself.

But what if there's an earthquake . . . ?

Or a mad bomber blows up a section of tracks . . . ?

"Ya okay?" Sue asked.

"Fine. Just a small case of the jitters."

"Ever been on any rolly coasters before?"

"Oh, sure. Lots of them."

"Not me," Sue said.

He couldn't believe his ears. *"You've never been on a roller coaster?"*

"Nope. Never been to a place that had one, till now."

"You've never been to an amusement park?"

She grinned. "Ain't I amazin'?"

Neal shook his head. "It's awful," he said.

"Well, it ain't the enda the world. I'm here now, right?"

He put a hand on her shoulder. "Yeah," he said. "You're here now. And if we miss anything tonight, we'll come back tomorrow."

And when we get back to L.A., he thought, I'll take her everywhere. Disneyland, Knotts, Magic Mountain, Universal Studios . . .

Universal was a motion picture studio, not exactly an amusement park. He wanted to take Sue there, anyway.

And the Venice boardwalk.

The Hollywood Walk of Fame.

The L.A. County Fair, though it wouldn't come along until September.

The Gene Autry Museum . . .

Take her everywhere, show her everything, share her delight.

Maybe *not* the Venice boardwalk, he thought. Might have to spend the day dodging bullets and knives.

Don't want our fine time wrecked by one of us getting killed.

And what about Marta? he wondered.

She'll come, too. We'll be a threesome. Marta and I, we'll be the couple. Sue and I we'll be like brother and sister.

Like Karen and Darren?

"What's the matter?" Sue asked.

"Huh? Nothing."

"Ya just sighed and shook yer head like yer pet dog got run over and squished."

Neal couldn't help but smile. "Actually, I was wondering how Marta's going to react when she meets you."

"She's gonna be charmed outta her socks."

Neal laughed. "You might be right."

Suddenly, they were at the front of the line. A worker in a

cavalry uniform beckoned them forward. Neal followed Sue through a turnstile. As they walked across the wooden platform, they were told by a girl in a fringed buckskin outfit to stand at number one.

The numbers were painted near the edge of the platform floor. Lower numbers to the left.

It came as no surprise to find that number one was the first number.

To Neal, however, it came as a shock to find that they would be sitting in the front seats of the lead car.

He groaned.

"What's the problem now?" Sue asked.

"We're first."

"Cool!"

"Aye-yi-yi."

Laughing, she squeezed his arm.

The Pony Express hadn't yet arrived. Neal could hear it, though. He heard its clatter and rumble, heard its passengers shrieking. He felt the platform tremble and shudder under his feet.

Oh, God, I don't want to do this! It's gonna crash!

He felt as if his insides were falling and shriveling.

No reason to be scared, he told himself. Nothing is going to go wrong. It's a *roller coaster*. It's a *ride*. It's not really dangerous at all. It's *make-believe* danger.

His legs felt weak. Goosebumps crawled all over his skin.

Just tell her you don't want to do it. She can go by herself.

And look like a chicken?

I faced Rasputin! Shot the bastard! I can't be scared of a stupid roller coaster.

Which suddenly arrived.

It lurched to a halt, the front seats of the lead car just below the edge of the platform in front of Sue.

After the safety bar swung forward, a man and a small boy started to climb out the other side. The boy, no older than ten, wore a grin like Dr. Sardonicus.

"Oh my God," Neal muttered, "it drove the little bugger mad."

Sue squeezed his arm. "How safe *is* this thing?"

Amazed by Sue's unexpected nervousness, Neal felt slightly less frightened, himself. "If it went around crashing," he said, "it wouldn't be here."

The answer seemed to reassure her. "Yeah, reckon yer right."

"We'll be fine," Neal said, feeling even better.

"Okay."

She went first. Neal followed. All too soon, they were seated side by side and the safety bar swung in toward their chests.

"Are you ready?" Neal asked.

"I don't think so!" Grimacing, Sue clutched the bar with both hands.

The roller coaster jumped forward and immediately began to clitter-clatter its way slowly up the main slope. It climbed higher and higher. The steep angle pinned Neal against the seat cushion at his back. Ahead, the tracks seemed to rise forever.

"I don't *liiiike* this," Sue sang out.

"The fun hasn't even started yet," Neal told her. "Just wait till we get to the top."

"I'm scared!"

"You're supposed to be."

As they neared the top, Sue began muttering, "Oh jeez, oh jeez, oh jeez!"

They reached the crest.

Neal couldn't see the downhill side. He could see nothing straight ahead except distant mountains.

"Here we go!" he shouted.

"*Shit!*" Sue yelled.

They both clutched the safety bar to brace themselves for the plunge.

It didn't come.

The ride jerked to a sudden stop.

They went nowhere.

Chapter Thirty-two

"Uh-oh," Neal said. He felt sick. He sat rigid in his seat, half expecting the odd stop at the summit of the ride's first and highest hill to be followed up by another surprise: maybe the whole structure would topple.

Sue turned her head toward him and bared her teeth. "This isn't s'pose to happen?"

"I'm afraid not."

"What's it mean?"

"A malfunction?" Neal suggested.

"Oh, dear."

"I'm sure they'll have it fixed in a minute or two."

Except that maybe everything's already starting to collapse . . .

"Weren't them *lights* on before?" Sue asked, nodding toward the low wooden railing a few feet to the left of the tracks.

A strand of colored lights was wrapped around the railing.

The lights no longer glowed.

Neither did the lights that were strung around the railing to the right.

Neither did the thousands of lights adorning the Stagecoach Ferris wheel at the other side of the park.

Neal spotted the upper stories of the Apache Inn way off in the distance. All its windows were dark.

Keeping his tight grip on the safety bar, he leaned to the left and peered down. The park below them, earlier so gaily lit, was cloaked with the gloom of late dusk. He saw people hurrying about, down there. And groups standing motionless, their heads back, staring up at the stranded roller coaster.

Most of the carny noise was gone.

He heard alarmed voices, a few faraway shouts and screams, birds . . .

Facing Sue, he said, "It's gotta be a power outage."

"Oh, boy. How'd *that* happen?"

"I don't know. An accident at a power station somewhere?"

"What'll we do?"

"Wait, I guess." Neal saw a wooden walkway at the edge of the structure. A walkway with a railing two-feet high, and a godless drop at the other side. It apparently became a stairway just ahead, where the tracks sloped down.

My God, what a stairway that's gotta be!

Neal had heard that it was a common practice at amusement parks for someone to walk the roller coaster tracks before the first run every day. To make sure everything looked shipshape.

What kind of nut would walk on that?

Such a narrow walkway. Such steep slopes. Nothing really to hold on to. Such a long way down . . .

The very sight of it made Neal feel giddy.

The idea of using it as an escape route horrified him.

Maybe as a last resort.

I'll stay right here and starve in my seat, if it comes to that.

"We're awful high up," Sue said.

She had a tremor in her voice.

"It's all right," Neal told her. He unfroze his right hand from the safety bar, slipped his arm across Sue's shoulders, and snuggled her in against his side. She was shaking. "It'll be all right," he said. He caressed her upper arm.

She hunkered down lower against him and tried to bury her face in his chest.

"If you think *we've* got it bad," he said, "how would you like to be in one of the cars behind us? At least we made it to the top."

"They still there?"

Keeping his arm around Sue, Neal twisted himself toward her as much as the safety bar allowed, and gazed over his right shoulder. The second car hadn't reached the top of the grade. He couldn't see it at all.

"Hello back there!" he called.

"Howdy," a woman called. She sounded elderly, and had a cheerful voice.

"Everyone okay back there?" Neal asked.

"So far. And how about yourselves?"

"Okay."

"It's a grand view of the sky," called a man. From the sound of his voice, Neal figured he was probably sitting beside the woman—likely her husband.

"Does this happen often?" the woman inquired.

"I don't know. We're just . . ."

"*Attention*," boomed a voice through a megaphone. "*May I have your attention, please?*"

"Ya got it, ya got it," Sue muttered.

Neal turned forward. Looking over the side, he spotted a husky man far below, head tipped back, a battery-powered megaphone at his mouth.

"*We are experiencing a temporary loss of electrical power. We regret any inconvenience or discomfort this may be causing you. However, you are in no danger whatsoever. I repeat, you are perfectly safe. So long as you remain seated. Please remain in your seats. Do not attempt to exit the ride. The situation will be rectified shortly, and you will be returned safely to terra firma.*"

"Terror firma?" Sue asked. "What the hell's he talkin about?"

"The ground."

"How come he didn't just say so?"

"He wanted to be fancy about it, I guess."

"Think we're really safe up here?"

"Sure."

If nothing else goes wrong.

"It don't *feel* safe. Feels high."

Neal turned toward her as much as he could. The side of his right leg pressed against the side of her left leg. She put a hand on his thigh and rested her face against his chest. He reached across with his left hand and stroked her hair.

"Are you okay?" he asked.

"Just scared," she said. Her mouth was touching his shirt front, and he could feel the heat of her breath. "I don't like gettin' stuck this high up in the air. I just don't."

"There's a way out," Neal said.

"Like what?"

He dug the bracelet out of his pocket and showed it to her.

"Put it on, kiss it, and take off. You can be safe on 'terror firma' in about two seconds."

"I reckon I could," she said. Then she gave his thigh a couple of playful smacks with her open hand. "Tryin' to get rid of me?"

"We might be stuck up here for hours. I *know* how scared you are. So, really. Go ahead and use it. There's no good reason for you to suffer though this. Just take off and have a good time. Visit some of the folks down on the ground. You could even go on back to the hotel and find yourself someone having a nice meal or some drinks at the bar . . ."

"I could find me a gal gettin' laid."

Neal blushed and let out a nervous laugh. "Yeah. Or that."

Sue raised her face from his chest. Even in the near darkness, he could see her smile. "You ever done that? Gone in somebody *doin'* it?"

"Nope."

"How come?"

"Just hasn't come up. I've hardly had a chance to *use* the thing. Besides, I'm not really big on sex with strangers."

"Ya could make it with *anybody*. Any old time ya felt like it. There's likely somebody doin' it someplace *all* the time. Just have to catch 'em at it."

"I suppose that's true," Neal said.

"Don't tell me ya ain't thought about it."

Though blushing, Neal had to smile. "I guess it's crossed my mind."

"Ya wouldn't even need to worry about catchin AIDS, or nothin', either."

"I'm not all that worried now."

"How come?"

"I'm careful who I sleep with. Nobody but Marta since my last physical."

"Might catch it from her."

"Nope. She's perfectly healthy."

"Think so?"

"I know so."

"What if she fools around?"

"Marta doesn't fool around."

"What makes ya so sure? Use the bracelet on her?"

"No. Of course not. And I have no intention of using it on her."

"I'll do it for ya."

"You will not."

Sue's grin spread. "Scared I'll find out she's got another fella?"

"Why don't we just leave Marta out of this?"

"Okay. Jess tryin' to help. I mean, I sure don't want ya to get sick and die, that's all. If she's steppin' out . . ."

"She's not stepping out."

"If you say so."

"I say so. Now look, do you want to use the bracelet and get out of here?"

She was silent for a little while, apparently thinking it over. Then she said, "Nah. I'm doin better. It ain't so scary . . . *isn't* so scary when we're talkin like this, ya know?"

"It does seem to help," Neal admitted.

"So we better keep on talkin', huh?"

"I guess so," Neal said.

"Let's go back to Marta."

"Well . . . how about if we don't, and—"

"Do ya use rubbers on her?"

"Sue!"

She laughed. "Sorry! Never mind! All I'm sayin', if ya *aren't* a hundred percent sure about her, ya better take precautions."

"Fine," Neal said. "Let's talk about something else."

"I don't use 'em, myself. Never have."

He blushed fiercely, and felt a quick rush of heat in his groin. "You should," he said.

"Last time I got myself boinked . . ."

"Sue. Jeez."

"Well, it was six years ago."

"You were *twelve?*"

"Yup." She put her head down on his chest again. "They was five guys in the school john."

"My God."

"Don't reckon they woulda put on rubbers even if I'd asked 'em."

"Did they hurt you?"

"Yeah. Sure did."

Neal's eyes suddenly brimmed with tears.

Just a little kid. Innocent and helpless. What sort of bastards could do that to her?

My poor Sue.

"I'm . . . so sorry," he murmured.

"Me, too. Bled like a stuck pig, and couldn't walk straight for a week. But I come through it okay. Least I didn't catch some disease or get knocked up."

Neal sniffed and took a deep, shuddering breath. He wiped his eyes. "What happened to the guys who raped you?" he asked.

"Huh?" She lifted her head. "Oh! They didn't *rape* me. I *got* 'em to do it. They were my buddies."

"*What?*"

"Sure. Only problem was, it was too many all at once and we were too young. Not to mention we got caught at it. The whole gang of us got expelled."

"My God," Neal muttered.

Sue laughed. "Anyhow, that was my first and last try at gettin' laid."

"Never once . . . ?"

"Come close a few times, and there's always guys wantin' to. I've even had the urge, myself, a few times. But mostly, the guys I know aren't much good so I been savin' myself."

Saving yourself for someone like me?

Neal didn't dare ask.

"Also, there's my problem," Sue said.

"Problem?"

He felt her head nod against his chest. "The time when I did it with all them . . . those guys . . . they sorta ruined me."

Her words gave Neal a tight, sick feeling.

Should he ask *how* they'd ruined her?

She probably expected him to ask, but he was afraid.

"Put that away and gimme yer hand," she said.

Neal stuffed the bracelet into his pocket. Then Sue took him by the wrist and pulled his hand over to her. Her head and

curtain of hanging hair blocked the view, so he couldn't see
what she was doing.

Her left leg shoved his right leg aside.

On his hand, he felt smooth, warm skin.

Then the feathery brush of soft curls against his fingers.

Sue guided his hand lower. He felt skin on both sides and
knew he was between her thighs.

"Here's what they done to me," Sue said. "Feel there? Right
there?" She slid his fingertips over soft folds of flesh and in
between them, into a split that was hot and slick. "See how they
left me gashed wide open?" Sue asked.

Neal could only answer with a groan.

Still holding his hand down there, Sue lifted her head and
kissed Neal on the mouth. He felt as if his breath were being
sucked away. Her tongue pushed between his lips. As he delved
deeper into her with his fingers, she released his wrist and caressed the side of his face.

She groaned and squirmed.

I shouldn't be doing this, he thought. Shouldn't be.

Can't help it. Feels too good.

But it was not just the wonderful slippery tight feel of her, it
was the knowing that she wanted his fingers there, wanted *him*
there. Trusted him enough. Liked him enough. Loved him?

A very weird trick to get me there . . .

"See how they left me gashed wide open?"

Yeah, right.

She'd told the truth, at least, about her drawers.

This is so . . . fantastic! Unbelievable!

What about Marta?

Marta never has to know, he told himself.

Sue writhed on his hand, grunted into his mouth, stopped
caressing his cheek and ran her hand down his chest and belly.
She tugged at his belt buckle.

He wanted a breast. Her left breast felt good the way it pushed
against his chest, but he wanted one in his hand. His right arm
was already stretched across her back. Lowering it slightly, he
went in beneath her armpit and slipped his hand through the
hole where her sleeve had been removed.

He felt her smooth, bare side. Stretching farther, he touched the side of her breast.

Tried to reach to the front, but couldn't.

Couldn't get to her nipple.

Almost, but . . .

Sue slipped his zipper down. He felt the front of his trousers go loose. The elastic waistband of his shorts went away.

He groaned when Sue's hand curled around his erection. He felt huge, hard and heavy, ready to explode.

Her cool, smooth hand glided slowly down, then up . . .

With a sudden jerk, the Pony Express lurched forward.

Neal and Sue both flinched rigid and gasped into each other's mouths.

Eyes leaping open, Neal saw the Christmas tree lights brightly aglow along the railing.

The seat seemed to drop out from under him.

And down they roared—a train plunging off a cliff.

Behind them, people screamed and clapped.

Sue's hand leaped away from his penis. In her haste to turn forward and brace herself, she trapped his hand between her thighs.

"Hey!" Neal yelled.

"Ha!" she squealed, and spread her legs.

Neal retrieved his hand. He clutched the safety bar and braced himself with his feet as the roller coaster kept on rocketing downward.

The warm night air rushed around his erection.

Great time for the power to come back.

Look on the bright side—we're not stranded anymore.

What am I gonna do?

At the bottom of the monster slope, the Pony Express sped into a right-hand turn, the tracks rising into a thicket of white beams. Daring to release his panic grip on the safety bar, Neal dropped both hands to his lap and shoved himself back into his undershorts.

One task at a time, he wiped his slippery left hand dry the best he could on the front of his shorts, shut the zipper of his trousers, buttoned his waist, and fastened his buckle—finishing with five or ten seconds to spare before the roller coaster stopped at the end of the ride.

The safety bar automatically moved away from them.

On shaky legs, Neal stood up and stepped onto the platform. He turned around. Sue, on her feet, looked flushed and unsteady. Meeting his eyes, she hoisted a corner of her mouth. Neal, with a breathless laugh, reached down and gave her a hand onto the platform.

Side by side, they staggered toward the exit.

He glanced down at himself. His shirttail hung out.

So did Sue's—but hers was always that way.

A couple of her buttons had come undone.

We must look like we've been wrestling.

As they neared the exit gate, a red-haired guy in a cavalry uniform looked them over and said, "Sorry about that problem."

"No problem," Neal told him.

"Are you both all right?" he asked.

"Fine and dandy," Sue told him. "Best rolly coaster ride I ever had."

It had left them both sticky, though.

Soon after leaving the ride, they found rest rooms. The doors were marked BRAVES and SQUAWS.

"S'pose anybody'll care if we go in the same one?" Sue asked.

"We'd probably get arrested."

"Yeah. More than likely." She squeezed his hand. "Ya aren't gonna disappear on me, are ya?"

"Why would I do that?"

"I feel so dang fine, seems like it's gotta end real soon, that's all."

"It won't," he said.

Chapter Thirty-three

For Neal, matters had been settled at the summit of the Pony Express. Doubts had been removed. He didn't know what to do about Marta yet, but he knew how he felt about Sue.

After coming out of the rest rooms, they didn't talk about returning immediately to the hotel.

The hotel, and what was sure to happen there, could wait.

They went on with their exploration of The Fort, walking slowly side by side, holding hands, often laughing at little things. There were strangely long silences, sometimes. And when they were standing still or sitting, they always found themselves staring into each other's eyes.

At a game booth, Neal threw darts at balloons, popped three, and won Sue a pink stuffed kitten not much larger than her hand. She named it Dart. At another booth, she sank a basketball and won a small, stuffed green dinosaur. "It's for you," she said, presenting it to Neal. "What're ya gonna call it?"

He gave the matter some consideration, then answered, "Spielberg."

Sue laughed and hugged him.

Neal stuffed the prize animals into the deep, loose pockets of his trousers. Putting Dart in his left-hand pocket, he felt the bracelet down there.

The smooth, warm feel of the gold made him smile.

Our fabulous bracelet. None of this would've happened without it.

Sue had used it and misused it, invaded his privacy with it, infuriated him. In the process, however, they had stopped being strangers.

Thank you, Elise. Thank you, thank you. You didn't just give me the bracelet, you gave me Sue.

Holding hands, they continued wandering the midway.

They played a few more games, but didn't win.

They rode the Wagon Wheel, a tilt-a-whirl ride that swung them round and round, throwing them against each other.

They ate cotton candy—flossy pink fluff swirled around paper cones. When they were done, they returned to the rest rooms to wash the stickiness off their hands.

They waited in line for the Crazy Horse Rapids, Sue with her back to Neal, her buttocks pushing against him, Neal with his arms around her belly. During the ride, they sat with four other people on a rubber raft that lurched and twisted and whirled and bounced its way down a flue of churning water. It rushed beneath bridges, passed under waterfalls, and plummeted off small cataracts. By the end of the ride, Neal and Sue were soaked.

They climbed out of the raft, dripping.

The water on their skin and clothes seemed to turn the night chilly. They walked bow-legged, laughing, hunched over in their clinging shirts.

Neal led the way to a nearby souvenir stand. He bought two big, blue sweatshirts. On the front of each sweatshirt was a pair of golden, crossed sabers. The backs read, THE FORT, NEW HOPE, NEVADA.

Standing in shadows to the side of the midway, Neal removed the sweatshirts from the large, plastic sack that they'd come in. He and Sue used them like towels to dry their hair, faces and bare arms. While Sue wiped her legs, Neal took off his clinging shirt and pulled the new sweatshirt down over his head. It was dry and soft on the inside. Sue frowned at him.

"One of the good things about being a guy," he said.

"I reckon."

"If you don't want to put it on over your shirt, we could head on over to the johns again."

"Heck with it," Sue said. Keeping her wet shirt on, she pulled the sweatshirt down over her head. But her arms stayed out of its sleeves. The crossed sabers bulged and writhed. She looked as if she had a couple of squirrels racing around inside her sweatshirt. Her empty sleeves swung by her sides. Then one of her hands reached down out of the bottom and tucked her wet, blue shirt between her knees. Moments later, her arms slipped into the sweatshirt sleeves.

But her hands didn't appear. She flapped her cuffs at Neal, then shoved the bulky sleeves up around her forearms.

They tossed their sodden shirts into the plastic sack that had come with the sweatshirts. Then Neal tossed in the stuffed animals, Dart and Spielberg.

"Feels so nice 'n cozy," Sue said, rubbing herself. "Like being all wrapped up in a big, warm blanket." She gave the bottom a tug with both hands, and her black leather skirt vanished under the sweatshirt. "Looks like I lost something!" Laughing, she raised the sweatshirt high enough to show a few inches of her skirt. "Oh, there it is!"

When they moved on, Sue carried the bag. Neal kept his right arm across Sue's back. By sliding his hand, he could feel her skin through the soft thickness of the sweatshirt.

The next ride they came to was the Stagecoach Ferris wheel, a mammoth affair with its individual cars designed to look like Wells Fargo stagecoaches.

Neal and Sue got into line. She stood in front of him, leaning back slightly against him like before. He wrapped his arms around her. The position was more snuggly this time because of the sweatshirts. Sue caressed his wrists. They both watched passengers disembark from the Ferris wheel, new passengers climb aboard.

After each new set of passengers climbed in, the door of their coach thumped shut and the enormous wheel turned a bit, swinging them up and forward while lowering the next coach to the platform.

Neal and Sue watched the wheel turn and stop. Turn and stop. Each time it stopped, all the coaches teetered wildly back and forth. And then, instead of stopping, it began to spin fast, hoisting the coaches high into the night, dropping them.

"Judas H. Priest," Sue muttered.

"What's the matter?"

She turned around and looked up at him. "How 'bout we go on somethin' else, okay? I mean, I'll *do* it if ya really wanna, only . . . I got me the squeamin' jimmies on the rolly coaster, and I just don't think . . . this here Ferris wheel's *high*."

"Are you sure?"

"I'm sure it's *high*."

"You're sure you won't mind missing it?"

"How 'bout you?"

"I don't mind."

"Then let's not, and say we did."

"Fine with me," Neal said, and led her out of the line. Once they were back on the midway, he shoved up his sleeve and checked his wristwatch. "The park's going to close in about half an hour. Maybe we should start heading back."

"I think we done most of it, anyhow."

"We've done most of it," Neal said.

"We've done. We. Have. Done."

"Very good."

"I don't reckon I'll ever get the hang of it."

"You're doing fine. Would you like some ice cream or popcorn or something?"

"We haven't got a lotta time."

"Half an hour."

"How 'bout we go in *there*?" she suggested, and elbowed him gently in the ribs. "Custer's Spookhouse."

The entire facade of the funhouse was a mural depicting cavalry soldiers and Indians sprawled dead on a grassy hillside, ghosts rising like gray smoke from their torn and bloody corpses.

"Talk about tacky," Neal muttered.

"Ya don't wanna?"

He grinned. "I didn't say that. The tackier, the better. Let's go."

As they approached the entrance, however, he felt compelled to explain, "The Battle of the Little Big Horn didn't even happen in Nevada, you know. That was Montana. Probably a thousand miles from here."

"I don't mind," Sue told him.

"I guess I don't either, actually. It's just funny, that's all. But Nevada *did* have the Pony Express."

"Best rolly coaster in the world."

Neal gave her shoulder a squeeze. "Sure was the best *time* I've ever had on one."

Then they entered Custer's Spookhouse.

As they walked through its maze of dark corridors, displays of mayhem suddenly appeared with noise and red lights. The first few times, Neal felt Sue flinch a little. Then she seemed to take the displays in stride.

They mostly consisted of mannequins that weren't realistic enough to fool anyone: an Indian brave hanging from a noose, his tongue protruding; a cavalry soldier on his back, half-a-dozen arrows jutting from his chest, his hair getting lifted by a leering, painted warrior crouched over his head; a frontier woman in a torn dress, tied to a stake, kindling piled around her feet; a brave, still on his feet in front of a saber-wielding soldier, his head split down the middle; a gory cadaver, rib cage and guts exposed, with a couple of turkey vultures pecking at it.

"Look," Sue whispered. "That one's got his eye."

Neal saw one of the corpse's eyeballs clamped in a buzzard's beak. "Cool," he said.

Sue elbowed him and laughed.

They walked on. After they'd gone a few steps, the red lights of the display went out, leaving them again in darkness.

There seemed to be a thick carpet or pad under their feet, silencing their shoes.

"It don't get much darker than this," Sue whispered.

"No, it doesn't."

"Doesn't." She squeezed his hand. Then she came to a halt. "It's quiet, too."

They both went silent, and listened.

Neal heard laughter, giggles and shrieks. Though they sounded muffled and far away, they seemed to come from somewhere inside the spookhouse.

"How come we haven't seen nobody?" Sue whispered.

"I don't know."

"Let go a second. I gotta tie my shoe."

He released her hand, and heard soft crinkly sounds when she set down the plastic sack.

"Apparently," he said, "this isn't The Fort's most popular attraction. Also, it's almost ten. Maybe we're the only people weird enough to save this place for last." Sue didn't comment, so he asked, "Did you ever see that movie *Funhouse?* These kids decide to spend the night in the funhouse of this creepy carnival that comes to town. So they hide until after closing time. The thing is, there's this monster lurking around, knocking them off one by one."

Probably not easy to tie a shoelace in the dark.

"Think there might be a monster in here?" he asked, smiling.

She didn't answer.

"Sue?"

She didn't answer.

Very cute. She thinks she can scare me with a gag like this?

"Hmmm," he said. "Where'd she go?"

Bending over, Neal swept a hand through the darkness. Sue was not crouched beside him, tying a shoelace.

What'd she do, sneak off?

She has to be all right, he told himself. This is just a game she's playing. Made up that story about needing to tie her shoe so I'd have to let go of her hand.

"Are we playing a little hide 'n seek?" he asked.

Still, no answer came.

Maybe something did happen to her.

That's crazy, he told himself. She was right here beside me. I would've heard . . .

Unless it was something silent.

Like what? he wondered. She certainly couldn't have been attacked . . . nothing like that.

She's just fooling around.

"Well," Neal said, "I don't know about you, but I'm leaving. Are you coming?"

No answer.

"Okay. Bye-bye. So long. Adios. Been good to know ya. It's been real. Cheerio."

Something in the black of the corridor wrapped its arms around him from behind. He flinched and gasped. He grabbed the wrists at his chest, ready to fight. But a voice whispered, "You ain't goin nowhere, buddy."

He let his arms fall to his sides. "Very funny," he said.

"Scared ya."

"Yes, you scared me. A little."

"Made ya jump." Though she spoke in the softest whisper, Neal could hear the glee in her voice.

"I knew you were just trying to trick me," he explained. "But then I started to worry about you, anyway."

"Really?"

"Yes, really."

"That's sorta nice," Sue said.

Her arms were loose around him, so he turned around. Though facing her, he could see nothing except pitch black. "I'm just maybe a little too sensitive about losing people," he said.

"Glad ya didn't lose me?" she asked.

"Yeah, I'm glad." He raised his hands and put them on her sides and felt bare skin. Sliding them downward, he felt the slopes of her hips, the smooth cheeks of her buttocks. No clothes, just skin. "Uh-oh," he said.

"Uh-oh, yerself."

Moving his hands upward, he caressed bare skin all the way up to her armpits.

He swallowed hard and whispered, "You're out of your mind."

"Just wanted to give you a little surprise."

"You're full of surprises."

"Yup."

He brought his hands forward and curled them over her breasts. He rubbed his palms against her stiff nipples.

A shiver seemed to pass through Sue.

Bending his knees, Neal kissed one of her nipples. He pressed it between his lips, then opened his mouth and drew it in, tasting it, exploring it with his tongue. Sue, moaning, put both hands on the back of his head. She pushed her fingers through his hair, and urged his mouth harder against her breast.

He slid his hand up between her thighs.

"Eeeww, look at *that!*" A little girl's voice.

Sue's hands froze against Neal's scalp. He pulled his head

back. Her breast came out of his mouth with a wet sucking sound.

Turning his head, he saw a very faint red glow down the corridor.

"Crap on a cracker!" Sue gasped in a harsh whisper. "What're we gonna do?"

"Where're your clothes?"

"In the sack."

Where's the sack? Neal wondered.

Too late, anyway.

"It's just pretend, darling," said a woman.

"Is not," said a boy. "What do you think they *used* their swords for, to toast marshmallows? No, sir. They used 'em to chop up injuns."

"Native Americans," said a grown-up man.

Shit! A family of four!

A few moments later, the red glow vanished.

The next attraction for the family would be the buzzards feasting on the corpse.

How far away? Neal wondered.

Not nearly far enough.

"What'll we do?" Sue asked.

Neal flung his arms around her, lifted her off her feet and rushed forward, hugging her to his body. After three quick strides, he rammed her against a wall. Though the wall was apparently carpeted, she grunted from the impact. Neal grimaced with unexpected pain from the scratches on his forearms.

"What was that?" asked the little girl. She sounded scared.

"Ghosts and ghouls," the boy said. "They're coming for you."

The girl made a squealy sound.

"That's enough of that, young man," said the man Neal assumed to be the father.

"I heard it, too, Tom," said the wife.

"Crazy Horse wants to scalp you, Molly."

"James!"

"Oooooooooooohhh!" From James.

"Oooooooooooohhh-yeeeeahhhhhhh!" From Sue—a trite and car-

toonish ghost "ooh" twisting and rising into the demented shriek of a banshee.

Both the kids erupted with terrified screams. Through their screams, Tom the father blurted, "Shit!" and the mother snapped, "Children! Get back here!"

Sue let forth a mad, witchlike cackle.

"Assholes!" the father yelled.

"Tom!"

"I'm coming, I'm coming! Like to get my hands on those assholes . . . !"

Gazing over his shoulder, Neal saw a dim red haze fill the corridor in the distance: the kids, fleeing, must've run through the sensor that activated the lights for the saber-in-the-head exhibit.

"Fucking assholes!" the father shouted—a parting shot as he gave chase to his retreating clan.

"Is he talking about me?" Sue whispered.

"I believe so."

She tittered softly. Neal felt small, warm puffs of her breath on the side of his neck. Her chest shook against him through his sweatshirt.

"Kids!" the mother yelled. "Stop running! Kids! Damn it! Wait for us!"

A few seconds later, the distant red glow vanished and the corridor returned to blackness.

"We'd better get while the gettin's good," Sue whispered.

Neal gave her a quick kiss. In the dark, his mouth found a peculiar part of her face. He didn't know what he'd kissed. "Where'd I get you?" he asked.

"My eye."

"What was it, open?"

"Yeah. I think ya blinded me."

"Hope not," he said. "Where's the stuff?"

"I don't know."

"Okay. No problem. Stay put for a second." He turned away from Sue and hurried in the direction where he'd seen the red glow. He shuffled along with his arms out, expecting to crash, but was still on his feet when he triggered the lights of the buzzard exhibit.

He glanced to the left.

No sign of the angry father or anyone else.

He checked to the right.

In both directions, the corridor vanished into darkness.

He turned around. Sue, prancing forward naked except for her shoes and socks, waved a hand at him. Her skin was rosy in the crimson light. Her breasts jiggled. Her nipples looked purple.

She halted over the big plastic sack, dipped down and snatched out her sweatshirt. She flung it high and seemed to dive up into it. An instant later, she was shoving the sleeves up her forearms. She bent down and grabbed the sack. "Let's go!"

She went to the right.

"Where's your skirt?" Neal asked. The sweatshirt hung only to her waist, leaving her naked from there down to the tops of her socks.

"I got it in my bag," she said.

"Gonna put it on?"

"No time." As she said that, the sweatshirt shook free from around her hips and dropped the rest of the way down—falling low enough to cover her buttocks.

Neal hurried after her. The lights went out.

"Wait up," he said.

Moments later, they found each other in the darkness. Neal took hold of her hand.

He hardly noticed the remaining attractions of Custer's Spookhouse. He was too nervous and excited—too stunned by Sue's wild behavior.

Amazed by her audacity.

Enthralled.

An angry-looking man was waiting on the midway just outside the spookhouse exit. No sign of the wife or kids, but Neal supposed this had to be Tom.

He was bald on top, wore glasses, and had a soft look about him as if he never got exercise. An expensive-looking Minolta camera hung from a strap around his neck, and rested on the slope of his belly. He glowered at Neal and Sue as they strolled down the ramp. His fists were clenched by his sides.

Terrific, Neal thought. The guy's going to cream us. And then we'll probably get arrested for disturbing the peace, or something.

Neat play, Sue.

Worth it. Man! She's fabulous! Nuts but fabulous!

Sue suddenly clutched Neal's arm. "The *bastards!*" she blurted, and looked up at him with hurt and rage in her eyes. "We oughta call the cops on 'em. Bastards! What'd they think they're doin', jumpin out and yellin' like that! Scared the pants offa me!"

Tom's scowl faded as they approached him. "Did somebody bother you in there?" he asked.

Sue nodded, her lips pursing out. She looked like a kid about to burst into tears.

"Us, too," Tom said. "They scared the hell out of my kids. I'm gonna grab them when they come out and fix their wagons. Did you see what they looked like?"

Sue shook her head. "Too dark. All I know, there was six of 'em."

"Six of them?" Tom didn't appear to like the sound of that.

Neal shook his head at Sue. "I thought more like five."

"Nope, six. I counted."

Tom grimaced. "Well . . . thanks for the information."

"Yer welcome," Sue said.

He glared toward the exit, then shook his head. "Aah, I can't wait around all night for them." He turned around and walked off.

Sue tugged on Neal's arm. "Now what?" she asked, grinning up at him.

"I think we've done enough here."

She laughed. Then she asked, "What time *is* it, anyhow?"

"Five after ten."

"Guess we better get, 'fore they throw us out."

Chapter Thirty-four

This time, of all times, they weren't alone in the elevator.

The whole way back to the Apache Inn after leaving Custer's Spookhouse, Neal had been conscious of little else except Sue walking near him in the bulky new sweatshirt, a sweatshirt that hung down just barely to the tops of her thighs. She hadn't put her skirt back on. She wore nothing at all under the sweatshirt, and Neal couldn't get it out of his head.

In the elevator, he intended to slide the sweatshirt up to her waist.

My turn to get a little wild.

In the elevator mirrors, they would see repeated reflections of Sue—back and front at the same time, over and over, receding.

She'll get a kick out of it, too, Neal thought. *Hell, she'll probably pull the sweatshirt off completely.*

In his fantasies as they walked through the night, they both ended up naked in the elevator, making love surrounded by their reflections.

But as they stepped into the elevator, a couple of women came rushing out of the casino area toward the open doors. Women with tall, stiff hair, too much makeup, western shirts bulging across their busts, big silver belt buckles, and blue jeans so tight that neither woman could walk properly. Or maybe it was the cowboy boots that made them walk funny. Or maybe their intoxication. Or a combination.

They each carried a big plastic tub of coins in one hand, a clear plastic tumbler of beverage in the other.

"Hold that door f'r me there, darlin'!" called the woman in the lead. Her enormous fluff of hair was snow white, with pink highlights.

Sue thumbed the button to make the doors shut.

They began sliding. "Shoot!" Sue blurted. "I pushed the wrong button!"

The pink-blonde sidestepped in. One foot inside the elevator, one foot out, she rammed her ass against the door behind her. Both doors stopped closing. She stayed where she was, running interference for her friend, but stumbled backward as the door retreated from her rump. Though she managed not to lose any coins from the tub she carried, her other hand leaped, flinging a glassful of ice and cocktail into her own face. "Bwah!" she gasped.

Neal took one of her arms, pulled, and helped her stand up.

As the doors slid shut, she said, "Thank y'there, darin'. Yer a gennleman 'n a scholar."

"Glad to help."

"Name's Myrna," she said, and winked at Neal. "This here's m'pal, Lola."

Lola, her brunette pal, pushed the button for the fourth floor, then gave Neal a little salute. "Whatever Lola wants," she said, "Lola gets."

"Ain't she a hoot?" Myrna asked as the elevator started to rise.

"Did y'all win much?" Sue asked.

"Nah," Myrna said. "The more y'win, the more y'lose. Ain't that so, Lola?"

"I done all right," Lola said. "I play that electric poker?" she said, her voice rising at the end as if she were asking a question. "Takes some smarts, but y'got better odds 'n the damn slots. Them slots, they're the shits."

"I like 'em," Myrna said.

"Then y'oughta not complain 'bout losin' all the time."

"Well, y'win a few 'n y'lose a few." Myrna tried to take a drink, found her tumbler empty, and frowned. "Where'd m'vodka 'n tonic go to?"

"Up yer nose, the most of it."

"Well, poopy!"

The elevator stopped at the fourth floor, and the doors rolled open.

Sue pressed the button to keep them that way.

Lola stumbled out.

Myrna scowled into her empty plastic tumbler. "I reckon I'll go on back down 'n get me a refill."

Sue and Neal looked at each other. Sue smirked. Then they both stepped out of the elevator, into the hallway with Lola. The doors shut.

Lola gave Neal and Sue a lopsided smile, said, "See y'laters, alligators," then strutted-stumbled her way down the hall. She turned a corner and vanished.

"Lordy," Sue muttered.

"Relatives of yours?" Neal asked.

She blurted out a laugh, and elbowed him. "Shame on you," she said.

They walked toward their room, Sue holding his arm with one hand and swinging her sack with the other.

"I had big plans for inside that elevator," Neal told her.

"You and me both."

Stopping in front of their door, Neal said, "The best laid plans . . ."

"Least we won't have nobody trippin' over us when we're in here."

"Sure hope not."

As he entered the room, Neal turned on the light. Sue came in, swung the door shut, leaned back against it, and dropped her sack to the floor. "C'mon over here," she said.

He stepped closer.

She clutched the front of his sweatshirt and tugged him against her, wrapped her arms around him and kissed him on the mouth. Her mouth was open and wet.

Neal's hands roamed up and down her sides, feeling her warmth through the thick fabric of her sweatshirt. Then he lowered his hands to her bare legs. He moved them up the backs of her legs, under the hanging sweatshirt. Her buttocks filled his hands, firm and cool, smooth as satin.

She raised one of her legs as if she wanted to climb him. He ran his hand under it. Just when he was almost to the back of her knee, she hopped and brought up her other leg. Hugged between them, Neal clutched her buttocks.

She was heavier than he expected.

What am I supposed to do now? he wondered.

Get her to the nearest bed before you drop her.

He began to stagger backward.

Sue broke contact with his mouth—almost. Her slippery lips moving slightly against his, she whispered, "Giddyap, horsey."

"Navigate for me?" he asked.

"Just keep on goin' back."

He kept on going back. "Say when," he told her.

"Keep goin'."

He kept going, but suddenly his legs were stopped by the bed. Gasping with surprise, he toppled toward the mattress. Sue rode him down. She didn't mash him, though; she caught herself with her hands and knees. Looming over him, she smiled. "Yer a good ride," she said. "Wanna do it again?"

"You were supposed to say when," he pointed out.

"When." She bent her arms, leaned down and kissed his mouth.

As they kissed, Neal rubbed and squeezed her buttocks, then made his way up her back, sliding her sweatshirt higher and higher. Sue stopped kissing him and pushed herself up slightly to let him work the sweatshirt over her shoulders and head.

When he had trouble getting the sleeves off her arms, she knelt above his belly, raised her arms, freed them from the sleeves and tossed the sweatshirt off the bed.

Neal gazed up at her.

She smiled down at him. "Whatcha starin at?"

"You."

"I'm kinda scrawny."

"You're beautiful."

"Thanks." She lowered herself onto him again and kissed him.

The feel of her breasts and belly and groin were muffled by Neal's sweatshirt. But she was all bare skin on top. He savored the warm sleekness of it, his hands sliding down the curves of her back and rump, then up along her hips and sides, and over her shoulder blades.

She lifted her face enough to talk. "Looks like I'm the only one butt-naked 'round here."

"So far," Neal said.

"Reckon that's a good deal for one or the other of us."

"I can't take my clothes off with you on top of me."

"Well." She raised her head a little higher and studied Neal's eyes—glancing from one to the other, back and forth. "I'll take 'em off ya," she said.

"Okay."

She kept studying his eyes.

"What's wrong?" he asked.

"Just . . . nothin'."

"What?"

"I just . . . I've got me a case of the squeamies, that's all."

"The squeamies? What's that? Diarrhea?"

She made a mock scowl. "*No!* I'm fine. I'm *scared*, that's all."

"Scared?"

"Last time . . . I got hurt. I got hurt pretty good."

"When?"

"When those guys done me . . . when I, you know, like I told ya on the rolly coaster. The five guys in the school john."

"Huh? That really happened?"

She suddenly sat up and frowned at him. "Did ya think I was *lyin?*"

"No!" he blurted, confused. Then he said, "I don't know. Not at first. But then when you had me touch your *wound* and it turned out to be your . . . you know . . . I just figured maybe the whole thing was a story."

"It was a *true* story. And it *was* my wound I had ya touch. Ya shoulda seen all the blood. . . ."

"I thought you were playing a trick on me. You know, joking around to get me to touch you there."

Both corners of her mouth tilted up. Her slender bare shoulders hopped up and down. "It was that, too." Her smile vanished. "I mean, I was havin some fun with ya, but . . . All the rest of it was the honest t'goodness truth. I haven't . . . nobody's, you know, *done* it to me since then. I haven't let 'em, 'cause of how they hurt me that time."

"And you're afraid I'll hurt you?"

Nodding, she lowered herself onto him again. She pushed her face against the side of his neck, and he caressed her back.

"We don't have to do it," Neal told her.

"But I wanna."

"We don't have to."

"I wanna. It's just, I'm scared a little. I don't like pain very much."

Neal's throat tightened at the sound of those words, and his eyes grew hot.

I don't like pain very much.

Like something you might hear from a frightened child.

His mind suddenly jolted him with a picture of Elise dead on the ledge of the tub, arms out, wrists tied, head drooping—mutilated and bloody, and a bar of soap in her mouth.

He squeezed Sue tightly against him.

She groaned. "Yer squishin me."

He released her. "I'm sorry."

Her head lifted and she kissed him on the mouth. Then she pushed herself up, crawled backward and climbed off the end of the bed. She stood there, Neal's knees hugged between her legs.

He pushed himself up on his elbows. "What do you want to do?"

"I aim to get on with it," Sue said.

"Are you sure?"

In answer, she leaned forward, reached down, and unbuckled his belt.

Moments later, his trousers were open. Sue tugged them down to his knees, then stepped back. Neal raised his feet off the floor.

"Thanks," she said, and pulled off his shoes and socks. When his feet were bare, she finished removing his trousers. Then she stepped forward, leaned over him, and slipped her fingers under the elastic waistband of his shorts.

Neal clutched her wrists.

"You're just going to yank them down?" he asked.

"I don't guess I gotta *yank*," she said.

When he let go of her wrists, she lifted the elastic band straight upward, then drew it toward her, freeing his erection.

She stared.

She pursed her lips.

"Oh, boy," she muttered. "It's s'pose to feel *good*, gettin a thing like that shoved up yer wuzzitz?"

"I don't gotta *shove*," Neal said.

The look on Sue's face was a cross between a grimace and a smile. Shaking her head, she slipped his shorts the rest of the way down. She tossed them aside.

Then she took a couple of steps backward, away from the bed. While Neal watched, she balanced on one foot, brought up the other and pulled off its white sneaker. Then she started to lose her balance and stayed up by hopping as she tugged off the sock. When that foot was bare, she stood on it and worked on her other shoe and sock, hopping, her golden hair bouncing, her small breasts leaping up and down.

When both her feet were bare, she ducked out of sight.

"What're you doing now?" Neal asked.

"Nothin'."

"Ah. Okay. While you're doing nothing . . ." He sat up and shucked off his sweatshirt. As he flung it to the floor, he glimpsed Sue's back. She was down on her hands and knees. "Anything I can help you with?" he asked.

"Nope. Thanks all the same."

"Okay." On hands and knees, himself, Neal pulled down the bedcovers. Then he stretched out on the bottom sheet. He squirmed on his back, enjoying the feel of the sheet against his skin.

As he stuffed a pillow under his head, Sue stood up.

Wearing the gold bracelet around her upper left arm.

"Oh, no," Neal muttered.

She frowned at him. "*I* think it looks nice."

"I *love* how it looks," Neal assured her. "Especially how it complements the rest of your ensemble."

She laughed and looked at the bracelet, herself. "Fits nice up here, too," she said.

"And it's conveniently located," Neal pointed out.

High on her arm, the bracelet was within easy reach of her lips.

"Are you planning to *use* it?" he asked.

Sue shrugged. Then she climbed onto the bed and crawled forward, Neal between her hands and knees. She halted when she was directly above him. Staring down into his eyes, she said, "I won't use it if ya don't want me to."

"Why would you want to use it?"

"To get out, case it starts hurtin'."

"If it starts hurting, I'll stop."

"Don't want ya stoppin'."

"Why not?"

She shrugged. "Because. I been in yer head. I know how bad ya want me."

Neal reached up under her breasts, and held them gently. Moaning, Sue shut her eyes.

"Just tell me if I hurt you," he said.

"Just don't stop," she murmured. "No matter what."

"If you bug out with the bracelet . . ."

"Just keep goin'."

"Where'll *you* be?"

"In you."

"While I'm . . . ? Jeez, I don't know."

"If ya don't want me to, just say so."

They gazed into each other's eyes. Sue, he realized, was moving her body just enough to make her breasts drift about within the loose cups of his hands, caressing him with their smoothness, stroking him with their stiff nipples.

"It's okay," he whispered. "You can come in if you want."

"Thanks," she whispered.

She remained braced above him, her breasts in his hands, and Neal didn't notice her changing position, at first. He noticed only the change in her face—how she made sort of a trembling smile and caught her lower lip between her teeth.

Then he felt a soft pressure against the tip of his penis.

He felt a snug, slick hole push itself onto him.

Sue sat down slowly, ever so slowly, slowly taking him into her.

He squeezed her breasts.

She threw back her head, her mouth hanging open, and kept on slowly easing herself down. He went up slowly into her slippery, hugging warmth. Up higher, up deeper. Higher and deeper until her body pressed on him. Seated, she could go no farther.

She gave a sigh, and smiled down at him.

Neal took a deep, trembling breath. "Are you okay?" he asked.

"Real fine," Sue whispered.

"Didn't hurt?"

"Mmmm. Nope."

Lifting his head, Neal saw her sitting on top of him, her legs splayed apart. Her groin was joined so tightly to his that nothing showed between them. He was in her completely.

"Lordy," Sue said. "If I'd known it'd be like this . . . Does it feel this good to you?"

"Maybe better," Neal said.

"Don't go away, I wanna see for myself." With a slight tuck of her head and a lift of her arm, she kissed the bracelet.

Chapter Thirty-five

She did it!

And went limp as if she'd suddenly passed out. Her eyes shut. Her head drooped. She started to drop forward.

Neal shoved against her breasts to hold her off, his open hands mashing them almost flat.

"This isn't any good," he told her in his mind. *"I can't . . . damn it! . . . Doesn't it hurt? Sit up. I don't want to hurt you! Stop, okay? Just stop?"*

But she didn't stop. She kept bearing down on him as if determined to crash her forehead into his face.

"Sue!" he gasped. "Somebody's gonna get hurt!"

He continued to brace her above him, giving her time to return to her own body.

She didn't.

"Okay," he thought to her. *"You're gonna play this out, huh? Okay. Here goes!"*

With a lurching buck, he flung Sue sideways. He stayed with her as she tumbled, wrapping an arm around her, clutching her to him, rolling, staying between her legs. When they were both on their sides, he almost came out of her. But then her back met the mattress and he was on top and he plunged down into her again all the way.

So deep.

So rigid and deep into her snug center . . .

Neal tried to hold back.

Sue, with a sudden gasp, thrust her pelvis up against him.

Shuddering, he throbbed inside her, throbbed and spurted, his semen pumping into her, spurting, flooding her as he throbbed and grunted.

When he could breathe again, Neal stayed inside her but propped himself up with his elbows. She smiled languidly. He kissed the tip of her nose, and said, "You came back."

"Wanted to be here for the big finish. Not that it weren't a thrill a minute in *you*." Her hands rubbed their way down his back and squeezed his buttocks. "Holy smokin' mackeral."

"I didn't know what to do with you," Neal said.

"Sure ya did." She squirmed a little and sighed. "Only thing is, it got over awful quick."

"Sorry about that."

"Wasn't yer fault. Shoot, I know that—I was *in* ya." Smiling up at him, she said, "I'm just way too excitin' for ya."

"You can say that again."

She squirmed some more. "I sure do like how ya feel in there."

"I like how *you* feel in there."

"I know. I drive ya crazy."

Blushing, Neal said, "You didn't happen to notice that I was . . . a little angry?"

"Ya had a right to be. Hell, I came droppin' down on ya like a safe."

"Well, you're not exactly a safe."

"Probably woulda knocked yer teeth out."

"I was worried about your . . ."

"My titties. I know. Ya had 'em squished flatter than flap-jacks."

"Are they all right?" Neal asked.

"Feel fine. How they look?"

Neal pushed himself up until his elbows looked. Braced above her, he studied her breasts. "They aren't flapjacks anymore," he said.

"Wanna taste 'em and make sure?"

Her words sent a sudden rush to his groin.

"Whoa!" she gasped. "What did that?"

"You said that about tasting them."

"Maybe ya better just *do* it, then."

"What?"

"Taste 'em."

"Now?"

"Just do everything ya feel like, okay? Whatever turns ya on. I'm gonna be right in there to see what happens."

"With the bracelet?"

"Unless ya don't want me to. Only thing is, I know ya like it."

"I'm not so sure."

"Just say no." She lifted her eyebrows.

Neal tried to think about it, but he found thinking difficult under the circumstances. And denying her request would be even more difficult. "Whatever you want," he said. "If you want to come in me again . . . I'd be glad to have you."

"Thanks." Smiling up at him, she said, "This time, I'll ride ya to the end."

She turned her head and raised her arm. The moment that her lips met the gold coil of the snake bracelet, she went limp. Her arm flopped to the mattress.

As if she'd passed out.

"I don't know about this," Neal muttered.

She's all right with it. It's her idea.

"*Wouldn't you rather stay in yourself?*" he asked her in his mind. "*We can do this like normal people.*"

We can do it like normal people some other time, he told himself. Not every day you get a chance like this . . .

Do whatever I want.

She wants me to do whatever I want.

Man, oh man!

"Okay, Sue. Look, here's the deal. I'll sort of . . . fool around with you. I mean, that's what you want, right?"

It's what I want, that's for damn sure.

"Sue? Look. If I start doing anything you don't like . . . anything at all . . . just stop me. Please. If you don't stop me, I'll figure it's okay. Okay?"

Oh, God. Here goes.

Shaking slightly, Neal crawled backward, eyes on Sue's limp, sprawled body. After sliding out of her, he sank back on his haunches. He stared at her.

Sleeping Beauty.

Don't think corny shit like that, she'll think you're a whacko.

And she knows you just thought that, dork.

This is so weird!

Better do something, or she'll think you're not interested.

No, she won't. She knows damn well I'm interested. She's in me right now.

Just pretend she's not.

Yeah, right.

"Hello, hello. It's only me from across the sea . . ."

She is in me, and . . . it's a ride. I'm gonna disappoint her if I don't do something. Do what? Kiss her tits, for starters.

Taste them. Suck them. Gnaw on them.

"How'm I doing, Sue?"

Forget her.

Do it. Do it to her. She wants it and I want it. She wants to know how I feel when I suck on her tits . . .

Neal lowered his mouth onto her left breast, kissed it, caught the nipple between his lips. And as he took the breast into his mouth, he fondled her other breast with his hand.

"How's this? You like this, Sue? I like this."

Oh, man.

He could feel himself getting harder and harder.

Oh, God, she's so smooth. So smooth all over here and here, and then like rubber here. Nipples like rubber.

"I don't mean that as an insult, Sue. I love them stiff and sticking up like this."

She knows that.

But as if to reassure her, he chewed gently on the one while he gently rubbed the other between his thumb and forefinger.

She squirmed. A moan slipped out.

Neal thought she must be returning to herself. When she remained limp with her eyes shut, however, he figured that her body must simply be reacting to the stimulation. She was still in him.

Her body feels it all, anyway.

And she gets the whole works from inside me.

It's more than just experiencing *my* sensations, he realized. She gets all that—how turned on I am, and everything. But she's also getting to see *herself*, feel herself, taste herself— through me.

She's my eyes, he told himself. She's my hands and fingers. She's my mouth and tongue, my nose. She's my cock, too.

And she's in my head, knows I'm thinking all this right now.

Thinking about my cock.

Neal realized he didn't feel embarrassed. He thought he *should* be blushing with shame. Instead, he felt daring and excited and even more aroused.

"*How do you like having a cock?*" he asked her with his mind.

She actually knows how it feels to have a cock. Not just having one stuck inside her, but how it feels to have one of her own, and how it feels when it slides into her . . .

Next time someone tells her to go fuck herself . . .

Terrific.

"I'm sorry, Sue. I think things. I can't help thinking things."

It's all right, he told himself. She's not going to hold it against me. Probably amused.

Or turned on.

She was writhing, gasping and moaning on the mattress as if trapped in a frantic dream.

Neal parted with her breasts and slid himself down her body, caressing her, kissing and licking her along the way. Moving slowly downward. Pausing to look. For himself, but also for Sue.

Very aware that she was his passenger.

They were touring her together, exploring her.

Sue couldn't make requests, so everything was up to Neal.

She was the tourist *and* the locale being explored.

Me, too. We're both getting explored here. Both tourists, and getting toured.

Make it memorable.

Don't miss a single marvel.

Don't hurry.

No hurry at all. Just linger and enjoy.

"And here," he whispered, "we have the famous Babcock Cavern. Also known as the Tunnel of Love."

Corny corny corny.

He raised his head and looked at her face. No smile. No smirk.

Humor doesn't carry over.

What humor?

He lowered his face again. "The famous Babcock Cavern appears to be flooded at the moment."

Maybe she doesn't appreciate me making fun . . .

Nothing so funny about it.

Nothing funny at all.

"Neal Darden," he whispered, "world renowned speleologist . . ."

Later, much later, he rolled Sue over.

Together, they slowly toured her back.

Her back and buttocks and legs glowed with a sheen of sweat. And Neal dripped onto her as he roamed.

He caressed her, squeezed her, probed her, tasted her.

She squirmed under him like a restless sleeper, sometimes sighing, sometimes gasping for air.

He mounted her.

Finally, exhausted, he crawled off Sue and flopped onto his back.

Sue turned onto her side.

Neal turned his head.

"Howdy," she said.

"Howdy yourself. Welcome back."

She stretched out an arm and lay it across his chest. Her left arm. The one with the bracelet wrapped around it.

Neal caressed her forearm.

"Wanna try it?" she asked.

"You've got to be kidding."

"You oughta."

"I'm wiped out."

"You and me both. Lordy."

"How was it?" Neal asked.

"Can't tell ya."

"Sure you can."

"Nope. It was too . . . I don't know . . . too big and strange. It wasn't like samplin' a kid's milkshake. Ya gotta try it yerself. Get in me, and try it."

"Not tonight. Okay?"

"Ya sure?"

"I'm sure."

"All tuckered out?"

"Sure am."

"Me, too." Her arm slid down. She fingered his penis. "My little buddy," she said. "All tuckered out. He ain't dead, is he?"

"Probably in a coma."

Her fingers fiddled. "Bet I can wake him up."

"That's all right. He's had enough excitement for one night."

"Didn't know these things could go off so many times," Sue said.

"Neither did I."

"Didn't know I could go off so many times, either."

"You really did, huh? I thought so. I wasn't sure . . ."

"Well, I don't go *squirtin'* all over the place," Sue said. "Not like *some* folks I could mention."

"But you actually had orgasms . . . your body did . . . while you were in me?"

"Had 'em both places."

"What do you mean?"

"In you *and* in me."

He nodded. "You mean, you experienced mine."

"Sure did! But that ain't what I meant. Isn't. I had my own *both places at once*. The part of me that was in you . . . my soul or whatever . . . it came the same time my body did. It's like we're wired up together. Like switches were gettin' thrown over where I was in you, and they—"

"Lit you up."

"Yer being funny again."

"Not very."

"Yer right," she said, and laughed. "I think yer funny. Sometimes. I reckon I mighta cracked up a few times, only I was too horny and outta breath. You had some *mighty* odd thoughts."

"You didn't have to stay," he told her.

Instead of answering, Sue gave him a calm, lazy smile and scooted closer. Then she pushed herself up, crawled onto him and lay down, her face close above his face, her breasts pushing against his chest, her legs together on top of his legs.

He supposed it was no accident that she held his penis between her thighs.

"That's better," she said, and wiggled a bit.

Neal moaned. He said, "Much better."

"Now, where were we?"

"Me and my odd thoughts."

"I loved every one of 'em."

"You did?"

"I did. That's 'cause I love ya, Neal. If ya don't believe me, just kiss the bracelet and come on in and see for yerself."

"Elise warned against that sort of thing."

"*I* done it to *you*."

"Right. And you found out I'm a filthy-minded pig."

"Yer a real *sweet* filthy-minded pig." Lowering her head, she kissed him on the mouth. Kissed him gently and for a very long time.

He woke up. The bedroom lights were on and Sue still lay on top of him. The room felt chilly. Neal was warm where Sue covered him. Her legs had fallen to the sides, however, so they no longer gave her heat to his groin and the tops of his legs.

He glided his hands slowly down her back and up the slopes of her buttocks. Her skin felt cool.

Oughta get up, he thought.

But he really didn't want to move. He liked the feel of Sue sleeping on top of him.

Oughta at least get up and go to the john. Brush my teeth. Wash up. Turn off the light. Make sure the door's secure.

He was fairly sure that the door, like most hotel room doors, locked automatically when it was shut. But he should make certain. And he should also fasten whatever chain or bolts . . .

What time is it?

Turning his head, he looked at the clock on the nightstand. 3:36 A.M.

He felt a sudden tremor of fear. For a few moments, he didn't know why.

Then he remembered Rasputin.

The bastard could be here by now.

Could've been here hours ago, snuck in the room and killed us both.

Hell, he isn't coming. No way.

Not the sort of guy who'd go around checking to see where I used my credit cards.

Probably.

Anyway, I shot him full of holes.

From Neal's position under Sue, he couldn't see the door. But he knew for certain that it wasn't secured from the inside by any sort of bolt or chain. Hours and hours ago, Sue had shut it, leaned back against it . . . then Neal had carried her to the bed and neither of them had returned to the door.

I should at least lock it from this side.

And get my gun over here where I can reach it.

Just in case.

And take a leak.

Turn off the lights.

Pull some covers up over us so we don't freeze . . . or turn off the air conditioner. Probably fine in here without the air conditioner.

But he couldn't get up and do anything.

Not without waking Sue.

Not without ruining the perfect feel of her sleeping on top of him.

No big hurry, he told himself. If she gets cold enough, she'll probably wake up. She's *bound* to wake up sooner or later. I'll just wait.

Waiting, he gently caressed her.

He wondered if this had been the best day and night of his whole life.

And decided there was no doubt about it.

A perfect day, a perfect night.

If only I hadn't dropped her at lunch. God, I wish I hadn't done that. It was such a mean, nasty thing to do. Shit! How could I do a thing like that to her? Split her chin open . . .

He began to cry.

He wrapped his arms around Sue's back and held her tenderly as he sobbed. Tears trickled down both sides of his face. On the left side, they were stopped by Sue's head. On the right side, they dribbled into his ear and tickled.

I'll never hurt her again, he promised himself. I'll never *let* anyone hurt her. I'll stay with her forever and protect her from harm.

Like I protected Elise?

He pictured Elise dead.

Again.

And then his mind, going off as if on a whim of its own—to torture him—made a few changes in the horrible picture. The mutilated corpse on the ledge of the tub became Sue.

No! Isn't going to happen. No way.

He held Sue gently. He felt her heat and weight, her heartbeat, her breathing. And he felt the crushing loss of her.

Whatever else happens, he thought, we'll never have another time like this. This was the best. You, aren't allowed repeats.

"Who the hell says so?" Sue whispered.

Neal thought for a moment that he had imagined her voice. But then she raised her head and stared into his eyes.

Her eyes were shiny and red.

"We are too gonna have more good times," she said. "We are, too. Repeats *are* allowed."

Then her eyes flooded and she began to shudder and sob.

Chapter Thirty-six

"What do you want to do about Mojave?" Neal asked. It was five o'clock in the afternoon. They'd been on the road since shortly after one, having stayed in their room at the Apache Inn until the noon checkout time, then eaten lunch at the Puncho Viva restaurant and spent a while exploring the town, buying souvenirs and some snacks.

"What *about* Mojave?" Sue asked, frowning slightly.

"What do you want to do when we get there?"

"Like what?" she asked.

"It's where you live," Neal pointed out.

Looking at him, she raised her eyebrows. "Well, I reckon ya could let me off there and go on without me."

Her words gave him a sick, sinking feeling. He knew she was joking around, but . . .

Reaching over, she squeezed his thigh. "Not that it hasn't been swell, George."

"It's Neal," he told her.

"Well, shoot! How'd I go and forget yer name?"

Smiling, relieved, he lowered a hand from the steering wheel and pressed Sue's hand against his leg. "The thing is," he said, "we'll be passing through. We should probably stop, don't you think? Don't you want to tell someone where you're going? Don't you have some stuff you'd like to pick up?"

"Nope," she said.

"*What?*"

"I told 'em I was goin' for good."

"*What?*"

"Yup."

"No, you didn't."

"Yup, I did." She gave Neal the wildest, most gleeful and disarming smile he'd ever seen her make. "I says to Sunny, 'I'm runnin' off with that fella over at table number five.' Sunny, she says, '*What?*' like I lost my marbles. I go, 'He's my dream-boat . . . takin' me away forever.' "

Neal gaped at her.

"Better watch the road, honey," she said.

He faced front. "You're making that up. You never said any of that."

"Wanna bet? If ya don't believe me, we can drop in on Sunny. You can ask her yerself. Better still, just use the bracelet on me. Hop on in, and you'll find out if I'm lyin or not."

Neal shook his head. "That's all right," he said. "I'll take your word for it."

"Good. 'Cause that's sure what I told Sunny."

"But you didn't even *know* me."

"I had me a feelin'."

"My God, you *are* nuts."

"Think I was wrong?"

"No, but . . ."

"I *mighta* been wrong, but I wasn't. So, anyhow, we don't gotta stop in Mojave. Nobody's expectin' me back."

"What about all your things?"

"I told Sunny to keep 'em."

"That was generous."

"Well, she was rentin' me a room. It was all her furniture. I didn't have nothin . . . *anything* much in it 'cept some duds, and they weren't much to write home about. She's got a daughter my size . . ." Sue shrugged. "I just went ahead and told her to keep everything."

"Don't you have keepsakes, or . . . ?"

"Nope."

"Nothing?"

"Nope." A corner of her mouth lifted. "Now, I got Dart. Dart's a keepsake, I reckon. All the other stuff ya gave me, too. They're keepsakes."

Neal suddenly felt awful for her. He shook his head. "How could you *not* have anything? You're . . . eighteen?"

"Depending which ID I use."

"I'm serious," he said.

"Yer also a guy that takes stuff hard, and I don't wanna make ya cry again."

"Oh, jeez."

"Well? It's the truth."

"You were supposed to be *asleep* last night when that happened. I didn't know you were spying on me."

"I wasn't spyin' on ya, I was on a tour of yer *marvels*."

"Ha ha."

Sue laughed for real, but softly, and rubbed his leg. "Anyhow, I used to have all kinds of good stuff. But it all got burnt up in the fire. All my keepsakes, all my clothes, my dog Sparkle, my sister Betty. My folks, too."

Neal turned to her, half smiling—she had to be pulling his leg.

He saw the way she was trying to look cheerful but had a frantic look in her eyes.

"Oh, my God," he muttered.

"It's all right," she told him.

"Your . . . whole family?"

"My cat Fraidy survived. But then he got squished a couple weeks later on the interstate. Him . . . He and I, we hit the road together. Only he didn't last. That's cause cats're generally not real bright. That's a little-known fact. They like to *pretend* they're regular little geniuses, but mostly they're dumb as dirt. That's how come they always get themselves stuck in trees and trapped in places and squished."

Neal, eyes wet and a lump in his throat before hearing about Fraidy, had been cheered up somewhat by Sue's denunciation of cats. He took a deep breath.

"Ya okay?" Sue asked him.

"Yeah. It's just . . ."

"Shit happens. Ya ever hear that saying?"

"Yeah," Neal said. "I've probably said it myself."

"Well, anyhow, I'm okay now. Sorta. I mean, what're ya gonna do? Crawl in a hole and die? Not me."

"You hit the road?"

"Yup. Me and Fraidy cat. Only he didn't last, and I did."

"How old were you?"

"Fifteen."

"*Fifteen?* My God, that . . . it's so young to be on your own."

"Well, they were gonna throw me in an orphanage. I didn't have no use for that."

"What about school?"

"Never went back after the fire." Grinning, she said, "But I reckon it don't show."

"Only when you open your mouth."

"Haw!" she blurted, and slapped his leg. "I'm gettin' better, and you know it."

"I know."

"I'm workin' on it." She narrowed an eye at him. "Betcha never even noticed I quit chewin' gum."

She was right. "You stopped? When?"

"I gave it up yesterday. Haven't stuck so much as *one* piece in my mouth ever since yer call to Marta."

"Really?"

"When ya called me a gum-snappin' twerp with hardly a brain in my head?"

Neal winced. "I didn't really mean . . ."

"Don't worry 'bout it. I know ya were just tryin' to put her off the scent. But I know ya sorta meant it, too. So I'm reformin' myself."

"You don't have to . . ."

"I wanna make ya happy."

"I won't be happy knowing I forced you to quit chewing gum."

"Well . . ." She shrugged. "Maybe I'll get back to it sometime."

"Let's get back to *you*," Neal said. "How long have you lived in Mojave?"

"Pretty near a year, now."

"And there's nothing at all that you want to pick up on our way through?"

"Nope."

"No money or jewelry, or . . . ?"

"I've got my money with me, all that isn't in the bank. I've got my checkbook. I don't have any jewelry."

"A TV, a radio, books?"

"Sunny owns the TV. It's my radio, only I don't have any

more use for it." She knuckled the radio on Neal's dashboard. "You got one. I reckon ya got plenty of books, too."

"You're right about that."

"You bein' a writer."

"Do you have any friends?" Neal asked.

"That s'posed to be a crack?"

"I mean in Mojave. Anyone you want to visit on the way through?"

"Hey, guess what. I'm on my way to Los Angeles, I ain't *dyin'*. I don't gotta give no last farewells to every Tom, Dick and Harry I ever said 'boo' to. Anybody I get to missin', I'll just call 'em on the phone or come back and visit. L.A. ain't Mars. I might just be headin' back on my own pretty soon, anyhow, if ya dump me."

"Dump you? I'm not going to dump you."

"Who's to say?"

"*I'm* to say. I love you."

"I know ya do. But things change. Yer gonna be seein' Marta when we get to L.A. Ya might just figure I don't stack up real well . . ."

"You know better than that; you've been inside my mind."

"Yer mind can change. Ya figured *Marta* was the true love of yer life till ya met me. So maybe you'll go back to her, or run into some *new* gal . . . Then I'll be on my way back to Mojave, more than likely."

"That won't happen," Neal told her.

"Well, I hope not."

"It won't."

Sue was silent for a while, then said, "I don't s'pose Marta's just gonna vanish on us."

"I doubt it."

"What'll we do about her?" Sue asked.

"I don't know. I don't think we'll be getting into L.A. before ten or eleven tonight, though. She doesn't know when we're coming back and she has to be at work by midnight, so we probably won't see her till tomorrow."

"Where we gonna go, to yer place?"

"I'm not sure. It might not be safe."

"Maybe that guy ya call Rasputin'll be there waitin for us, and we can nab him."

"He might be. You never know."

"I'll tell ya *one* thing I know."

"What?" Neal asked.

"We've gotta split the reward with Marta when we get it. That's the only fair thing. I mean, even if ya dump her as yer girl, she has to get her share. She has to get half."

"Why is that?" Neal asked. Even though he agreed with Sue, he was curious about her reasons.

"For one thing, I like her. She's nice. I don't wanna see her get cheated. Besides, she was there for ya after the murder. She took yer side and helped out."

"Yeah, she sure did."

"I reckon she probably loves ya."

"I suppose so."

"Also, she's a pretty sharp gal. I got a feelin' she might be smarter than *either* of us."

"You might be right about that."

"So what we've gotta do is work together, the three of us."

Neal nodded. "We'll make a great team," he said. "Marta's brains, your guts, and my gun."

"Only problem is," Sue said, "she probably hates me already."

"I doubt if she *hates* you. Yet. Right now, she's just feeling a little nervous. You're sort of a vague threat to her."

"Well, ya made me out to be an imbecile."

"Wait till she meets you."

"Then she'll *know* I'm one."

"No. She'll see, right away, that you aren't the brain-dead teenybopper I made you out to be on the phone. She'll see . . . the real you. But she'll figure out right away that we . . . you know, have a *thing* going."

Sue grimaced at him. "Think she'll know we did the nasty?"

"The minute she sees us."

"What'll happen then?"

"I don't know."

"She's gonna hate me, that's for sure."

"Probably hate us both."

"That don't sound like much fun."

"No, I'm sure it'll be terrible for everyone involved."

" 'Specially for poor Marta."

"Yeah."

"She won't kill us, will she?"

"I don't think so."

"Ya know what?" Sue asked.

"What?"

"We got lotsa time on our hands. What we oughta do is think real hard and figure out how to make it happen different."

"What do you mean?"

"I don't know. Make it so she doesn't find out we're in love, and everything."

"How do you propose to accomplish that? Shoot her? Blind her?"

"Maybe if I hide out. If she never meets me . . ."

"Stash you away in a hotel somewhere?"

"Yeah, there ya go. I could be yer silent partner. Just tell Marta I got run over and squished on the interstate."

"I'd hate to lie to her."

"That's a real problem, then. Ya can't fool *nobody* if y'ain't willin' to lie."

"I'd rather not. She'd catch me at it, anyway, if I tried. She knows me too well."

Sue frowned in silence for a few moments. Then she said, "That's okay. I don't much wanna get stuck away in some hotel, anyhow. Not unless yer with me. What I *really* think we oughta do is stick together."

"What about Marta?"

"We'll figure out somethin'."

Chapter Thirty-seven

They arrived in the alley behind Neal's apartment building fifteen minutes before midnight. Nobody seemed to be lurking about. He saw nothing to arouse his suspicions. But as he neared his parking space, he said, "Let's keep going. I want to look around."

"What kinda car does Marta drive?" Sue asked.

"A green Jeep Wrangler."

"A four-wheel drive Jeep?"

"Yep."

"Wow!"

"I don't think it's around here, though. She *ought* to be getting to work about now."

"What days off has she got?"

"Thursday and Friday nights."

"This is what, Wednesday?"

"For a few more minutes."

"So she doesn't work tomorrow night or the next."

"Not unless they had a shift change she didn't tell me about."

He suddenly realized they were nearly to Karen's building.

What if she sees me?

She won't. Not unless she comes out to dump her garbage, or something.

Nobody seemed to be in the alley.

"What's the matter?" Sue asked.

"Just watching out for an old friend," he said.

"Karen? The gal that scratched yer arms?"

Did I tell her about that?

Oh. Right.

Anything Sue doesn't know *about me?*

"The one I punched. Yeah."

"She sure lives awful close."

"I may move."

"On account of her?"

"On account of a *lot* of stuff."

Neal stopped at the end of the alley, waited for a car to pass, then turned onto the road. He quickly made another turn, and drove past the fronts of the apartment buildings.

"Everything looks okay," he said.

"I didn't see no Jeep Wrangler."

"Neither did I," he said, and stopped at the end of the block. "I didn't see no Rasputin, either."

"*Any*," Sue corrected him. "*Any* Rasputin."

He stretched an arm over to her side of the car, slipped a hand under her ponytail, and rubbed the nape of her neck. Then he took his hand away, turned and headed for the alley.

"We gonna go *in* this time?" Sue asked.

"Probably."

"I sure hope so. Gotta see the man about a dog."

"Guess we'd better quit dawdling." He swung into the alley and picked up speed. "We'll leave our stuff here," he said. "Except for the gun."

Moments later, he pulled into his parking space. He stopped, killed the lights and engine, and threw open his door. He opened the back door. His overnight bag was on the floor. Bending down, he unzipped it. He felt around for the pistol.

Sue came to his side of the car. She stood behind him, but didn't say anything.

As if she simply wanted to be near him.

He found his Sig down at the bottom of the bag and pulled it out.

"So that's yer gun," Sue said, when he turned around.

"This is it," Neal said. He shut the door. "Let's go."

Sue stayed close to him as he led the way to the rear gate. "It's all loaded and everything?" Sue asked. "Yer gun?"

"Yeah." Afraid someone might see him with it, he slipped it into the right front pocket of his trousers. But he kept hold of it.

"Don't go and blow off yer dingus," Sue whispered.

"It's not cocked."

"Neither will *you* be."

Neal shook his head. He saw the white of Sue's teeth. In the dark, he couldn't tell whether she was smiling or grimacing.

With his left hand, he opened the gate. It squawked on its hinges.

Sue followed him through, then eased the gate shut.

Coming up beside him, she whispered, "Ya got a swimmin' pool."

"Yeah."

"I love swimmin' pools."

He nodded. He started walking toward the stairs.

The pool was dark, the courtyard deserted. Lights glowed above several of the apartment doorways, but most of the windows were dark.

At Neal's apartment, no lights showed.

He stopped.

His windows facing the balcony were dark. So was the bulb above his doorway.

"What's the matter?" Sue whispered.

"My porch light isn't on. It has one of those sensors so it comes on automatically after dark."

"Uh-oh."

"Maybe it just burnt out," he said. But he felt shaky inside.

"We're still goin' up, aren't we?"

"I guess so."

They started to climb the stairs.

As Neal climbed, he listened. He heard the wheeze of air-conditioning units, some distant traffic, a helicopter that sounded as if it might be circling a few blocks away, his and Sue's footsteps on the stairs.

When they reached the balcony, he whispered, "Maybe you should wait here. I'll go in and make sure everything's okay."

"What if everything *isn't* okay?"

"Run for it."

"Run for it, my butt. Think I'm gonna run for it while yer gettin' knifed to death, or something?"

"I've got the gun."

"Ya got me, too. Now, let's go 'fore I wet my drawers."

"You aren't wearing any."

"That's besides the point," she said.

"At least let me go first."

"Be my guest."

As they walked along the balcony, Neal slightly ahead of Sue, he pulled the automatic out of his pocket.

They walked past his picture window.

The curtains were drawn. Neal could see nothing through them.

What if he's in there?

He's not.

Might be.

Maybe you got away just in time, and he's been inside waiting for you ever since.

Unscrewed the light bulb . . .

The bulb probably just burnt out, Neal told himself.

He switched the pistol to his left hand and reached into his pocket for the keys.

"Give 'em to me," Sue whispered. "I'll unlock the door, and you get ready."

"No. You stand over there." He nodded toward the far side of the doorway, where there was stucco wall instead of window.

Sue stepped past him and took the position.

Neal unlocked the door. He pushed it open, leaving his key in the lock. As the door swung his keys into the darkness, he switched the gun back to his right hand. He stood there, gazing in.

Saw nothing but shadows and motionless shapes.

Heard nothing.

After a few moments, he stepped inside. With his elbow, he brushed the light switch up. The lamp came on.

Nobody in his living room.

It seemed to look the same as when he'd left for The Fort.

While he scanned the area, Sue came over behind him. "Is it okay?" she asked.

"So far. Wait here."

Leaving her in the doorway, Neal hurried through every room, turning on lights, checking to make sure all the windows were locked and intact, glancing into places where someone might hide: behind furniture, under the bed, inside closets. Even before he finished, he grew certain that there'd been no intruder.

He returned to the living room.

Though the front door was still wide open, Sue had come into the room. She stood facing the entryway, her left arm stretched out to the switch panel.

The switch nearest the door was tilted upward: It was the one Neal had hit with his elbow to turn on the living room lamp. The switch on the other side of it was down.

"Yer light didn't burn out," Sue said. "Nobody unscrewed it, either. Looky here." She pinched the down-slanted switch and jerked it up and down a few times. The outside light flicked on, off, on, off, on, off, on. "Wasn't turned on."

"I always leave it on," Neal said.

"Did ya leave it on when ya left for the trip?"

"I never turn it *off*. The switch stays up all the time, and the light goes on and off by itself."

"*Somebody* turned it off."

Shaking his head, Neal shut the door and snapped the dead bolt into place. He stared at the light panel. Sue had taken her hand away. Both switches pointed upward. "I don't know," he said. "I don't have a specific recollection of whether it was up or down when I left for the trip."

"A *specific recollection?*"

"You obviously haven't watched much of the O.J. trial."

Sue shook her head. "Just seen stuff on the news. I been workin' at Sunny's."

"I watched it every day for the first couple of months, till it started driving me nuts. Anyway, those scumbag defense attorneys were always whining about whether people had a 'specific recollection' of this or that. *I* don't have a specific recollection of how I left the light switch."

"So maybe *you* didn't leave it on."

"Possible. I don't think so, but it's possible. Anyway, nobody's here now. And I didn't find anything weird. As far as I can tell—except for the porch light—we didn't have any visitors."

"So ya figure it's safe?"

"I guess so. Anyway, this is like the fourth night since the murder. If Rasputin hasn't been here yet . . ." Neal shrugged. "No reason to think he'll suddenly pop in on us now."

"So we're gonna stay?"

"Might as well."

"Okay. Hang on just a sec. I'll hit the john, and then we can go on down to the car and get our stuff."

Neal almost suggested going down for the luggage by himself, but he knew that Sue would want to stay with him. He said, "Okay, I'll wait here. The bathroom's through there." He pointed at the hallway. "The light's on."

"Back in a jiff."

He watched her stride away, her ponytail bouncing and swaying. She wore her sleeveless blue shirt. Its tail hung down, draping her rump, hiding most of her black leather skirt. Even though she wasn't very tall, her slim legs looked long. And very bare.

She disappeared into the hallway.

A few seconds later, Neal heard the door shut.

A few seconds after that, he heard it open.

"Neal?"

She didn't sound alarmed. Not exactly.

"Yeah?" he called.

"Ya wanna come here? Ya better take a look at this."

He didn't much like the sound of that.

He found Sue scowling down into the toilet bowl, a look of distress on her face.

Someone hadn't flushed.

But the mess in the water wasn't excrement.

Blood and adhesive tape, pieces of bandage wrappers, wads of toilet paper, bloody pads.

Sanitary napkins.

"Yuck," Neal said.

"It wasn't me," Sue told him. "I just picked up the lid and there it all was."

"And there it all is," Neal muttered.

"Ya aren't s'pose to throw 'em in the toilet like that. Used pads."

"I didn't do it," Neal explained.

"Who ya think did?" From the look in her eyes, she already had a pretty good guess.

"Him."

"Rasputin?"

Feeling weak, Neal leaned back against the sink. "So, he *has* been here. That stuff in the toilet . . . He must've changed his bandages."

Sue glanced around. "He was mighty *tidy* about it."

"Yeah. Looks like he cleaned the place up when he got done. Probably didn't want me to know he'd been here."

"Just shut the lid and forgot he hadn't flushed?" Sue suggested.

"Yeah." Neal slipped the pistol into his pocket, turned around and opened his medicine cabinet. Right away, he saw that things had been rearranged—slid this way and that to close gaps. It took him a while to figure out what was missing: a bottle of aspirin, a tube of antiseptic cream, a tin of adhesive bandages, a big roll of gauze and a spool of adhesive tape.

He shut the cabinet, faced Sue and told her what was missing. "Maybe some other stuff, too," he said. "I don't know."

Sue bared her teeth. She looked as if she were in pain. "Well, at least he ain't here now. Is he?"

"No."

"Ya sure?"

"I'm positive. I looked everywhere."

Sue glanced into the toilet. "Ya can stop worryin' about who found yer business card."

"Yeah. He knew where to come."

"So when he comes back to try again, we can nail his sorry ass."

"Or he'll nail ours."

"Nothin' *sorry* about ours." Sue reached back and patted her own rump.

A little too upset to smile, Neal shook his head.

"In the meantime," Sue said, "we gotta do somethin about *this*. If ya try to flush with them *pads* and stuff in there, it's all gonna get clogged up, more than likely."

"I know."

"And I *still* gotta go."

"Okay. Hang on a minute." Leaving her in the bathroom, Neal hurried to his kitchen. He found a pair of tongs in the utensil drawer. In a cupboard under the sink, he found the plastic bucket that he used now and then when he mopped the floor or washed the car. He emptied the bucket of some old sponges, detergents and rags, and returned to the bathroom.

"Tongs?" Sue asked.

"I'm not gonna stick my *hand* in there."

Resting the bucket on the toilet's rim, he bent down and dipped his tongs into the bloody water. He stirred some cloudy wads of toilet paper out of the way, spotted a gory pad, and clamped it with the tongs.

"Where ya think he got them things?" Sue asked.

"Maybe Elise's house."

The pad came out of the water, dripping. Neal dropped it into the bucket. It hit the bottom with a spashy thump.

"One down," he said, "three to go."

"How many times ya *shoot* that fella?" Sue asked.

"I don't know." He fished out another sodden, bloody pad and dropped it into the bucket. "I got him once for sure in the head. I don't know how many body shots. Maybe three." He clamped another pad between the tongs and lifted it out. "And there might or might not be exit wounds. I guess he could have as many as eight wounds, altogether, if every slug went in and out."

"Gotta be four, anyhow," Sue said.

"At least. It looks like he ran out of . . . these things." He lifted out the final pad and dropped it into the bucket. "Had to make a few bandages out of gauze and tape."

"How come he ain't dead, shot up that bad?"

"That's why I call him Rasputin." Poking around, Neal found clumps of gauze and tape. He removed them with the tongs, then hunted down several strips of tape, clamped them and took them out.

Nothing seemed to remain in the bloody water except toilet paper and several small bandage wrappers. Nothing likely to cause a clog.

"That should do it," Neal said. He dropped the tongs into the bucket, reached up and pushed down on the handle.

The toilet flushed, sucking down the mess, filling the bowl with clean water.

"Ya did it!"

"Yep." Neal stood up. Lifting the bucket, he said, "It's all yours."

"Right in the nicka time, too."

Neal hurried out of the bathroom. Sue quickly shut the door.

Wandering into the kitchen, he wondered what to do with the contents of the bucket. He could toss it in the trash, throw it out with the garbage.

It's blood evidence.

Evidence of what? he asked himself. What could it possibly prove? Just that Rasputin's been here.

And that he's the same guy who bled in Elise's house.

What'll that prove?

Maybe nothing, Neal thought. But I'd better keep it, just in case.

A few minutes later, Sue came into the kitchen and blurted, "What in tarnation are ya *doing?*"

Neal smiled over his shoulder at her. "What does it look like?"

"Looks like ya lost yer marbles."

A large paper grocery bag was spread across his counter. He had arranged the four sanitary napkins on it, side by side. Dangling from his tongs was a wad of blood-stained gauze and tape. He placed the wad on the paper.

"I'm just laying this stuff out to dry."

"Aimin' to *reuse* it?"

"Let's not get gross," Neal told her.

"Too late."

"Actually, I'm just trying to preserve the blood evidence. It should stay good longer if it dries out."

"Ya learn that watchin' the trial, too?"

"Yep."

"What's it gonna prove?"

"I don't know. I just think we need to save it. Maybe it'll come in handy, somehow."

"Well, if you say so."

When the bucket was empty, he carried it to the sink. With

hot sudsy water, he washed the bucket and tongs. Then he put them away and dried his hands. "All done," he said.

"What're we gonna do now?" Sue asked.

"Would you like a beer?"

"Sure."

As he took a couple of cans out of the refrigerator, Sue said, "It don't bother ya, me bein' under age?"

"I guess you'll have to drink the beer as your alter ego. What's her name? The older one?"

"Elaine Taylor?"

"That's the one." He tossed a can to her, and she caught it.

In the living room, they sat down beside each other on the sofa and popped open their beers.

"Here's how," Neal said.

"Chug-a-lug," said Sue.

They both drank. The beer was very cold. Neal drank a lot of his before coming up for air. Then he said, "Do we stay here or not? That is the question."

Sue lowered her can. She wiped her mouth with the back of her hand. "I say we stay."

"He *has* been here."

"Yer tellin' me."

"He'll *probably* come back. Maybe even tonight."

Frowning at Neal, Sue nodded. "If he *don't* come back, how'll we ever catch him? I mean, he knows who *you* are, but ya don't know *him* from Adam. So he's gotta come after us. If he don't, we're out the fifty grand."

"You're right about that," Neal told her.

"So we gotta stay right here till he comes."

Neal drank some more beer. "I guess so," he said. "But . . . you do realize he intends to kill me. I mean, that's the only reason he came over here. I'm not just a lose end, either. I'm not just some Joe Blow who might be able to identify him. I'm also the guy who nearly killed him. I'm responsible for all those bullet holes in him—God only knows the pain I've caused him. And I'm sure he wants to pay me back in full."

"We won't let him," Sue said.

"If you're with me . . . the things he'll do to you . . ."

"He won't do nothin' to either of us, Neal. We'll surprise him and nail him."

"Maybe he's *better* at surprises than we are. Maybe *we'll* be the ones who get surprised and nailed."

"Naw."

"This isn't a movie, Sue. There isn't any rule that says *we* end up winning. He might win. He's won before. He won against Elise." He gazed into Sue's eyes. "At the very last, just before I got out of her, she was thinking . . . you know, like it was a movie. Like she would survive, somehow. Because she was . . . the star, and the star always makes it, one way or the other. But she didn't. He killed her. He won."

Sue looked more somber than he'd ever seen her before.

"I know how much you want the reward money," Neal said. "But do you want to risk your life for it?"

Sue took a deep breath. She blew it out loudly, then took a drink of beer. "I want it," she said. "Sure I do. I mean, our half of fifty grand . . . But it's not just the money. If it was only just the money, maybe I'd say forget it. But if we don't stay, we'd have to run away and hide. We'd have to keep on hidin', too. Till Rasputin's either dead or jailed."

"I guess so," Neal admitted.

"So what I still think is, we oughta stay right here and lay for him."

Chapter Thirty-eight

"What's wrong?" Sue asked.

Neal set down his empty beer can. "I don't know. I'm not sure. Maybe I scared myself with that talk about *him* winning. I just . . . I don't like it here. I think maybe we'd better not stay."

"How come?"

"Just because he was here, I guess."

"But he's gone."

"Probably."

"Ya looked around . . ."

"That doesn't make it a hundred percent certain he isn't here. Maybe he found a *really good* hiding place." Neal found his gaze wandering the room, studying the curtains, the dark corners . . .

"Yer givin me the squeamies," Sue said. Wrinkling her nose as if bothered by a foul stench, she looked over one shoulder, then the other.

"He's probably gone," Neal told her.

"Or he might be watchin' us, huh? Might be hearin' every word we say."

"It's not likely."

"If he's here," Sue whispered, "how come he ain't jumped us yet?"

"Scared I'll shoot him again?" Neal suggested. "He might want to bide his time, wait until later, come out after we're asleep."

"Oh, jeezle." Looking pained, Sue hugged her chest and rubbed her upper arms.

They were bumpy with gooseflesh.

"We could search the place *really* carefully," Neal said. "But even if he's not here . . . and he probably isn't . . . he might be nearby. Maybe he broke into someone else's apartment. He might be right next door, or . . ."

"Y'on a mission to scare the pee outta me?"

"I'm sorry. I don't want to scare you. I'm just trying to explore some of the possibilities."

"Maybe he just went on home."

"That's a possiblity, too," Neal said.

"Or maybe he took off and went lookin' for ya someplace."

"He'd have no idea where I went."

Unless he traced the credit card, Neal thought. But that seemed awfully farfetched.

If he did trace the card, he'd end up in Nevada, a good, safe distance away from—

"Any chance he knows about Marta?" Sue asked.

Her question stunned Neal, put a hard cold place in his stomach. "No."

But even as he denied it, he realized Rasputin *might* have followed him when he drove to Marta's place Monday night. Or

Marta might've stopped by here for some reason, yesterday or today. Or Rasputin might've found her name in Neal's address book.

There must be fifty names in it. He'd have no way of knowing who . . .

Neal jerked his head sideways and stared at his telephone.

His answering machine.

From where he sat, he couldn't see the tiny red dash that might be blinking to indicate new messages. He stood up and stepped toward the phone.

And saw the blinking red light.

He tapped the panel marked new messages.

"Neal?" Marta's voice. "It's me. Are you back yet? Hello? Guess not. Anyway, I just thought I'd give you a call. I was hoping you might get back before I had to head off for work. Did you decide to stay another night, or something? Anyway, I miss you. Let me know as soon as you get back, okay? This is Wednesday night, elevenish. Love you. Bye."

The machine beeped.

No more messages.

Neal blew out a long breath. Then he saw Sue staring at him. "I was afraid she might say her name," he explained. "Then Rasp could've looked her up in my address book and gone over to pay her a visit."

"Ya think she's okay?" Sue asked.

"Well, she was fine when she made the call. Elevenish. She should've left for work pretty soon after that. So unless . . ." Neal shook his head. "I'm sure she must be fine."

"Yer not, either. We better make sure."

How? Neal wondered. A quick visit to her apartment, either by car or bracelet, wouldn't prove much.

Unless she's there. Dead. Or captured by the bastard.

Maybe he's working on her, torturing her, trying to make her talk . . .

Has her tied up naked . . .

Cutting her . . .

"I'd better get over there," Neal said, and started for the door.

"Use the bracelet," Sue said. "It'll be quicker."

He shook his head. "Have to go in person."

"Wait for me," Sue called. She hurried after him and switched off the light.

Out on the balcony, Neal paused long enough to watch her shut the door.

In the car, he said, "She's probably fine." He backed out of the parking space and sped up the alley. "It's just that I can't go by bracelet. If the bastard's got her, I'd be useless. I found that out the hard way."

"How far away does she live?" Sue asked.

"Just a couple of blocks. Keep an eye on things, okay? Make sure we aren't being followed."

"Roger dodger."

"She's probably fine," he said again. "I mean, she was okay when she made the call, and she should've taken off for work right after that. She didn't give her name, either. Even if Rasp was in my place and *listening*, he wouldn't have known where to find her."

"Maybe he picked up the phone and talked to her."

"*What?*"

"After she gets done leavin' her message, maybe he picks up and says, 'Ah! Don't hang up! I'm here.' Pretendin' to be you."

The suggestion made Neal squirm inside. "Marta's too smart to fall for a lame trick like that," he said, and hoped so. "For one thing, she'd recognize my voice."

Unless the guy's really good.

"Or maybe he tells her he's a cop . . ."

Neal grimaced at Sue.

"Sorry," she muttered.

He reached over and rubbed the back of her neck.

"I sure hope she's okay," Sue told him.

"Me, too."

Moments later, he swung around a corner and Marta's apartment building came into sight. He sped closer. Her parking space was empty. No sign of her Jeep.

Neal blew a long breath. "She must've gotten away all right. Her car's gone."

"Ya better check inside her place, anyhow."

"Yeah." He drove nearly to the end of the block before finding an open stretch of curb. After parking, he faced Sue. "Let's take our stuff up. I've got a set of keys. We'll stay there tonight."

"In *Marta's?*"

"It'll be safer for everyone. We won't have to worry about Rasputin popping in on us."

"Won't have to worry about *catchin'* him, either."

"We'll get him. We'll figure out a way. The thing is, I want *us* to end up on top. I'm just afraid he'll nail us if we stay at my place."

"Okay. But ya don't s'pose Marta's gonna mind?"

"We'll see. Come on."

As they unloaded the car and walked back toward Marta's building with their bags, Neal turned his head constantly, on the lookout for approaching cars.

"I don't think we got followed," Sue told him.

"Probably not," Neal said.

"This ain't the movies, ya know." She grinned at him.

"What do you mean?"

"Yer sayin' how we might get killed, as this here's real life? Well, Rasputin, he's real life, too. Works both ways, is what I'm sayin'."

"I'm still not sure . . ."

"He's not a *movie* monster. Even if ya *did* hang a funny name on him, he ain't . . . he isn't Freddy Krueger or Jason or that *Halloween* guy, whatever his name was."

"Michael Myers."

"Yeah, him. *Those* guys, they show up anywhere and everywhere for no reason at all. I mean, they're chasin' after ya one second. Then the next, they pop up in *front* of ya. They always turn up in places where they got no reason to be. But that's the movies. Rasputin's real, so he's not gonna turn up where he shouldn't be. See what I mean?"

"I think so."

"If he *was* at yer place, only he didn't hop in a car and chase after us, then he isn't gonna turn up here. Not just yet, anyhow."

Unlocking the gate, Neal grinned at her. "You're absolutely

right." He held the gate open, then followed her into the court-yard.

She looked over her shoulder at him. "He *doesn't* have a hitchin' bracelet, does he?"

"A hitchin' bracelet? No. I don't think so."

" 'Cause if he did, he might be inside you or me right this very second."

"There's only one, as far as I know." He patted his pocket, and felt the shape of the thick, coiled snake.

"A thing like that," Sue said, "it'd be dangerous in the wrong hands."

"It's dangerous in *any* hands, if you ask me."

"Gosh, look at *this* swimmin' pool. They keep gettin' bigger and better. S'pose we'd get in trouble if we took a dip?"

"At this hour? They'd probably shoot us."

"Only if we woke 'em up."

Neal, smiling, shook his head. "I don't think it would be a good idea."

"Chicken."

"That's me."

He led the way up the stairs to the balcony. In front of Marta's door, he set down his suitcase. He pulled the pistol out of his pocket. Holding it ready in his right hand, he quietly unlocked the door with the key in his left.

Her apartment was dark.

Neal reached inside and found a light switch.

Everything looked okay.

In a hushed voice, he called Marta's name a couple of times. Then he turned to Sue. "I'll take a look around," he whispered.

"Make sure and look in the john."

He did.

He found nothing in the toilet bowl except clean water.

He found nothing in any of the rooms to suggest that a stranger had visited.

"Everything's fine," he told Sue. Then he shut the door and latched its dead bolt.

In his wallet, he found the scrap of paper on which Marta,

months ago, had scribbled her home and work numbers. He took it over to her phone.

"Gonna call her up?"

"Yeah, I'd better."

"Good idea."

He tapped in the work number.

"Hope she's there," Sue muttered.

"Hoffburg Travel," said the man at the other end.

"Yes," Neal said. "I'd like to speak to one of your agents, Marta Wheaton."

"Who may I say is calling?"

"Neal Darden."

"Just a moment please, I'll page her."

He met Sue's eyes. "I think she's in."

Sue looked relieved.

"They're paging her. Might take a while."

"Gonna tell her I'm here?"

"I guess so. She'll find out, anyway, when she comes home in the morning."

"I could be gone by then."

"It'll be all right."

"Neal?" Marta asked.

"Hi, yeah, it's me. I'm back. Sorry I had to bother you at work."

"No problem."

"I got your message."

"Good. I was a little worried about you, that's all. I thought you'd be getting back earlier."

"We had a late start," he explained.

"We, huh?"

"Sue and I."

"That's the girl you were telling me about? Sue?"

"Yeah."

"I thought you said she's a pain in the ass and you were going to get rid of her."

"Well . . . I couldn't."

"Terrific." Marta sounded only slightly annoyed. "Now you've brought her back with you?"

"Yeah, but . . ."

"Terrific."

"She's going to help us get the reward."

"Do we need her help?"

"I don't know," Neal said. "She might be useful. Besides, going for the reward—it was sort of her idea in the first place. We really do need to keep her in on it."

"Hmm. Well. It's up to you."

"The main thing is, I had a visitor."

"*What?*"

"Our friend."

"Rasputin?"

"Yeah."

"What happened? Are you all right?"

"Yeah, we're fine. He was gone by the time we arrived."

"Thank God for that. What did he do? Did he break into your *apartment?*"

"He got in somehow. Nothing seemed to be broken. Maybe he picked the lock, or got himself a key that fits?" Neal shook his head. "We wouldn't have even known he'd been here, but he left some bloody bandages in the toilet."

Marta was silent for a few moments. Then she said, "You'd better get out. Go on over to my place. You have the keys, don't you?"

"Yeah."

"Okay. Go on over. Right away. And be careful. He might be hanging around, waiting for you, you know?"

"I know."

"You've got your gun?"

"Yeah."

"Okay, good. Jeez. So I guess he *did* find your business card."

"Looks that way."

"Bad news."

"Well, we sort of expected it."

"You'd better get the hell out of there," she said.

"Sue's here, too."

"I know."

"Okay if I take her with me?"

"No, leave her behind at your place so Rasputin can take *her* apart. Of *course* take her along. Are you nuts?"

"Just wanted to make sure it was all right with you."

"It's fine. It's dandy."

"Okay. That's great. We'll go on over."

"I'll give you a call in ten minutes to make sure you got there all right."

"What if we haven't?"

"I don't know. Maybe I'll call the cops."

"Shouldn't be necessary. Ten minutes oughta be plenty of time."

"Okay. Get going. And watch out."

"Okay. Thanks."

"Bye." She hung up.

Neal hung up and smiled at Sue. "That worked out nicely. She invited us over."

"Yer a tricky fella."

"She just assumed I was calling her from my own apartment, and I . . . chose not to disabuse her of the notion. Anyway, we're now her official guests. She's going to call back in a while to make sure we arrived safely."

"Hope we do."

Chapter Thirty-nine

Exactly ten minutes after hanging up, Marta called back.

"You made it," she said.

"No problem."

"Thank God. I was afraid he might . . . you know, jump you on the way to your car."

"No sign of him so far."

"Thank God," she said, her voice breaking.

Neal suddenly felt a hot flood of guilt. "Everything's fine," he told her.

Sounding shaky, Marta said, "Anyway. Be careful. There's no

guarantee that he won't show up at my place. I mean, who knows? So keep your eyes open."

"I will."

"I'll be back around nine in the morning."

"Fine."

"You guys . . ." She sniffed. "Just make yourselves at home. Plenty of food and stuff to drink. Have yourself a party, or whatever."

"I think we'll probably turn in. It's been a long day."

Marta sniffed again, then said, "Okay. Well. There're clean towels and wash cloths in the linen closet. Blankets," she added. "Sheets."

"Thanks. And don't worry, okay? About anything."

"Easier said than done, buddy."

"See you later."

"Night." She hung up.

Neal hung up and looked at Sue. "She was scared to death we wouldn't get here in one piece."

"That's cause she loves ya."

"I know." He sat down on the sofa. "I don't want to hurt her, Sue."

"Well, maybe ya can have the both of us."

He gave her the smirk that she seemed to expect.

"Anyway," she said, "y'aren't gettin' me anymore. Not while we're stayin' here. Wouldn't be right."

Neal sighed, then nodded and muttered, "That's probably for the best."

"Yep. I'll take the sofa. You can have her bed."

"You should sleep in the bed," Neal protested.

"No way. It's Marta's, and she isn't gonna want a stranger in it. You get the bed, and I'll sleep on the sofa here."

"We'd be in different rooms."

"Ya want her walkin' in and findin' us in the *same* room?"

"What if Rasputin shows up?"

Sue grinned. "I'll scream. You run in and shoot him."

"I mean it."

"Me, too."

"I've got a better idea," he said. "You take the sofa, and I'll take the chair." He nodded at Marta's big, stuffed recliner.

Sue frowned at it. Then she smiled and said, "That's a good place for ya."

"I'll sleep in my clothes, too," he said. "Just in case."

"In case of Rasputin or Marta?"

"Both."

When he came out of the bathroom, the living room was dark except for a single, dim lamp beside the padded chair. Sue was stretched out on the sofa, her head on a pillow, a powder blue blanket covering her almost to the shoulders.

"Okay if I kiss you good night?" Neal asked. "Marta will never have to know."

"C'mon over here."

He went to her. In the vague light from the lamp across the room, he could see that her shoulders were bare. He knelt beside the sofa. "What're you wearing?" he asked.

"What I got on."

"What's that?"

"My blanket."

"And that's *all?*"

"What else I need?"

"What about Marta?"

"Yer keepin' *yer* duds on. We don't *both* gotta." Smiling, she slipped a bare arm out from under the blanket and caressed his cheek.

"What about Rasputin?"

"He the jealous sort?"

"Do you want to be naked if he breaks in?"

"Won't matter. Yer gonna shoot him dead."

"Then what about me?"

"What about you?"

"How am I supposed to fall asleep in the chair over there when I know you're right here naked?"

"Just put it outta yer mind," she said. Her smile faded a little. "Thing is, I can't sleep at night if I'm wearin' stuff."

"You're kidding."

"Nope. I toss and turn too much. If I got somethin' on, first thing ya know I'm all wrapped up and gettin' twisted half to death. Can't stand it."

"Really."

"Yup."

"I think you made that up."

"Nope. Ya gonna give me a kiss?"

"Mmm-hmm." Bending over, he kissed her on the mouth. Her hand curled over the back of his head and stroked him through his hair.

She made no protest when he crept a hand beneath the blanket. He glided his hand over the rises of her breasts, down her rib cage and belly. Hand sliding lower, he felt her bare skin against the whole length of his arm. She was long and smooth and warm. She moaned a little and squirmed.

Turning her head to break away from his mouth, she whispered, "Whatcha tryin' ta do?"

"Nothing."

"Coulda fooled me."

He brought his arm up and out from under the blanket.

"Sure felt good, though," Sue said, and kissed him again.

After the kiss, Neal whispered, "Guess I'd better return to my corner."

"Reckon so."

He left her and went to his chair. Standing in the lamplight, he pulled off his shoes and removed everything from his trouser pockets. He set the bracelet and pistol on the lamp table, then turned off the light and sat down. After covering himself with a blanket, he tilted back the chair. Its footrest popped up, lifting his feet off the carpet.

"How's the chair?" Sue asked through the darkness.

"Comfy. How's the sofa?"

"Lonely. Only don't get no ideas 'bout comin back over, okay? I'd love to have ya, but it wouldn't be right."

"I know. I agree."

"Night," she said.

"Night."

He shut his eyes, took a deep breath and tried to relax. But he couldn't get Sue out of his mind. He thought about how she was stretched out beneath the blanket, all bare and warm. And how it would feel to be under the blanket with her.

Forget about it.

We should've stayed at my place, he thought. If we'd stayed there, this wouldn't be happening.

But then we'd be scared of Rasputin busting in on us.

Better this way, he told himself.

Not that Marta would find out if we . . .

"Neal?" Sue said from across the room.

The sound of her voice made his heart quicken.

She's changed her mind. She's gonna invite me over.

"Yeah?" he asked.

"Wanna come here with the bracelet?"

"You want the *bracelet?*" he asked.

"I don't mean that. *You* wanna use it? C'mon over here and get in me?"

"A bracelet ride?"

"Yeah. Be glad to have ya."

"I'd much rather ride you in person."

He heard a soft huff of laughter. Then Sue said, "Smarty."

Reaching out, he fingered the tabletop until he found the bracelet. He picked it up and slipped it onto his right wrist. Then he raised it above his face and stared at it in the vague, faint glow that came through the curtains.

"You're not supposed to use it on someone you love," Neal said.

After a moment, Sue said, "That's nice."

"What?"

"Sayin' ya love me."

"Well . . . you already knew that."

"Nice to hear it, anyhow. I love you, too. So how 'bout comin' on over here?"

"In the flesh?"

"Keep yer flesh in the chair."

"I'd . . . I really don't want to do it with the bracelet."

"It'll be great. Just wait and see what . . ."

"It's against the rules."

" 'Cause ya love me."

"That's right."

"Well, I used it on you."

"You also carry a fake ID. That doesn't mean I should do it."

"Chicken?"

"No. I just don't think it would be such a good idea." He knew that she would want a reason. After giving the problem a few moments of thought, he said, "What if I get in, and find out I don't like you?"

"That ain't likely."

"But who knows? Maybe your head's such a jumble of crazy thoughts and atrocious language that I'd want to scream and run for the hills and never see you again."

Sue laughed softly from her sofa.

"Anyway," Neal said, "we won't stand a chance of pulling off this abstinence thing if I get into your head. So . . . we'd better forget it, okay? Maybe tomorrow night we'll be back in my own place. Then we can do whatever we want."

"Well, it's up to you."

"I think we'd better try to sleep," he said.

"All right. Night."

"Night."

"Sleep tight," she said.

"You, too."

"Don't let the bedbugs bite."

Neal couldn't sleep. The chair felt soft and comfortable, but he kept thinking about Sue on the sofa. He was tempted to go to her. He was also tempted to break Elise's rule and visit Sue with the bracelet.

He imagined how it might be.

Many times, he thought about Marta.

Had he stopped loving her? He didn't think so. Then how could he fall in love with Sue?

Did he want to lose Marta?

She'll hate me—the minute she figures out about me and Sue.

He pictured her raging: "*You bastard! How could you do this to me?*"

Of course, she had never behaved that way before.

No telling how she might react: betrayed, outraged, pleading, snide, martyred, indifferent, brave, forgiving . . .

No matter what, Neal thought, it'll be bad.

I could keep her if I dump Sue.

I'm not dumping Sue.

He thought about her sleeping only a few yards away. He wanted to go to her.

He knew that he wouldn't, though.

He also knew that, with his mind in such turmoil, he would probably remain awake most of the night.

Finally, to escape, he kissed the bracelet.

As he touched his lips to the serpent's head, he had no idea where he wanted to go. But somewhere. Away from here. Away from the temptations and guilt and worries.

A moment after his lips met the warm gold of the bracelet, he floated up out of his body. As he rose toward the ceiling, he saw Sue's head and bare shoulders—gray in the gloomy light that seeped through the curtains above the sofa.

If I try going out that way, I'll end up inside her.

To avoid her, he aimed himself in the opposite direction. He passed through Marta's special framed print of a bayou scene, signed by the artist, Robert Malcolm Rucker; through the wall; through a kitchen cupboard stacked with plates and bowls. Drifting below the kitchen ceiling, he saw horizontal stripes of black and light across the room. He rushed at them, raced through the open wooden blinds and glass and found himself outside.

Suddenly high above an alley, he panicked for a moment, expecting to drop.

Too long since I've done this, he thought. *Thanks to Sue. Haven't used the thing since she got her hands on it.*

When was the last time? The trip to Karen's? Was that really the last? Monday night?

That didn't seem right.

Then he remembered sitting on the men's room floor at Sunny's Café, kissing the bracelet with every intention of checking Sue, then slamming smack into the Highway Patrol officer on the other side of the door. The guy with the trots.

That was the last time. Such a miserable failure that it almost shouldn't count.

Why am I even doing this? he wondered.

Thinking back, it seemed that *all* of his bracelet trips had been disasters of one kind or another.

Except the first.

The experimental trip into Elise.

That had been wonderful, spectacular.

But they'd been lousy ever since.

Maybe I should go back to Marta's place and . . .

He felt a sudden pull, a tug of the invisible connection, as if the controller of such things was starting to pull him back.

No! I didn't mean it! This is fine!

He resisted the pull, and found himself gliding forward again through the night. Uncertain where he was, he studied the layout of the buildings and streets below him.

Familiar territory.

Without making any conscious choice about his destination, he must've headed straight for his own neighborhood.

Let's just make sure I don't end up at Karen's, he told himself.

Why not? As long as I'm not there in the flesh . . . It was a kick being in her.

"Forget it." He heard his comment in his mind, but not in his ears.

Back in Marta's living room, had he muttered "Forget it" in his chair?

Maybe. Tuesday night at the Apache Inn, when Sue had been inside him, her body had squirmed, moaned, gasped, groaned and sighed. She hadn't spoken, though.

Maybe words can't make it through.

Or maybe they can.

Hope. I didn't wake her up.

Seeing his own apartment building below him, Neal wondered what to do. Visit one of his neighbors?

How about Miss Universe?

That's just what I'd need, he thought. I've got problems enough without jumping inside some gorgeous bimbo. She's probably asleep, anyway.

Everyone's probably asleep.

Not everyone.

From high above the building, Neal could see a lot of activity: a helicopter in the sky near Century City; some airliners heading into LAX, probably ten miles away, their landing lights pushing beams into the darkness ahead of them; cars and delivery trucks here and there, gliding silently along pale, uncrowded streets; a black-and-white police car stopped on Pico, swirling the area with blue and red flashes as two officers climbed out and walked toward a pale van. He saw a few people, widely scattered, walking dogs. He saw a cat scurry across a road and vanish beneath a parked car. In various directions, he saw lighted windows, some with moving shapes behind them: possibly janitors cleaning offices in high-rise buildings; people in upper stories of homes, condos and apartment houses who were still up and around for whatever reasons, and hadn't bothered to shut their curtains. From some windows came the glow of televisions.

No shortage of people to choose from, Neal thought.

Go on a hunt for someone interesting?

You'd better make it good, he warned himself. You only get one shot per trip. Don't want to end up in a dud.

Why not? Why not experiment? I've got all night—at least what's left of it. I could hop back and forth, try out half a dozen people . . .

Below him, the courtyard and swimming pool of his own building looked deserted.

He wondered if he should make a quick pass through his rooms.

And realized that he *had* to, now that he'd thought about it. Otherwise, the failure to check would gnaw at him.

So he swooped down, passed through the balcony railing and through the stucco wall into his bedroom. He whipped like a gust of wind beneath his bed, rushed into the closet and through its wall to the bathroom. Nobody in the tub, nothing in the toilet bowl.

On he went, curling around corners, seeping through walls and furniture, searching the darkness everywhere for signs of an intruder.

Nothing.

Coast is clear.

He flew out through the front door and softly crashed into a man and screamed.

Chapter Forty

Rasputin!

He stood just outside the door to Neal's apartment, hunched over and working with a couple of slender steel tools buried deep in the keyhole of the lock.

Neal had no chance to see him.

Simply collided with a dark mass on the other side of his door, and shrieked with fright.

Inside him, Neal knew him at once.

He felt the hot aches of bullet wounds.

And he felt a trembling tightness in the man—part fear, mostly excitement.

An icy tremor in the bowels.

A stiffness in the penis that made it push against the front of his trousers.

A wild, raging strangeness in his mind.

"Come on, come on. Baby. Come. Open up for Papa."

The fucker better be here this time. Ooh, it's gonna be sweet. Better be here this time.

"Come on, baby."

As the silent monologue went on, his mind played a memory-scene of a stranger, a dark and undefined shape standing yards away in the darkness of the trees, aiming at him and shooting. Even as fire spat from the muzzle and the booms crashed through the stillness, his mind flipped to a new scene—a naked man nailed to a floor, screaming and writhing. Rasputin pictured himself kneeling between the man's spread legs, reaching forward with pliers . . .

Is that supposed to be me? Neal wondered.

The guy in the dark with the gun was *definitely* Neal shooting at Rasputin on Sunday night. The guy on the floor about to get worked on with pliers, well lighted in Rasputin's fantasy, was Neal's size but the hair and face were wrong.

It's me. They're both me. He just doesn't really know what I look like.

That's what he wants to do to me.

Neal didn't want to watch what was about to happen with the pliers.

Get the hell out of here!

No! Bug out and I might lose him. Who's to say he'll still be here by the time I can get back . . .

Back with my body and my gun . . .

I might never get another chance like this. Find out who he is, where he lives.

Find out enough, and he's MINE.

So is the reward.

When Neal's attention returned to Rasputin's mind-movie, the guy nailed to the floor was bucking and screaming . . .

Neal saw what the pliers were doing.

He felt himself shrivel.

Rasputin was so wrapped up in his fantasy that his mind had gone voiceless and he seemed unaware of his own hands. But through his fingers, Neal suddenly felt something give inside the lock.

And so did Rasputin.

Yah! "Here I come, ready or not, you cocksucking piece of shit! You better be here this time!"

He slipped the lock-picking tools into a soft leather case, folded the case and stuffed it into a pocket of his trousers. Then he pulled out a pair of thin rubber gloves. He snapped them onto his hands.

The fingertips of the gloves felt strange to Neal—stiff, not flimsy. Had they been painted with something—maybe fingernail polish or glue—as an extra precaution against leaving latent fingerprints?

This guy's careful, Neal thought.

As Rasputin shoved the door open, he pictured Neal standing

in the darkness, waiting with the gun, blasting him point-blank in the face. A cold wind of fear swept through him.

The bastard's scared of me, Neal realized.

Good!

But the fear was a lone gust that blew through him and left him behind—gone as soon as Rasputin stared into the darkness of the room and didn't find Neal facing him.

Looking in the wrong place, asshole. I'm not in front of you, I'm inside you.

Rasputin stepped over the threshold and silently shut the door. Then he stood motionless, listening.

"Oh, you better be here."

I'm here all right, Neal thought.

Rasputin seemed to sense that the rooms were deserted. But he didn't want to admit it to himself. Not yet. He didn't want to face the disappointment, the frustration . . .

He suddenly detected an aroma.

So did Neal.

A vague, sweet scent . . .

What's that? Rasputin wondered. His mind switched to a memory of his previous visit. He remembered himself standing in much the same place, trying to detect . . .

This odor was new.

Beer!

Neal felt himself shrivel again. *He knows!*

Excitement swelled in Rasputin.

He doesn't know about Sue, Neal realized. He thinks it was just me drinking the beer . . . He thinks I'm still here.

Now I gotcha! Now I gotcha! Ohhhh.

Rasputin surged inside with a brew of rage and glee and lust that made Neal want to scream and bolt.

STAY! he commanded himself. *This bastard can't hurt me, can't touch me, doesn't even know I'm here. I'm perfectly safe.*

But he sure didn't feel safe.

Rasputin started creeping across the living room.

"Here I come, ready or not. Ooh hoo hoo. Oh, how I'm going to make you scream!"

Back he went to his fantasy of Neal naked, hands and feet nailed to a floor.

Neal turned his attention to Rasputin's body. The man was tall and extremely thin, but had muscles like strips of iron. He wore heavy, snug boots. Leather trousers that were tight and very hot inside—so hot that Rasputin was dripping sweat all the way down from his waist and the leather felt slimy against his buttocks and cock and legs. No underwear. Several objects in his trouser pockets—something in the right front pocket that might be pliers. A belt cinched around his waist. At his left hip, a weight that Neal suspected might be a sheathed knife.

Above his waist, a snug shirt with long sleeves. Under the shirt, bandages and wounds.

These bandages didn't seem to be made from the odds and ends Rasputin took from Neal's medicine cabinet. They wrapped his torso, shoulder, and the top of his head as if someone had tried to make a mummy of him.

Rasputin had apparently found medical care.

They're supposed to report bullet wounds.

He'd probably gone to a crooked doctor—plenty of those in L.A.

How do you find a crooked doctor? Easy. Just ask your crooked lawyer.

All patched up and rarin' to go.

He doesn't have a hammer, Neal suddenly realized. Rasputin's only weapons seemed to be the pliers and the knife.

How does he expect to nail me to the floor if he didn't bring his hammer and nails?

Borrow mine? He'd have to find them first.

Maybe that's what he's looking for.

Because Rasputin hadn't gone directly to the bedroom, where he was sure he would find Neal sleeping.

Pay attention, Neal told himself. What's the bastard up to?

Relishing the anticipation.

And wanting to make sure nobody would pop in from another room and take him by surprise.

"*Are we all by ourselves tonight, Neal? No guests? Lonely boy?*

I'll give you some company. Yoo-hoo! Leslie Glitt, at your service. Less is more. And all that glitters isn't gold."

He pulled the knife from its sheath and stepped into the kitchen.

Leslie Glitt, Neal thought. That's his name? *Leslie?*

Walking through the kitchen, Rasputin considered taking his boots off. He couldn't walk quietly in them, not on the linoleum floor. But he decided against it. The struggle to take them off would fire up the pain in his wounds. Besides, he would need to put them on again in the bedroom.

Needed to be wearing them when he took Neal.

He imagined himself sneaking to the side of the bed, bending over and pressing the knife to Neal's throat. *"Wake up, sleepyhead—Leslie's come over to play."* He imagined Neal waking up, startled and terrified, gasping. *"Remember me? You shot me, you fucking cocksucker."* He pictured himself jabbing Neal a few times with the knife. *"Didn't kill me, though. Too bad, so sad. Didn't save the slut, either. Did you? Thought you'd saved her ass, big hero. No no no. Wrong. So sad. You should've seen what I did to her. You should've heard her scream."* All the time, poking Neal with the knife. Not really shoving it in, just poking him with it, making him flinch and bleed. *"But she died easy. Wait'll you see what I do to you. Now get up."* Neal hesitates, so Leslie gives him a slice across an eyeball. *"Get up, now. We're going on a trip. I'm taking you to a very special place."*

A place with a wooden floor, Neal supposed.

Rasputin, shivering and hard, stepped through the bedroom door and halted and stared at Neal's bed. Neal stared at it with him—saw it as he did.

In the gray glow filtering in through the curtains, the bed looked like a flat, unwrinkled plain. Nobody was sprawled on it. The blankets covered no telltale landscape of humps.

No! Impossible! He's here! He has to be here!

Rasputin flung out an arm and flicked the light switch. The sudden light hurt his eyes. He squinted.

The bed was empty, neatly made.

He rushed to the closet and flung open its door.

No Neal.

"You're here! I know you're here! You've GOT to be!"

He hurried to the other side of the bed, sank to his knees and, pain crushing through him, bent and peered underneath the bed.

No Neal.

"Where ARE you?"

"Right here inside you, Lesss-ley," Neal told him.

Rasputin hunted for him.

He stomped through every room, turning on lights, knife clutched tightly in his right hand, teeth clenched. He looked in the bathtub. He looked in cupboards and closets. He looked behind furniture. He looked behind doors. He no longer shivered with excitement. He no longer had an erection. He ached not only from his bullet wounds but from disappointment.

An agony of frustration and regret.

"Where the fuck are you? Where ARE you, you slimy cocksucking shit? I know you're here!"

He's not here.

He's not.

Oh, the dirty fuck!

Where is he?

Done with the frantic search, Rasputin turned his back to the front door and scanned the living room.

Okay, okay, calm down. He's not here. Big deal. What's the hurry? He lives here. He'll be back.

He already came back. Came back since I was here last, and had a beer. Two beers.

Rasputin scowled at the two beer cans. They had *not* been on the table during his earlier visit to Neal's apartment.

They stood side by side . . .

Ha! Just look at them!

Not close together, as if Neal had polished off one, then the other. Two feet apart, as if set down on the table by two different people sitting side by side.

"You drank with a friend, didn't you? A beer for you, a beer for . . . him or her?"

Rasputin sniffed the air, but detected no hint of perfume.

Ah, I do hope it's a she. A pretty she. I do love shes. The pretty ones.

Pretty ones like Elise.

He groaned aloud as his mind played a memory . . . not a whole scene . . . a clip . . . a peek . . . two or three seconds . . . Elise in her bathtub while . . .

For a moment, Neal wasn't sure what he was seeing.

Then he cried out "NO!!!" so loudly that he thought his voice might explode Rasputin's mind.

It did nothing.

"How could you do that to a person?" Neal raged. "How could you even THINK of a thing like that? What kind of sick bastard are you?"

Rasputin was becoming aroused again.

Have to try that on the drinking buddy. Hope she's a she. A pretty one. Try that one on her and see how she likes it. Do it in front of Neal, so he can enjoy it, too.

That might be tricky. How'll I manage two of them?

Easy.

Get them one at a time.

The buddy first. Beer girl.

Next time they come by, track them when they leave. Follow them, find out where they're hiding . . .

Neal, sobbing inside him, blurted, "You're never gonna touch her! Never! I'LL KILL YOU!"

Rasputin suddenly wondered how long ago they'd left.

He picked up one of the cans. It left a wet circle on the table. He couldn't tell much about the can's temperature, thanks to his rubber glove, so he pressed it against his cheek. It had no coolness to it. He shook the can near his ear. Though he heard no sloshing sound, he put the can to his lips and tilted it high.

Some lukewarm, sour-tasting beer dribbled into his mouth.

He concluded that several hours had probably gone by since Neal and his friend had been sitting on the sofa, drinking the beers.

Earlier tonight?

Late this afternoon?

Maybe they'll be back tomorrow. Ooh, I do hope so. Hope she's a pretty one.

Might be a guy.

Fine, too, if he's pretty.

Tomorrow, when they come . . .

Shit! Fuck! Not tomorrow night! The money.

Wait. Yeah. Sure I can. Don't have to be there till two.

If I get over here good and early . . .

Can't let them know I was here. Don't want to spook the little critters and scare them off.

Rasputin set the beer can down on its own wet circle. After that, he made his way through every room, checking to make sure he was leaving behind no token of his presence, then turning off the lights.

Finally, he opened the front door. He leaned out, glanced around, then stepped onto the balcony and silently shut the door. Hurrying toward the stairway, he pulled off his gloves and tucked them into a pocket of his trousers.

As he started down the stairs, he tried to remember where he'd left his car.

He remembered.

Yes! Neal thought. *We're going to his car!*

This is it!

Chapter Forty-one

Rasputin, turning the corner, saw several cars parked along the curb.

What kind of . . . ah, sure. A white something. A Subaru, or . . . there!

It's not his own car, Neal realized. Probably stole it.

Rasputin didn't search for the keys as he approached it.

Of course not, Neal thought. *He doesn't* have *keys. Must've popped the ignition. . . .*

The driver's door wasn't locked. Rasputin opened it and

climbed in, reached out to the steering column and started the car.

With the key. Which was already in the ignition.

The engine turned over and ran smoothly, quietly.

Rasputin thought, *Not a bad little car. Maybe I'll keep it.*

He laughed, then frowned.

Where's the headlights? I had them on coming over . . . Ah yes. Cute.

The twin bright beams leaped forward. Rasputin stepped on the gas and swung away from the curb.

"And awaaaay we go!" he proclaimed aloud.

Get me a real car with the loot. How about a Lincoln Continental, or one of those Towncars? Or, hey, why not a Ferrari? What's something like that cost, anyhow? Not half a mil, that's for sure. Half a mil, I could buy a fucking airplane.

Yeah, sure. I can't buy shit. Get back to Kingman and lay low, keep a good low profile till I heal up.

If I do heal up.

That cocksucker, he'll wish. . . .

Wait'll he sees what I do to his beer buddy. A little taste of what he'll be getting for himself. Teach him to blow holes in me . . .

Rasputin imagined Neal nailed to a wooden wall. Not to a floor, this time, but to a wall. Naked, the same as before. His arms stretched out and nailed at the hands, but his legs together. His feet in a green plastic bucket.

The bucket, Neal supposed, was meant to catch his blood and whatever other bodily fluids . . .

Clever, he thought, feeling sick.

At least this guy doesn't look like me.

For that matter, the victim in Rasputin's fantasy didn't even resemble his previous mental version of Neal. This fellow was older than the other, a little flabby, and had a neatly trimmed black mustache. Not at all the handsome blond chap he'd pictured last time.

He can't keep straight what I'm supposed to look like, Neal thought.

And he obviously had *no* idea what Sue looked like.

Thank God for that, Neal thought.

The woman was nailed to the wall across the room from Neal. So that they were facing each other. So that he could watch.

Like Neal, her arms were stretched out and she was standing in a green bucket.

She must've been forty years old. In good shape. Slender, with very large breasts.

This is what he thinks my beer buddy looks like?

She didn't resemble Sue *or* Marta. They were both a lot younger than that. Neither of them had breasts like *those*, and both had blond hair.

A lot *less* hair, too.

Neal had never seen such a hairy woman in his life: thick black tresses hanging over her brow and flowing down both sides of her head; heavy black eyebrows that nearly met above her nose; a huge thicket below her navel.

Rasputin smiled over his shoulder at his imaginary Neal, walked up to the woman and lit her pubic hair on fire. It flared as if bathed in gasoline. She writhed against the wall and danced inside her bucket, her huge breasts leaping, her skin orange and gleaming in the firelight.

Rasputin, caught in his fantasy, was hard again.

Do that to his girlfriend, he might wish he hadn't been so quick to shoot me, the fuck.

Do that to her for starters, and make him watch. Make him watch everything till she's dead. Before I even start on him.

Maybe we can make it interactive.

"Where would you like me to make the first incision, Neal? Pick an eyelid. Pick a nipple. Pick . . . "

Suddenly recognizing the house, he was jerked out of his fantasy. He hit the brakes and swung into the driveway. His headlights brightened the broad, white door of a garage.

Gotta catch the address, Neal told himself.

"Come on, Rasputin, look at the house! Come on, Leslie! Damn it! Look!"

Instead of looking toward the house, Rasputin lowered his eyes to the passenger seat. He picked up a small, pale device—the garage door opener. He pointed it out the windshield.

We're going in the garage? I'll never get the address!

The garage door started to rise.

The car started toward it.

"Look at the house, you bastard!"

He didn't. He kept his eyes on the rising door.

All Neal could make out, through Rasputin's peripheral vision, was a single-story stucco building with some bushes in front.

Then Rasputin shut off the headlights.

The house went dark. It seemed to have no lights on, at all: none in the windows, none over the front door, none in the garage.

Rasputin drove slowly into the black, wide mouth of the garage.

"Home, sweet home," he said.

He shut off the engine. When he thumbed the remote, the garage door began to rumble down. He stayed in his seat until it was completely shut.

And wondered what he ought to do, now that he was home.

Go straight to bed?

He probably should turn in, but he felt too edgy and excited to sleep.

Anyway, I can sleep all day tomorrow. Nothing to do till after dark.

I might as well stay up for a while and have some fun.

Rasputin, feeling a delicious tremor of excitement, climbed out of the car. He made his way through the darkness, walking carefully with his arms outstretched.

He found the door to the house.

He didn't open it, though.

He touched the knob only to orient himself. Then he found the door frame. And then the light switch.

He flicked the switch up.

And squinted in the brightness.

And turned.

Neal glimpsed a man against the wall, arms outstretched, feet in a bucket, head drooping.

Rasputin looked at the man for only an instant before turning and walking across the garage toward the woman.

Slender, with very large breasts.

But no black tresses, no heavy black eyebrows, no thicket below her navel. Where all that hair had been—in Rasputin's fantasy—this woman had bare, scorched skin.

Neal knew, at once, that it had been no fantasy.

Not a fantasy, a memory.

She lifted her head and her eyes opened.

Neal shrieked.

Gotta get outta . . . No! I didn't mean it!

Too late.

He was plucked out—instantly free from Rasputin's trembling, tense body and foul mind. Gone was the feel of his bullet wounds, his trembling excitement, the hot and slimy lick of his leather trousers, the hard ache of his erection. Gone was the jumble of his memories, fantasies, contrivances and commentary.

Neal was suddenly himself again.

Like a hooked fish, he was flung up through the garage beams and roof and into the clear night sky.

He looked down, but already he'd been hurled high and far away from the house. Below him was a rushing blur of moonlit roofs, treetops, gray streets, bright puddles of light, parked cars . . .

He tried to slow down, but couldn't.

The bracelet was reeling him in fast, as if an angler feared he might slip the hook and escape.

It swung him down from the heights and flipped him through the front window of Marta's apartment. A lamp was on. He glimpsed Sue. She was crouching beside his chair, her blue blanket hanging down her back. Her head was in the way. He struck it with his hip, but it felt like air. A moment later, he landed inside his own body.

His heart pounded hard and quick. He was gasping for breath. His hair was soaked with sweat and his clothes stuck to him.

Opening his eyes, he met Sue's gaze.

She looked jittery. "Yer back," she said.

"Thank God," he said.

She looked so fine.

So alive and safe.

So sweet and beautiful.

Her hair was mussed, tangled, golden in the lamplight. Her shoulders were wrapped by the blanket.

"I reckon ya went on a bracelet ride," she said.

"Yeah."

"Musta been hell on wheels." Her right arm came out from under the blanket. It lifted the blanket away from her breast and side as she reached up and caressed Neal's face. "Are ya okay now?"

"Getting better."

"Ya screamed yer head off a couple times. Scared the squirmin' jaspers, outta me."

"I'm sorry," Neal said.

"Nothin' to be sorry for," she said, her voice gentle, a gentle look in her eyes, her hand stroking the side of his head as if she were trying to calm a spooked puppy.

"I guess I woke you up, huh?"

"That's okay," she said. "I'm just glad yer back."

His eyes followed her outstretched arm to where it met her blanket-hooded shoulder, then drifted down to her breast. It seemed casually, innocently exposed by the disarray of the blanket. It was hazy bronze in the lamp shadow. It moved slightly with the motions of her arm.

"I was real tempted to pull ya back," she said. "Take yer bracelet off. That woulda done the trick, right?"

"Yeah."

"Thought so."

"Why didn't you?"

"Figured it oughta be *yer* call, when to come back. Didn't seem right for me to interfere."

"So you stayed by my side and watched?"

She nodded. "I wanted to keep an eye out, case somethin' mighta gone *really* haywire. Anyhow, I like watchin you. Only it was sorta painful, cause I could see ya were havin a bad time."

"Putting it mildly."

"Shoulda gone in me," she told him.

Neal met her eyes. "How do you know that I *didn't?*"

"Only about fifteen ways. For one, ya didn't have a smile on yer face."

"I found him."

Sue's hand dropped to Neal's shoulder. "Him? Rasputin?"

"Yeah."

"Holy smoke." Her eyes were wide, her head shaking slightly back and forth.

"But his name isn't Rasputin, it's Leslie Glitt."

She made a face. "What?"

"Leslie Glitt."

"That's a girl's name, Leslie."

"Leslie Howard, he was a guy."

"Never heard of him."

"He was great. *The Petrified Forest?* With Bogart?"

Sue shook her head.

"And he played Ashley Wilkes in *Gone With the Wind.*"

"I seen that one," Sue said. "So what happened, anyhow?"

"His plane was shot down in World War Two."

"Not that other Leslie, *this* Leslie. What'd ya say his last name is?"

"Glitt."

"Sounds dirty."

Neal shook his head.

"So, what happened?" Sue asked. "Did ya ride *him?*"

"Yeah, I sure did."

"No wonder ya kept screamin'."

"It was only twice, wasn't it?"

"Well . . . maybe. I got woke up by one of 'em, maybe a half hour ago. Figured ya were havin a nightmare, there at first. But ya kept on squirmin and gaspin' . . . ."

"Did I say anything?" he asked.

"Ya sorta mumbled some stuff, only I couldn't make out what. Mostly, ya just gasped and whimpered. Anyhow, I got up and came over to see what was goin' on. When I turned on the lamp, that's when I saw the bracelet and figured ya'd gone on a trip."

"I had to get out of here," Neal explained. "I couldn't sleep. I was going nuts."

A smile lifted the ends of Sue's lips. "Hope it weren't . . . wasn't. . . . my fault."

"It was mostly your fault."

"How come?"

"I wanted to go to you."

"That's nice."

"But we'd decided against it."

"That was drivin' ya nuts, huh?"

"Yup."

"Wish ya'd come on over to *me* with the bracelet."

"Me, too. My God, if I'd had any idea . . . It was like. . . . crawling through a sewer. Being in him."

"Wanna tell me all about it?" she asked.

"There's a lot to tell."

"Ya got an appointment?"

"Yeah. In Samarra."

She raised her eyebrows. "Huh?"

"Nothing. A bad joke. A *literary* bad joke."

She narrowed her eyes and went, "Hmmmp." Then she pulled her arm back. As she stood up, she drew the blanket shut. "Why don't you get on outta that chair? Nobody's gonna sleep for a while, anyhow. C'mon over here." She turned away and glided toward the sofa.

Neal climbed out of the chair. The blanket he'd used earlier was rumpled on the floor. He picked it up and tossed it onto the chair.

Sue, wrapped from her shoulders to her ankles in the other blanket, sank down onto the sofa, leaned back and rested her bare feet on the coffee table.

Neal stretched and groaned.

As he walked toward Sue, she crossed ankles and said, "Y'oughta give me some books to read. I'll read 'em all, and then I'll know what yer talkin' about when ya go and get literary on me."

"All right." He sat down beside her.

"We can even read to each other."

"I'd love to have you read *True Grit* to me."

"Jess grab me a copy, and I'll do it. Now, tell me all 'bout what went on tonight with you and . . . Leslie Glitt."

Neal slipped an arm around the back of her shoulders. The blanket felt soft and nice. He supposed it must feel very good for her to have it wrapped around her body.

She leaned against him. "Don't leave nothin' out," she said.

"Anything," he corrected her.

"Don't leave anything out," she said. "Or better yet, how about if I get in yer head for the story? Like in the car yesterday."

Yesterday? Was it only yesterday that he'd let Sue kiss the bracelet and get inside him?

To prove I didn't kill Elise.

It seemed like so much longer ago.

It was the day I met Sue. Right after she kissed the bracelet and got in me by accident. Yesterday? On our way to The Fort. . . .

Tuesday. That was Tuesday. We only spent one night there, left the next day. . . . Wednesday. Arrived at my place, then came over here. This is Wednesday night.

More like Thursday morning.

He looked at the bright red numbers of the clock on Marta's video player.

3:56 A.M.

Thursday morning, all right.

"Maybe you should just listen," Neal said.

"Please?"

"I'm not sure you want to be in there. It gets awfully bad."

"I can take it. Come on."

With a sigh, Neal took his arm back.

As he slipped the bracelet off his wrist, Sue said, "But tell it to me, anyhow. The story. Don't just think it. Tell it to me like ya did in the car."

"I'm not sure about this."

"I am. It'll be the best way." The front of her blanket bulged and parted, and her right arm came out. It pushed against the side of her breast as she reached across herself and offered her hand to Neal.

He slipped the bracelet onto her wrist.

"You're sure about this?" Neal asked.

"Sure I'm sure."

"If it gets too rough, just bail out."

"It'll be fine," she said, then raised her hand to her mouth and kissed the head of the serpent.

She went limp. As her arm fell, it shoved the blanket aside. The back of her hand slapped against her bare thigh.

Neal saw that the entire right side of her body was naked—except for a flap of blue blanket that still covered her right leg from the knee to the ankle.

Oh, beautiful. Look at that. "Hi, Sue. Lovely. But how am I supposed to concentrate on . . . ?"

I could cover her.

He didn't want to cover her. He wanted to stare. And touch.

Didn't we do enough of that earlier?

You can never do enough of that.

He sighed. Then he reached over Sue's body, lifted the blanket, and covered her.

"I'm such a gentleman," he said. "Anyway, here's what happened. I was feeling really restless in the chair. Sleep was out of the question. So I kissed the bracelet and took off."

Chapter Forty-two

Neal was shocked awake by the *snick-clack* of the dead bolt.

Oh, no.

Brilliant daylight hit his eyes as the front door swung open. Marta stepped in and shut the door. The room stayed bright, but was no longer blinding.

Marta walked quietly as if she didn't want to disturb her guests. She wore her uniform. A large leather purse hung from her shoulder. Stopping at the other side of the coffee table, she lowered her purse to the floor. Then she turned and stood motionless, staring at Neal and Sue.

Neal mouthed the word, "Hi," and tried to look innocent.

Sue continued to sleep.

They were both seated on the sofa, leaning against each other, their legs stretched out, their feet on the coffee table.

Neal had planned to return to his chair before falling asleep. He had planned to set an alarm clock so that he and Sue would wake up in plenty of time to be ready for Marta.

He had fully intended to make sure that Sue was properly dressed.

He looked at her.

Some of the blue blanket was pinned between her arm and Neal's. None of it covered her. All she wore was the bracelet around her right wrist.

Neal grimaced.

Facing Marta, he shook his head and shrugged and tried to look perplexed.

She stared at him. Her eyes seemed a little glazed. Her mouth hung open.

She seemed surprised, confused, wary . . .

Her eyes went to Sue.

Studied her.

Checking out the competition? Neal wondered. Seeing how she stacks up?

Thinking, *I lost him to this skinny kid?*

This bitch? I'm twice as pretty as she is! My figure's ten times better!

But she must be ten years younger.

The dirty bastard traded me in for a new model.

Neal saw her composure begin to slip. Her face reddened and she started breathing harder.

Contemplating double homicide?

She tossed a glance at Neal, then picked up her purse and walked off.

Never said a word.

Oh man, Neal thought. How could I let this happen? How could I do this to her? I *love* her, damn it! She loves *me*. And I dump her for the first stranger I meet . . .

Sue's no stranger.

Not anymore, he told himself, but she was sure a stranger Tuesday morning when I stopped for breakfast. How could I let this happen?

I'm such a shit.

But I fell in love with Sue, he told himself. What was I supposed to do, get rid of her?

This sucks. This sucks so bad.

"Go to her," Sue whispered.

He turned his head. Sue's body remained stretched out naked beside him, but her head swiveled and tilted slightly. She opened one eye.

"You're awake," Neal whispered.

"Yeah. Now, go on. Get her cheered up. Lie if ya gotta."

Neal nodded and struggled to his feet. He felt shaky, frightened, ashamed.

The last thing I ever wanted to do was hurt Marta.

But you did, he told himself. Demolished her. It didn't show, but she's crushed inside.

He walked quietly down the hallway to her bedroom. The door was shut. He gave it a few taps with his knuckles.

And waited.

He was about to try knocking again, but she said, "Come in."

His hand was sweaty. It made the knob wet and slippery. But he turned the knob and pushed the door open. He stepped into the bedroom, then quietly shut the door.

Marta was standing at her closet. After hanging up her blue blazer, she turned around and met Neal's eyes. "So," she said. "I guess that was Sue." She didn't sound snide or indignant or angry—just a little breathless, agitated.

She doesn't know what to make of this, Neal thought.

Or is she struggling to control herself?

"We fell asleep talking," Neal said. He took a deep breath. "I'm sorry. About all this."

Marta frowned. "How'd your arms get scratched up?"

"Some woman."

"Sue?"

"No. It was just a little misunderstanding with someone. It'd be a long story."

"Do they hurt?"

"Not much. They're getting better. It happened a couple of nights ago."

"You've been busy."

"I still love you, Marta."

Her eyes on Neal, she moved her head very slightly up and down a couple of times. She started to untie the blue and gold silk scarf around her neck. Her hands were trembling.

"Sue's a beautiful girl," she said.

Neal nodded. "So are you," he said.

A corner of her mouth turned up. "Didn't you call her a gum-snapping twerp? A brain-dead hillbilly?"

"Something like that."

"Now you're in love with her." She wasn't asking.

"I think so," he admitted.

Marta started to unfasten the buttons of her white blouse.

Neal couldn't believe she was doing it in front of him.

"And you've slept with her, haven't you." It wasn't a question, either.

He nodded. Then he managed to swallow. Then he said, "She gave up the gum-snapping."

Marta didn't seem to find it funny. But she finished with the buttons, and started to untuck her blouse.

"She's a very nice person," Neal said. "I mean . . . in other circumstances . . . if you just happened to meet her someplace . . . you'd like her. You couldn't *help* but like her."

"I can see why *you* did." Not even *that* came out sounding snide.

Marta took off the blouse, walked to the corner of her room, and tossed it into her hamper. Standing at the hamper, her back to Neal, she took off her bra. She dropped it in.

Still facing the hamper, she asked, "What about me? Should I . . . consider myself dumped?"

"I wish you wouldn't."

"You think you're . . . in love with both of us?"

"Seems that way," Neal said.

"Does Sue love you?"

"Apparently."

"I do. You know that, don't you?"

"Even now?" Neal asked.

"Even now. I guess I must be crazy." She turned around and

walked slowly toward him. Her black leather shoes were silent on the carpet. She wore pantyhose and her straight, blue skirt.

Bare above the skirt, she somehow seemed more naked than the times when she wore nothing at all.

Her eyes looked a little frightened.

"You're so beautiful," Neal whispered.

She halted in front of him, reached out with both hands, and started to unbutton his shirt. Her breasts were pushed together between her arms, making her cleavage a straight, tight slot.

Neal stood there, staring at her as she opened his shirt and pulled it off and tossed it aside. When she took hold of his belt, she flicked a glance at his eyes.

"Are you all right?" he whispered.

"Sure."

Standing face-to-face on the carpet near the foot of the bed, they undressed each other. First, Marta finished with Neal. Then she took off her own shoes, but she let Neal pull down her pantyhose. Staying crouched in front of her, he drew her panties down. She stepped out of them.

As he kissed her soft mat of hair, he suddenly thought of the woman in the garage. Rasputin's crucified plaything, his burnt toy.

Nothing I could do.

I should've at least *tried* to find my way back. I *might've* recognized the house.

What if he does it to Marta or Sue? What if he nails them to a wall and sets them on fire?

I'll kill him. I'll rip him apart.

"Watch the teeth," Marta whispered.

Neal felt as if he'd been in a daze. Her hair was a wet tangle in his mouth. He kissed her gently, then stood up. She gazed into his eyes. He felt her breasts against him. And he felt a couple of hairs in his mouth.

Smiling slightly, Marta picked them out.

He ran his hands down her back, and squeezed her buttocks. They felt large after Sue's, but just as firm and smooth.

"Are you sure you want to do this?" Neal whispered.

"I'm sure."

"A lot has changed."

"Not how I feel about you," she said. "I'll always love you, no matter what."

"I'll always love you, too," he told her.

And was pretty sure that he meant it.

"What about Sue?" she asked.

"Do you want me to dump her?"

Marta shook her head, which surprised him. Then she said, "That isn't what I meant. Are you going to feel guilty about it if we make love?"

"I don't know."

"I hope not."

"You had me first," Neal said. "Besides, I don't think she'll mind."

"Most women would."

"She knows how I feel about you."

Curling her fingers lightly around his penis, Marta asked, "Would you dump her if I asked you to?"

He didn't have to think about it.

"I'd hate to do that," he said.

"Good thing I'm not asking," Marta said.

They went to Marta's bed. Bending over it, she pulled down the blanket and top sheet.

They lay down together.

The sheet under Neal felt smooth and cool at first. He stretched out, relishing the feel of it. Then he rolled onto his side. Marta, on her side, scooted closer to him until the tips of her breasts touched his chest, and his penis pushed against her belly. She gazed into his eyes.

"So here we are," she whispered. She put a hand out and rested it on his hip. "It's good to have you back."

"It's good to be here."

"I was so worried about you. I was so afraid I'd never see you again—that he'd find you, somehow. Rasputin. And kill you." Tears suddenly shimmered in Marta's eyes. "Even if I lose you to her . . . to Sue . . ."

"I don't want to lose you," Neal whispered.

They moved in snug against each other. Marta was all soft

and smooth. When she opened her mouth, she was wet. And
Neal was wet and slick against her belly.

The feel of her mouth was familiar to him. Every part of her
body was familiar, and so were the sounds she made, and the
ways she touched him and how she moved. All of her, familiar
and safe and like going home.

Chapter Forty-three

When Neal woke up, he sensed that he'd been asleep for hours.
He was sprawled on his back, hot from the sunlight that filtered
in through the curtains above Marta's bed.

He could hear her sleeping beside him, softly snoring.

He pushed himself up on his elbows.

She was curled on her side, facing away from him. Her hair
was a tangle of mussed gold. Her skin look tawny in the mellow
light. Her left arm rested on top of her side. Its hair was very
fine and nearly invisible on her upper arm, thicker below her
elbow. Neal wanted to run his lips along the length of her arm
and feel the downy hair.

But he didn't want to wake her.

Looking beyond her shoulder, he saw the clock on the nightstand.

3:18 P.M.

Marta hadn't fallen asleep until almost eleven that morning.

So Neal didn't touch her. He stared at her for a while longer,
savoring the light and shadows on the curves and rises and slants
and creases of her body. He wished she weren't asleep. He would
love to touch her, to explore every bit of her, caressing and
kissing and tasting . . .

Like I did to Sue.

Sue.

She'd been deserted for hours.

Neal carefully made his way to the edge of the bed, swung

his feet to the floor, and stood up. Marta didn't stir. She sounded as if she were still asleep.

He stepped around the clothes scattered on the carpet, then eased open the door and stepped into the hallway. He shut the door.

As he walked silently toward the living room, he wondered if Sue was asleep.

He wondered if she'd ever gotten dressed.

What *has* she been doing? he wondered.

And who was she in, Marta or me?

He knew her well enough to be sure that she'd used the bracelet on one or the other of them; she had been present, a mute participant in all that had happened in Marta's bedroom.

It didn't bother him, though.

He hadn't given the matter any conscious thought at the time, but he must've wanted Sue to be with them. Otherwise, he could have taken the bracelet from her.

She might be in me right now, he realized.

"Hello? You in here? How was it?"

Even as he put the questions to Sue inside his mind, he stepped into the living room and saw the empty sofa. Both blankets were neatly folded, stacked at one end, the pillows piled on top of them.

Sue was not in the room.

Take it easy. She's probably around here someplace.

Neal hurried toward the bathroom, but changed directions when he saw its open door, and entered the kitchen. The linoleum felt smooth and warm under his bare feet.

No Sue.

She's gone!

What if Rasputin got in, somehow, and . . .

Took her to that garage . . .

Nailed her to the wall . . .

Neal was just starting to cringe inside when he saw the piece of paper standing upright in the middle of the kitchen table. He snatched it up.

The note was printed in pencil.

Dear Neal and Marta,
Gone shopping. Back before you know it.
Luv,
Me

Neal took a deep breath, and sighed. "Thank God," he muttered. Then he wondered where she'd gone.

Heading for a store seemed like an odd thing for her to do, especially since she'd never been in Los Angeles before. How would she even know where to go?

She's not exactly shy. Probably asked someone.

Neal did some exploring. He discovered that Sue's leather skirt and sleeveless blue shirt were gone, along with her panties, bra, socks and shoes. Her purse was missing, too. So were Neal's keys.

She took my car!

For a moment, he was annoyed. Then amused by her audacity at taking his car without asking. Then pleased that she'd felt no need to ask. Then worried.

What if she gets lost?

Gets in an accident?

Gets jumped by Rasputin and taken . . . ?

"She'll be fine," he said quietly.

But he wished she were here.

He wondered how long she'd been gone.

What if she doesn't come back?

Lighten up, he told himself.

Had she taken the gun? He turned his eyes to the lamp table beside the chair. His pistol was there.

Beside it, the bracelet.

At least she's not in me or Marta now.

Neal went into the bathroom to take a shower. He needed a shower; he was hot and sweaty and sticky. And it would help to pass the time.

Take a good long one, and maybe Sue will be back when I get out.

We could've gone shopping together, he thought. Maybe if I'd gotten up the minute Marta fell asleep . . .

But he'd felt so tired and comfortable.

If anything happens to Sue . . .

She'll be fine, he told himself.

Then he was standing in the hot spray, surrounded by aromas that reminded him of Marta.

This is all so unreal, he thought as he slicked his body with a bar of Marta's soap.

It's crazy, that's what it is. You can't get away with having two women.

And what the hell kind of a problem is this to be worrying about when you've got a guy like Rasputin out there? Leslie Glitt.

He pictured the crucified, scorched woman in the garage. Raising her head and opening her eyes. But when her eyes opened, she was suddenly Elise on the ledge of her tub, arms spread, a bar of soap in her mouth.

He yelped at the rumble of the shower door.

Jerked his head sideways.

Saw a smudged figure through the frosted glass until the glass slid out of the way and Marta stood there. She had a mild look on her face. "May I join you?" she asked.

"Are you kidding?"

She climbed in, rolled the door shut, and embraced him. As they kissed, Neal slid his hands up and down her back. She felt slippery and wonderful.

When they were done kissing, he said, "Did I wake you up?"

She shrugged. "I don't want to sleep my life away." She took the bar of soap from him and began to slide it on his body. "Where's Sue?"

"I guess she went shopping. She left a note in the kitchen."

"Did she know where to go?"

"I don't know."

"You don't think she left because of us?"

"I doubt it. She probably went to buy some clothes. She doesn't have anything."

"I noticed that. She'll probably cause quite a stir at the store."

"You're causing quite a stir yourself," Neal said.

"I noticed." She set the soap aside, and caressed him with her slippery hands.

He picked up the soap and used it on her.

"We'll both be squeaky clean," she said, her lips moving against his.

Later, they found that the tub was too small so they made love standing up, Marta's back to the tile wall. She clung to him and grunted as he thrust up into her.

Later still, they stood on the mat and rubbed each other dry with thick, soft towels. They wrapped the towels around their waists before leaving the steamy bathroom.

Marta, in the lead, headed for the kitchen. "When was the last time you had a meal?" she asked.

"I don't think I can remember back that far," Neal said. "Last night, actually. We stopped at a Denny's around eight o'clock."

"Nothing since?"

"We had beer at my place."

As they entered the kitchen from the hallway, Sue entered from the other end. She wore her usual blue shirt and black leather skirt. Smiling, she raised a hand and said, "Howdy."

"You're back," Neal said.

"Yup." She came toward Marta with brisk strides, extending her hand. "Hi, I'm Sue."

"Nice to meet you. I'm Marta." Though blushing, she didn't try to hide her breasts.

After shaking hands with her, Sue said, "Nice towels."

"We didn't know you were back yet," Neal said.

"No problem."

"I'd better go change," Marta said. She turned around and headed for the hallway.

"Me, too," Neal said.

"Ya look good in a towel," Sue said. "Both of ya."

Marta, in the doorway, looked over her shoulder and smiled slightly. Then she turned and walked out of sight.

"Go on with her," Sue said.

"I need my suitcase and stuff."

Sue went with him into the living room.

He saw a few shopping bags on the sofa.

"Did your trip go all right?" he asked.

"Yeah! I went to that Westside Pavilion? Never seen nothin' like it."

"You didn't get lost?"

"Nope."

Bending down, Neal picked up his suitcase and overnight bag. Then he met her eyes. In a whisper, he asked, "Did you use the bracelet on us?"

"I went to the mall."

"Before you went to the mall."

A slight smile tilted the corners of her mouth.

"I knew it. Which one of us?"

Her smile grew. "That's for me to know and for you to find out."

"Bitch," he whispered.

She laughed. "See ya later, alligator."

Shaking his head, he turned away from Sue. He carried his luggage down the hall to the bedroom. Marta had left the door open. Walking in, Neal found her already wearing a pair of old, cutoff blue jeans. She turned to face him, a T-shirt in her hands. "How does grilled cheese sound?" she asked, putting her arms inside the T-shirt.

"Great."

Her breasts lifted when she swung her arms and the T-shirt overhead, then shook as she pulled the shirt down.

"No bra?" Neal asked.

"Too hot. Besides, it's a little too late for modesty around here." She stepped up to Neal, slipped a hand behind his head, kissed him gently on the mouth, then said, "I'll see if Sue's had anything to eat yet."

When she was gone, Neal plucked off his towel and tossed it on the bed. He got dressed in a pair of gray hiking shorts and a loose, short-sleeved shirt. Then he picked up both the damp towels and carried them out of the bedroom. He planned to hang them in the bathroom, but the door was shut.

He found Marta in the kitchen.

"What do you want me to do with these?" he asked. "Sue must be in the john."

"Yeah. She asked if she could take a shower. Care to join her?"

Neal blushed. "I've already had mine," he said.

"If you want to . . . don't let me stop you."

He shook his head. "No, thanks. But what about the towels?"

"Just hang them over a chair." She nodded toward the kitchen table.

Neal draped them over the back of a chair. "Can I help?"

"Feel free to sit and watch."

He pulled out the middle chair, turned it around and sat down, but didn't lean back against the towels.

Crouching, Marta took a skillet out of a cupboard. "We don't have to wait for Sue, by the way. She ate at the mall. How about a beer?"

"Sure."

Marta took two cans out of her refrigerator, brought one to Neal, and kept one for herself.

A moment after Neal popped open his can, he heard the sound of water running; Sue had started her shower. He imagined how she must look standing under the spray—then felt guilty about it.

Marta popped open the other can of beer. She took a sip, then set it down on the counter and looked at Neal. "I like her," she said.

"You do? You've hardly even met her."

She shrugged. "You get a feeling about people. *I* do. I can usually tell right away whether I'm going to like someone."

"First impressions."

"Mine are usually right."

"So you're not going to throw her out?"

"Nah. Wouldn't do that even if I hated her. Which, by the way, it surprises me I don't."

"I'm glad you don't."

"We'll just have to work things out, one way or another."

It took Marta only a few minutes to prepare the sandwiches. Then she brought them to the table on paper plates.

After she was seated, Neal picked up his sandwich and bit into it. The crisp, grilled bread crunched in his teeth, and his mouth suddenly filled with the flavors of melted butter and cheddar cheese.

Marta picked up her sandwich, glanced at it, then looked at Neal. "Now," she said, "how do we get our hands on the reward money?"

Caught with a mouthful, Neal shook his head and continued to chew. When his mouth was almost empty, he drank some more beer. Then he said, "Things have changed. I don't know. Maybe we'd better wait for Sue."

Chapter Forty-four

Finished with their sandwiches, they went into the living room and sat down on the sofa. A while later, Neal heard the bathroom door open.

Sue came striding in, barefoot, wearing a pleated white miniskirt and a bright yellow knit pullover with short sleeves. "What do ya think?" she asked. She spread her arms and twirled, the skirt floating up higher.

"Very nice," Marta said.

"Yeah," Neal agreed.

"I got me a bikini, too, and some other stuff. Never seen a mall like that. Wow! Anyhow, what's up?" She dropped onto the recliner, raised her left foot and hooked it under her right thigh. Then she glanced from Marta to Neal, her eyebrows raised.

"We need to figure out a few things," Neal said. "About tonight."

"Did ya tell Marta what happened?"

He shook his head.

"What?" Marta asked.

"I found out some things about Rasputin," Neal explained. "He showed up back at my place."

"At your place? When?"

"Late last night, I don't know. Three o'clock, around then."

Marta scowled. "You went *back?*"

"Yeah. Sue was asleep and I wasn't tired, so I headed over to my place and he was there. I saw him picking the front door lock. He got inside and looked around, then left."

"What did *you* do?" Marta asked.

"Watched. I was hiding, and . . ."

"My God! What if he'd caught you?"

Neal shrugged.

"Did you have your gun?"

"No, but . . ." He saw the strange, intense way that Sue was staring at him from her chair.

Marta looked at Sue, then back at Neal. "What's going on? Something's going on. You're not telling me something."

"I think y'oughta tell her," Sue said. "What's it gonna hurt?"

"Tell me what?" Marta asked.

Neal groaned. "Jeez, Sue! Nobody's supposed to know about it but *me*. Not even *you*—and now I'm gonna have to tell *Marta?*"

Marta, looking hurt, said, "You don't have to tell me *anything*. I don't want to bust into your little secrets . . ."

"It's not that," Neal said. "*Nobody's* supposed to know about it. Sue only found out by accident."

"Then don't tell me," Marta said. "Simple as that."

"I've *got* to, now."

"No, you don't."

"Ya better tell her," Sue said.

He sighed. Then he said, "It's the bracelet."

Sue reached to the lamp table, picked it up, and raised it. "This," she said. She untucked her leg, stood up, crossed to the sofa, and handed the bracelet to Marta.

As she returned to her chair, Marta looked at the heavy gold snake. She held it in her hand and turned it slowly. "Nice," she said, then turned to Neal and asked, "What's the big secret?"

"It's not exactly a normal bracelet," Neal said.

"Is it real gold?" Marta asked.

"I think so."

"Are these real emeralds?"

"Probably."

"*I'll* say it's not normal. It must be worth a ton of money."

"That isn't the main thing about it," Neal said.

"Just give it a kiss," Sue suggested.

"*Kiss* it?"

"Yeah. That's how ya get it to work."

"It *works?* What do you mean, 'works'?"

"It's magic."

Marta frowned at Neal. "Is she nuts?"

"Yeah, but that's beside the point."

"Hey!" Sue blurted.

"She's right about the bracelet," Neal said.

"It's magic," Marta stated, staring him in the eyes.

"Right."

"Right," she said.

"Go on and kiss it," Sue suggested.

"Some kind of a Blarney Stone thing?" Marta asked.

"More of a mind-reading thing," Neal said. "When you kiss it, you . . . sort of take a trip out of your own body and into someone else."

"Right," Marta said.

"Try it," Sue urged her.

Marta cast her a smirk. "Don't think so."

"Sue did it by mistake," Neal explained. "That's how she found out about it. I never would've told her. Or anyone. It's supposed to be a complete secret."

"It came with instructions?" Marta asked.

"It came from Elise Waters."

Marta's face suddenly turned solemn.

"She gave it to me as a reward for saving her life," Neal said.

And then he told her about it: how Elise had presented him with the bracelet, allowed him to experiment with it by entering her, shared the little she knew of its history, and given him the warnings about its dangers.

He told how he'd used the bracelet later to learn that Rasputin's body had vanished from the place below the freeway embankment where he'd left it for dead. And he told of his return to Elise—how he'd been inside her when she was attacked in her house, but could do nothing to help her.

"You can't *do* anything while you're in there," he explained. "That's the problem. You can't even warn a person . . . You're helpless. You're just an observer."

"Ya *feel* everything, too," Sue added.

"Yeah," Neal said. "It's as if you *become* the person, except that you can't have any effect. You're a passenger taking a ride in someone else's body."

"It's really somethin' else," Sue said. "Ya *gotta* try it."

Leaning forward, Marta placed the bracelet on the table. Then she settled back in the sofa, shaking her head. "Thanks, but no thanks."

"Yer not gonna?" Sue asked.

"Right."

"How come?"

"A, I think it's hogwash. B, it's nonsense. C, it's bullshit."

"Yer gonna change yer tune if ya try it."

"I'm not going to try it."

"It don't hurt or nothin," Sue assured her.

"Neither does taking a spin around the galaxy in a flying saucer. Or chitchatting with the ghost of Eleanor Roosevelt. That doesn't mean I'm going to do it."

Sue made an odd face at Neal and said, "She don't believe us."

"I wouldn't, either," he said.

"Well, we ain't *lyin'* ."

"I'm not accusing anyone of lying," Marta said. "I'm just not interested in fooling around with some bracelet that's supposed to transport me into someone else. I mean, give me a break. It's impossible, for one thing. But if it did work, I'd *really* want to stay away from it. The last thing I'd like to do is go floating off into someone else and *eavesdrop* on all their private thoughts and feelings. I wouldn't do it if I could. And nobody'd better do it to *me*, either."

"Too late," Sue said.

Marta's eyes went wide. "*What?*"

"I paid a little visit to ya."

Marta stared at her. "Bull," she said.

"I did."

"With the bracelet?"

"Yup."

"You got *in* me."

"Yup."

"No, you didn't."

"Yeah, I did."

"No way."

"If you wanna say so."

"When?"

"After ya got here."

"This morning?"

Sue nodded.

"No, you didn't."

Sue shrugged.

"Maybe we'd better try to figure out what to do about Rasputin," Neal said, hoping to change the direction of the conversation.

Marta ignored him. "Where were you?" she asked Sue.

"Out here."

"Where was I?"

"In yer bedroom."

"With Neal?"

"Well, ya were in there with him pretty near the whole day."

"What were we doing?"

Sue wiggled her eyebrows up and down.

Marta's face went scarlet. She shook her head. "It wouldn't take any magic bracelet to figure out what we were doing in there."

"I was *in* you," Sue said. "Not for real long—figured to let ya have some privacy. But I was in ya for a spell, there."

"Bullshit. Nobody can kiss some damn bracelet and go flying into people."

"Yeah, ya can."

"Prove it."

"All ya godda do is kiss the bracelet," Sue told her.

"Not me. If you were in me this morning, prove it."

"Nah."

"Ha! That's because you can't."

"Ya don't want me to blab stuff, do ya? With Neal sittin' right there?"

"I've got no secrets from Neal."

"I can think of a couple things," Sue said.

Marta suddenly looked shaken. "Like what?" she murmured.

"I'm not tellin'. I wanna be yer friend. I'm not gonna go and tell stuff yer tryin' to keep a secret."

"Now you've got *me* curious," Neal said to Sue.

"Well, yer just gonna have to stay that way."

"I want to know," Marta said. "What are these big secrets I'm supposed to have?"

"Let's you and me leave the room for a minute."

Nodding, Marta got up from the sofa. Sue climbed out of the chair, and Marta followed her into the hallway. When they were out of sight, Neal heard their bare feet on the carpet. Then a door bumped shut.

Must be *some* secrets, Neal thought.

He felt a little amused at first. Then annoyed.

Left out.

He saw the bracelet on the coffee table, within easy reach.

No.

Staring at it, he folded his arms.

Let them have their little secrets. I won't stoop to spying on them.

He sighed. He waited.

What's taking them so long?

At last, he heard the door open, then their footsteps. Sue in the lead, they walked into the living room.

Sue cast an impish smile at him.

Marta, frowning, sat down on the sofa. She watched Sue climb onto the chair. Then she turned her head toward Neal and said, "Okay. She convinced me. I guess maybe the bracelet works, after all. But I'm not going to try it. You two can go around spying on people's private lives if you're into that sort of thing, but not me. I think it's a rotten thing to do. I want nothing to do with it. If you ask me, you oughta get rid of the bracelet—or at least stop using it that way. It'll get you into nothing but trouble."

"You're probably right," Neal said.

"Looks to me," Sue said, "like it's gonna get us into half a million bucks."

"*What?*" Marta asked.

"Tell her 'bout it."

Neal nodded. Facing Marta, he said, "You know how I was starting to tell about last night? How I'd gone over to my apartment and run into Rasputin? Well, that is what happened, but I wasn't there in *person*. I'd kissed the bracelet and left my body here."

"Here," Sue said, and patted the arm of her chair.

"Terrific," Marta muttered.

"Sue was asleep, so I took off. And I ran into Rasputin picking my lock. Literally. And found myself *in* him. He'd come back to look for me again. This made two nights in a row he'd paid a visit, apparently. The first time, he threw his old bandages into the toilet and forgot to flush. This time, he found out I'd been back. And he figured out that I'd been there with a friend. He saw our beer cans on the table. So now he's planning to return again tonight. He's hoping he'll finally get a chance to lay his hands on me."

"And me," Sue added.

"He wants to . . . murder us, basically. To get back at me for shooting him."

"Jesus," Marta muttered.

"Well, it's pretty much the way we figured."

"I guess so."

"The thing is, he has to make a pickup later tonight. In a parking lot somewhere. Half a million dollars."

"You're kidding."

"I was in his head. Somebody's going to pay him half a million bucks, and he gets it tonight. At two in the morning, actually."

"Who would be paying him half a million dollars?" Marta asked.

"I don't know."

"Has to be Vince Conrad," Sue said. "Elise's husband."

"That's just a guess," Neal pointed out. "Sue and I talked about it for a while last night after I got back. It might *not* be him, but it'd stand to reason. Elise was going to divorce him. If it went through, she would get half his property. The house *alone* is probably worth a couple million dollars, at least. And who knows what else he might've lost if they'd gotten a divorce."

"So you think he hired Rasputin to murder her?"

Neal nodded. "While he was off in Hawaii getting himself a suntan and a perfect alibi. Probably instructed Rasputin not to kill her in the house: he didn't want it turned into a crime scene . . ."

"Didn't want his nice home to get all mucked up with blood," Sue suggested.

"He probably told Rasputin to take her somewhere and really work her over—torture her, rape her, make it look like she was grabbed by a serial killer."

"Which he *is*," Sue pointed out.

"Huh?" Marta asked.

"Looks like he really *is* a serial killer," Neal said. "Rasputin."

"Leslie Glitt," Sue said. "That's his real name. Ya believe it?"

Marta cast an amazed look at Neal. "You found out his name?"

"Yeah. Sure did. At one point, he thought about himself in the third person—by name."

"Leslie Glitt," Sue repeated. "With a G."

"Have you tried looking him up?" Marta asked.

Neal and Sue glanced at each other.

"Not yet," Neal said. "I can't imagine he'd be listed, though."

"Never know till you try."

"And I know for a fact that he isn't staying at his own place," Neal added. "He took over a house. I was there. I went . . . back with him after he left my place. He had a man and woman . . . the woman wasn't dead yet. But they were in the garage. He'd been torturing them."

Marta met his eyes. "Where? Where's the house?"

"I don't know." He shook his head, grimacing. "I just don't know. I wasn't paying attention to directions on the way over. And neither was he. All of a sudden, he swung into this driveway. I didn't even get a good look at the house before he pulled into the garage. I don't even know what street it's on, much less the address. If I had any idea, I would've gone back to the place with my gun last night and . . . put an end to it there and then."

Marta reached over and gently rubbed the back of his neck. She said nothing. Sue watched, a slight smile on her face.

"I just don't know where he is," Neal muttered.

"But we know where he's gonna be tonight," Sue said. "We'll get him then, and we'll grab us half a million bucks, too."

"Let's just see if he *is* in the phone directory," Marta said. She stopped rubbing Neal's neck, stood up and left the room. A couple of minutes later, she returned with the hefty book. She sat down beside Neal, spread it open on her lap, and started leafing through its pages. "That's G-L-I-T?" she asked.

"Two *T*'s," Neal said. A moment later, he said, "Actually, I'm not sure. I haven't seen it spelled out. But when he said it to himself, I got the impression that it was G-L-I-T-T."

"And here it is," Marta said. "L. Glitt."

"His address there?" Sue asked.

"Yeah."

"Holy smoke. Let's go and visit."

"He won't be there," Neal said.

"Let's go anyhow!"

"Might be a waste of time," Marta said. "Let's call first and see what happens." She hunched over the book for a few moments, then put it on the table, stood up and walked over to her telephone. After tapping in the number, she said, "We'll just see who answers."

Sue whispered at Neal, "Told ya she's smart."

Marta, raising a hand for silence, said, "Hello. This is Doctor Irma Klein, calling from the emergency room of Westside Medical Center. We have a Mr. Leslie Glitt who was just brought in for treatment following a motor vehicle accident." She listened briefly, then said, "Leslie Glitt." She listened again, this time nodding and frowning. "No, he didn't have any identification. He told me . . . I really can't describe him very well—he was heavily bandaged. But I would say that he's approximately six feet tall, very thin, with black hair . . . Hard to say. Just from his voice, I'd guess maybe thirty, forty? . . . Uh, huh . . . No, I looked it up in the phone directory . . . In surgery . . . Why do you say that?"

A few seconds later, Marta made a face as if she'd just sat down in something wet and sticky.

"I see," she said. "You're sure about that? . . . Uh-huh. Well, then this *must* be someone else." She shook her head. "I have no idea why he might be using your brother's name . . . I will. I'll look into it . . . Really? Why the police?"

She listened for a long time, nodding and saying very little, often shaking her head, glancing from Neal to Sue.

Finally, she said, "Don't worry about anything, Lois. I'm sure this can't be your brother. But I will notify the police, and have them look into the matter." Marta made a frustrated face. "Let me just ask you one thing. I did notice something else about this man. Did your brother have webbed feet? . . . Webbed feet . . . No, it's a somewhat rare anomaly—what we used to call a birth defect. I happened to notice because this patient was brought in barefoot. He has a cutaneous membrane between the toes of both feet . . . He didn't?"

Marta beamed a smile at Neal and Sue.

"Well, then the man we have here is obviously not your brother. This really does confirm it. All I can figure is that the name must be a coincidence . . . It *is* a very unusual name, but there's no way that your brother could've developed webbed feet later in life. A person is either born with the condition, or not . . . Right, still dead. I'm sorry for disturbing you over this situation. I didn't mean to ruin your day . . . Well, thank you. And thanks so much for your help, Lois. Bye, now."

Marta hung up, tilted back her head, took a deep breath, and blew air at the ceiling from her pursed lips.

"Wow," Sue said.

"You ought to be a detective," Neal said.

Marta returned to the sofa, flopped on it, and swung her feet up onto the coffee table. "I feel like a jerk for lying to the poor woman. Not to mention, I scared the crap out of her."

"She's Leslie's sister?" Neal asked.

"Yeah. Lois. According to her, Leslie's dead. And she wants him to stay that way."

Neal had guessed as much from Marta's side of the telephone

conversation. He could hardly believe it, though. "His sister thinks he's *dead?*"

"He is officially among the deceased. He shot it out with the cops in San Francisco seven years ago."

"Then how could this guy be him?"

"They lost his body. Apparently, he was struck by gunfire as he was climbing over the rail of the Golden Gate Bridge. And down he went."

"Off the *Golden Gate?*"

"Yeah. And into San Francisco Bay, where he was never seen again."

"Maybe this *isn't* the same guy," Neal said.

"Name's the same. And her brother had the same build."

"Did her brother have the webbed feet?" Sue asked.

Marta stared at her, eyebrows rising. "No," she said.

"Well, then . . ."

"I made it up about the webbed feet."

"Did ya?"

"I didn't want Lois to know her brother's still alive. She's terrified of him. She didn't tell me what, but I got the impression that he used to do some pretty horrible things to her. On top of which, the cops thought he was this guy called 'The Beast of Belvedere.' "

"My God," Neal muttered. "You're kidding. The Beast of Belvedere?"

"You've heard of him?"

"Sure. He was breaking into homes on Belvedere Island . . . It's one of those very exclusive neighborhoods . . . Up in Marin County, just across the bridge from San Francisco. Woodsy hills, narrow little streets, a lagoon, houses that cost a small fortune . . . This guy got into four or five of these places and murdered anyone he found in them. Whole families, in a few cases. Tortured the people. Mutilated them. Raped them. Never left any survivors. The press started calling him the Beast of Belvedere. I knew all about it at the time, but . . . it *was* seven or eight years ago, I guess. From what I remember, they never had a suspect. And I don't recall anything about a police shoot-out on the Golden Gate. The killings just ended, suddenly."

"Apparently when Leslie got shot off the Golden Gate."

"I can't believe anyone could survive a thing like that," Neal said.

Sue met his eyes. "Yer the guy that calls him Rasputin."

Chapter Forty-five

"It's about four-thirty now," Marta said after a glance at the clock on her VCR. "The money pickup isn't till two tonight, so we've got plenty of time to figure things out."

"You *do* have tonight off?" Neal asked.

"Right. Thursdays and Fridays."

"I guess we could go on over to my place any time," Neal said. "Glitt probably won't show up till sometime after dark, but the earlier we get there, the better."

"Is that what you have in mind?" Marta asked. "We wait for him to show up at your apartment?"

"I guess so."

"Then what?"

Neal shrugged. "We grab him."

"Make him tell us where to go for the money," Sue explained.

"Or I'll get into his mind with the bracelet," Neal said, "and find out that way."

"Okay." Marta nodded her understanding. "We learn whatever we need to know. Then what?"

"Go and get it," Sue said.

"What about Glitt?" She looked at Neal. "You're saying we grab him inside your apartment, make him talk . . . whatever. Then do we leave him there? Take him with us?"

Neal realized he hadn't actually given much thought to the matter. "Well," he said, "I guess that depends. Would all three of us be going to the pickup?"

"We don't wanna leave *anybody* behind to stand guard on him." Sue said. "I wouldn't do it, not even if we had him hogtied 'n blinded."

"It'd be too dangerous," Marta agreed. "And we can't exactly let him go." Eyes on Neal, she asked, "Would you want to kill him?"

"Maybe. I mean, yeah. He has to be killed, I think. I've always figured I would kill him. But not in my apartment. If I *did* do it there, we'd have to haul out the body. We couldn't just *leave* him. And somebody might see us."

"Dead or alive," Sue said, "we can't just let him stay in yer rooms."

Neal shook his head. "No. And either way, it'll be a major problem."

"Not to mention," Marta said, "the whole idea of trying to 'grab' him in your apartment when he shows up to kill you tonight. How do you plan to manage that?"

"Stick my gun in his face."

"What if he puts up a fight? If you have to shoot him, we'll never find out where to go for the money."

"I'll try to just wound him."

"He can't get killed anyhow," Sue pointed out. A single side of her mouth lifted. "Right?"

"It almost looks that way," Neal admitted.

"But even if you only wound him," Marta said, "your neighbors will hear the shot. One of them might phone the cops."

"Nobody in L.A. calls in about gunfire," Neal said.

"I bet they do when the shots come from their own building. Or if not call the cops, they might do some checking around on their own. Which they might do if there's *any* sort of major disturbance—shouts, a struggle . . ."

"I gotta hunch y'ain't keen on the big plan."

"It seems to have some big problems."

Nodding, Neal said, "Maybe we need to jump him outside, huh? Right after he leaves his car. Before he gets to the building."

"And then what'll we do, interrogate him on the sidewalk?"

"Well . . ."

"Ya want my plan?" Sue asked.

They both looked at her and nodded.

"Here's what I think," Sue said. "I think Marta's already figured out how to get the job done and we oughta do it her way."

Marta grinned. "How did you know?"

"Oh, I know more than I think."

Neal turned to Marta. "Let's hear it."

She grinned. "We don't wait for Glitt to show up at your place tonight. Instead, we make a preemptive strike."

"A *who?*" Sue asked.

"Means we beat him to the punch," Neal explained. "We go out and nail him before he comes for us." To Marta, he said, "Only one problem with that. We don't know where to find him. That house last night, I haven't got the slightest idea . . ."

"We don't know where to find Glitt, Rasputin, the Beast of Belvedere. But I'll bet we can find Vince Conrad."

Neal stared at her. He suddenly felt a little shaky. "Pay *him* a visit?"

Marta nodded. "He's the guy with the money. If he's planning to hand over half a million bucks to Glitt tonight, he probably has it in his house right this very minute."

"You're probably right."

"When'll we go?" Sue asked.

Marta grinned and said, "Now?"

"Haw! That's the ticket!"

"I don't know," Neal said.

"It's perfect," Marta said. "This way, we find out whether he really did hire Glitt to kill Elise. If he's got the payoff money, we find out where it is. That's where your bracelet should come in handy. You get inside him and find out whatever we need to know. If we're lucky, maybe we can take it from him."

"Yeah!" Sue blurted. "We swipe the bundle right out from under his nose!"

Neal moaned.

Still grinning, Marta said, "Then here's poor old Vince minus the half a million bucks he owes Glitt. Comes two o'clock in the morning, what's he going to do?"

Sue gleefully threw in, "What's Glitt gonna do?"

"Not the sort of chap I'd like to have mad at *me*," Marta said.

Neal took a deep breath. He felt trembly and sick, but excited by the plan. "In other words," he said, "we steal the money from

Vince. He can't make tonight's payoff. Glitt gets pissed off at him and all hell breaks loose."

"Beautiful?" Marta asked.

"Brilliant," Neal said. Wrinkling his nose, he added, "Now if we could just hire someone to do it *for* us."

"*You* got no reason to be scared," Sue told him. "Yer gonna be all safe and sound in the bastard's head. Anybody gets hurt, it's gonna be me or Marta."

"Maybe that's *why* I'm scared."

"We'll be safe," Marta said. "Vince didn't have the guts to kill Elise—had to *hire* someone else to do it. So he's not about to try anything with a couple friendly babes like us."

"Anyhow, yer gonna be in his head. If he takes on any funny ideas, just get back in yer own self and come to the rescue."

"You're kidding," Neal said, when they returned to the living room. They both wore suntan oil that made their skin glisten, swimsuits that showed most of it, and nothing else.

Neal had seen Marta's suit before. A skimpy, two-piece affair the color of butter, its imitation leather was cut in a shaggy style that made her look like some sort of Hollywood jungle woman— Tarzan's Jane or Raquel Welch in *One Million Years B.C.*

Sue wore a shiny black bikini. Smiling, she raised her arms and twirled around, modeling it for Neal.

"You're not wearing that over to Vince's, are you?"

"Sure am."

"We're going there to *distract* the guy," Marta pointed out.

"Well, you'll distract him all right. Both of you will. If your naked breasts don't . . ."

"They are not naked," Marta said.

"As good as."

"A gal's decent long as her nips don't show," Sue explained. "Marta's don't and mine don't . . ."

"Your *ass* shows."

"A dang nice ass it is, too," she said, and gave one of her bare buttocks a soft slap.

"A lot of people wear thongs these days," Marta explained. "I've thought about getting one, myself."

"Jeez." Sighing, Neal shook his head. "Don't get me wrong, okay? You both look . . . great. But can't you wear some clothes, or something? At least on the way over?"

Smiling at Marta, Sue said, "He just don't want anyone *else* to get an eyeful."

"Terribly selfish of him."

"I'll say. Here he gets to have the both of us, and he don't want nobody else to even look. *Doesn't* want *anybody*."

Keeping a straight face, Neal said, "If people start looking, they'll start crashing. Might even crash into *us*. I'm only concerned about your safety, ladies."

"Well, he's got a point," Marta said.

"I hate to hide my new bikini from the world," Sue said.

"If you don't put on *something*," Neal told her, "you'll burn your butt on the car seat."

Marta and Sue started shaking their heads and laughing. Neal suddenly realized they had intended from the start to wear clothes over their swimsuits. Without a word more, they headed back for the bedroom.

"Very funny!" he called.

"We thought so," Marta called back.

At Sue's request, they used Marta's Jeep Wrangler. They agreed to let her ride in front, so Neal took the backseat. Which was fine with him, even though the space was so narrow that he had to sit sideways. The car had no top—only a windshield and roll bar—so the rear seat was a great place for catching the late afternoon sunlight and wind.

Neal also had a wonderful view of Marta and Sue. They sat side by side in the bucket seats, their hair blowing behind them, gold in the sunlight. He could see the right side of Marta's face and neck, the left side of Sue's. They both wore sunglasses. They both wore sleeveless tops. Marta's right arm was out, bent slightly at the elbow, her hand on the steering wheel. It gleamed with suntan oil all the way up to her shoulder. The soft golden hairs were slicked down. Sue's arm hung by her side, elbow resting on the center console. It gleamed like Marta's, but didn't seem to have so much hair.

My God, they're both so beautiful.

We oughta be going to the beach, not . . .

"Hey," he said, speaking loudly to be heard over the road noises and the wind. "Why don't we skip Vince's place and head for a beach?"

Marta turned her head and called, "The beaches are too dangerous. Do you want us to get shot?"

"You think we'll be safer dropping in unexpectedly on a murderer?" Neal asked.

"You bet."

Sue turned her head and laughed.

Both women had their heads turned toward the middle and Neal could see the profile of their faces.

They could be sisters, he thought. Marta and her kid sister, Sue. Marta older, larger, with a lush body that Sue probably envied. Marta the more sensible of the two, the better educated, the more refined. But Sue the wilder of the pair. A tomboy to Marta's woman. A kid, somehow tough and vulnerable at the same time.

But both women were very much alike with their fine blond hair and smooth skin and blue eyes, with their gentleness, with their mischief, with their passion and love for Neal.

How could I be this lucky? he wondered.

Can't last.

Sure it can, he told himself. They *like* each other. Hard to believe, but they do.

The best of all possible worlds . . . But somebody could get hurt.

"Let's not do this," he called.

"What's the matter?" Marta asked.

"I don't care about the money. You know? Not really. Let's turn back, okay? Before we get ourselves into some kind of a real mess."

Sue looked over her shoulder at him. "It's half a million buckaroos, hon."

"It's not worth dying for."

"Nobody's gonna die," Sue said.

"How do you know?"

Marta's head turned. "What else *can* we do?" she asked. "If we just go back to my place and forget the whole thing, Glitt's still going to be looking for you. If he doesn't get stopped, he'll *kill* you, sooner or later."

"Not if he can't find me. We could all take off . . . move away. Maybe to Arizona or New Mexico, or—"

"That wouldn't guarantee anything," Marta said. "No matter where we might go . . . even if we change our names . . . there would always be a risk of him finding you. Anyway, you still want to write for the movies. You almost *have* to live in L.A. for that."

"Wouldn't have to."

"The thing is, as long as he's alive, Glitt's going to be after you. You shot him full of holes. He isn't going to forget that. He's going to keep hunting you. Eventually, he'll find you."

"Not to mention me and Marta, we'll more than likely be with ya when he does. Ya don't want him gettin *us*, do ya?"

Neal started to remember what Glitt had done to Elise . . . started to see it in bloody color on the screen of his mind. To stop the images, he quickly said, "We could go to the police and tell them everything. Then *they* could take care of the whole mess."

"They haven't taken care of much so far," Marta pointed out. "Glitt's still in the world. Vince is still a free man. Last I heard, he isn't even a suspect. And if the cops *do* grab them, who's to say there won't be a team of slick attorneys come along and get them both off the hook with a bunch of lies?"

"I know," Neal said. "I know."

"This *is* Los Angeles."

"I know."

"You want these guys to get away with murdering Elise?"

"No, of course not."

Sue called over her shoulder, "We gotta take these assholes down. If we don't, who's gonna?"

Marta nodded. "We'll never be safe, the three of us, until they're both dead."

"I know you're probably right," Neal said. "I'm just scared, that's all."

"Tell ya what," Sue said to him. "Quit lookin' on the dark

side of stuff and start thinkin' about half a million smackeroos."

"I'll try," he said.

He realized they were now rushing along San Vicente and bearing down on Greenhaven, the road to Vince Conrad's house.

If we just don't make the turn, we'll be at the beach in a few minutes . . .

With no instructions from Neal, Marta made the turn.

Chapter Forty-six

"I'm surprised the place isn't crawling with reporters and gawkers," Marta said as she drove slowly up Greenhaven.

From here, they could see a fair distance ahead. There were no news vans, no crowds.

"This guy ain't exactly O.J.," Sue pointed out.

"Still, he *is* an actor and Elise was an Olympic star."

"What kind of coverage *has* it been getting?" Neal asked. "We've mostly tried to avoid it."

"Fairly big. A day doesn't go by that it doesn't get some kind of coverage. Elise's funeral was yesterday. That was one of the top stories."

"Vince attended?" Neal asked.

"Oh, sure. How would he look if he didn't?"

"Has there been anything about my letter to the cops?"

"Nary a word."

"It obviously didn't do much good, since . . . here we are. This is it on the right."

Though Neal had never seen the place in daylight, he recognized the heavy foliage bordering the road, the small entrance gate and the larger gate at the driveway. Through its iron bars, he glimpsed the garage door.

"No car in the driveway," Marta mentioned.

"Maybe he's not home," Neal said.

"Easy way to find out," Sue said.

A few feet past the driveway gate, Neal said, "This'll be a good place to park."

"Shouldn't we go farther away?" Marta asked.

"Just so we can't be seen from the house. I want to be near enough to get inside fast if there's trouble."

Nodding, she slowed the Jeep and eased it to the right. The side tires dropped slightly. They made crackly sounds crunching the leafy ground cover. Then bushes squeaked against the door.

Marta stopped and shut off the engine. She and Sue both turned to look back at Neal.

"I guess we're really going ahead with it," he said.

Marta nodded. "How long will it take you to go in and scout around?"

"With the bracelet? A minute or two."

"And you'll come back right away if there's a problem?"

"Yeah."

"If there isn't a problem," she said, "just go ahead and . . . enter him, or whatever you do with that thing. We'll get ready. If you aren't back in four or five minutes, we'll assume everything is okay and we'll go to the door."

Neal took a deep, trembling breath. He blew it out slowly. He shook his head. He muttered, "Oh, man."

"Relax," Sue told him. "Yer makin' *me* nervous."

"Everything'll be fine," Marta assured him.

"Okay," Neal muttered. "Okay." He settled back in the seat, leaning to the side and stretching out his legs.

"Maybe you should get lower," Marta suggested.

"I don't want to seem like I'm trying to hide. You know, if someone comes by. This way, I'll look like I'm taking a little snooze while I wait for my friends to come back."

"Better not stay out for very long at a time," Sue told him. "Check on yerself every so often."

"We'll see. With any luck, Vince won't even be home."

"Don't say that," Sue said. Thrusting her arm though the gap between the seatbacks, she gave his leg a gentle slap.

"Be careful," Marta told him.

"You, too. Both of you. Just remember, I'll be inside him. If he decides to pull anything, I'll bail out and come after you as fast as I can."

He could feel the pistol against his thigh, and patted it through his pocket.

"Hope it's loaded," Sue said.

"It's always loaded," Neal told her. He sighed again. "Guess that's it, unless . . ."

"If everything goes all right," Marta said, "just give the horn a couple of toots when you're ready to leave. We'll try to make a graceful exit so we don't arouse his suspicion."

"It'll get aroused damn fast when he finds out that his money's gone. So use fake names. Try not to give him *any* way of figuring out who you are."

"We'll be amazingly cagey," Marta said.

"Just watch and see."

"I will. One more thing . . . While you're busy being so cagey, see if you can bring up a subject that'll make him *think* about the payoff. But be subtle about it."

"Will do," Marta said. "Ready?"

"Not really."

"Let's get this show on the road."

"All right. Good luck. So long. Be careful." He took another deep breath, then raised his arm and kissed the serpent's head.

He felt himself rise weightless.

Looking down, he saw his body sprawled in the rear of the Jeep.

Marta and Sue unfastened their seatbelts, swung the straps out of the way, and pulled off their shirts. Then, staying seated, they started to remove their shorts.

Neal wanted to stay and watch—a very strange and wonderful view from up here, looking straight down at them as they struggled with their clothes—but he felt guilty. He had a job to do. If he wasted time here, the gals might end up walking into trouble.

Better get a move on.

The mere wish was enough to send him speeding off. He rushed over the top of the brick wall, through the branches of a tree, across the driveway and over the front lawn, then through the front door of the house.

Before he even had a chance to start his search, he spotted a man through a sliding glass door at the other end of the living room.

It has to be him!

The way the man sat, however, Neal could only see his bare legs stretched out on the green pad of a poolside lounge.

Take it easy. Don't rush in. Wait till you're sure it's him.

Wary of entering the man by accident, Neal veered off to the right and passed through the glass wall a good distance away from him. Then he drifted out over the swimming pool and turned around.

The man on the lounge was Vince Conrad, all right.

Neal recognized him from a couple of dozen movies. Early in his career, Vince had played the leading man in a few films that never quite made it. He possessed the handsome features of a lead, but lacked something. Character? In spite of his rugged features and well-toned muscles, there was a simpering weakness to him that couldn't be disguised. Unfit to be cast as the protagonist, he'd quickly found himself getting steady work as a heavy. For the past decade, he'd been the sly, sleazy villain of nearly every film in which he appeared.

He looked the part now, sprawled on his lounge by the pool wearing sunglasses and a skimpy white Spandex swimsuit, his dark skin gleaming with suntan oil, a cocktail on a tray by his side, a cordless telephone in his hand.

Time's wasting! Go for it!

Neal plunged into the man.

Whoa! What's going on here?

Sunbaked, sweaty, mellow, half tanked and half erect.

And feeling great. Way too great, Neal thought, for a guy who buried his wife yesterday.

And who's this on the phone?

"Just relaxing here by the pool," Vince explained. "Having meself a cold toddy."

"All by your lonesome?"

"Just lonely me. Mourning the loss of my beloved spouse. Attempting to drown my sorrow."

"Shame, shame."

Though Vince was well-soused, it was the woman on the phone who sounded loopy. She had a breathy drawl as if she were trying to imitate Marilyn Monroe.

Give her half a blink, she'll start angling to come over. Vince thought. *Not today, sweet stuff.* "I wish you were here, Pamela," he said.

"That might be arranged."

"I'd *love* to have you here. You know that, don't you? But it's too soon. What'll the coppers think if a sweet bit of stuff like you trots over to play?"

"They aren't watching your house, are they?" She sounded appalled.

"Might be. Might be. One never knows about such things. For that matter, they might be eavesdropping on this very conversation at this very moment."

"Do you think so?"

"They might be. Coppers are a tricky lot." Vince grinned, amused by himself.

"They better not be listening!" Pamela snapped. "Hello? Cops? If you're listening in on us, you oughta be ashamed— persecuting an innocent man this way. You know good and well he was all the way over in Hawaii. He couldn't *possibly* have murdered Elise. Haven't you ever heard of an 'airtight' alibi? Well, that's exactly what Vince has. Airtight. So you shouldn't be pestering him. Why don't you just hang up the phone right now and go and fuck yourself!"

Vince chuckled.

What a moronic twit, he thought. *Why do I put up with her?*

Vince answered his question with the mental image of a tawny woman climbing naked out of his pool, walking toward him. She had sleek black hair cut short like a pixie. She had a tan everywhere.

She looked familiar to Neal. An actress? he wondered. A model? He thought that maybe he'd seen her not long ago on Letterman.

"How was that?" she asked.

"You gave them an admirable piece of your mind," Vince told her. *A piece you can ill afford to loose, you gorgeous, nincompoop.*

"Why should they even care if I come over?" she asked.

"It'll look bad, my sweet. That's all."

"I don't care. I miss you, Vincent. I miss you so much, I can hardly stand it."

"I miss you, too. Every moment. But it won't do either of us any good if you're seen—"

"I don't care. I want to be with you. I don't care—"

"Perhaps in a few days."

"I can't stand this! You didn't kill her. It isn't fair that they won't let you live your own life."

"We'll simply have to keep our passions bridled—"

The sound of the doorbell chimes stopped Vince's voice. He felt a quick flutter of anxiety. "I have to hang up, now. Someone's at the door. I'll phone you later. *Au revoir.*" Without waiting for a response, he thumbed the power off switch.

He swung his legs off the lounge and slipped his feet into a pair of flip-flops.

Who the fuck? Cops or reporters. Bastard fucks, why don't they leave me alone?

He set the phone on the tray. Then he stood up.

Don't they know I'm in mourning?

He picked up his slippery, cold glass and took a sip.

Vodka and tonic.

It tasted to Neal exactly like the drinks he'd had with Elise. He felt a sudden ache of loss.

My ache or his? he wondered.

Must be mine.

Because Vince, walking toward the nearest glass door, seemed to be thinking of other matters.

I'm not exactly decent. He gazed at the front of his white swimsuit. *Look at that boner. I should put something on. No telling who'll be at the door. Homicide dicks? A crew from Hard Copy?*

Chuckling, he rolled open the door and stepped into the living room. The air inside felt cool on his hot, sweaty skin. The swimsuit was clinging to him like a rag of clammy skin.

Fine just the way I am. If they don't want a peek at Vincent Conrad in his natural habitat, fuck them. What you see is what you get.

As he slid the door shut, the chimes rang again.

What if it is the cops?

He imagined himself opening the door . . .

And there stand a pair of middle-aged and tired-looking L.A.P.D. homicide detectives—the heavy one with the stacked silver hair and the wiry bald one—*Van Ness and Long, that's them*—and they stare at him with their weary see-all eyes and Van Ness says, "Vincent Conrad, we're arresting you for murder. You have the right to remain silent . . ."

Feeling suddenly all shrunken and cold inside, Vince stopped in the foyer and gazed at the door.

They haven't got anything on me. Impossible. It has to be somebody else.

Who?

He swung open the door.

And stood there gaping out at Marta and Sue.

To Vince, they were strangers.

Strangers who were not Van Ness and Long.

Who were, instead, a couple of beautiful females in sunglasses and scanty swimsuits.

But who the fuck are they?

"May I help you, girls?" he asked.

The larger of the two, smiling, stuck out her hand and said, "I'm Tracy. You must be Vince."

Nodding, feeling a bit confused but pleasant, Vince took hold of her hand. "Very nice to meet you," he said. Shaking her hand, he watched her breasts wobble slightly. They were tanned and shiny. Her leather top didn't hide much. He could see down between them.

Neal felt Vince's penis start to rise again.

Damn it! Marta's turning him on!

She's supposed to, he reminded himself.

The rotten bastard doesn't have to look at her that way.

"And this is my cousin . . ." Marta said.

"Katt," Sue broke in. "With a *K.* And two *T*s."

"Katt," Vince repeated. Smiling, he took her offered hand. "Very nice to meet you, too." When he shook her hand, her breasts didn't wobble.

Oh, they're so nice and small and firm. By God, what is she, sixteen? Look at those nipples! Look at them!

Vince imagined himself lifting the black patches of the bikini top away from her breasts and taking one of her nipples between his teeth. Squeezing it between his teeth. Neal could feel it in there, long and rubbery. He could taste it.

He could also feel Vince growing even larger, pushing out against the front of his clingy damp swimsuit.

Had Marta or Sue noticed *that?*

Neal couldn't tell; not with their eyes hidden behind the dark sunglasses.

Still holding Sue's hand, Vince said, "Do I know either of you?"

"I'm just Tracy's cousin from Sacramento," Sue said.

"Elise invited us over to swim in the pool," Marta said.

Holy shit, Neal thought.

Vince's mind seemed to be reeling, stumbling about at a loss for coherence, wondering what sort of game these two gals might be trying to play, hoping they were for real—*Don't they know she's dead for God's sake? They been on Mars?*—wanting to invite them in—*"Glad you stopped by! Sure, sure, you're welcome to use the pool. I was about to go in for a dip myself"*—but who are they really?

I don't care who they are.

The one's too young to be a cop, anyway.

I want to see more of her, whoever she is. More of the other, too. Tracy and Katt.

"Come in," Vince said. "Please, come in." Still holding Sue's hand, he stepped backward and drew her across the threshold. "I wasn't expecting company." Marta entered. Releasing Sue's hand, Vince closed the door. "But you're certainly welcome to use the pool. May I offer you two girls a drink? I do believe the sun's over the yardarm. How about a vodka and tonic?"

"That'd be great," Sue said.

"Sure," said Marta. "I could go for that."

"Right this way, girls." Vince wanted to walk behind them for the rear view, but figured he really needed to lead the way. So he walked in front. They followed him into the den.

It looked familiar to Neal.

Like a room from a wonderful, sad dream: here the sofa where he'd stretched out and tried the bracelet; here the place where Elise had stood when he entered her; there the bar stools; there the bar where they'd had their drinks, where later she'd taken the aspirin and Alka-Seltzer just before starting the walk back to her bedroom with Neal's card in the pocket of her pajama shirt, stiff against her nipple . . .

And now it's sleazy Vince behind the bar, making drinks for my women after he's killed his own.

Chapter Forty-seven

Marta and Sue perched themselves on the high stools in front of him. Vince, behind the counter, stole glances at them while he made the drinks.

Perhaps someone hired them to cheer me up. A Strip-o-gram sort of deal.

Who would do such a thing?

Bill?

Unless they are cops. No, no, not cops. Reporters?

Who cares? They're fabulous stuff. Just gotta do what comes naturally.

Toss in a good load, loosen them up.

He dumped an extra shot of vodka into each of the three ice-filled glasses.

"Is Elise around?" Marta asked.

She really doesn't know? Or is this a trick?

Better play it like a trick, just to be safe.

Shaking his head and trying to put a sorrowful expression on his face, Vince poured tonic water into the glasses. Then he said, "You haven't heard?"

"Heard what?" Marta asked.

Sue shrugged her fragile, tanned shoulders.

"This last Sunday night, someone broke into the house and . . ." Vince's voice cracked. He brought tears into his eyes. He thought, *Excellent.*

He's a pretty good actor, after all, Neal decided.

"Elise is dead," Vince said, and lowered his head and clasped a hand across his eyes as if to hide the shame of his tears.

Maybe he's *not* so good, Neal thought.

"She was . . . brutally murdered."

"Oh, dear God," Marta said. "I'm so sorry."

"Who done it?" Sue asked.

Vince, still covering his eyes, shook his head. "We don't know." His mind flashed a picture of Glitt's gaunt, bearded face.

That's it! Neal thought. *Gotcha, you bastard! You did it! You hired him!*

"I was away on a trip at the time," Vince said.

"I just can't believe she's dead," Marta muttered, very convincingly disturbed by the news. "I'm so sorry. This is terrible. We never would've come over . . ."

"It's quite all right." Vince rubbed his wet eyes, then cast a brave smile at her. "I'm glad you came. Both of you," he added, and turned his grief-stricken smile on Sue.

"We was on a campout since Friday," Sue told him. "We only just got back this mornin'. Must be how come we missed the news. Not as how I *knew* Elise myself, but Tracy's told me lots and lots about her."

Lots and lots? What does Tracy know? Who the fuck is she? What if Elise told her about our fights . . . the breakup?

"How long did you know my wife?" he asked Marta.

She shrugged, which drew Vince's eyes to her breasts. "Six months or so, I guess."

"But I've never met you," he said.

"We got together for lunch quite a lot. Also, you weren't around very often. I've been over here to the house . . . oh, I don't know . . . ten or twelve times, probably. You were always away. The fact is, Elise made a point of never asking me over when you were home."

Ah. Little wonder. Didn't want me laying my eyes on a babe like—

"You weren't actually supposed to be home *today*," Marta went on. "Elise told me you'd be in Hawaii."

"And so I was. But . . ." He managed to choke up again. "I came back early . . . Because of . . . I'm sorry." He shook his head and wiped his eyes.

"I'm really sorry we came along and disturbed you," Marta said, climbing down from the stool. "We had no idea. This is so awful. We never would've come if we'd known."

"You're not leaving?" Vince managed to ask.

"We'd better," Marta said. "I mean, dropping in on you at a time like this . . ."

Sue, giving him a somewhat forlorn look as if she hated to go, swiveled around and slid off her stool.

For the first time, Vince saw her from behind.

His gaze latched on her buttocks—naked except for the slip of black fabric up her crack. Lust slammed through him. He went almost breathless. His heart pounded. His penis grew rigid, tilting upward. He felt it pushing at the flimsy fabric of his swimsuit.

"Don't go," he said. "Please. At least stay for a while, enjoy your drinks, have a swim. I insist."

"We really shouldn't," Marta said.

"No, please. Elise wouldn't have wanted you to run off. I'm sure of that. She would've insisted that you stay and enjoy yourselves. Please. For her sake. And for mine. You two . . . you're like a breath of fresh air. Truly. Ever since I came back, it's been nothing but tearful well-wishers trying to console me. And reporters. And police. I'm so . . . so weary of it all. But you two . . . a couple of lovely, cheerful young women who came here at Elise's invitation simply to enjoy yourselves . . . Stay. Please. You do my heart good."

When he said that about his heart, he clapped a hand to his bare chest.

Marta and Sue looked at each other.

"Please. Stay."

"Fine by me," Sue said.

"Well," Marta said, "all right." To Vince, she said, "If you're sure."

"I'm absolutely, one hundred percent sure." He sighed. With all the fuss, his passion had subsided somewhat. Instead of urgent lust, he now felt proud of himself for convincing them to stay. He also felt a certain quiet thrill of anticipation.

They're mine now. Get them nice and soused, and we'll all go in for a little swim.

He imagined himself with them, cavorting with them in the pool, all three naked and gleaming.

"Not a chance, asshole."

Vince, unaware of Neal's remark, cut wedges of lemon and squeezed them into the drinks while he imagined himself wrenching off Marta's swimsuit top and setting her breasts free.

He gave each drink a quick stir with the blade of his paring knife.

"Shall we take them out to the pool?" he suggested.

He watched the two women step forward and pick up their glasses. Then he lifted his own glass. He stepped around the end of the bar, slid the door open, and said, "Girls first."

They filed past him, almost brushing against his body with their smooth, oiled skin.

Look at them! My God! Tracy and Katt.

He wanted them both. Badly. And knew that he would succeed. If not this afternoon in or by the pool, then tonight. He would ask them to stay for dinner.

He isn't suspicious of them anymore, Neal realized as he observed the plans forming in Vince's mind.

Plans for grilling steaks on the barbecue, keeping their glasses loaded with vodka and tonic, eating outside by candlelight. Later, after a leisurely dinner—including a nice cabernet sauvignon—they would be good and soused and ready for a night swim. Get them to take their suits off.

"It feels so much better that way. You feel so free. The water slides over your skin like a lover's caress." They always go for that line. They always want to be naked in the pool. And they want me to see them naked. All of them. Always. And after the skinny-dipping, they always want to . . .

Fuck!

I've got the fucking drop-off tonight! Gotta take that fucking maniac his money.

The thought of it made Vince feel squirmy inside.

He's terrified of Glitt, Neal realized. Why the hell did you hire Glitt if you're scared to death of him?

Because he's the best man for the job? If you want a sadistic rapist to take care of your wife for you . . .

Stop it! Neal warned himself. You're missing stuff. Pay attention.

. . . get there by two . . . Leave around one-thirty? Drink in hand, Vince stepped outside. *That oughta do it, can't take more than half an hour. Why'd he pick a place so far away?*

Vince started to close the door, sliding it slowly.

I'd better get there early. Good and early. Don't want to run into that fucking beast. Just drop it off and get my ass out of there.

So what time?

Maybe one at the latest.

The door bumped shut.

Try to fuck these babes and get rid of them by midnight. Midnight at the latest.

Should be easy.

Neal snarled into his mind, "You'll fuck these babes when hell freezes over, dirtbag."

Vince turned away from the door. Marta had already set her drink on the round, glass-topped table. Sue stood at the other side of it.

"Is this all right?" Sue asked.

"Wonderful," Vince said.

They all sat down on patio chairs around the table.

"Sure is nice out here," Sue said, turning her head and gazing at the pool. "Sure wish I had me a place like this."

"You're welcome to come over any time," Vince said. "Both of you."

"Thanks," Sue said. "That's awful nice. Know what? Ya fooled me. I figured you'd be sort of a creep."

They know all about me!

"Yer always such a mean stinker in yer movies."

False alarm.

She smiled at him. "I never been to a movie star's house, before."

My lovely, sweet darling!

"Oh, I'm not what one would call a *star*."

"Sure y'are. I seen bunches of yer movies."

"We're both fans of your work," Marta added.

"Why, thank you."

"Ya know my favorite?" Sue asked. "It's the one where you hire this guy to knock off yer business partner."

Nodding as if he appreciated her praise, he tried to figure out which film she meant. In several, he'd paid men to murder people who were causing him trouble.

"I can't recall the name of it," Sue said, frowning.

"Neither can I," Vince admitted. "I've been in so many. Do you remember the cast?"

"There was you."

He chuckled.

"I don't know. Was it Chuck Norris?"

"I haven't appeared with Chuck Norris."

"Well, must've been somebody else. Anyhow, how it ends, yer in this parking lot, all set to hand over a million bucks to the killer . . ."

Vince suddenly stopped trying to figure out which film she was trying to describe.

He saw himself swinging his car into a parking lot at night.

Tonight? Neal wondered. *What is this? A memory? Or is he thinking about tonight?*

The scene was continuing in Vince's mind. He was climbing out of his car in a brightly lighted parking lot. The lot of a Video City store; Neal could see the big, neon sign in the background.

Vince carried a wrinkled old grocery sack by his side. Its top was crinkled down, its bottom swollen.

My God, that's it! The money's in the bag! That's the payoff! You did it, Sue! You did it!

". . . only instead of *him* showing up for the payoff, the killer?

. . . it's the guy he was s'pose to've murdered. Who *was* that? Could've sworn it was Chuck Norris."

"Van Damme?" Marta suggested.

"Nah."

"That Steven Seagal?"

Vince, his mind-film rolling, sees himself stuff the grocery sack inside a garbage container beside Video City's front entrance. As he releases the sack, a voice from behind says, "The joke's on you." He whirls around. Elise is striding toward him, very alive, dressed in her blue satin pajamas. The pajamas flow against her body, purple in the lights of the parking lot. She carries a bloody meat cleaver in one hand. In her other hand, swinging by its hair, is the head of Leslie Glitt.

"That movie doesn't sound at all familiar to me," Marta said, pulling Vince's mind out of the awful fantasy.

He picked up his glass and took a drink. "Frankly," he said, "it doesn't ring a bell with me, either."

"I coulda *swore* it was you," Sue told him.

"I don't believe it was."

Sue shook her head, and took a drink. "Well," she said, "don't *I* just feel like a prize shit?"

Vince chuckled. "No call for that."

"Katt's always sticking her foot in her mouth," Marta told him. "I think she must enjoy the flavor."

"Yer's, they're so big they don't fit in *nobody's* mouth."

"Let's not fight, girls," Vince said, enjoying himself.

"Show him yer big feet," Sue taunted.

"Settle down, Katt."

"They're so big, she can't fall down. Just pops right on up again. She can't drown, either. It's as good as wearin' flippers. She's safe anywhere."

"Ha ha," Marta said. "You're hilarious."

"Yer so safe, I'd hide my jewelry in ya—if I had some."

Vince laughed.

"If you ever did that," Marta told her, "I wouldn't give you the combination."

"What combination?" Sue asked.

"To open me up and take your jewelry out."

"I ain't got no jewelry."

Laughing, Vince shook his head.

Come on, come on, Neal thought. *Your safe. Think about your safe and combination. It's the least you can do, these two jumping through hoops for you this way.*

"If I *had* some jewelry," Sue said, "last thing I'd do with it is to stick it in you. Less maybe I shove it where the sun don't shine."

"Girls, girls."

Marta sighed and shook her head. "I have to apologize for my cousin. She's not usually this way. I imagine it's the vodka. She's not actually old enough to drink, you know."

"I am too old enough. I was old enough when I hit nine."

Vince, surprised and amused, raised his eyebrows. "You started drinking at the age of nine?"

"Yup. That's when I figured out how to lay my hands on Daddy's booze. He kept it locked up, 'cause of Mom being a lush. There was this lock on the cabinet. The combination kind? Well, Daddy had him a real bad memory, so he wrote the combination numbers on a piece of paper that he kept in his billfold. So one night when he was sleepin', I snuck a peek at it and copied it all down. I got away without him catchin' me, went straight to the booze cabinet and squatted down and started workin' on the lock. It was a left this way, a right that way, and then a left. Like that. Took me eight or nine tries. All that left and right stuff, and do ya pass the number once or stop at it right off the bat—hard to keep it all straight. But then I finally got the thing to unlock for me. I opened it up and there was ten different sorts of booze all lined up in rows. I had me a sip from every bottle. Time I got done, ya never seen a girl so drunk. It's a miracle I made it back to bed." She sighed. "Anyhow, I didn't touch another drop for about five years after that."

While Sue was telling her story, Vince had let her words become moving images in his mind. He'd watched her sneak through a house at night, find the numbers in her father's wallet, then squat in front of a cabinet and struggle with the combination lock.

In Vince's version, however, she did not appear to be nine years old. She looked as she looked now.

Except that her bikini was gone.

In his mental film, Vince had viewed Sue from the front, as if his eyes were in the door of the liquor cabinet, level with her breasts as she tried to work the combination lock. Her skin had looked like bronze in a shimmering, ruddy light. Her knees had been wide apart, almost touching the cabinet door.

Squatting that way, she'd soon opened the door. And Vince had been inside the cabinet, watching her reach in and take out bottles, remove their caps, take swigs.

While listening to the story and living it inside his mind, Vince had grown hard again.

But he never gave a thought to his own safe or to the numbers of its combination lock.

He hasn't got a safe, Neal thought.

So where's the money hidden?

Somewhere in the house, ready to go. Already in a grocery sack, maybe.

Let's find out.

Chapter Forty-eight

Neal wished they'd parked in the shade. He found himself in the rear of the Jeep, sunbaked and streaming sweat, his clothes sodden. Feeling as if the sun had drained away half his strength, he reached up and grabbed the roll bar and pulled himself to his feet.

He stood there, hanging on to it.

Marta's purse and clothes were piled on the driver's seat, Sue's on the passenger seat.

Never should've let them do this.

The slimy, scheming bastard and his fucking hard-ons . . .

Neal stepped up onto the side of the Jeep. From there, he

jumped to the pavement. Leaning over the top of the driver's door, he reached for the steering wheel.

"Put a stop to this shit right now," he muttered, and shoved the wheel's hub.

He expected a blast from the horn.

He got silence.

He pressed the wheel's center again, felt its give, but heard no horn.

"Great," he muttered. "Terrific."

Why the hell didn't Marta tell me her horn's on the fritz?

Now what? he wondered.

How about going for the money, stupid? That's what you were supposed to do in the first place, not wimp out and go for the damn horn. You came here for the bastard's money. The gals've been parading around as good as naked in front of the sick fuck to where they've got him half nuts—they've tricked everything out of him, we've got all his secrets—now all we need is the money and it'll be mission accomplished. We'll have the cash and he'll have shit.

He'll have his big memories of a cocktail hour and a hard cock with his dear friends, Tracy and Katt.

And he'll have a big empty bag full of nothing when it comes to paying Glitt.

Neal stretched out his arm and snatched Marta's ignition key out of the steering wheel.

Can't have someone driving off . . .

Then he opened the car door, leaned in, and stuffed their purses underneath the front seats.

He shut the door gently, silently, dropped Marta's key case into a pocket of his shorts, and ran back along the roadside. He raced past the driveway with its closed, iron gate.

The smaller gate was shut, but not locked.

He opened it, stepped through, and walked toward the house.

If I were a bag full of money, where would I be?

Not outside, that's for sure.

Hidden in the bedroom? Under the bed, maybe?

Apparently, the slug hasn't got a safe.

First things first, Neal told himself. Get inside the house.

He headed up the walkway toward the front door.

Vince had let the gals in that way. He'd shut it after them, but was it locked?

Neal tried it.

It was locked.

Which left the sliding doors.

Neal remembered a total of three sliding glass doors along the rear of the house: in the living room, the den, and the master bedroom. Vince had used two of them while Neal'd been inside him. And he'd locked neither of them.

Why should he? He's sitting back there where he can keep an eye on them.

The bedroom door, the one Elise had opened for Neal on Sunday night, might or might not be locked.

Neal pictured the position of the glass-topped table.

Only yards from the den door.

And Vince was seated so that he faced the bedroom area.

Those two doors were out.

Which left the living room door, not very far from where Vince sat, but at least behind him.

That's if nobody's changed position yet.

Neal jogged across the front lawn, then stopped and glanced around the corner. Nobody. He rounded the corner and hurried on, walking swiftly through the shadows of the fruit trees. As he approached the back of the house, he detected the quiet murmur of voices.

He peeked around the corner.

They all sat around the table, just as when Neal had left them. Vince, as expected, was facing away. His head and bare, tanned shoulders showed above the back of his chair. Marta sat with her back to the pool. Neal had a good view of her left side and much of her front. Sue sat across the table from Vince, but somewhat closer to the house so that Neal had a clear line of sight.

She might be looking right at me.

He slowly raised his hand and waved.

Sue nodded and said something Neal couldn't make out. Vince laughed. Marta turned her head slightly in Neal's direction. With her forefinger, she pushed at the bridge of her sunglasses. Neal wiggled his forefinger at her. She faced Vince and reached out and picked up her drink.

Neal was fairly sure that Marta had spotted him. He wasn't so sure about Sue.

If she hasn't yet, she will.

He pulled the pistol out of his pocket. Holding it ready by his side, he stepped around the corner of the house and began sneaking over the concrete toward the sliding door to the living room.

Keep him interested, ladies. Don't let him look.

Mouth parched, heart thumping fast, Neal raised his left hand and pressed his forefinger to his lips. Marta and Sue gave no hint that they saw him. They both acted as if they were enjoying cocktails with a fascinating movie star.

Neal kept moving, though he trembled badly. Soon, he was close enough to understand the words being spoken.

"No," Marta said. "Not me. I broke up with my fellow almost a year ago."

"And why was that?" Vince asked.

Neal still had such a long way to go—twelve, maybe fifteen feet.

The handle of the sliding glass door, still so far away, appeared to be only six feet behind Vince's back.

I'll never make it. He'll look around and . . .

"Ah, he thought he owned me. I can't stand *possessive* men. He was so jealous, he went nuts any time I so much as glanced at another guy. He even beat me up one time."

Not me, Neal thought. Who is she talking about? Somebody beat her up? Who the hell did that? I'll kill the son of a bitch.

Maybe she's making it up.

She'd better be.

"That's awful!" Vince blurted. Reaching out, he put a hand on Marta's forearm.

Get your mitt off her, you fucking shit.

"Heinous. How could anyone *dare* to harm such a lovely young lady?"

"Comes easy for some of them," Marta said.

"Despicable."

"Well, he didn't get a chance to hit me again, I'll tell you that much. It was 'So long, pal, been good to know you.'"

"Only not *that* good, huh?" Sue put in.

"He was a low-down dirty bastard."

She can't be talking about me, Neal thought.

And he finally arrived at the handle of the door.

"Keep talking, Marta. He'll hear the slightest sound." God, I can't believe I'm standing right behind him.

Vince turned his head from Marta to Sue. "And how about you, Kitty Katt? Do *you* have a boyfriend?"

"Not just now," Sue said. She smiled—a smile that seemed to be aimed over Vince's shoulder and straight at Neal. "I had me one, only he was always *at* me, if ya know what I mean. It ain't that I don't like that sorta thing much as anyone, only there's a time and place for it. He just wouldn't ever leave me alone. I never seen such a lech! Last time we went out, get this, he tried to boink me on a rolly coaster."

"Tried to *what* you?" Vince asked.

"Boink me, do me, screw me. Ya know?"

"Ah. I see."

"Almost got us both killed."

Vince chuckled. "I've never heard of anyone doing it on a roller coaster. Sounds rather intriguing."

"Don't ever try it if ya value yer life."

Neal reached out carefully and gripped the door handle. But he didn't dare pull it. Neal could well imagine the sucking squeak the door would make as it let go of the jamb.

He grimaced at Sue, then glanced toward Marta, who was taking a drink.

"Looks as we're all about ready for a refill," Vince said. "Can't fly on one wing."

Neal's stomach dropped.

"Not me," Sue said quickly. "Thanks anyhow. Maybe later. Time for me to hit the water." She shoved back her chair, sprang to her feet, whirled around and pranced toward the pool. Vince's head turned to watch.

Neal watched, too.

She was tawny and shining, bare except for the skinny black

bands of her suit. Neal supposed that Vince's eyes must be locked on the flexing mounds of her buttocks. His own certainly were.

This is distracting the bastard all right, but he's still going to hear the door . . .

Sue leaped off the edge of the pool. In midair, she jerked up her legs and hugged her knees. She dropped rump-first.

Cannonball!

She struck the water with a heavy, solid splash—*thugg-dump!*

At the same moment, Marta yelled, "That-away-t'go-Kattsy-babe!!!"

At the same moment, Neal jerked the door open.

It let out a loud, squeaking suck, but Vince didn't turn his head.

Nor did he turn his head to investigate the low rumble of its sliding. He probably couldn't hear it through the splatter sounds of Sue's falling splashwater pelting the surface of the pool and Marta's voice saying to him, "I'm going in. Are you ready? You're coming in, too, aren't you?"

Neal stepped through the gap and into the living room.

"Come on," Marta said. Looking back, he saw her stand up and pull at Vince's arm. "Let's go. Time to cool off. It'll be great. No time like the present."

Vince, laughing, allowed himself to be dragged from his chair.

When they were nearly to the pool, Neal eased the door shut.

In!

Chapter Forty-nine

Neal stood just inside the glass door, staring out.

Marta didn't release Vince's arm until they reached the edge of the pool. Then she turned away from him and dived.

A lovely dive. She soared out low over the water and knifed in with barely a splash.

Vince dived in after her.

Neal muttered, "Shit."

All three of them were in the pool, and Vince would no doubt go after the gals, hoping to grope them.

They're earning their take, that's for damn sure.

Neal had known, before now, that he loved them both. But he'd never felt quite so aware of how fabulous they really were. Where did they come up with such guts and ingenuity and wit?

They're both nuts.

Fabulous nuts!

As impressed as Neal was with them, he hated to see them splashing around in the pool with Vince.

The quicker I find the money, the quicker we'll be out of here.

He turned away from the glass door and walked through the living room.

No sign of a grocery bag.

It isn't going to be lying around in plain sight.

Why not?

Vince let two strangers into his house, that's why.

It's hidden somewhere. Try the bedroom. Try under the bed.

But the kitchen was just ahead, and Neal realized that a kitchen might be just the place for a grocery bag full of loot.

Hide it in plain sight. "The Purloined Letter."

So he hurried into the kitchen and looked around.

He found several brown paper sacks like the one he'd seen in Vince's mind, but they were all neatly folded and tucked into a space between the side of the refrigerator and a cupboard.

He wondered if Elise had done that.

He pictured her in the kitchen, surrounded by unloaded groceries, head down, a frown of concentration on her face as she carefully folded an empty sack.

She wore a white blouse and tan shorts. The legs of the shorts were turned up so she had cuffs high against her thighs. On her feet were white sneakers.

The image stuffed Neal's throat and made his eyes burn.

She'd be alive today except for Vince.

Neal hurried out of the kitchen.

Then, halting, he gazed across the living room and out through the glass.

Vince was standing in waist-deep water, Marta swimming toward the deep end, and Sue climbing out near one of the diving boards. Vince seemed to be admiring Sue's backside.

I could kill him right now, Neal thought. It'd be easy.

He imagined himself striding through the house, shoving open the door, marching straight to the edge of the pool—Vince tearing his eyes away from Sue's sleek wet ass and turning to face the intruder, angry until he sees the pistol. Then puzzled and terrified. Raising his arms. Shaking his head. Neal saying, "This is for Elise," and firing. *Blam blam blam blam* fast as he can pull the trigger, the slugs pounding Vince backward through the water.

Yes! Blow the bastard to hell right now and be done with it.

Neal's hand ached from its hard grip on the Sig Sauer.

But his fantasy continued. He saw Vince dead in the pool, all right, floating on his back with his arms out, bloody craters in his face and chest, the water pink around him—and the cry of sirens in the air. Marta and Sue look at him, panic in their eyes.

Oh, God, no. I can't. Not with them here . . . they'd be busted as my accomplices . . .

Out in the sunlight, Sue climbed onto the low board.

Vince gaped at her.

Marta, in the water below the boards, hooked an arm over the side to hold her up. At first, Neal thought she intended to watch Sue's dive. Then he realized she was gazing straight at him.

Could she see him?

He doubted it. But she seemed to have a frowning, anxious look on her face as if she wondered what could be taking him so long.

Why am I just standing here?

He turned away. He didn't bother searching the den, simply scanned it for a grocery sack as he walked by. Then he glanced into the guest bathroom, a couple of closets, and the laundry nook where Elise had washed his filthy clothes on Sunday night.

He remembered standing behind her while she'd removed his clothes from the dryer, the way she'd looked squatting down in her glossy blue pajamas. And how he'd accidentally touched her when she handed over his clothes. He'd apologized, but she'd told him, "I'm all yours, remember? You're free to touch or look to your heart's content."

He felt like crying again.

Elise's presence was everywhere.

So was her absence.

The settings of her life remained, but she was gone. She'd been torn out, demolished in a fury of screaming pain and humiliation and terror, removed forever.

How can she be gone from all this?

It seemed impossible to Neal, and horrible. But he also felt that he might come upon her. As he stepped into her bedroom, he half expected to find her standing in front of her closet. He imagined her whirling around, slightly alarmed for a moment, then pleased. *"Oh, Neal. It's you. Where'd you come from?"*

But it didn't happen.

It never would happen, because she was dead.

He saw nobody in the room but himself—his reflection clear in a mirror above the dresser.

He scanned the sunlit room. The bed was a mess, its covers on the floor, a white terry cloth robe hanging off a corner of the mattress.

It looked like the same robe that Elise had given him to wear after his shower.

Vince's?

Articles of Vince's clothing were scattered about: socks and a pair of briefs on the carpet near the bed, shoes here and there, trousers and a sport shirt thrown across the chair, a cast-off necktie crooked and twisted on the dresser top surrounded by a litter of coins.

Neal saw no grocery bag.

He stepped past the end of the bed and looked out the glass door. Marta, shiny and dripping, sat on the edge of the pool, her legs hanging into the water. Sue, apparently on her feet, glided sideways through chest-high water.

Both of them were facing the house. They had worried looks on their faces.

Neal couldn't see Vince.

He suddenly heard the far-off squeak and rumble of a door sliding open.

His stomach sank. He stood motionless, listening.

The door slid shut. Probably the den door.

Neal waited.

It's Vince.

Probably just came in to make some drinks, that's all. He'll make them and go back outside.

Neal glanced at the bracelet on his wrist.

No. One ride in the mind and body of Vince had been enough for him.

A movement outside caught Neal's eye. Turning his head, he saw Marta, on her feet, reach behind her back with both hands. A moment later, the top of her swimsuit went loose. She removed it. Tossing it to the concrete, she called out, "Hey Vince, come on back here. You . . ."

Neal missed her next words; they were somewhere beneath the noise of the den door being jerked open.

". . . miss my high dive, do you?"

Vince hurried into view. Halting at the edge of the pool, he put his hands on his hips. He seemed to say something to Marta, but Neal couldn't make it out. Marta, striding along the far side on her way toward the diving boards at the deep end, smiled and flapped a hand at him.

My God, Marta.

Look at her, look at her.

Doing this for me.

God, she shouldn't be letting Vince see her this way.

Look at her!

As Neal watched, she began to climb the ladder of the high dive. He could see her through the spaces between the rungs: her fine legs lifting, one at a time; the flap of pale leather angling down from her hips; her bare belly and ribcage and breasts glossy in the sunlight; her shadowed throat, her solemn face, her matted hair the color of wet straw.

Each time one of her arms reached up, the breast beneath it seemed to rise slightly on her chest.

Don't just stand here and stare at her!

Groaning, Neal forced his gaze away from Marta. He glimpsed Sue standing in the water and Vince motionless by the edge of the pool with his head turned toward Marta.

Neal put his back to them.

He dropped to his knees and glanced under the bed.

Nothing but carpet.

Scurrying up, he rushed around the end of the bed. Something as large as the grocery sack wouldn't fit into a dresser drawer. Not unless Vince mashed it flat . . .

What if it's already in the car?

Of course!

Neal was tempted to quit his search of the house and go straight for the garage.

If I'm wrong . . .

I'd better look while I'm here.

But he dreaded entering the main bathroom.

He didn't know if he could *stand* to go in there—to walk on the tiles that had been splattered and puddled with Elise's blood, to step over the place where he'd found her pajamas, to look into the bathtub . . .

There's no point, he told himself. Vince wouldn't hide the bag of money in his bathroom. Nobody would hide a bag of money in a bathroom.

It's in his car. In the trunk of his car. Makes all the sense in the world.

Not in his bathtub, for God's sake.

I'm not going in there.

No way.

But if nobody would ever think to hide a bag of money in a bathroom, then maybe that would be a very good place for hiding it.

I'll have to look. Have to. Just run in very quickly and try not to think about Elise or what Glitt did to her . . .

Did Vince pay him to do that?

Probably just paid him to kill her and make it look like the work of a sadist.

Left the details to Glitt.

Neal doubted that Vince was even capable of imagining such atrocities as Glitt had committed on Elise.

I can't go in there.

Have to.

Not just yet. Pretty soon, but not yet. If the money's in there, it won't go anyplace in the next minute or two. I just need a little time . . .

Neal opened the doors of the bedroom closet and scanned the shelf above the hanger bar. No grocery bag. He tried to ignore the clothes suspended on hangers, not wanting to see the array of outfits that Elise used to wear when she was alive. There were so many. Neal knew without looking that he had never seen her in any of them.

Never would.

Vince's clothes filled the other half of the closet. Neal had no interest in them.

Crouching, he checked the closet floor. He saw rows of shoes and boots and not much else.

Except for something that appeared to be a brown paper grocery sack at the far end, nearly hidden behind a pair of cowboy boots.

Can't be!

Neal rushed to Vince's end of the closet, squatted, shoved the boots aside, reached out and grabbed the crumpled top of the bag. He pulled the bag toward him. It seemed to be nearly full. It felt heavy.

Half a million bucks in here?

Fat chance.

The bag of money was almost certainly in the garage, locked in the trunk of Vince's car. And Neal would almost certainly be unable to break into the trunk. He would have to give up, somehow signal Marta and Sue that it was time to leave . . .

A big fat waste of time.

He pulled open the sack and peered down into murky shadows and saw bundles of money.

YES YES YES! This is it! We're rich!

He crumpled the top shut, picked up the sack and rushed across the bedroom.

Gazing through the glass door, he saw Marta on the high dive. Vince still stood by the side of the pool and Sue was still in the water, both with their heads toward her.

Marta stood at the very end of the board. Hands on her hips, she bent over slightly at the waist and looked down. She shook her head. Then she straightened up and spoke to Vince.

Neal couldn't make out her words.

Sue, smiling up at her, said something. Vince spoke, too. Neal saw their mouths move, but heard only strange murmurs through the closed glass door.

Marta nodded. She took a few steps backward. Then she halted and stood as if at attention, eyes forward, shoulders back, stomach in, arms straight down against her sides, legs together. She took a deep breath. Then she marched to the end of the board, hopped, and came down with both feet—onto the board. It bent and flung her up. She came down onto it again, and again it tossed her upward—but higher than before.

Neal gaped at her.

High above the water, naked except for the jungle-woman flap of hide below her waist, she bounced on the springboard as if it were a trampoline. Her tawny skin gleamed. Her arms, out away from her sides, moved up and down in ways that seemed intended to control her balance. Her knees bent slightly with every landing. Her breasts leaped as if being punched about by an invisible boxer.

Vince and Sue stared up at her. Their mouths hung open.

Neal wondered if others could see her, as well; so high up, she was above the fences and shrubs enclosing the property. Neighbors might be watching her from their pools, from the windows of their houses, from the street.

Look! Up in the sky!

Why doesn't she dive? Neal wondered.

She'll end up falling!

Maybe not, Neal thought. Her bouncing looked a little less reckless than earlier. She was no longer being flung higher and higher with each hop. Now, she seemed to be keeping a steady rhythm and height.

Almost as if she planned to continue for a long time.

Till she knows I'm safe?

She'd stripped off her top to grab Vince's attention, to pull him out of the house. She'd climbed the diving board to keep his eyes glued to her. And now she was holding him at poolside with the spectacle of her leaps, the promise of her dive.

A moment after her splashdown, Vince would return to the house.

Gotta get my ass outta here!

Neal hated to miss the dive.

He watched one more bounce. Then, clutching the sack of money to his chest, he whirled around and rushed for the bedroom door.

Chapter Fifty

Before crossing to the foyer, Neal stopped and peered into the den. Nobody there. Beyond the glass, Vince stood by the pool.

Clapping!

Neal raced to the front door, jerked it open, stepped outside and eased the door shut. He ran up the walkway and through the open gate. The street was empty, shrouded by shadows. He ran to Marta's Jeep and stuffed the paper sack into the narrow storage compartment behind the rear seat.

Now all I've gotta do is get the gals out of there.

Can't signal with the horn.

What should I do, ring Vince's doorbell?

Why not?

Feeling squirmy in his stomach, Neal listened to the chimes ringing inside Vince's house.

What if he doesn't open up?

He'll open. He'll be worried it's the cops. Might even hope it's a couple more luscious babes arriving.

As Neal reached forward to ring the bell again, Vince asked from the other side of the door, "Who is it?"

"I'm here to pick up Tracy and Katt."

Moments later, the door opened. But not all the way. It only opened the width of Vince's shoulders. He stood in the shadowy gap and frowned out at Neal. A towel, draped over one wrist, hung like a rumpled curtain from his belly almost to his knees.

"Are they expecting you?" he asked. He spoke slowly, as if being careful not to slur his words or stumble on them.

"Well," Neal said, "I dropped them off a while ago. They said I should come back in an hour."

"I see. And you are?"

"Ken. Tracy's my kid sister."

Vince tried to smile, but he suddenly looked uneasy. "Ah. I see. You're her brother."

"Yeah. She and Katt came on over to swim with Elise. Are you *Mister* Waters, Elise's husband?"

"I'm Elise's husband," he said. But he didn't say his name or stick out his hand. "Unfortunately, she and the others—Tracy and what?"

"Katt."

"Ah. Yes. You just missed them. They all went off to dinner just a short while ago."

"They did?"

"I'm afraid you just missed them. But you might be able to join them at the restaurant. They were on their way to . . ." Vince frowned and shook his head. "Some Italian place. Let me think." Still shaking his head, he nibbled on his lower lip. "No, I'm frankly not sure. They just decided to take off on the spur of the moment. I'm sorry you missed them."

Neal scowled at Vince. "But they knew I'd be coming over in an hour. I can't believe . . ."

"Elise gets these *whims*. She'll run off at the drop of a hat—usually dragging along a few unsuspecting friends. There's simply no stopping her. But anyhow—be not alarmed. They'll be turning up back here . . . oh, by midnight at the latest."

"*Midnight?*"

"The moment they return, I'll have Elise take them home. Or I'll return them myself. How's that?"

"Not good. We have plans for tonight. Are you sure they aren't here?"

"I'm absolutely, one hundred percent sure they're not here. They've gone out to dinner. At Andre's? You might try Andre's."

"Just tell them I'm here, all right?"

"I can hardly do that. And I resent the implication that I'm being less than truthful. Good-bye, now." He started to shut the door.

Neal rammed the door open. Vince yelped and stumbled backward. As he fell, he flung out his arms. The towel flew. For a moment, he looked like a dancer trying to squeeze himself under the limbo stick. Then his bare back smacked the marble floor. He grunted.

Neal flung the door shut. Pulling the pistol out of his pocket, he rushed to Vince's side. He crouched and jammed the muzzle down hard midway between Vince's nipples.

"Don't say a word," Neal told him.

"Please. Don't hurt me."

"That's four," Neal said.

And whipped the pistol straight up from the center of Vince's chest. It struck him under the chin. His teeth clacked together. His head must've been raised slightly; an instant after his teeth collided, the back of his head *thonked* the floor. His eyes bugged out. Then he squeezed them shut. His entire sweaty red face seemed to be squeezed into furrows of pain. Blood spilled from a gash on the point of his chin.

At the sound of a door sliding open, Neal looked up. Sue leaned into the house. She squinted toward the foyer. "What's goin' on?" she asked.

"It's me," Neal called. "Time to go. Tell Tracy."

She called over her shoulder, "Tracy! Let's get." Then she rushed over the carpet. As she approached the foyer, she slowed down. She stopped beside Vince and stared down at him. "He don't look real good," she said.

His eyes opened. He squinted up at Sue as if staring into painful sunlight.

"Shut your eyes or I'll shut 'em for you," Neal said.

He shut them.

Marta came running into the house. She was gasping for air, dripping. She must've just climbed out of the pool. She still wore only the pants of her swimsuit. The top swung in her hand, flipping and jerking as she hurried through the den.

She stopped beside Sue. Out of breath, she bent over at the waist and clutched her knees. Water spilled down her body, dribbled off her chin and breasts, formed a puddle around her feet. "Jesus," she gasped. "What happened to him?"

"I did," Neal muttered. "Come on, let's get out of here."

Sue started to say, "Did ya find . . . ?"

Neal guessed what was coming. He didn't want Vince to hear it.

The blow from the gun opened Vince's cheek and knocked his head sideways. He went limp.

"I found it," Neal said. "It's in the car."

"I guess he's . . . out cold," Marta said, still bent over and breathing hard. "First time I've ever . . . seen him . . . without a hard-on."

"He's a real ladies man," Neal said. "He had big plans for you two."

"We oughta get," Sue said, "or else he's gonna come to and you'll have to whack him again."

"You ready?" Neal asked Marta.

She gave him a quick grin. Her swimsuit top had fallen to the floor. She dipped down and snatched it up. Standing straight, she slipped her arms into the straps, cupped her breasts in the soggy hide, and reached behind her back. A few seconds later, she said, "All set."

Neal opened the door. He watched Vince while the women rushed out.

No sign that the guy was regaining his senses.

Neal waited until Marta and Sue reached the road. Then he backed out of the house and pulled the door shut. He shoved the pistol into his pocket and ran.

At the gate, he glanced back. The front door was still shut.

Marta and Sue were already climbing into the Jeep. Neal fished the keys out of his pocket, then raced for the Jeep like a sprinter, the keys jangling. Marta turned in the driver's seat. She stretched out an arm. He slapped the keys into her hand. As he vaulted the side, the engine grumbled to life.

The Jeep lurched forward and picked up speed.

Neal gazed down the road behind them.

No sign of Vince.

Moments later, they swept around a bend and there was no more reason to watch the rear.

"I believe we made it," Neal said.

Marta turned her head. "Do you think he'll call the police on us?"

"No way. Cops are about the *last* thing he wants to see. He's terrified they'll show up and arrest him."

"So he *was* involved?" Marta asked.

"Sure was. He hired Glitt to do the murder, just like we figured."

Sue grinned over her shoulder. "Wait'll he finds out his money's gone. Ya *did* get it, right?"

In answer, Neal reached down into the storage space behind his seat. He gripped the bag by its crumpled top and lifted it into sight.

"All *right!*"

Marta glanced back. "Hope you looked inside."

"Oh, I did. Chock full of cash."

"Where was it?" she asked.

"In his bedroom closet. I found it while you were doing your high-dive act. Which, by the way, was spectacular."

"You watched?"

"Some of it."

She made a face as if she'd tasted something bad. "Terrific," she muttered. "You weren't supposed to see that."

"It was great," Neal said.

"It was humiliating. I only did it . . ."

"I know why you did it."

She scowled. "You were supposed to be looking for the money."

"I know."

"Y'oughta be flattered," Sue told her.

"I couldn't help myself," Neal said. "You were a sight to behold."

"Terrific. Glad you appreciated it. I just wish you hadn't watched, that's all. It made me feel . . . like a slut or something, doing that for a slimy creep like him. Not to mention, I thought I'd end up breaking my neck. That board was so damn high . . . I could see the top of his *roof*. I kept jumping up and down, and I'm thinking any second you'll honk the horn so I can quit. I'm praying it honks before I slip and fall and kill myself. But you're apparently at a window enjoying the show . . ."

"The horn doesn't work," Neal explained.

"What?"

"I tried it. It doesn't work."

Marta beeped the horn.

"That's odd," Neal said. "It didn't work when *I* tried it."

"Did you have the ignition on?" she asked.

"No."

"That's why."

"You're kidding."

"Nope. The horn's like the radio. Won't work when the car's shut off."

"That's stupid."

Looking back at him, Sue said, "Reckon ya had to ring the doorbell and conk the daylights outta Vince, all 'cause ya didn't know how to work the car horn."

"I guess so."

"Haw! What a hoot!"

"I thought you knew that about the horn," Marta told him. "Why do you think I left the key in the ignition?"

"I needed to turn it?"

"Yeah. Like for the radio."

"Well . . ." Neal shook his head.

"You'll be danged," Sue supplied for him.

He laughed.

Staying off main roads as much as possible, Marta picked turns at random. They made their way slowly, sometimes taking out-of-the-way detours, but generally moving closer to her apartment building.

Even most of the side streets were thick with traffic.

Guys in nearby cars stared at Marta and Sue. Some hooted, whistled, called out remarks and offers. Marta ignored them. Not Sue. She smiled at some of the guys. Waved at others. But then a laughing teen with friends in the bed of a pickup truck curled one hand into an O and poked his finger in and out of it. "Ain't that charmin," Sue muttered, and flipped her finger at him.

"Jesus H. Christ!" Marta blurted. She swung out a hand and smacked Sue's upper arm. "Don't do that! You're in L.A., for God's sake. You'll get us killed."

"Ya see what he done?"

"It doesn't *matter* what he did." Marta swerved to a curb and stopped the car.

Neal watched the pickup truck continue on up the road.

Marta faced Sue.

"Ya gonna kick me out?" Sue asked.

"No, of course not. Just don't do anything like that again. It doesn't matter *what* someone does, just ignore it from now on. Okay?"

"Well . . ."

"Marta's right," Neal said. "The city's full of nutcases who are just *looking* for a reason to blast you."

"Me?"

"Anyone."

"So the last thing you want to do," Marta said, "is antagonize a stranger."

"You know," Neal said, "it'd probably help the situation if you both put your shirts back on."

"We're sitting on them," Marta told him.

"Had to leave in a hurry," Sue added.

"We're stopped now," Neal pointed out.

Sue grinned at Marta. "He just don't want all the other fellas getting a load of us."

"Selfish bastard," Marta said.

They both laughed.

"Comedians," Neal said.

Still laughing, they unlatched their seatbelts, squirmed, shifted, scooted upward, and managed to tug their shirts out from under their rumps. Then they leaned forward and put them on.

"Thank you, ladies."

"Yer welcome," they said in unison.

During the remainder of the drive, there were no more shouts or whistles, hoots or remarks or obscene gestures. But the guys in nearby cars still turned their heads and stared.

Chapter Fifty-one

Neal placed the sack of money on top of the coffee table in Marta's living room. Then they stared at it for a while, sometimes glancing at each other.

"Should we look at it?" Marta asked.

"It's ours," Neal said.

"Can ya'll hang on till I take a leak?" Sue asked.

"No hurry," Neal told her.

"None at all," Marta said. "In fact, why don't we call an official time-out for five or ten minutes? I want to get out of this wet suit, myself. Soon as I'm into some dry clothes, I'll make a batch of margaritas. We can have a little party and count the take."

"My kind of gal," Neal said.

Sue glanced at him.

He wasn't sure what to make of the look, but he said, "You, too."

Sue and Marta looked at each other as if they shared an amusing secret.

"What?" Neal asked.

"It's just . . . ya don't gotta do that."

"What?"

"All that 'you, too' stuff."

"And all that 'both of you' stuff," Marta added.

"It's kinda silly."

"I'm just trying to be nice."

"Ya don't gotta be *that* nice."

"We aren't going to flip out if we don't receive equal treatment."

"Right," Sue said. "I ain't . . . I'm not jealous of Marta, and she's not jealous of me."

"We've got an understanding," Marta said.

They grinned at each other.

Then they headed off together.

Neal felt strange: relieved but curious, and a bit as if he were the odd man out. He realized that he'd been feeling that way, off and on, ever since Marta and Sue had first encountered each other.

No, not from the very first.

It had started after Sue's confession that she'd gone into Marta with the bracelet; to prove the bracelet worked, she'd taken Marta out of the room and revealed a couple things. Secrets that Marta had supposedly been keeping from Neal.

What the hell sort of secrets?

Can't be anything really major, he told himself.

But the gals hadn't been the same, since. They'd developed a bond of some kind.

Neal wished he could be in on it.

Just be thankful they haven't turned into raving, jealous dogs.

Lucky thing.

It isn't luck, it's a miracle.

Marta and Sue sat on the sofa. They had both changed out of their swimsuits: Marta into a white, oversized T-shirt and Sue into her white pleated miniskirt and yellow knit pullover. They were both barefoot. They sat close together, their knees at the edge of the coffee table. Each held a margarita, but hadn't taken a drink yet. The salt was thick and white around the rims of their glasses.

Before sitting down, they had cleared off the table. Now there was nothing on it except Neal's drink, down near the end in front of Marta.

Neal stood across the table from the women, holding the grocery sack. "Ready?" he asked.

"Let 'er rip," Sue said.

He leaned over and upended the sack.

The money spilled out. Bundles of bills, bound by rubber bands, dropped from the ragged mouth of the bag and tumbled toward the table. Thick stacks and thin stacks, they cascaded out and fell, flopped onto the table, whapped the wood surface like notepads tossed onto a desk, thumped it like paperback books.

After a few seconds, they no longer pounded wood; they landed instead on stacks and bundles of money, hitting with softer sounds. The final few packs, after hitting, slid silently down the gray and green slopes.

When the sack was nearly weightless, forty or fifty loose bills floated out and drifted toward the heap. A broken rubber band fell out. And then a foot-long, curled strip of white paper with rows of blue ink.

As it slid down the slope of money, Neal caught it. He stretched it taut between his hands and looked at it.

"A grocery receipt?" Marta said.

He nodded. The receipt was dated July 6, 1995. Only a few days before Elise's death. The purchases were itemized.

Neal didn't want to know what she'd bought. Bad enough to be reminded of her, still alive, pushing a grocery cart down a supermarket aisle . . . Alka-Seltzer. She'd bought Alka-Seltzer.

Memories rushed into him.

Elise in her blue satin pajamas.

The feel of the foil packet in her shirt pocket.

The way he'd felt breathless while she was gulping down a glassful of the fizzing medication.

How she had been, that first time, when she'd let him come over from the sofa and enter her. How nervous she'd felt, and embarrassed, and excited. She had never allowed anyone to do that before. Neal had been the first. And the only.

"Y'okay?" Sue asked.

She and Marta were both staring at him.

He shook his head. Crunching the receipt in his hand, he said, "It made me think about Elise, that's all."

"Well, don't go and get sad on us. We're trying to have a party, here."

Marta, looking solemn, gestured with her glass and said, "We should drink to her."

"A toast," Sue said. "Neat idea."

Neal stepped to the end of the table, picked up his margarita, and returned to the middle. Across the table from him, Marta and Sue got to their feet.

"To Elise," he said. "I wish they hadn't killed you. But since they did . . ." He struggled to keep control. "Wherever you are— I hope to God you're up in heaven if there is such a place— may you be looking down on us with a smile tonight." Voice trembling, he said, "I couldn't save you. I let them kill you, but . . . we're making them pay . . ." He swallowed hard. "They'll pay big for what they did to you."

"Big time," Sue muttered.

Marta nodded. "Big time."

"This is the first installment," Neal said. "This is where they paid in green. The next installment, it'll be in red."

"Fuckin A," Sue said.

Neal stretched his arm out. As he held his margarita glass above the money pile, Marta and Sue both reached forward and clinked their glasses against his. Crumbs of salt, knocked off, sprinkled down on the cash.

"That's sure a heap of money," Sue said.

Nodding, Neal held his glass steady while Marta refilled it from the blender's pitcher.

"Five hundred thousand dollars," Marta said. Done pouring, she headed for the kitchen.

"I wonder if it's all there," Neal said.

"Do we want to count it?" Marta asked over her shoulder.

Sue frowned at the pile of cash. "It'd take us halfway till Christmas to count all that."

Neal set his glass on the table and picked up one of the bundles. It was about an inch thick. He flipped through it with his thumb. "This one's all twenties," he said. He tossed it onto the pile and picked up another. "Fifties."

Sue, inspecting a bundle, said, "This one's only tens."

"Glitt must've wanted some denominations that'd be easy to spend."

Sue delved into the pile, spreading the stacks around as if she were looking for a dark sock in a load of laundry. After a while, she said, "Well, a lot of 'em's hundreds."

Marta came into the living room, a platter of tortilla chips in one hand, a bowl of salsa in the other. "So, have you got it all counted yet?"

"Has hell froze over yet?" Sue asked her.

Marta set down the snacks at the far end of the table. "I don't see any big reason to count it. If it's actually the payoff money . . ." She looked at Neal and raised her eyebrows.

"It almost *has* to be," he said.

"How do you know for sure?"

Neal set down his drink. "First off, I saw Glitt's face in his mind." He crossed the room and grabbed a straight-backed chair. As he carried it toward the table, he said, "That was right at the start of things, when you two were at the bar and Vince was making the drinks. He'd just told about Elise being murdered." Neal placed his chair near the chips and salsa, and sat down. "One of you . . . Sue . . . asked who'd killed her. When he said he didn't know, his mind flashed a picture of Glitt."

"Fantastic," Marta said. She dipped a chip, poked it into her mouth, then passed the chips to Sue.

Sue pulled out a handful.

"Salsa?" Marta asked.

Sue shook her head and asked Neal, "How'd ya find out about the money?"

"That movie you asked him about."

"Haw! Thought so!"

"The million-dollar payoff in a parking lot. Chuck Norris."

Sue beamed.

"It was *inspired*," Marta told her. "And so subtle!"

Narrowing her eyes, Sue nodded. "Did ya catch on how I

changed it to a *whole* million. Tricky, huh? Didn't wanna make him suspicious."

Neal and Marta burst out laughing. Sue watched them laugh. She looked quite pleased with herself. She took a sip of her margarita, then raised the handful of tortilla chips to her mouth and grabbed a chip with her teeth. She chewed, watching them laugh. After swallowing, she said, "Just call me a genius."

A little while later, Marta asked, "What movie *was* that, anyway?"

"Made it up."

"Thought so."

"It sure worked," Neal said. "It made him start thinking about the payoff." To Marta, he said, "You know how people imagine things? It's like a mental movie?"

"Sure," she nodded. "Daydreams and things."

"Right. Well, I got to see *his*. I saw him park his car at Video City and take out a grocery sack. He was planning to leave it there for Glitt." Neal nodded at the pile on the table. "So I went hunting through his house for a bag of money."

"Did ya find it in his safe?" Sue asked.

"He doesn't have a safe."

"Huh?" She looked as if she'd been cheated. "Yer kiddin'."

"No safe."

"Crippled Judas! After I got him to think all about his combination?"

"You *might've*, if he'd had one. It was an admirable attempt."

"*I'm* so safe," Marta said, "she'd like to hide her jewelry in me."

Sue smirked at her. "Up yer kazoo."

"A hell of a show," Neal said.

Grinning and shaking her head, Marta told Sue, "That *was* a terrific story about breaking into your father's liquor cabinet. Nine years old?"

"Brilliant," Neal said. "Vince might've pondered every turn and number of his combination lock—I could've run straight to his safe and opened it up slick as a whistle. No doubt about it."

"That's how I had it figured," Sue said. She shrugged. "Ain't my fault if he didn't have a safe."

"You're amazing," Marta told her.

"Well . . . thanks. Sometimes I'm more amazing than at other times. You ain't a slouch, yerself."

"Thank you."

Sue nodded and took a drink. Then she frowned. "The tricky part was how I worked the combination lock into the story. That's what took the genius. 'Cause there weren't no combination lock on that cabinet where he kept his booze. It took a key Daddy wore on a chain. He wore it around his neck, there with his little gold cross that he always wore on account of he worried about vampires. So I had to sneak the necklace off him that night while he was snoozing."

Marta and Neal stared at her.

"What?" Sue asked.

"It was a *true* story?" Neal asked.

"Not the part about the combination. All the rest, though, yeah, I reckon it was."

"Sounds like you've had an interesting life," Marta said.

"Mostly not," Sue told her. "I reckon I've had some adventures, but they mostly been bad things. The best stuff, it's all happened since I run into Neal. Minute I laid eyes on him, I knew he was the fella I been waitin' for. I figured to head off with him, if he'd take me. I fell in love, that's the thing. Never figured on gettin' messed up with a magic bracelet or a murder— or heistin' half a million bucks. Or meetin' you, either, Marta. It's all been pretty wild."

"I'm glad things turned out this way," Marta said. "I was a little upset at first, but . . ."

"To know me is to love me. Ain't that right, Neal?"

"You're modest, too," he said.

"Anyhow," Sue continued, "I just feel like the luckiest girl ever was, fallin' in with you two desperados." She hoisted her glass and drank.

"You can afford your own Jeep, now," Neal told her.

"You want a Jeep?" Marta asked.

Sue lowered her glass. "Yup. A Jeep Cherokee. Leastwise, I *did* want one. I'm not so sure, anymore."

"What do you mean?" Neal asked, dismayed. "That was your

dream. To have a brand-new four-wheel drive Jeep Cherokee and drive all over the country, seeing all the sights, stopping to visit with strangers . . . Now you don't *want* to anymore? Now that you're rich? Now that you're free to really *do* it?"

Marta frowned. "If we split the take three ways," she said, "you'll end up with more than a hundred and fifty thousand dollars. You could buy a *ton* of Jeeps."

"Well, I'd only need one."

"What's the problem?" Neal asked.

With a sad look on her face, Sue said, "I don't wanna go off and break up the team. I mean . . . ya know? I'd like the three of us to stick together. If I went off by myself—or even with just you, Neal—I'd feel like a part's not there."

"Yeah, me," Marta said, and tried to smile. But her smile faltered. "You can't leave *me* behind, for God's sake."

"Wouldn't think of it," Neal told her.

"No way," Sue said. "Ain't no way in tarnation we'd leave *you* behind."

"I should hope not. After all, I'm the one who's pregnant around here."

Chapter Fifty-two

Neal gazed at her, stunned.

Marta stared at him over the top of her glass. "Let's just say I *might* be."

"You *might be pregnant?*" Neal asked.

"That's one of her two big secrets," Sue explained, grinning like an imp.

"What's the other?" Neal asked.

"Still a secret," Sue said.

Marta set down her glass. "It's not definite yet. I shouldn't even have mentioned it, but . . . I'm pretty late, and . . ."

"We're gonna buy one of them home pregnancy tests tomorrow," Sue said.

Marta gave her an uneasy look. "I shouldn't have said anything till we'd made sure."

"It don't matter. I betcha a thousand bucks yer knocked up. *Ten* thousand—there for a second, I forgot I'm rich."

Neal tried to think of something to say. Finally, he managed to ask Marta, "You really think . . . ?"

"I'm pretty sure."

"Not only that," Sue said, "but Marta figures it's at least fifty-fifty odds that yer the father."

"Sue!" Marta blurted, and laughed. To Neal she said, "If I am, you are."

"Good thing."

"You're the only one—"

". . . she'll admit to."

They both looked at Sue.

"Okay. Okay. Sorry." She held up her hands. "I'll butt out. Fact is, I oughta get outta here for a while and give you two some privacy." She set her empty glass on the table, then stood up. "I'll just take me a little walk and come back in maybe an hour."

"You don't have to," Marta said.

"Yeah, that's okay." Sue gave them a wave as she headed for the front door.

"You don't have to go," Marta said again. "Really."

Hand on the doorknob, Sue looked back. "You two gotta have a while . . ."

"Don't," Marta said. "Just stay here. Please. I don't want you going outside . . . not alone. Not until all this is over. You tell her, Neal."

"It might not be safe," he said. "You'd better not—"

"I don't wanna be in the way."

Probably better if you *are*, Neal thought. He wasn't so sure that he looked forward to being alone with Marta just now. What would they talk about? The future? Commitments? And what if she wasn't completely happy about the situation?

Neal wanted a baby. He supposed that he'd always hoped to become a father, someday. But this seemed like a very odd and inconvenient time to spring such a thing on him.

If we can just put it off till after Glitt and Vince . . .

"You won't be in the way," Marta told Sue.

"Glitt's out there someplace," Neal said.

Sue smiled slightly. "Where do ya think he was when I went to the mall this afternoon?"

"Sue!" Marta snapped. "Please!"

"Y'oughta be alone together." With that, she swung open the door.

Marta lurched to her feet and rushed at her, blurting, "I mean it! Damn it! Don't go out! I'm not letting you go out there and get yourself killed."

Neal stood up. But he stayed put, uncertain what to do.

Sue, turning to face Marta, raised both hands and shook her head. "Okay, okay! Whoa! Calm down!"

Marta halted, put an arm out to bar Sue's way, and pushed the door shut. She fastened the dead bolt. Then she leaned back against the door. She was breathing fast. Her eyes looked a little frantic. "I'm sorry," she gasped. "I just . . . I'm sorry. Everything's . . . I'm a little scared, okay? Everything's . . . going too well." She glanced toward Neal, then back at Sue. "You know? We put over such a big one on that prick Conrad. We're suddenly rich. I mean, it's a ton of money. And I'm probably going to have your baby, Neal. We'll have a little boy or girl. We'll be a family. And there's *us*. The three of us. We're all . . . we make a great team, like you said, Sue. The three of us. So the thing is, I just can't stand the idea that it might all suddenly go down the tubes. I want us to stay together and be safe." Her mouth twisted crooked and tears shimmered in her eyes. "Okay?"

"Okay," Sue said.

"We'll be fine if we stick together." Her wet eyes swung to Neal. "You know?"

"I know," he muttered through a tightness in his throat.

"You know?" she asked Sue.

"I know."

"If something happened to either of you . . . it'd kill me."

Sue went to her. She pressed her face against the white of Marta's T-shirt, just below the shoulder. Marta's arms went around her.

They held each other and wept.

Neal watched. He was glad Marta had talked Sue into staying, but the closeness between them bothered him more than ever.

What's going on? What about me?

He glanced down at the gold serpent wrapped around his left wrist.

No. I won't. Not with them. They can have their secrets.

I don't want to know.

Can't invade them. It'd be wrong, and I won't do it, no matter what.

"Neal," Marta said.

Mouth against the white of Marta's T-shirt, Sue said, "Get yerself over here, hon."

"Me?" he asked.

"Yeah, you," Marta said.

"Okay," he said.

As he neared them, Marta met his eyes. She opened her arms and reached out beyond Sue, stretching both arms toward Neal. He moved in gently against Sue's back. He felt the heat of her body through her knit top. He felt the curves of her back, the firm mounds of her buttocks.

Marta's hands caressed his sides. Reaching past Sue, he put his hands on Marta's hips. He slid them upward, feeling her smoothness through her T-shirt.

He pushed his face into the soft warmth of Sue's hair.

Reaching behind herself, Sue curled her hands around the backs of Neal's thighs. Her hands roamed higher and clutched his buttocks.

He kissed the nape of her neck. The hair tickled his face. Close to her neck, it felt moist.

"I feel like the meat on a sandwich," Sue murmured.

"The meat's the lucky part," Marta said. "You get to have us on both sides."

"Reckon so." Sue squirmed, rubbing herself against them. "Only thing is, ya godda unwrap me."

Neal noticed that nobody was crying anymore.

He fingered the bottom of Sue's knit pullover. It was partly tucked into the waist of her skirt. He plucked it loose, then lifted it. She raised her arms. He slid her shirt all the way up and off.

Instead of lowering her arms, she kept them high and eased them forward against the door. Elbows straight, she pressed her open hands against the wood some distance above Marta's shoulders. She tilted back her head. Marta's face angled down toward her.

It occurred to Neal that they were kissing.

It also occurred to him that it seemed like a perfectly fine idea, and he wondered vaguely why he didn't feel shocked or offended or jealous.

Pressed to Sue's back, he glided his hands from the waist of her skirt up her naked sides. When he felt her rib cage, he slid his hands forward and cupped her breasts—soft, smooth hills, springy, with rigid nipples that thrust against his palms.

Curving his hands over the tops of Sue's breasts, he met the soft undersides of Marta's breasts.

She still had her T-shirt on, but no bra. Neal had known all along that she'd put on nothing except the T-shirt after coming back from Vince's. No bra and no panties. It had been obvious from the way the T-shirt draped her body.

Pushing upward, he lifted her breasts. They were heavy against the backs of his open hands. He moved his hands to the front, still lifting. He felt her nipples rub against his knuckles. Spreading his fingers, he trapped the stiff juts of flesh. He squeezed them through the T-shirt. Marta let out a shuddery breath.

Moments later, Sue's hands came up from somewhere below. They collided with Neal's hands, knocking them away from Marta's breasts. He thought she'd done it to interfere. Then he realized she was lifting Marta's shirt. He helped. Marta raised her arms. Neal pulled the shirt off them and flung it aside.

Now she was entirely naked, Sue in nothing except her pleated white miniskirt.

Both women seemed to become aware, at the same moment, that Neal remained fully clothed. Marta, reaching past Sue's bare sides, plucked out his shirttails. Sue, still pressed against Marta, reached behind her own back and unfastened Neal's belt.

An awkward way to go about things.

Neal almost suggested that they break up their sandwich and move to the bedroom.

Are you nuts? Keep your mouth shut—you could ruin the whole deal. Interrupt a thing like this, might be the end of it. Somebody gets a case of the guilts . . .

And you might never get a chance like this again.

Don't blow it.

He said nothing. He helped by taking off his own shirt. While Marta caressed him, Sue worked on his shorts. He let Sue open them and pull them down his thighs, along with his briefs.

A hand encircled his penis.

He didn't know whose hand.

It glided lightly up and down.

At the same time the mystery hand went away, Sue used the heel of one foot to shove Neal's pants the rest of the way down to his ankles. He stepped out of them and used his own feet to pry his shoes off.

Then he slid his hands up Sue's legs and under her pleated skirt.

She wore nothing under there.

Neal was not surprised, but he was very pleased. He curled his hands around the fronts of her thighs. As he brought them slowly upward, someone removed Sue's skirt. It stopped brushing against the backs of his hands.

He was vaguely aware of Marta and Sue clutching and exploring each other, kissing and moaning.

A hand that he thought might belong to Marta squeezed one of his buttocks, fingertips digging at his crack.

He squirmed, rubbing himself against Sue's sweaty back. He slipped fingers into her. She gasped. She writhed on his hand. Soon, she was thrashing about, making whimpery sounds. And so was Marta. Neal didn't know what was being done to Marta, or who was doing it, but she seemed as frantic as Sue.

Someone took his hand.

It was pulled forward, leaving Sue, and lifted and shoved up between Marta's legs. She let out a cry. Not a cry of pain, but of surprise and delight.

Sue must've been the one who'd moved his hand.

Nice of her to share.

With his other hand, he went for Sue's left breast. But a hand was already there, so he found his way above it and took hold of Marta's breast.

One of Sue's hands reached around behind her back. Reached for Neal and found him.

Marta, writhing frantically, blurted, "Stop it! Stop it! Let go! Everyone . . . let go."

She shoved his hand away.

Sue stopped moving.

"What?" Neal gasped.

"Let go. Everybody . . . let go. Step back."

Knew this was too good to last.

Sue let go of him. He took a couple of steps backward. The air felt cool against his sweaty skin where he'd been pressed against Sue. His penis stood erect, so hard and straining that it seemed ready to explode. His right hand hung by his side, dripping.

Sue freed herself from Marta and stepped backward slowly. Her hair was matted against her head with sweat. Her back gleamed.

Neal moved to the side so he could see past Sue. Marta stood with her back to the door, arms raised and legs apart. Strands of wet hair clung to her face. She was panting for air. Her skin dripped.

"Y'okay?" Sue asked her.

Marta nodded, her mouth hanging open. "Neal," she gasped. "You want . . . one of us?"

Breathless, he nodded.

"Shoot, I reckon he wants . . . the *both* of us."

"I reckon you're right," Marta said.

"Right," Neal said.

"Can't have us both."

Oh, shit! Here it comes! I knew this was too good to . . .

Marta's eyes went to Sue. "Your turn," she said.

"Ya sure *you* don't wanna go first?"

"Come here, honey," Marta said to Neal.

He went to her. She pulled him tight against her hot, sweaty body. Hands roaming up and down his back, she kissed him. Her tongue pushed into his mouth. She squirmed, sliding herself against him.

And suddenly she wrestled him.

Shoved him and turned him around and wrapped her arms around his chest and hugged him tight. He felt her strong embrace, her breath on the side of his neck, the push of her breasts against his back, the tickle of her pubic thatch against his rump.

"Come and get it, honey," she said to Sue.

A grin spread across Sue's face.

She had to jump.

Neal caught her. Hands cupping her slick buttocks, he lifted her. He eased her down onto him. He did it very slowly, and watched. As he felt himself slide into Sue's hugging tightness, he saw his penis vanish.

Marta stopped hugging Neal's chest. Reaching out, she clutched Sue by the sides, just beneath the armpits.

Sue came forward. Breasts pushing against Neal's chest, she kissed Marta over his shoulder. Then she kissed him. Then Marta nibbled his ear.

Then it all became a little wild.

Everybody groped and panted and squirmed. While he thrust, buried in Sue, Marta rammed her pelvis against his ass. He had Sue's tongue in his mouth. Later, he had her breast in his mouth while he held her high and she kissed Marta and then the breast popped out when he brought her down and then he rammed her down onto him and he plunged up high into her and she cried out and shuddered.

At some point, they fell. They landed on the carpet in front of the door, Neal still embedded in Sue, and Marta must've been on all fours behind him while he continued. She made him squirm and wiggle. He came so hard that he thought he might never be able to move again.

For a long time, they all lay sprawled on the floor.

The carpet felt scratchy under Neal. The room was nearly dark. A soft breeze blew in, stirring the curtains, drifting like fingertips over his hot, wet skin.

                     *   *   *

He was almost asleep when something brushed against his lips.
He opened his eyes. In the murky light, he saw a breast looming
down in front of his eyes. It was too large to be Sue's. It swung
slowly from side to side, its nipple grazing across his lips.

   His penis, limp against his thigh, began to rise.

   It rose into a moist, round hole with a tongue inside.

   He sucked Marta's nipple into his mouth.

   At the other end of him, Sue sucked.

   Neal couldn't believe it.

   "What are you doing?" he asked after a while.

   "We're having our way with you," Marta said.

   "How's it so far?" Sue asked.

   "Not bad."

Chapter Fifty-three

When Neal woke up, the bedroom was dark. The curtain above
him drifted up and wavered, letting in moonlight and a breeze.
The breeze roamed over his skin. It was mildly cool, and felt
wonderful.

   Someone's arm lay across his chest.

   His head was elevated as if resting on a high, firm pillow. A
hard knob pressed against the back of his neck. A hip bone?

   Turning his head, he felt skin against the side of his face.
Inches from his eyes was a tangle of moonlit, silvery hair. Beyond the hair was empty space, thighs on both sides. This close
up, the thighs looked like huge, snow-covered slopes stretching
off into the distance. But maybe darker than snow. Maybe sand
dunes washed in moonlight.

   They seemed to end at the knees.

   That was where the mattress ended.

   She was lying crosswise, her legs—knees to toes—hanging off
the bed.

   Fingers fiddled with Neal's hair.

"You awake?" Marta's voice, a familiar whisper.

"Yeah."

"Hi."

"Hi."

"This is nice."

"Yeah."

The arm across his chest glided downward. Its open hand patted him a few times, stroked his hip, caressed his belly, slid lower and squeezed him.

Neal looked down at his own body. The hand belonged to Sue.

She lay on her back beside him, a dim shape, darker than the white sheet. She looked as if she might still be asleep—motionless, feet apart, her left hand curled on her belly, her right arm angled out and resting on Neal.

But she had to be awake, or her hand wouldn't be doing that to him.

He raised his head for a better look at her.

Sue's face was just above Marta's shoulder, the top of her head touching the left side of Marta's face.

What if they were connected that way? Neal thought. Like Siamese twins, joined at the head.

The notion made him smile.

I wouldn't have to worry about being one guy in love with two women—there'd only be one of her. One fabulous creature.

I'd need a name for it.

The Marta-Sue?

How about the Two-she?

He laughed.

The Two-she came apart, Sue turning her head to look at him and Marta lifting her head off the mattress. Sue's hand released him.

She made a *"Mmmm?"* sound.

"Nothing," Neal whispered. "The way your heads were together like that, I thought for a second you might be a Two-she."

Marta laughed.

"A tushy?" Sue asked.

Marta laughed harder.

"A *Two-she*," Neal said. He lowered his head onto Marta. Her laughter made it bounce. Grinning, he gazed at the ceiling. "A tushy is something altogether different."

At that, Sue cracked up.

They were both laughing like a couple of nuts.

Neal felt as if he had a trampoline under his head.

When the bouncing stopped, Marta took a deep breath and sighed. She said, "So what *is* a Two-she?"

Sue laughed some more.

"A fabulous mythological creature," Neal explained. "Two gorgeous Greek goddesses, joined at the head."

"With *two* tushies," Sue said.

The bouncing resumed.

Afraid he might get a headache, Neal sat up. He turned around and knelt on the mattress. Marta and Sue, still laughing, stayed where they were, their heads together, their bodies stretched out at right angles to each other.

"Two tushies, two pussies, two everything," Neal said.

"Four titties," Sue corrected him.

"This is certainly taking a turn for the vulgar," Marta commented.

"Yeah, Sue, watch your language."

"You watch yers, fella!"

"Children, children," Marta said.

Neal dived for Marta. Even before he got to her, she cried out, "No!" and started to bring her knees up. Then she squealed as he shoved his wide-open mouth against her belly and blew hard. Joining her squeal was a loud, fartlike blast.

"Gross!" Sue yelled. "Who cut one?"

Marta shoved Neal. His mouth broke away from her belly with a noisy, squelching suck. As he teetered on his knees, Sue attacked him from the side. He landed on his back, knees in the air, his head and shoulders hanging off the end of the mattress. Sue climbed onto him.

She seemed to be trying to say something, but she was laughing too hard to speak.

Neal wanted to warn her that he was slipping off the mattress.

He couldn't talk, either.

She bounced on him.

The slipping continued.

"Hey," he gasped.

"Hey, hey!" Sue bounced on him, her rump slapping his belly.

"Hey!" Marta blurted.

Neal's feet flew up.

And were grabbed at the ankles by two hands. Grabbed and tugged. As he was jerked back from the rim of the mattress, Sue almost tumbled off him. He reached up fast and caught her around the waist. She stayed aboard.

Then they were both sprawled on their backs, gasping and laughing. Marta, the rescuer, knelt between them, down near their feet. She had her hands on her hips. She was shaking her head.

"This is what happens," she said, "when people get carried away. You could've broken your necks."

Sue reached out and slapped Neal's chest. "Look at her, she's already actin' like a mother and she ain't even had the baby yet."

"Mama Marta," Neal said.

Marta waded in on her knees and shoved Sue off the side of the bed. As Sue yelped and thudded, Marta turned to Neal.

"Hey!" he gasped. "I give! Spare me! I'm the father of your child!"

"Tough tacos," she said. Kneeing and shoving him, she rolled Neal off the mattress.

He hit the floor.

He heard Sue gasping and laughing from the floor on the other side of the bed.

"Now," Marta said from above, "everybody calm down before you get me evicted."

"We've got half a million dollars," Neal pointed out from the floor.

"Smackeroonies," Sue added from her distant section of floor.

"That's no reason to get carried away," Marta explained.

"Seems like a plenty fine reason to me," Sue said.

"Can we come back up?" Neal asked. "It's lonely down here. And the floor's hard."

"Okay, but no more rough-housing."

"Rough-housing?" Sue said.

"You're right, Sue," Neal called. "She's turning into a mother before our very eyes."

"Eat me," said Marta.

They lay on the bed, side by side, Marta in the middle. It had taken a while to stop laughing and calm down. Though Neal was no longer breathless, his body still ran with sweat. The breeze from the window felt wonderful.

"Ya know what?" Sue asked from the other side of Marta.

"What?" Marta asked.

"This is . . . it's just the greatest."

"Yeah," Marta said.

"Yeah," Neal said. "My God."

"I never had nobody like you two," Sue said. "Ya know? It's . . . I love ya so much it hurts."

"Yeah," Marta said. "It hurts, but it sure feels good."

"And we won't never split up," Sue said.

"Not if I have anything to say about it," Marta whispered.

"How 'bout you, Neal?" Sue asked.

"I'm the luckiest guy in the world," he said.

Marta squeezed his hand. "You damn bet you are. You were the luckiest guy when all you had was me. Now you've got *both* of us, a baby on the way, *and* half a million bucks."

"And Vince *don't.*"

"Doesn't," Neal corrected.

"All he's got is the shaft," Marta said.

"Reckon he's the *unluckiest* guy in the world."

"Unless," Neal said, "he can come up with another half a million before two o'clock."

"How would he do that?" Marta asked.

"How did he get the *first?*"

"We only stole it from him a few hours ago," Marta pointed out. "He hasn't had time to replace it. The banks would've all been closed . . ."

"Maybe he has a wealthy friend with a safe full of cash. Maybe *he* has a safe full of cash. Just because he didn't think about it while I was in his head . . ."

"I doubt it," Marta said. "I think we've *got* his money. And I think there's gonna be a very pissed-off Leslie Glitt when two o'clock rolls around."

Sue sat up. Twisting sideways, she braced herself on a stiff arm and looked over her shoulder at the clock. "It's twelve after twelve," she announced.

"I don't think Vince is planning to show up before one," Neal said.

"If he shows up at all," Marta said. "Which I wouldn't, if I were in his shoes."

"He'll probably show up and drop off *something*," Neal said.

"An apology?" Marta asked.

"Maybe an IOU."

"If I was ol' Vince," Sue said, "I'd put a bomb in a sack and blow Glitt to smithereens."

"I'd love to see that," Neal said.

"When we gonna go?" Sue asked. Not waiting for an answer, she said, "We don't wanna miss nothing. Maybe we oughta get goin' right now."

"It's still pretty early," Neal told her.

"I'll take my camcorder," Marta said. "At the very least, we oughta be able to get some video of Glitt showing up to look for his money. If we're lucky, we might get *both* of them. That'd *prove* there was a conspiracy."

"Prove to who?" Sue asked.

"The cops. A jury."

"I'm the jury," Neal said.

"Think you're Mike Hammer?" Marta asked.

"Yeah. Except he used a .45, and all I've got is a measly .380.

Marta rolled onto her side. She swung a leg across his thighs. Rubbing his chest, she squirmed closer. He felt the smoothness of her body against him, the tickle of her pubic hair, the weight and heat of a breast on top of his arm. She nibbled his shoulder. "Let me be your Velda?" she whispered.

Sue gave Marta's rump a smack.

Marta flinched. "Ow!"

"Time's a-wastin, gang. We gotta move it or lose it." The mattress wobbled as Sue scurried off the bed. Neal watched her rush across the moonlit room. She stopped at the doorway and reached out.

The sudden brightness hurt Neal's eyes.

Marta groaned and pushed her face against his chest.

"Let's go!" Sue called out, grinning.

"We've got plenty of time," Neal said.

"We ain't the first ones there, no tellin what we might miss. C'mon, let's move it!" She clapped her hands. "Let's go, let's go! Time's a-wastin!"

With another groan, Marta rolled off Neal and sprawled on her back. She flung an arm across her eyes to block out the light.

By the time Neal could force himself to sit up, Sue was gone. He swung his legs off the bed. Then sat there, head drooping.

"I don't wanna move," Marta muttered from behind him.

"Me either."

"Why's *she* so damn perky?"

"Part of her charm," Neal muttered.

Sue came prancing into the room.

Neal raised his head. She was grinning, naked, and had clothes clutched to her chest: her own white pleated skirt and yellow knit pullover, Marta's T-shirt, Neal's shorts.

"Here ya go, got yer duds for ya." She tossed the shorts at Neal. They almost hit him in the face. Just in time, he shot a hand up and caught them. "Get up, get 'em on, we gotta get outta here."

"Settle down," Marta muttered.

Sue threw the T-shirt at her.

Neal looked over his shoulder. Marta was on her back, propped up with her elbows. She regarded Sue with narrow eyes, but made no attempt to protect herself. The T-shirt opened up in midair and fell, dropping over her head, draping her entire face, covering one shoulder and one breast.

She let it stay.

The fabric showed the general shape of her face. Neal could

see the curve of her brow, slight indentations over her eyes, the rise of her nose, the slopes of her cheeks. He could see where her lips were. Her mouth seemed to be closed and unsmiling.

"Extremely amusing," she said, lips and chin moving the fabric.

Neal suddenly pictured her dead, face covered by a sheet.

He turned away, stood up and stepped into his shorts. As he pulled them up, he said, "We don't all have to go. Why don't you two stay here? I'll drive down and take care of things."

"Yer kiddin'," Sue said, fastening her skirt.

"We're not staying behind," Marta said.

The T-shirt no longer shrouded her face. She was sitting up in the middle of the bed, scowling at Neal, the shirt heaped in her lap.

"All I'm going to do is park and watch what happens," he explained. "And I'll use the camcorder. I'll get everything on tape. And maybe I'll use the bracelet on Glitt to see where he goes after he finds out he's been stiffed. It won't take three of us to . . ."

"*I* wanna watch," Sue protested.

Seated cross-legged on the bed, Marta put her T-shirt on. When her head reappeared, she gazed at Neal and said, "I know what's going on in that mind of yours."

"Probably," he admitted.

"You're afraid one of us'll get hurt."

"That's right, I am. You don't know Glitt. He's . . . the things he would do to you . . ."

"So you think we'd be better off—safer from Glitt—if you go away in the middle of the night without us? Leaving us alone and unarmed?"

"He doesn't know where you are," Neal said.

"How do you know?"

"I don't know for sure," he admitted, "but . . ."

"Wasn't Glitt planning to visit your apartment again tonight?"

"Yeah."

"Over in your apartment, is my address written down anywhere?"

"Yeah, but—"

"And you still want to leave us here for a couple of hours, all by ourselves, without the gun?"

Neal grimaced at her.

"If you go," Marta said, "we all go."

"Fair's fair," Sue added.

"Everything else aside," Marta said, "you might need us. If you *do* go on a bracelet trip, we should be in the car to keep an eye on your body."

"We'll be yer bodyguards," Sue said. She stood by the bed in her white, pleated skirt, casually twirling her knit blouse by the side of her leg. Her hips shifted slightly from side to side. Her skirt swayed, its front brushing across her thighs.

She looked like a cheerleader who'd decided to go native.

And Neal suddenly knew that he didn't want to go anywhere without her.

Without her *or* Marta.

"We'll make sure you're safe and sound," Marta said, "while you're riding Glitt to God-knows-where."

"Who'll guard *you?*" Neal asked.

"Any sign of trouble," Marta said, "and we'll drive off."

" 'Sides," Sue said, "we'll have yer gun. It ain't . . . *isn't* a thing ya can take with ya on a bracelet trip."

"We'll be fine in the car," Marta told him.

Neal glanced from Sue to Marta. They both had their eyebrows high, impish looks on their faces. They knew that they'd won.

He supposed they would *always* win.

Two against one.

The Two-she versus me.

Could be worse, he decided.

Just, please, God, don't let anything happen to them.

Chapter Fifty-four

Neal knew that he should've made them stay behind. But he was glad they were with him. It was very good to be in the back seat of the Jeep, both of them in front of him, close enough to touch, their hair blowing.

Marta drove. She and Sue sometimes turned their heads and said things that Neal couldn't hear.

If anything happens to them . . .

He wondered if he was risking them, allowing them to come. Or would they have been in more danger, left behind?

This way, he thought, *at least we're together. I'll be here to protect them.*

Which, he suspected, was more an excuse than a reason. The real reasons were probably more selfish than that: He *wanted* them to be with him. Partly because he was afraid, deep down, to go out by himself at this hour of night, on this sort of mission. But mostly because, at least for now, he felt as if parting with either of them would be too painful.

But I'm taking them to Glitt. He might've never found us, and here we are, going to him.

Suddenly, the insanity of it seemed so vast that Neal imagined himself leaning forward between the seatbacks and saying, "Turn it around. We're going home."

He wanted to do that.

But he couldn't.

Tonight, and only tonight, Glitt would be making a rendezvous with a paper sack in a garbage container in front of Video City.

Miss him, and he'll still be out there. But we won't know where. Sooner or later, he'll find us. But we won't know when.

Back out now, he'll nail us for sure.

* * *

They had started their trip at Marta's apartment. From there, any of several routes would've led them to Video City. But Neal soon noticed that they were traveling on the very same backroad that he always took to the video store.

The same road that he'd used Sunday night.

They would soon be coming to the freeway underpass.

They stopped for a traffic signal at National Boulevard. Turning in her seat, Sue looked back at Neal. "How ya doin'?" she asked.

"Okay."

"Sure you are," Marta said. He could never fool her.

"I've been better," he admitted. "Just scared. I wish we were back in bed."

"Well, it'll all be over in a couple of hours."

"That's what he's scared of," Sue said.

"I know we have to do this," Neal explained. "But I don't like it."

"I sorta do," Sue said.

"You *what?*"

"Like it. I feel like when we was about to climb aboard that rolly coaster at The Fort. The Pony Express? All sorta trembly and excited."

"Wish I'd been there," Marta said. The traffic signal turned green, and she drove through the intersection.

"The dang thing busted on us," Sue told her. "We was stuck way up there at the tippy-top. Scared the squeamin' jimmies outta me. But it turned out fine. This here, it's gonna turn out fine, too."

Listening, Neal had half-expected Sue to tell Marta what they'd *done* while stuck at the summit of the roller coaster. He was a little surprised that she left it out.

"After this is all over," Marta said, "we should go to Disneyland."

"Yeah!"

"Now that we've got half a million bucks," Neal said, "we might be able to afford it."

Marta turned her head slightly, and Neal saw the side of her face smiling. "The baby's gonna *love* Disneyland. After it's born, we'll have to go two or three times a year."

"And we'll *all* go, right?" Sue asked. She sounded as if she wanted to make very sure that she wasn't being eliminated from Marta's visions of the future.

"We'll make you push the pram," Marta told her.

Neal realized that they had already gone through the freeway underpass. He hadn't noticed it at all, hadn't given a moment of thought to the gangster threats scribbled on its walls, hadn't felt its menace.

They'd left it behind while talking of Disneyland.

"Can I name it?" Sue asked.

"The baby?" Marta asked.

"Yeah."

"No!" Marta blurted, and laughed.

The Jeep jolted as she drove across the old railroad tracks. Then she turned left.

"I suppose we might listen to your suggestions," she relented. "But Neal and I will have the final say."

"Well, sure. Fair's fair."

Head turned, Neal gazed out across the field. The wasteland. In the gray of the moonlight, he saw bare dirt, gravel and scruffy bushes, scabs of pale litter, vague shapes of discarded junk.

He remembered his charge across the no-man's-land and into the trees.

There. Right there.

Right in there is where the bastard had Elise.

There in the narrow wilderness between the field and the slope of the freeway embankment. An area made for dark hiding, for playing games dreamt up in nightmares.

There, he thought. Right there.

I could've saved her. If only I'd finished him off.

Should've crouched down over him and stuck the muzzle in his mouth.

Boom!

And one to die on.

If only, if only . . .

The main thing to remember is this, he told himself: Don't

make the same mistake again. This time, kill him dead.

Leaning forward, he said, "Over there, that's where I almost saved Elise. In those trees over there."

Marta and Sue turned their heads. They gazed toward a place in the trees below the freeway. But not the correct place. Neal hadn't spoken fast enough. The correct place had been left behind.

"That's where you *did* save her," Marta corrected him. "Not *almost*."

"No. I only gave her a reprieve. A short one."

"It ain't yer fault," Sue said.

"I know. It's *their* fault. But I had a chance to get in the way and keep her alive. And I blew it."

Blew my chance to save the gal in the garage, too, he thought. But maybe there'd never been much chance to save her. Even if I could've found the place again . . . Such awful burns.

She must be dead by now.

But if I get into Glitt's head, maybe I can find out where the garage is. It'd be worth a try. There's a chance that she's still alive . . .

Slim to none.

But I should try, he told himself. I *have* to try.

Marta turned right and drove slowly up the last road to Video City.

Sunday night on this very road, Elise had been hiding in the backseat of Neal's car, injured and bloody, naked except for Neal's shirt and Glitt's shoes.

Rasputin's shoes, he reminded himself.

The Beast of Belvedere.

"I wonder how Vince met him," Neal said.

"Met Glitt?" Marta asked.

"Yeah. Where do you go to find a guy like that?"

"Look under rocks," Marta suggested.

Neal saw the bright lights of Venice Boulevard ahead.

Almost there! God!

He suddenly felt breathless and sick.

"That's it on the corner," he muttered.

Light spilled out from display windows along the side of Video

City, washing over the walkway by the edge of the road.

"Is it open?" Sue asked.

"Should've closed at midnight," Neal said. "I think they leave the lights on like that all night."

"The more light," Marta said, "the better."

"Speaking of which," Neal said, "you'd better kill the headlights."

She shut them off. Their bright tunnels disappeared, but the night was still pale with the glow of streetlights and the full moon.

"Where should we park?" Marta asked when they were adjacent to the building.

"*Not* in the parking lot," Neal said.

"How 'bout this street?" Sue asked.

"Yeah," Neal said. "Maybe over there. You could U it here."

Slowing almost to a stop, Marta eased the car toward the curb on the right. Then she swung it to the other side of the road. With the tail of the car toward Venice Boulevard, she straightened out beside the curb. Then she slowly backed up.

Across the road, the Video City seemed to slide out of the way.

When they had a clear view of the entire parking lot, she stopped. "How's this?" she asked.

Neal checked over his shoulder. "Back up some more. There's a big shadow behind us."

Marta did as he asked. The shadow from a tree crept over the Jeep.

"Here."

She stopped and shut off the engine.

"Beautiful," Neal said.

Though the shadow failed to hide them completely, at least it kept away the direct brightness of the full moon and the nearest streetlight.

From a distance, they probably looked like vague, dark shapes—if anyone should notice them at all. The eyes of a stranger might simply sweep past this section of road, notice that a vehicle seemed to be parked in a patch of darkness, and move on to brighter places.

That was Neal's guess, and his hope.

Close up, he could make out the dim features of Marta and Sue. They both had their heads turned to the left. Both seemed to be studying the well-lighted parking lot across the road.

He wished they'd worn dark tops. He hadn't thought of it until now, though.

There'd been no discussion of what to wear; they'd simply gotten dressed in what Sue had brought in from the living room—as if they were about to run a little errand in the middle of the night, had no plan to leave the car, and figured nobody was likely to see them, anyway.

Which had been fine with Neal.

Even if he'd *thought* of dark clothes, he supposed he would've kept quiet for fear of ruining a good thing. It was nice to know that Marta wore nothing under her T-shirt, that Sue was naked under her knit top and pleated skirt. He wore nothing, himself, except his shorts and sneakers.

Why *didn't* we get dressed? he wondered.

He supposed it had to do with comfort and with the good feel of keeping a bit of sexual tension in the air. More than that, however, it seemed like a way to deny that they were going on such a risky mission.

Dress as if you're stepping out for a few minutes—maybe to return a video.

With a gun in my pocket.

It felt strange to wear nothing under his shorts, but to have the pistol resting on his thigh. The pistol was cool and heavy through the thin fabric of his pocket.

Marta turned sideways and looked over her shoulder at him. "Wanna hand me the camcorder?"

He picked it up and passed it forward.

As Marta opened its leather carrying case, Neal turned his attention to the parking lot. Five or six cars were scattered about, but the area was so large that it seemed nearly deserted. He saw nobody. The parked cars appeared to be empty, and he couldn't see anyone moving around inside the store.

The only activity was behind them on Venice Boulevard. There, a few vehicles were rushing by, making sounds like wind.

Somebody in one of them had a radio playing too loudly, the bass blasting out booming noises that hid any sound of music.

"I hope there's enough light," Marta said.

Neal looked at Video City's glass doors, the walkway in front, the night return slot, and the round concrete garbage container where the money was supposed to be dropped. Light flooded out through the store windows. A harsher light fell on the area from the standards that surrounded the parking lot.

"It seems pretty bright," Neal said.

Marta raised the camcorder to her eye. "Looks good," she said. There was a buzzing sound when she zoomed in. "Oh, yeah. This'll be great."

"Now," Sue said, "if somebody'll just show up."

"What time is it?" Neal asked.

"Twelve thirty-five."

"We shouldn't have long to wait. Not for Vince, anyway. He planned to get here good and early."

"Last thing he wants," Marta said, "is a face-to-face with Glitt."

Sue chuckled. "Now that he's shit outta cash."

"*If* he's shit outta cash," Neal said.

"He couldn't have possibly scraped up another half a million," Marta said. "Not this fast."

"Anything's possible."

"It might already be there," Sue said.

"What?" Neal asked.

"The bag. Whatever's in it. Vince coulda come and gone already, ya know?"

"Or maybe he won't come at all," Marta said.

Sue flung open her door. "Back in a sec," she said and hopped out of the Jeep.

"What are you doing?" Marta asked.

"Gonna take me a look in the garbage," she said, and broke into a run.

"Don't!" Neal called. "Get back here."

Halfway across the road, Sue grinned over her shoulder. "Don't worry none. Just gonna have me a peek." Then she faced forward and picked up her speed, bare feet striding out, her pleated white skirt lifting and prancing around her thighs.

Chapter Fifty-five

"Look at her go," Marta said. She sounded impressed.

"The idiot." Neal couldn't take his eyes off Sue. She was really flying—already past the corner of the building and sprinting up the front walkway. "If Vince shows up now . . ."

"Wouldn't *he* be surprised?"

"Say that again."

"It's still early," Marta said.

Neal suddenly imagined one of the cars in the parking lot roaring to life and racing toward Sue. It slams into her. Rips her off her feet. Folds her in half. With Sue sprawled over the hood, it crashes through the plate glass and plunges on into the store.

So far, however, all the cars remained motionless.

Sue stopped at the garbage container. Putting her hands on both sides of its lid, she bent over at the waist and lowered her face toward the hole.

A few moments later, she straightened up.

Shoulders swiveling, head turning, she scanned the parking lot.

"What's she looking at?" Marta asked, worry in her voice.

"I don't know."

"Maybe she heard something."

"I don't see anything wrong," Neal said.

He reached into his pocket and slowly pulled out the Sig Sauer. He rested it on top of his thigh.

Sue was again bent over, peering into the trash barrel.

"She's sure taking her time," Marta muttered. "I'd like to honk."

"Don't," Neal said.

She made a small, quiet laugh. "I won't. But I'd like to."

"I'd like to swat her ass."

Turning her head, Marta grinned at him. "We'll take turns."

"The damn bag's either there or it isn't. If Vince shows up while she's there . . ."

He quit speaking as Sue shifted sideways a bit and reached an arm down into the hole.

"She's going for something," Marta whispered.

Face twisted away from the hole, Sue reached deeper and deeper.

At the far end of the parking lot, a pair of headlights swept in from a side street.

"Shit!" Neal gasped.

Burger Boy was down there. For a moment, Neal hoped the car might be heading for its drive-through lane. But he suddenly remembered that the place no longer stayed open past midnight. After the kid had gotten shot there last month . . .

The car drove straight into the Video City lot.

And rushed toward Sue.

Neal's stomach dropped.

Clutching the automatic, he leaped over the side of the Jeep.

"Be careful!" Marta gasped.

As he rushed into the road, he saw Sue, bright in the headlights of the approaching car, come up quickly out of the trash barrel, a white sack in her hand. She faced the car and squinted into the glare of its lights.

The lights slid off to her side. The car kept coming, but slowed down. Then it stopped, its front bumper still a few yards from Sue.

The car was a black Cadillac.

It didn't look familiar to Neal.

The driver climbed out. Leaving the door open, he made his way toward Sue. A big guy, so heavy that he seemed to have trouble walking. He wore a tank top and enormous blue jeans. His black ponytail swished from side to side as he waddled along.

He carried a videotape. Just one. He held it off to the side, swinging it this way and that as if using it to ward off an invasion of his right flank.

Neal, at the corner of the store, slipped the pistol into his pocket but held onto it.

Sue smiled at the stranger. Then she opened the paper bag,

glanced in, muttered something, wadded the bag and tossed it into the garbage container.

"No luck?" he asked her. He had a high-pitched voice that sounded girlish.

"Nope," Sue said. Still smiling, she stepped off the walkway and extended a hand. "I'll drop it in for ya," she said.

"Much obliged," the stranger said, and handed the tape to Sue.

She started to turn away.

"Wait," he said.

She faced him.

He removed a wallet from a back pocket of his jeans.

"Hey, no," Sue said. "I ain't lookin for no handout. Honest."

He pulled out a bill and held it toward her. "I'm sure you can put this to good use. Please. I want you to take it."

Sue shook her head. "I got more money than I know what to do with already," she told him.

"I saw what you were doing in the garbage. Looking for scraps . . ."

"Naw. Just . . ." She snatched the bill from his fingers and said, "Thanks, mister."

He waved a pudgy hand at her, then turned around and began slogging his way back to his car.

Sue hurried over to the night return slot. She popped his video in, then looked down at the money in her hand. Whistling softly, she shook her head. She glanced toward Neal, shook her head again, then turned toward the man. "Thanks a real lot," she called. "God bless you."

His door thudded shut.

Neal turned to a window. Staring in at the shelves of videotapes, he waited for the stranger to drive away. While he waited, Sue walked over to him.

"Look at this," she said. "The fella gave me a fifty. Ya believe it? Look." She thrust the bill at him. "Nobody *never* gave me no fifty before."

"Let's get outta here," Neal said.

They started walking side by side. Sue held the fifty dollar bill in front of her and gazed at it. "Never got me a tip this big when I was waitin' tables at Sunny's."

"He must've felt sorry for you," Neal said. "Saw you rooting through the garbage."

"Well . . ."

"And how *skinny* you are."

"He sure was a nice guy. Too bad I didn't run into someone like him back there in the days before I got rich." Reaching behind Neal, she patted his rump. "Thanks for runnin' to my rescue."

"That might've been Vince, you know."

"Mighta been, but wasn't. Anyhow, I didn't find nothin' in the trash can. Just some trash. So I reckon we got here first."

They crossed the road and climbed into the Jeep.

"Look what that fella gave me," Sue said, and held the fifty out for Marta to see.

Marta didn't seem impressed. "You could've gotten yourself killed," she said.

"Coulda, but didn't."

"I don't think it's funny. There was no good reason to go running over there like that. You were just showing off."

"Was not."

"It turned out okay," Neal said. "And at least we know that Vince hasn't been here yet."

"He might've watched the whole episode," Marta pointed out. "He could be in one of those cars over there . . . anywhere. Just keeping an eye on things. The same goes for Glitt. Anybody with half a brain would show up good and early for this sort of a deal. And if they're here, they know *we're* here." She looked at Sue.

"Sorry," Sue muttered, and shrugged. "Didn't mean to cause trouble."

"It's no big deal," Neal said. "If they got here this early to keep an eye on the situation, you can bet they probably watched us arrive."

Marta was silent for a moment. Then she said, "That's probably true."

Sue turned sideways and said to Neal, "Why don't ya try a

bracelet trip? Take a run through them parked cars, and . . . Duck!"

As Neal dropped across the backseat, he heard an engine. The sound came from the rear.

Just behind them, a car seemed to be making a right turn onto their road from Venice.

Could be anyone, Neal told himself.

After all, they'd chosen a place that was directly across from the main entrance to Video City's parking lot.

But how many people return tapes at this hour?

"Coast is clear," Sue announced.

Neal lifted himself up. Looking across the road, he saw a Toyota pickup truck. It sped through the lot and veered toward the front of the store.

Marta and Sue were both sitting up, watching it. Marta held her camcorder just below her chin as if ready for action.

The pickup braked to a quick, skidding stop.

The passenger door flew open. A woman jumped out. She wore a red bathrobe. Her hair was up in curlers. Carrying a videotape in each hand, she trotted toward the deposit slot.

"She dressed up for the occasion," Marta said.

"Just like us," Neal pointed out.

"I'd never go *anywhere* in curlers."

Shaking her head, Sue commented, "She don't look at *all* like Vince."

They watched the woman hurry back to the pickup and climb aboard. As she swung her door shut, the truck backed up. Then it lurched forward and raced for the exit at the far end of the lot.

"Why're *they* in such a god-awful rush?" Sue asked.

"Probably afraid of being bushwhacked by gang bangers," Neal said.

"If they're scared, they oughta stay home."

Marta shook her head and lowered the camera. "What's *with* all these people, returning their tapes at this hour?"

"They probably stayed up late watching the things," Neal suggested. "I've done it, myself."

"But this is after *closing* time. Why don't they just wait till morning?"

"Next one comes by," Sue said, "y'oughta hop in with the bracelet and find out why."

"Thanks anyway," Marta said. "Not me."

"*I'll* do it," Sue volunteered. "Then I'll let ya know what I find out." She smiled over her shoulder at Neal. "Here, let me have it."

He shook his head. "Not till this is over. I have to use it on Glitt when he shows up."

Sue sighed. "Have it yer way. Poop."

Neal reached forward and gave her ponytail a quick tug.

"Ow!"

"Look over there! It's him!"

As Marta raised the camcorder and pointed it across the road, Neal jerked his head to the left. The parking lot still looked empty except for the scattered cars that had been there all along.

"Where?" he whispered.

"There," Sue said. "See him?" She pointed past Marta's face.

Neal heard the buzz of the camcorder zooming in.

And then he saw the man.

Vince Conrad, all right. Though he was still a good distance away, Neal recognized him immediately. He was striding along the walkway in front of Video City with a quick step. He looked fit and somewhat jaunty. Dressed in a dark warm-up suit, he might've been someone out for a night of exercise.

Except for the bag he carried.

A large brown grocery sack was clutched to his chest.

"Where'd he come from?" Neal whispered.

"Over by Burger Boy?" Marta suggested, her eye to the camcorder's viewfinder.

"You getting him?" Neal asked.

"Yep."

"I wonder what he's got in the bag," Sue said.

Raising her voice slightly, Marta said for the benefit of the tape, "What we're seeing here is Vince Conrad, husband of Elise Waters, on his way to drop off a bag of cash for the man he hired to murder Elise. The killer, Leslie Glitt, also known as the

Beast of Belvedere, is supposed to come along at about two o'clock this morning to pick it up."

Off in the distance, Vince walked briskly up to the trash container. Without any hesitation at all, he dropped the sack through the hole in the lid, turned around, and walked the other way.

"There he goes," Sue whispered.

Reaching out, Neal clamped a hand on her shoulder.

"Hey, hey, take it easy. I ain't goin nowhere."

"We sit tight and see what happens."

"I know. I know."

He gave her shoulder a gentle squeeze, then let go.

Marta lowered the camera. "If nothing else," she said, "at least we've got evidence of Vince's involvement."

"We won't need any evidence," Neal said. "When Glitt finds out he got stiffed, he'll probably kill the bastard. And if he doesn't, I will."

"What if the bag's got half a million smackeroos in it?" Sue asked.

"Vince could *not* have come up with that much money," Marta insisted. She sounded slightly annoyed, as if she might be getting tired of repeating herself on the matter.

"Couldn't hurt to take a look," Sue said.

Neal clamped her shoulder again. "It could hurt plenty. Stay put."

For a while, nobody spoke. Neal kept his hand on Sue's shoulder, and they all studied the parking lot. Then Sue said, "If the bag's full of money, we oughta grab it 'fore Glitt shows up."

"It's not full of money," Marta insisted.

"Ya never know."

"I know."

"No, ya don't. Just let me run on over there for a sec."

Neal shook his head. "That might be exactly the 'sec' when Glitt shows up. If he catches you . . ."

"If he catches me, shoot him. That's what ya wanna do anyhow, isn't it?"

"No. What I want . . . I want Glitt to go after Vince. That's the whole idea. I mean, this is not a guy you want to cheat out of half a million bucks. What he'll probably do is head straight over to Vince's place and take him apart. *That's* what I want. I want him to work on Vince the way he worked on Elise . . . the way he'd *like* to work on all of us. And I'd like to be inside him while he's doing it, so I won't miss a thing."

"Well, if that sack's full of money, ol' Glitt'll go off happy."

"I'll ride him, anyway. Whatever happens, we need to know where he goes. Once I find out, I'll come back and we'll go take care of him."

"Whatever might be in the bag," Marta said, "we can take it then."

Sue frowned over her shoulder at Neal. "Don't ya *want* Glitt to take apart Vince?"

"I'd love it. Nobody could ever hurt him the way Glitt could. And it'd be so . . . appropriate. He can't cough up the dough to pay Glitt for butchering Elise, so Glitt butchers *him. That's* justice."

"If he butchers Vince," Marta said, "he'll *never* get the money."

"He'll *at least* torture the bastard."

"He might not do anything."

"Oh, I think he'll do plenty. I have loads of faith in my beast."

Sue chuckled softly, then said, "Ya want Glitt doin' the dirty work, then we'd darn sure better find out what's in the bag. And take it, if there's money."

"I guess you're right," Neal admitted. He pressed down firmly on Sue's shoulder. "*You* stay here. I'll take care of it."

Chapter Fifty-six

"Hurry," Marta urged him as he left the Jeep.

Neal shook his head, quickened his pace slightly, but didn't break into a run. If he ran, it might draw attention to him.

Inside the pocket of his shorts, his right hand clutched his pistol.

Shouldn't worry about Glitt, he told himself. It's way too early.

Neal felt awfully vulnerable, though, as he walked along in front of Video City. It was so brightly lighted. He was out in the open, in plain sight, nothing between him and the traffic on Venice Boulevard. People in passing cars could see him. He felt as if people *everywhere* could see him.

It didn't help, being half naked.

Nobody would know, by looking, that he wore nothing under his shorts. But *he* knew. He could feel the air in there, the pleasant sensation of swinging free. It felt good, but it made him feel exposed.

Mostly, he wished he was wearing a shirt.

Guys were *allowed* to go shirtless in public, but you didn't see it very often. Not unless you were at the beach, or maybe a construction sight.

Who's gonna care? he asked himself. Who'll even notice? It's the middle of the night. It was a really hot day . . .

I didn't have my shirt on the night I came here with Elise.

He'd given it to her because she had no clothes of her own.

He remembered how she'd looked in it, her legs long and bare.

Then he pictured her dead in the tub.

Think about something else!

Think about the money. What if there's another half a million?

Fat chance.

He walked past the front doors of Video City, past the night deposit slot, and stopped at the garbage barrel. Leaning forward, he peered into the lid's opening. The grocery bag was a dim shape in the shadows, about halfway down.

He considered taking a quick look around.

Don't, he warned himself. Just grab it and go.

He left the pistol in his pocket, twisted sideways a bit, reached down through the hole and clutched the crumpled paper top.

He lifted the bag.

It felt nice and heavy.

My God, what if there is money in here?

He wanted to take a look, but fought against the impulse.

Just get out of here. Get back to the gals.

No. No. I'd better check. What if it's something dangerous? Maybe Vince put a bomb inside. Or rattlesnakes.

Neal suddenly wasn't so sure that *he* wanted to open it.

Taking a step backward away from the garbage barrel, he jostled the bag. It seemed to have about the same feel as the bag of money he'd taken from Vince's house.

He set it at his feet, crouched down, and unrolled the crumpled top. He leaned away so his face wouldn't be directly above the opening. Then, with both hands, he spread the edges.

Nothing sprang out.

Easing forward, he gazed inside.

Slam the Big Door.

By John D. MacDonald.

The Killer Inside Me.

By Jim Thompson.

My Gun Is Quick.

By Mickey Spillane.

He reached into the bag and pushed some of the top books aside to see more.

His Name Was Death.

By Fredric Brown.

The Long Goodbye.

By Raymond Chandler.

And more. Many, many more old paperbacks. Rummaging through the bag, Neal figured that twenty or thirty of them had been thrown in.

To give it the proper heft. To trick Glitt. And maybe to give Vince a smirk by paying Glitt off with tales of treachery and murder.

Must've been Elise's books, Neal thought.

Whoever had put together such a collection in the first place was not a person who would use the books this way.

I never knew she was into this stuff.

Hell, I never knew much of anything about her.

And now the bastard's ripping off her library . . .

A car honked. Not a loud, urgent blast, just a beep—like a stealthy warning. Neal knew that it must've come from the Jeep.

He looked back, but couldn't see it. A car was on the road, in the way, blocking the Jeep from his view.

It looked like it might be a white Subaru.

Can't be Glitt, Neal thought.

Why not?

The car turned onto the parking lot and came forward.

Just somebody bringing back a video or two. Has to be. Because it can't be Glitt showing up now while I'm right here squatting over his bag. Can't be! Not even close to two o'clock yet. He wouldn't come this early. He can't be showing up while I'm right here. No way!

But a different part of Neal's mind was certain that this was Glitt, indeed, showing up not only early but at almost the worst of all possible times. Blowing everything.

It figures, he thought.

Then he told himself that nothing was blown. Not yet.

As Neal stood up and turned to face the car, its headlights swung toward him.

They stayed on him, white and glaring, while the car rolled closer.

It stopped at an angle, several yards away, its lights still fixed on Neal.

The driver's door opened and Glitt stepped out.

Rasputin.

Even with the top of his head wrapped in a white bandage, he looked like the mad monk. His eyes glared at Neal from the caverns of their sockets. His face was dead white, but little of it showed. Most was hidden under his wild growth of beard.

He wore his usual outfit: long-sleeved black shirt, black leather trousers and black boots. At his left hip was a large, stag-handled knife in a black leather sheath.

His gloves were missing. His hands were empty.

He showed his teeth through a hole in his beard.

"Where'd you get the bag?" he asked.

"In the trash. Somebody threw it away."

"It's mine."

"Finders keepers," Neal told him. And slipped his right hand casually into the pocket of his shorts. And wrapped his fingers around the grips of his .380 pistol.

Glitt shook his head. "It was left here for me."

"What makes you think so?"

"I watched the man deliver it. He's an associate of mine."

Neal stomped on the bag, crushing down its top against the books piled inside. He kept his foot on it. "Tell me what's inside."

"You know what."

"But do you? Identify your property, and I'll let you have it."

"Sure you will."

"What are you expecting?"

"Money," Glitt whispered. "Lots of money."

"Wrong. It's full of books."

"Liar."

"Good ones, too." Neal tried to grin. "If you were expecting money, mister, you got cheated."

Glitt lurched forward, stiff and grimacing.

"See for yourself," Neal said, backing off.

Glitt dropped to his knees and tore open the bag. The brown paper split and gaped, exposing the paperbacks. Some of them spilled out. Glitt gazed down at them.

"*FUCK!*" he bellowed.

"If you don't want them, I'll take them."

As if he couldn't believe the money wasn't there, Glitt shoved the books with both hands, dug through them, spread them until he'd exposed the bottom of the bag.

Then he tilted back his head as if to howl at the full moon, and cried out, "*That fucking cocksucker, I'll kill him!*"

"That sounds a bit drastic," Neal said.

Incredible, he thought. It's gonna work.

Groaning, Glitt struggled to stand up.

"Can I have the books?" Neal asked.

"Fuck you," Glitt said.

And started to turn around.

Neal noticed the distant *boom boom buh-boom boom* of a loud car radio off in the distance, over on Venice Boulevard, probably . . . and suddenly a quick *bam-bam-bam-bam-bam* that sounded a lot like rapid gunfire.

Glitt dived to the pavement.

He thinks someone's firing at us?

Neal looked out across the parking lot and saw, sure enough, a car rolling by on Venice Boulevard with the front and back windows down, with guys leaning out. Guys with dark guns going *bam-bam-bam* muzzles flashing.

What the hell they got there, Uzis? AK-47s?

Looks like a pack of fucking gang bangers.

Looks like a bad movie.

He supposed that Vince must've sent them to gun down Glitt. Not a bad idea. Smart man.

I'm here, too! They're shooting at ME!

Neal wished he'd been as quick as Glitt to dive for cover.

Something zipped past his face.

Shit!

He jerked the Sig out of his pocket. Sidestepping, he pointed at the car and started to pull his trigger. The pistol bucked, blasting out fire and slugs.

Screw this, he thought. I oughta hit the deck . . . dive behind the trash can . . .

Bullets whacked him in the chest, pounded across him, knocked him backward. He tried to stay on his feet. Then he was falling into the store through an avalanche of shattered glass.

Marta and Sue

Chapter One

They watched from the Jeep.

When the slugs smacked a line of dots across Neal's bare chest, he looked as if he'd been struck by a burst of wind. His hair blew. His cheeks shook. He flung out his arms, threw his pistol away, and stumbled backward. Behind him, the plate glass window was breaking apart and falling even before he stumbled through it.

Sue shrieked, *"NO!"*

She flung open her door, but Marta grabbed her hard by the upper arm. "Don't!"

"I've gotta . . . !"

But Sue's voice stopped and they both gaped at the car of the gunmen. It was leaping the curb at the edge of Venice Boulevard.

"Yes!" Marta cried out. "Go!"

She could see the vague shape of a man in the right rear window of the airborne car. But nobody at the window in front of him.

Nobody at all seemed to be in the front seats!

No passenger, no driver.

Neal got them?

The car smashed down, bounced and wobbled on its tires, then roared straight for Burger Boy.

"Go!" Sue yelled.

It crashed into the front wall. Burger Boy windows exploded.

The wall crumpled. The car stopped with a shock. A body came up out of the passenger seat. Its head and shoulders punched through the windshield and stayed there.

"He got 'em!" Marta yelled, but could barely hear her own words through Sue's wild, strange scream of agony and glee.

She wiped tears from her eyes. As she reached for the ignition key, the white Subaru suddenly lurched forward. Its driver—who *had* to be Glitt—must've survived the storm of gunfire.

Of course he made it through, Marta thought. Rasputin always makes it through.

Not always.

The white car squealed through a tight turn and raced across the parking lot, heading for Venice Boulevard.

Marta started the Jeep.

Glitt's car hopped off the curb, skidded for a moment, then sped west on Venice.

Marta steered across the road and entered the parking lot.

A *whump!* like a muffled explosion pulled her eyes to the Burger Boy.

The car of the gunmen was wrapped in fire. The body stuck in its windshield didn't try to get out. Nobody did. But someone in the back seat seemed to turn very slowly, gaze out through the flames at Marta and Sue, and raise an arm as if asking for help—or waving good-bye.

"*Adios*, fucker," Marta muttered.

Then she veered toward the shattered front window of Video City.

Saw Neal sprawled on his back inside the store.

And felt as if a thug was stomping on her heart.

"*Neal!*" Sue cried out.

He lay motionless on a bed of shattered glass.

Don't do this to us, Marta thought. Move. Get up. At least for God's sake raise your head. Show us you're okay.

But she knew that Neal was not okay. He didn't move at all. He looked as if he'd been hosed with blood.

The Jeep was still rolling when Sue leaped out and ran for Neal. Marta had to wait. She had to stop the Jeep, make sure it wouldn't get away . . .

She shut off the engine, jerked up on the emergency brake lever and climbed out. Sue was already squatting by Neal's left side, pulling at one of his arms. "C'mon, honey," she gasped. "Ya gotta get up. Yer gonna be okay."

His head wobbled, and Marta thought that he was responding.

But maybe the wobble was only because of Sue tugging his arm.

She hurried to his other side.

The glass clinked and clattered under her bare feet, and cut her. She knew she was being cut. She didn't care. Standing over Neal, she gazed down at the bullet holes.

Seven or eight of them.

Pulpy, raw-edged craters brimming with blood.

Connect the dots . . .

Connect them, and there's a straight line crossing his ribcage at a slightly upward angle from under his right nipple to above his left.

A line crossing directly over his heart.

Sue gazed up at Marta, her face red and twisted. "Help!" she blurted. "We gotta get him outta here! Grab an arm! C'mon, don't just stand there! Gotta get him to a hospital."

Too late, Marta thought.

Can't tell that to Sue.

So she crouched and took hold of Neal's right upper arm. It was coated with blood. When she pulled at it, her hands slipped down to his elbow. And suddenly she found herself crying out of control. And sinking. Sinking to her knees and feeling the bite of the glass, then dropping across Neal, holding his face in both hands, kissing him.

Blood washed into her mouth. Blood soaked through her T-shirt. She wanted to feel him breathing under her, wanted to feel his heartbeat against her chest. But there was no heartbeat, no movement at all, not even the twitches from Sue jerking him by the arm.

Someone was shaking her by the shoulder.

"Marta!" Sue gasped. "Sirens."

Yes. She could hear them. Sirens. Far-off cries.

Coming here?

You bet your ass they're coming here.

"C'mon," Sue said, shaking Marta's shoulder some more. "We gotta get him outta here. Cops're gonna show up. Please! Get up!"

As Marta pushed herself up, the front of her T-shirt peeled away from her body, clinging to the blood on Neal's chest and belly. Then it peeled away from Neal. It returned to Marta and stuck to her as she got to her feet.

"Grab him! C'mon!" Sue's face streaked with tears.

Marta shook her head. "He's . . . better off here. They'll . . ." She struggled to gather her thoughts. "He'll get taken care of quicker."

"Think an ambulance is coming?"

"Firetrucks first. But they . . . they'll take care of him. They'll know what to do. The firemen. They're trained . . ."

Who am I trying to kid? He's dead.

Sue sniffed and wiped one of her eyes.

"Let's get out of here," Marta said. "If the cops catch us . . . they'll have us till morning. We've gotta . . . finish what we started."

"Huh?" Sue asked, but she was already backing away from Neal, limping slightly in the glass.

"We've gotta take down Glitt and Vince," Marta explained.

"They didn't have nothin' to do with this."

"They had *everything* to do with it. Vince sent those motherfuckers to kill Glitt. He didn't have the payoff money—*we* took it—so he sent killers. Only they missed Glitt and got Neal."

"Yer outta yer . . ." Sue went silent. Suddenly, a look of pain and rage filled her wet eyes. In a voice that seemed very quiet, she said, "Let's get 'em."

She ran for the passenger side of the Jeep.

Marta rushed up the walkway toward the trash barrel, ducked and snatched Neal's pistol off the concrete. The slide was back. She muttered, "Shit." But she kept the gun and raced for the Jeep.

Sue was already in the passenger seat.

Marta jumped in behind the wheel, clamped the pistol between her thighs, cranked the ignition, and shifted to reverse.

Backing away, she watched Neal on the floor just inside Video City become smaller, smaller. She felt as if she were viewing him through a zoom lens that was pulling back, pulling away, letting him retreat into the distance.

Then she turned for the exit.

As they sped out of the parking lot, Sue asked, "Do ya think he's dead?"

"I think so."

Sue gave out a high-pitched squeal. The noise made Marta think of a pig stabbed by a pitchfork, though she'd never heard or seen such a thing.

She reached over and squeezed Sue's hand.

Both hands were wet and sticky with Neal's blood.

With only her left hand on the steering wheel, Marta drove down the side street away from Venice Boulevard.

In a shaky, broken voice, Sue asked, "Where we goin'?"

"To Neal's."

"Huh?"

"We can't go after those guys with an empty gun."

"Empty?"

"He used up all his ammo on the bastards who . . . shot him."

"He had an extra one of them gizmos."

"A magazine?"

"Yeah. I saw one someplace." Sue sniffled. "He had it with him . . . in his bag. Ya know?"

"His black overnight bag?"

"Yeah."

"That's at my place. He didn't bring the magazine with him, did he?"

"Tonight?"

"Yeah."

"I don't know. Maybe. Or maybe it's still over at yer place."

"Well, I *know* he keeps a box of ammo in his bedroom. I might need more than what's in the other magazine, anyhow."

"So we're goin to his apartment?" Sue asked.

"Right. It's not far. Won't take ten minutes."

"Go on and do that. Get the ammo. Then come on over and meet me at Vince's. I'm goin' on."

Going on?

What does she mean by that? Planning to walk?

Marta turned her head, frowning, just in time to see Sue raise her right arm and press her lips to something just below the sleeve of her knit shirt.

Something that gleamed in the moonlight.

The bracelet!

"Don't!" Marta gasped.

Sue's left hand went limp. Her right arm dropped and she slumped sideways until her shoulder shoved against Marta.

Chapter Two

From overhead, Sue saw the Jeep make a sudden stop. Marta shoved Sue's body sideways, then leaned across her.

She's gonna take off my bracelet.

"Don't do it!"

As Sue drifted a little higher, she saw that Marta was pulling the safety belt down across Sue's chest.

That's all. That's real nice. She don't want me gettin' hurt.

Sue wondered if Marta even *knew* the trick about taking off the bracelet.

Did we tell her?

She couldn't recall herself or Neal explaining it to Marta.

It don't matter. She didn't pull it off me, and that's what counts.

Marta started the Jeep moving again.

Sue swung around and climbed, heading back toward Video City.

Moments later, high above the parking lot, she saw that fire trucks and police cars had already arrived. Some were in the lot. Others had stopped on Venice Boulevard, blocking traffic. The night was gaudy with orange flames and flashing red lights, blue lights, yellow lights. The car of the gunmen still burned, but now Burger Boy was also engulfed in flame. Firefighters scrambled about in their helmets and yellow coats. Some were hitting the flames with cloudy white blasts from fire extinguishers while others struggled to free the men from the car.

Hope the dirty rotten assholes are cooked.

Though afraid of what she might see, Sue looked down at the group directly below her—the cops near the front of Video City.

A couple of uniformed officers were standing by the open door of a patrol car, talking to each other. Another was behind the trunk of a nearby black-and-white, removing a huge roll of yellow "crime scene" tape from its trunk.

They gotta get him to a hospital!

Sue swooped down. Careful to stay clear of everyone, she glided past the demolished display window and looked in.

She saw Neal.

He still lay sprawled on his back in the broken glass, arms out.

A cop standing near Neal's body was talking to a fireman, but Sue couldn't make out his words. Too much noise, and she was too far away. She started drifting closer to him.

But backed off fast.

Any closer, and she might end up inside the guy.

Besides, she didn't *want* to hear what was being said.

It don't matter. Neal's dead. If he wasn't, they'd be workin' on him. They're just waitin for the homicide cops to show up, or the coroner, or something.

But what if they just *think* he's dead? she asked herself. What if they're wrong?

She started moving toward Neal.

I'll just take me a little peek inside him.

Chapter Three

Marta was just pulling away from a stop sign when Sue blurted, "*Aaaah!*"

Startled, she slammed on the brakes. The Jeep jerked to a stop in the middle of the intersection. No other cars were coming, though. She couldn't even see any headlights in the distance. These were very quiet, empty streets. Letting the car stand where it was, she stared at Sue.

And wondered what had made her cry out that way.

Is she all right?

Oh, God, what if something happened to her?

What *can* happen to her? Marta asked herself. Her body's safe with me.

Slumped back in the passenger seat, Sue was gasping for air. She squirmed a little. If Marta didn't know otherwise, she would've thought Sue was simply asleep and having a very bad nightmare.

What if something did happen and she never comes back?

What if her—soul or whatever it is—stays gone?

And I don't even know where to go looking.

Or how to get it back.

She glimpsed a future for herself without Neal *or* Sue, and it looked vast and lonely and frightening. She stepped on the gas. The Jeep lurched forward, out of the intersection, and gained speed as it rushed up the curving road.

"Screamin' Judas!"

Marta jumped. She jerked her head sideways.

Sue turned her head and said, "Howdy."

"You're back!"

"Had me a close one."

Marta swung over and stopped at an empty stretch of curb. The house beyond the lawn was dark except for a porch light. She reached out and squeezed Sue's shoulder. "You're all right?"

"Musta cut up my feet . . ."

"We both did."

"Just noticed. Ya come back after . . ."

"What happened? You yelled. It scared the hell out of me."

"Oh, jeez, yeah, I had me a good scare. Went back to Video City, you know . . ."

"I thought you were going to Vince's."

"Just got sidetracked some. Anyhow, there's cops and firemen all over the place back there. Burger Boy's on fire. Looked to me like that whole sorry carload of bastards bit the big one."

"Good," Marta said.

"But they . . ." Her voice broke. She looked away. Marta rubbed her shoulder.

"You saw Neal?"

With her face still turned away, Sue nodded. "He was just layin' there. Nobody was workin on him, or . . . They weren't takin him to no hospital."

"It's all right," Marta whispered.

"No, it ain't." Sue faced her. In the glow of the streetlights, the tears running down her cheeks looked silver. "Nothin's all right."

"*We're* all right. Sort of. I was afraid you might not come back."

"Almost didn't. Maybe. Don't really know. What happened . . ." She took a deep breath. "I figured I'd check to see if Neal . . . to see if he was still alive, or not. Ya know? 'Cause I wanted to find out for sure. So I was gonna go in him. It's against the rules. Yer s'pose to stay shut of dead folks. But I was gonna do it anyhow, 'cause I needed to find *out*. Anyhow, I didn't wanna think he's dead, ya know?"

"I know," Marta murmured.

"So I was on my way, maybe no more than a foot or two short of poppin' in on Neal, when all of a sudden I got this awful feelin' inside like I suddenly knew he was gone, dead as a carp, and I was about two blinks from endin' up *stuck* in him. That's when I yelled. I knew I wouldn't never get out. I'd be stuck in him . . . forever. While he rotted away . . ."

"Stop it, Sue. You're talking about Neal, for God's sake."

"Well . . . Anyhow, it all just suddenly knocked the squeamies outta me. I yelled and sorta flung myself to get away from him and ended up inside this cop that was standin' there. Didn't wanna be in him, either, so that's how come I'm back here."

"Glad to have you back," Marta told her.

"Me, too. I sorta needed to . . . How in tarnation do I *get* to Vince's place, anyhow?"

Marta released her shoulder, returned her hand to the steering wheel, and swung away from the curb. "Stick with me," she said, "and I'll drive you."

Sue shook her head. "Might all be over and done with by the time we can drive there. Glitt's got a mighty big headstart. Which way's that Pico street? I reckon I can find my way from Pico if I just go like we went this afternoon."

"Are you sure?"

"Pretty sure. It's Pico to Bundy to San Vicente to Green-peace."

"Greenhaven."

"Whatever. I'll know it when I see it."

"Pico's basically straight ahead," Marta said.

"Meet ya at Vince's."

"Be careful."

"You, too. And don't let nothin' happen to my better half." Reaching across herself with her right hand, Sue patted her own left shoulder. Then she kissed the bracelet.

Chapter Four

Sue climbed above the treetops and pointed herself in the same direction that Marta had been heading in the Jeep.

She passed over blocks and blocks of housetops, lawns, back-yard swimming pools, walkways, parked cars and roads. She saw only a few people wandering around. There was almost no traffic at all. The narrow, winding roads were often hidden beneath overhanging trees.

It seemed very peaceful and pretty.

She wished she could enjoy it.

She wished *Neal* could enjoy it, but he would never enjoy anything again.

He can't be dead. How can he be dead? We were all gonna have us such a great life.

Then below her was a broad, brightly lighted river of pavement.

Pico.

She swung left and poured on the speed.

Chapter Five

Marta slowed down as she approached the row of parking stalls behind Neal's apartment building. All the slots were full except for the one where Neal usually kept his car. She swung into it, stopped and killed the headlights.

She looked at Sue.

And felt abandoned.

Damn it, you should've stayed with me. We should've stuck together.

But she realized that Sue was probably right; by the time they could drive to Vince's house, it might all be over. Apparently, bracelet travel was very fast.

How fast? Marta wondered. *Is she already there?*

She isn't here, that's for sure.

She seemed all right, though. She looked as if she were sleeping peacefully in the passenger seat. No gasping for air, no moans or outcries. Wherever she might be, things were apparently going fine, so far.

"Back in a minute," Marta whispered.

She pulled out the ignition key. Holding the key case in her right hand, she opened the car door with her left, then took the

pistol from between her thighs and climbed out. She kneed the
door shut.

As she stepped out of the gloom of the carport, she looked
down at herself. Gun in one hand. Arms streaked with Neal's
blood. Sodden T-shirt clinging to her. Her thighs smeared a bit
with Neal's blood, but her cut knees dark with her own, which
had run down her shins.

Anybody sees me, they'll call the cops for sure.

She glanced up and down the alley. No cars were coming.
She saw no people, either—though she supposed that *anyone*
might be lurking in some of those dark places.

Too many dark places.

She turned her eyes to the Jeep. The carport was fairly dark;
unlikely that anyone would notice Sue in the passenger seat.

Can't take her with me, that's for sure.

Marta turned away and hurried toward the rear gate of Neal's
apartment building. Before opening it, she gazed into the courtyard. She couldn't see much: the passageway on the other side
of the gate, most of the swimming pool, and the front gate area
beyond the far end of the pool.

Both sides of the courtyard were out of sight.

She didn't like the idea of walking in with a gun in her hand.

So she clamped the key case between her teeth. With her
right hand, she tugged the neck of her T-shirt, stretching it
down. Then she slipped the pistol through the neck hole. She
tucked it, barrel first, beneath her right armpit and lowered her
arm to hold it in place. The handle pushed against the side of
her breast.

The pistol felt heavy and slightly cool.

She wished it was loaded.

Take care of that in a few minutes.

She took the keys in her hand, went through the gate, and
walked quickly into the courtyard.

Lights glowed above many of the front doors, but all the doors
were shut. Most of the windows were dark. Scanning the lower
and upper levels, she saw nobody looking out at her.

You never know.

She kept the pistol tucked under her armpit as she silently climbed the stairs.

The light above Neal's door wasn't on.

He always keeps it on at night.

Maybe Glitt turned it off, she thought.

Had he been here? Very likely. He'd been planning to come over tonight before going for the payoff.

We could've been here, waiting for him. Nailed him when he showed up. If we'd done that, Neal might still . . .

Neal's dead.

Dead.

Impossible. There has to be some mistake. Or this is some sort of really horrible, vivid nightmare.

I'd sure like to wake up.

Please, let me wake up. Let it all be a dream. We're all still fast asleep on my bed, and I'll wake up and Neal will be there with his head on my hip, Sue with her head by my shoulder. We're the in-famous Two-she . . .

But she knew she wouldn't wake up.

This was real.

I'd give anything if we could all go back. Start over again.

This time, stay away from Video City.

Hell, stay away from Vince.

Let him keep his damn money.

Go back and do any of it differently, and Neal'd still be alive right now.

It didn't seem right, *not* being allowed to go back. It seemed hugely unfair.

What's the matter with you, God? My God, have a heart! What'd Neal ever do to hurt anyone? You want his kid to grow up fatherless?

Anyhow, I loved him! What's the matter with you!

I'll tell you what the matter is—you don't give a rat's ass!

She was in tears by the time she reached the top of the stairs. Walking along the balcony, sniffing and sobbing quietly, she searched through her leather key case and found the key to Neal's door.

Don't blame it on God, she told herself. *We got ourselves into this mess.*

Ourselves? Fuck that! Put the blame where it belongs—on Vince and Glitt and the assholes who gunned down Neal.

She reached down the neck of her T-shirt and pulled out the pistol. Then she unlocked Neal's door. She pushed the door open. There were no lights on.

Nothing to worry about, she told herself. Nobody's here. Glitt's on his way over to Vince's house. Probably.

He *must* be. Vince not only cheated him out of half a million bucks, but hired a carload of gangsters to blow him out of his socks.

But they got Neal!

Don't think about him, she told herself. Don't. Gotta hold it together and take care of business.

She stepped into the dark room, reached out with her elbow and flipped a switch up. Behind her, the light came on. She hit the second switch, and a lamp suddenly filled the living room with light.

Everything looked fine.

Marta shut the door.

Better look around.

Be quick about it, for God's sake!

She hurried across the living room. As she entered the dining area, she glanced back. Her cut feet had left faint, reddish scuffs on the gray carpet. She supposed that she'd probably made a trail through the courtyard and up the stairs, as well.

Doesn't matter. I don't care.

The sight of Neal's word processor sent a sudden thick wave of sickness pushing through her.

He'll never write another screenplay. Never make it big. Never anything.

She spun away from the word processor and hurried through the kitchen.

Fine, fine, fine. Nobody here. Get on with it.

She rushed into the bathroom and flicked on a light.

Fine, fine . . .

She saw herself in the mirror.

It was no surprise to find her face bloody; she'd been able to feel the stiffness of the drying blood on her cheeks and chin and around her mouth. But this was so much worse than she'd imagined.

"Carrie at the prom," she muttered.

All of it from throwing herself onto Neal's body and kissing him.

Unlike Carrie, Marta had little or no blood in her hair. But her face was a red mess, and blood had dripped down her neck. Her T-shirt, all the way down . . .

She set the pistol and keys on the edge of the sink, then shut the bathroom door and thumbed down its lock button. With both hands, she grabbed the bottom of her T-shirt. She lifted and the shirt came unstuck from her skin. She pulled it over her head.

I don't have time for this, she thought. *Haven't checked the rest of the place yet, either. What if someone's in the bedroom?*

"Screw it," she muttered.

It felt good to be rid of the gory T-shirt. She wadded it and tossed it to the back of the bathtub. Then she climbed into the tub, pulled the curtain shut and bent over the faucets.

Make it quick, make it quick! Just to get the blood off.

The water came rushing down on her back, cold. She yelped and flinched. Not waiting for it to grow warm, she stood up straight. The cold spray wet her hair, then hit her in the face.

Eyes shut, lips tight, she kept her face in front of the shower.

This'll get most of it. Forget soap, I'd have to waste time rinsing.

She rubbed her face with both hands, rubbed her neck and shoulders, her arms and breasts. Her skin was rumpled with goose bumps. Her nipples were hard and jutting.

I'll never feel Neal's hands. Or his mouth.

Don't think about him!

The water was no longer quite so cold.

As she stepped back, the spray descended her body. Warm, it pelted her breasts. It grew fairly hot against her belly. By the time it reached her groin and thighs, it was too hot. She bent down quickly into steamy, stinging water and twisted the faucets off.

Standing up, she wiped her eyes clear. She looked down at herself. Her skin looked flushed and shiny. The goose bumps were gone. So was the blood. The cuts on her knees didn't seem to be bleeding anymore.

She swept open the shower curtain and stepped out.

Quick all right. The mirror didn't even steam up.

She jerked a towel off its bar, quickly rubbed her head with it, then draped the towel over her shoulders and opened the bathroom door. She grabbed her pistol and keys. Dripping, she hurried into Neal's bedroom and elbowed a light switch.

The lamps came on.

Nobody.

She started toward Neal's bed, thinking she might drop to her knees and check underneath it.

Don't waste your time. If the boogeyman was here, he would've nailed you in the shower.

She turned to the dresser. In the mirror above it, she saw herself set down the pistol and keys. Her hair was a dark tangle. She was dripping.

She considered pulling the towel off her shoulders and drying herself with it.

Why waste the time? Who cares if I'm wet?

She tugged open the top drawer where Neal usually kept his ammunition. There, hidden under some socks, was a flat brown box labeled .380 auto.

Standing on one foot, then the other, she inspected the cuts on the bottoms of her feet. Nothing really major. Most of the bleeding had stopped. She didn't want to waste time with bandages, so she took out a pair of socks and put them on. They felt thick and good on her feet.

She took the box of ammunition from the drawer, opened it, and slid out the clear plastic rack that held the cartridges.

Water trickled down her body. Some of the dribbles made her skin itch.

Ignore it.

The rack was about half-full. The cartridges stood upright: rows and rows of disks that looked like golden wheels with dull iron hubcaps in the center of each.

She picked up the pistol. Its slide was back, indicating that it was empty.

She studied it for a few moments.

Neal had taken her to a shooting range back in April. She'd used the Sig, and he'd shown her how to reload it. But the lessons seemed like ages ago.

Something trickled into her left eye. It made her eye burn. Sweat? She blinked, then rubbed the eye with the back of her slick right hand.

The rubbing did little good.

"Terrific," she muttered.

Forget it. Get the pistol loaded and get the hell out of here!

She tried thumbing the small lever just forward of the hammer. It didn't seem to do anything. Then she tilted the pistol and studied the bottom of its handle where the magazine was inserted.

She found a black, ribbed switch at the back of the magazine. A bit of memory returned.

That's it!

She shoved it with her thumb. It moved. It clicked. The magazine lurched downward a bit.

All right!

She slid the magazine all the way out and set down the pistol.

With her free right hand, she jerked the towel off her shoulders. She quickly mopped her dripping face, her chest and breasts and sides and belly. Then she pressed the towel between her thighs, where it would be easy to reach.

She plucked a cartridge out of the plastic rack. Holding the magazine with her left hand, she braced its bottom against the top of the dresser. With her right hand, she pushed the cartridge down against the top of the spring-loaded slide.

The spring seemed awfully powerful.

But it gave a little, then gave a little more.

Water and sweat dribbled down her back, down her sides, down her buttocks, down the backs of her legs. She ached with tickles. She wanted to drop everything and flop onto Neal's carpet and squirm around to make the itching stop.

Finally, shoving down as hard as she could with the tip of her thumb, Marta jammed the cartridge into place.

"Christ!" she gasped.

She glanced at the end of her thumb. It was red and deeply dented.

One down, five to go. Or six? I'll be lucky if I can fill the damn thing!

She snatched the towel from between her legs and frantically wiped herself dry from head to toe, front and back.

Then she stuffed it between her thighs again.

She picked up the magazine and the second cartridge, took a deep breath, and started back to work.

Chapter Six

Sue swung off San Vicente at treetop level and raced for Vince's house.

Where the hell'd it go?

Most of the houses below had backyard swimming pools. Several even had tennis courts. But Sue couldn't find a house with a pool area that looked like Vince's.

It's gotta be here someplace. Didn't just get swallowed up.

She overflew the narrow road once more.

Where in tarnation . . . ?

She aimed for the full, white moon. It looked huge. The Man in the Moon had a surprised look on his face.

Here I come, ready or not.

She wondered how high she *could* go. Could she get up there all the way to the moon?

No way.

There was a pulling sensation, as if she'd already gone about as far as possible and something wanted to drag her all the way back to where her body was.

Anyhow, this oughta be high enough.

She gazed down. For a few moments, she was staggered by her height. Her stomach dropped. She wanted something to hang onto. This was way worse than being on top of the Pony Express.

Nothin to be scared of, she told herself. Ya can't fall.

From up here, she could see the Pacific Ocean. And the airport, maybe ten miles down the coast. And several clusters of tall buildings: some nearby; a much larger group of skyscrapers a few miles to the east. She supposed that the larger group was downtown Los Angeles.

The ocean mostly looked black. So did the range of hills that seemed to start almost below Sue and stretch along the side of the city. She could see a few roads through the hills, and a scattering of lights. But away from the hills, the basin itself was almost as bright as the Video City parking lot.

A few cars were creeping around on the roads. They looked tiny.

Sue wondered if she might be able to see Glitt's Subaru.

San Vicente was easy to recognize; it had lots of lanes and a center strip that was wooded and grassy like a city park. Right now, it looked deserted except for two or three cars coming up from the coast. Nothing at all was approaching from the east.

Glitt's probably already at Vince's. If I don't hurry and get there . . .

She gazed down at the area where she'd been searching for Vince's house.

Where is the darn . . . ?

Suddenly, she noticed a thread of poorly lighted road just to the east. It ran into the broad, bright lanes of San Vincente exactly where Greenhaven was supposed to be.

Even before locating Vince's house, she knew she would find it. In her rush to get there, she must've simply overshot Greenhaven.

She dived.

On the way down, she spotted Vince's house.

It was the only house without lights. *All* its lights seemed to be off. None shone at the porch or street or driveway. None spilled out from windows. The pool area was dark.

But Sue could see it all in the pale glow of the moon.

None of the other houses had such large pools. And this pool had two diving boards at its north end.

As she neared the pool, she saw the tremendous height of the high-dive. She remembered Marta up there, bouncing. Bouncing and bouncing. Her breasts hopping up and down, all to keep Vince's attention while Neal searched for the money.

She'd sure looked dandy up there.

Too bad a dirty pig like Vince had to put his eyes all over her. But he would've caught Neal, maybe, if Marta hadn't . . .

Too bad he didn't catch Neal.

Wish he had.

If we'd never laid our mitts on his damn money . . .

Sue suddenly found herself wondering *why* all the lights were off at Vince's house.

He better be there!

She made a low pass over Greenhaven. It was carless from San Vincente to the front of Vince's house. No sign of Glitt's Subaru. Vince's driveway was empty, his garage door shut.

Inside the garage, Sue found a white Mercedes. It made quiet tinking sounds of the sort that cars usually made for a while after they'd been driven somewhere.

Vince had probably gotten home only minutes ago from dropping off the sack of paperback books.

Glitt would be coming along soon.

If he comes.

He'll come, all right. Only he won't be comin' just to ask where the money is. He's gotta know the drive-by was meant for him. Marta figured it out and so will he.

Leaving the Mercedes behind, Sue glided into the house. She found herself in a dark hallway. No lights came from either direction.

He's gotta be tryin to hide.

Unless maybe Glitt got here and shut off the power.

The thought of Glitt in the house made a chill scurry up her back.

I ain't even got a back.

In the car, I do.

She wondered if her body, in the passenger seat of Marta's Jeep, had goose bumps all over it. More than likely.

Marta might notice and figure she was cold.

I ain't cold. Just got me a case of the jitterbugs, thanks to Glitt.

Vince didn't scare her, but Glitt sure did. She hated to think that he might be creeping through the house at this very moment.

He jumps out, I'll likely pitch a coronary.

He can't hurt me, she told herself. Shoot, he can't see me or touch me or even know I'm here.

Besides, he really shouldn't be here yet.

Though Sue wasn't sure about the distances involved, she figured that Vince's house must be eight or ten miles from Video City. In spite of Glitt's head start, and in spite of her own problems locating the house, Sue figured that she might've beaten him here by a few minutes.

Unless he drove like a bat outta hell.

He ain't gonna speed, Sue told herself. Not *that* much, anyhow. He'd be scared the cops'll pull him over.

So where's Vince?

Come out, come out, wherever y'are.

She made a pass through the bedroom, its long closet where Neal had found the money, and its the bathroom. No Vince.

Where ya hidin', chicken-ass?

Under the bed? It didn't seem likely, but she went for it anyway. She slipped into the dark space between the box springs and the floor, scooted through, came out the other side and sped on through the glass door to the pool.

No sign of Vince out here.

But the *pull* felt stronger than ever.

She knew why; she was too far away from her body. And maybe she'd been away too long without landing in someone.

Better find him quick, or yer gonna get jerked back.

Fighting against the pull, she swerved toward the den door. She slipped through.

Nobody here.

Not even any good places to hide, except behind the bar.

She didn't expect to find Vince there, but figured she might as well check. Besides, she could just continue on through the cupboards and wall—a short cut into the living room.

Going in low, she rushed through the legs of a bar stool. Then she entered the wooden front of the bar counter, slid through as if it were air, and collided with someone.

She yelped with fright.

But it only took a moment to figure out that she was inside Vince Conrad.

He was frightened, trembling.

He hadn't taken time to change his clothes after returning from Video City. He still wore the warm-up suit. He was sweating inside it. Sweating and shaking.

He held a revolver in one hand.

He was sitting on the floor, knees up, inside the nook behind his bar. Such an obvious hiding place that it seemed a little pathetic to Sue.

This the best ya could do?

But she realized that he was too scared to think straight.

You never know, he was thinking. *Maybe they've got phone trouble. Damn cell phones. Maybe the stupid assholes didn't have it turned on.*

Yeah, maybe that's it. I shouldn't have tried. Should've just waited for them to call me, like we planned.

Vince glanced at the luminous face of his wristwatch.

1:16 A.M.

What am I scared of? Leslie isn't even supposed to show up till two.

But he won't wait for two. Not my Leslie.

Bet he watched me drop the bag in. Maybe waited a minute or two just to be safe, then came right along to pick it up. At which point my pals performed their little drive-by number.

Should've happened ten, fifteen minutes ago.

Sue figured that ten or fifteen minutes ago was probably when Vince had started to panic. He would've been in his car, hurrying home. So he must've been expecting the call on his own cell phone.

For all I know, Leslie hasn't even shown up yet.

Sure wouldn't be his style, but . . .

Delays happen. I shouldn't panic. Maybe he decided to play by the rules for the first time in his life . . .

Sure.

They didn't get him, that's the thing. Stupid assholes missed him.

"Oh, yeah, man, no sweat, we blow his fuckin' head off." *Yeah, right, sure.*

Who the hell knows if they even tried? Took my money and went home and laughed. "Yeah, man, we sure pulled one on that dumb ass."

Shit.

I'll kill their asses, that's what I'll do. Think they can fuck with me.

In a mind-film, he saw himself facing the four men at night in an alley. He's pointing his revolver at them. They're shaking their heads, waving their hands and pleading, "Hey, it's cool. Chill, man. Please! Hey, now. It's cool."

"Not cool," Vince tells them.

On a different level, one that seemed somewhat vague to Sue, Vince considered "Not cool" to have been a very cool thing to say to these guys.

Pleased with himself, he opens fire on them.

The revolver jumps in his hand and spits out fire. His bullets smack the four men, throwing them backward. Slammed against the brick wall, they jerk and prance as each new slug punches in.

He pumps more and more rounds into them.

Fifteen, twenty.

The magic revolver keeps on firing.

"Nobody fucks with me!" he yells.

When all four men are sprawled on the alley pavement, he walks over to them, bends down and gives each guy a slug in the head.

That's what I'll do to them, he thinks.

But Sue knew he had no intention of doing any such thing. He had never fired a real gun at anyone in his entire life. He would *like* to blow them all away, but he's too frightened. He hopes that he will never see them again.

Even though the shoot-out was nothing more than a fantasy, it seemed to make Vince feel better, for some reason. He wasn't quite as frightened as before.

Teach them to fuck with me, he thought.

But his fear returned in a cold rush at the sudden image of Glitt floating like a black shadow into the den.

Nah, nah, nah. He'll have to break in, first. I'll hear it. Then I'll know where he's coming from. He won't stand a chance.

Vince imagined himself standing up very suddenly behind the bar, surprising Glitt.

Don't say a word to him, just blow him away. That's the mistake they make in all the movies—talking. You always gotta give a fucking speech, explain everything. Hey, you're gonna kill the bastard anyway, why not spill your guts for five minutes, tell him everything you know? Meanwhile, you lose your chance and he nails you.

This is all a movie to him, Sue thought. He's playing the bad guy in a crummy film.

Screw the chitchat. Wait till he's good and close, then pop up and blow him out of his fucking shorts. Boom boom boom, end of story. Call the cops. "This is the guy that butchered my wife. Know who he is? The Beast of Belvedere?"

Shit, don't say that. They'll wonder how come I know.

Another mind-film rolled. In this one, Vince saw himself at night, leaning over the stern of a powerboat and pulling a man out of the water. A skinny, naked man with two bullet holes in him and a knife clamped in his teeth.

Don't tell the cops anything. Not about who he is, anyway. They're gonna figure it out anyway—probably run his fingerprints.

What if they also find out I had a houseboat in Sausalito back in those days?

Shit.

Gotta make it so they can't identify him. Wreck his face, smash his teeth. Maybe cut off his fingertips and put them down the garbage disposal.

Long as they can't ID him, they'll never figure things out. All those years ago. It's not exactly something they're gonna guess—nobody goes off the Golden Gate and lives.

Only reason he made it . . .

Maybe he won't kill me. Shit, you don't kill the guy who pulled you out of the drink. I saved his fucking life, that's what I did. Nursed him back to health. Hid him out for a whole month.

Vince felt a surge of hope, but it didn't last long.

Only thing is, he said we're even. Way back when he did Jackie for me.

Vince saw Glitt standing in front of him, smirking, saying, *"That makes us even, Vincent. Her life for mine. No more favors. From now on, you want me to take care of a problem, you pay."*

Sue was astonished. She could hardly wait to tell Neal and Marta all the news. Then she remembered that she wouldn't be able to tell Neal. Her eagerness suddenly crumbled. She felt like crying.

"I hope Glitt does get ya!" she shouted inside Vince's mind. *"Hope he nails yer ass!"*

. . . have sent those guys to hit him. Should've just told him the truth. He might've given me an extra day or two to come up with the money.

While Vince was telling that to himself, Sue found something else going on in his mind. There seemed to be a distant observer who was thinking that the loss of the money had been nothing more than an excuse for hiring the gunmen. Vince had wanted, for a long time, to have Glitt killed. He'd been putting it off, but he'd wanted to get it done.

Dead men tell no tales to the D.A.—tales that could put Vince on death row. *And dead men don't get pissed off and come after you.*

He might've knocked me around some. Wouldn't have killed me, though. I mean, shit, it wasn't my fault those fucks came along and stole . . .

Those fucks, Sue thought. He means us.

You don't kill the goose that lays the golden egg.

But you sure as shit kill the goose that arranged to have you whacked.

For that . . .

I oughta call it off! Tell those assholes to keep the five grand and go home. Leslie'll give me a break.

He looked again at his wristwatch.

1:19 A.M.

Still might be time! He's not supposed to be there till two, damn it!

Plenty of time to call it off . . .

If their phone's working, this time.

Though part of Vince seemed eager to call off the hit, he remained in his hiding place behind the bar. Because another part of him figured he wouldn't be able to get through, anyway. And another part was certain that his hired gunmen had already made their attempt, but failed. And still another part wanted very much for the gunmen to go ahead with the ambush—if they hadn't already done so—if they could do it right.

But if they don't try to kill him, he might take it easy on me.

But if they try and succeed, he'll be out of . . .

Bells and shrill beeps erupted throughout the house.

Vince jumped as if kicked by the sudden noise. Even as the shock blasted through him, however, he realized that the chaos of alarms came from his various telephones.

Relief surged through him.

It's them! They nailed the son-of-a-bitch!

He looked again at his wristwatch.

1:20 A.M.

Still early. It worked! Just like I planned! Took a few minutes longer, that's all.

Relief changing to elation, Vince scooted out of the nook and stood up. As he hurried around the end of the bar, Sue felt a strange, tight giggly sensation inside his throat and chest.

He crossed the den at an angle, heading for the nearest telephone. He couldn't see the phone in the darkness, but he knew exactly where it should be: on top of the lamp table just past the end of the sofa.

A stride or two away from the phone, he squealed, "Yes! They gotcha! Ha!"

He switched the revolver to his left hand, wiped his sweaty right hand on the leg of his warm-up trousers, turned his back to the den and picked up the telephone.

"Hello?"

No answer.

All he heard was an empty hiss.

It's their car phone, all right!

"Hello?" he asked again. "Are you there?"

"I'm here," Glitt said.

The voice entered Vince's right ear from the telephone. It entered both ears from behind him.

He suddenly felt as if the floor had dropped out from under his feet.

He whirled around.

There stood Glitt, close enough to touch, blacker than the darkness of the room, a cellular phone pressed to the side of his shaggy black beard.

Chapter Seven

By the time Marta had finished shoving five more cartridges into the magazine, her hands were shaking from the struggle, the livid tip of her thumb looked as if it were dented into the bone and her body was pouring sweat. The sweat made her eyes sting. Everywhere else, it ticked. A hundred dribbles seemed to be sliding down her skin, and every one of them made her itch like crazy.

She couldn't ignore them, but she refused to deal with them.

If only she hadn't taken the shower . . . that's what had made her so hot in the first place.

What was I supposed to do, drive around in the Jeep for all the world to see looking like Carrie after the prom?

It didn't help matters that Neal's room was so hot.

Get it done and I can go outside where it's cool.

Get back to Sue.

Left her alone way too long.

And God only knows what's going on wherever she went with that bracelet.

At last, Marta shoved the magazine up the handle of the pistol. It stopped without clicking into place, so she pounded it home it with the heel of her hand.

"There!"

She smacked the pistol down on top of the dresser. Hands

free, she wrenched the towel from between her thighs. She furiously wiped the sweat off her body.

This is all taking way too long!

She flung the towel aside, shut the dresser drawer, sank to a crouch and opened the bottom drawer. She'd seen Neal go there for swimming trunks, for different kinds of shorts.

She wanted pockets.

She found a pair of gray hiking shorts and shook them open. They had very large pockets in front.

She put them on. They were so large that, even with the zipper up and the waist button fastened, they barely touched her anywhere.

Holding them up, she hurried over to Neal's closet. She found some belts on a hook. Spreading her legs to keep the shorts from dropping, she slipped a black leather belt through the loops. Then she jerked the belt tight and fastened its buckle.

She pulled a plaid shirt off a hanger.

On her way back to the dresser, she shoved her arms into the short sleeves. In the mirror, the shirt was wide open, trailing behind her. Her breasts gleamed and bounced.

Neal'd love to see me like . . .

Dead. He's dead.

He'll never . . .

Don't think about him!

She slapped her hand down on the pistol, snatched it off the dresser and shoved it into her right front pocket. A few rows of cartridges still remained in the plastic rack from the ammo box. She upended the rack into her hand, then dumped the cartridges into her left front pocket.

Grabbing the keys, she rushed out of the room. She fastened a few shirt buttons on her way to the front door. Moments later, she was outside. The night felt cool and wonderful.

She rushed down the stairs, then ran as fast as she could for the rear gate. Her pockets swung with the weights of the pistol and ammo. They bumped against her thighs.

Switching the key case to her left hand, she used her right to open the gate.

She raced into the alley.

As she ran toward the rear of her Jeep, she glanced into the gloom of the carport. And saw something against the passenger door. A clump of blackness. That moved as if it were alive, swaying and squirming.

She lurched to a halt.

She stared.

What is it?

The black clump had a shine to it—satin?

Ah, it's only Count Dracula having a late-night snack.

The idea started to make Marta smile.

Then she thought, *Shit!*

She yelled, "Hey! What're you doing!"

The blackness swirled and broke away from Sue.

No longer black, it rushed Marta. A man, pale and skinny, a black cape flowing behind him. Hairless. Naked in front all the way down to the tops of his black boots.

I don't believe this, Marta thought. *We've got enough troubles without . . .*

"I am the Creeper!" he announced.

"Stop!"

He didn't stop. He charged toward her, teeth bared, hands high and reaching out, penis erect, boots clumping on the pavement.

"The night belongs to me!"

Marta jerked the pistol out of her pocket. Before she could bring it up, the Creeper clutched her shoulders and drove her backward. She jammed the muzzle into his belly and pulled the trigger.

She heard the hammer clank down.

But no gunshot.

Her back hit the alley. The Creeper slammed down on top of her. As his penis poked hard against the crotch of her shorts, his belly struck the upthrust barrel of her pistol.

His eyes bulged. He grunted, his sour breath gushing against Marta's face.

She rolled and flung him off. He landed on his back. Sprawled there, he clutched his belly and writhed.

Marta got to her feet. She jacked a cartridge into the chamber and took aim at his face.

"No!" he gasped. He flung up his arms and crossed them in front of his face as if he thought they might keep bullets out. "Don't shoot!"

"What did you do to her?"

"Nothing!"

"Get up!"

"Please!"

"Now!"

He rolled over, got to his hands and knees, then stood up and pulled the cape around his body as if he'd suddenly turned modest.

"Over to the Jeep," Marta told him.

"What for?"

"See what you did to my friend."

"I didn't do anything!" He turned around and started walking toward the carport. "She was already like that."

"Like what?"

"I don't know. Like she's passed out." He glanced over his shoulder at Marta. "Is she drunk, or . . . ?"

"None of your business. What were you doing back here?"

"Nothing," he said, and entered the shadows beside the Jeep.

"My ass," Marta said.

As if suddenly discovering enthusiasm, he proclaimed, "I was trying to help her. I could see that something wasn't right. I thought she might need help."

"Sure."

Now once again a black shape in the gloom, he stopped beside Sue's door. Marta poked his back with the pistol.

"Keep moving," she said.

He took a few more steps. Marta halted at the door and told him, "That's far enough."

"Yes, ma'am."

She hunched over the door. Sue was still seated. She was breathing hard, as if exhausted or frightened or excited. In the near darkness, nothing looked wrong.

Marta switched the pistol to her left hand. With her right, she felt for Sue.

"I just wanted to help her," the Creeper repeated.

Marta's hand found a roll of fabric bunched a few inches below Sue's chin. Beneath the roll, she found bare skin. She touched one of Sue's breasts. It was wet and slippery.

Not saying a word, she opened the glove compartment and took out a flashlight the size of a marking pen. She thumbed the switch. A tube of white light leaped out.

Sue no longer wore her seat belt. Her knit shirt was rucked up above her breasts.

"I was . . . checking her heartbeat."

Marta didn't say a word.

Sue's breasts had goose bumps. Her nipples were erect—and shiny.

The skin around her open mouth was shiny, too.

Her pleated white skirt was torn up the middle and spread open. Her legs were wide apart. She was no longer sitting up straight, but looked as if she'd been dragged forward so that she was halfway off the seat. Her pubic hair looked wet and sticky. The lips of her vagina glistened. There were streaks like snail trails nearby, on her thighs.

Marta switched off the flashlight and dropped it into a pocket of her shorts.

As she turned to face the Creeper, she switched the pistol to her right hand.

He had turned around. The cape was wrapped around him. His face, a pale blur above the blackness, was moving from side to side, denying.

"You messed with her," Marta said.

"No."

"Slobbered all over her."

"I didn't. She was . . . already like that when I got here."

"Yeah, sure. Did you rape her?"

"How could I rape her? She's in the car like that, and . . ."

"All you'd have to do is open the door, maybe drag her out."

"I didn't. You can see for yourself . . ."

"You would've gotten around to it."

"No! Honest!" The cape spread open as he put out his hands. He patted the darkness in front of him as if to calm her down. "I didn't do anything. Please. Just let me go. I didn't *do* anything."

"What *did* you do?"

"Nothing."

Marta raised the pistol and took aim at the dim oval of his face.

"I *kissed* her, okay? I kissed her and touched her. That's all. I swear."

"Touched her with what?"

"My hands. Just my hands. I swear! I never even opened the door. All I did was lean over it."

"And *play* with her. She couldn't stop you, couldn't even tell you to quit."

"Maybe she liked it."

"I'm going to kill you."

"No. Please. I'm *sorry!*"

Marta stepped toward him. "Open your mouth."

"What?"

"Open it."

He started to cry. But he opened his mouth.

Marta put the gun in. "Contemplate your sins," she said, "and prepare to meet your maker."

He squealed around the muzzle.

Marta shoved the pistol, driving it deep into his mouth. He choked. He stumbled backward, but Marta stayed with him, shoving, forcing him back past the front of her Jeep until he was stopped by the wall.

He choked and sobbed. He said, "Bleesh!"

"Sue couldn't defend herself, just had to sit there and take it. Now it's *your* turn."

"Nuh!"

"Any last request?"

He started crying like a kid. A kid with a mouth full of barrel.

Marta jerked the pistol back. It came out smoothly, silently, missing his teeth. As she stepped away, Creeper fell to his knees. He cowered, head down, bawling.

She pushed the muzzle against the top of his head.

With her other hand, she reached down and ripped the cape off his back.

"I can't spare a bullet right now," she said. "So wait here. I'll be back in a few minutes to kill you."

He didn't move.

Marta hurried around to the other side of her Jeep. She tossed the cape in. It fell onto Sue's lap and legs.

She climbed in behind the steering wheel, tucked the pistol between her thighs, slipped the key into the ignition, and called, "You'd better be here when I get back, or I'll hunt you down forever."

She started the engine and put on the headlights.

As she backed out of the carport, her headlights illuminated the Creeper. Pale and skinny, he was hunkered down on his knees, his face hidden behind his hands. He was naked except for his cowboy boots. He looked pathetic. But Marta didn't feel sorry for him.

I should've shot him for what he did to Sue. And for what he might do to others, someday. Put a bullet through his head.

But it wouldn't have been a good thing to have on her conscience. Also, it would've cost her a bullet.

She had plenty of ammo in her pocket. Getting a new cartridge into the magazine would be difficult, though. Tough on her thumb. Painful.

She looked over at Sue. "How're you doing?" she asked.

Sue didn't answer. Her body bounced with the roughness of the alley pavement.

Keeping her left hand on the wheel, Marta reached over and pulled Sue's shirt down.

When she came to the end of the alley, she stopped the Jeep. She leaned far over, kissed Sue gently on the cheek, then grabbed the seat belt and strapped her in.

Chapter Eight

Vince, shocked with fright, tried to bring up his gun. His hand moved no more than two inches before it was stopped by Glitt's quick, steel grip.

He pulled the trigger anyway.

Just as he fired, Glitt smashed him in the face with the cell phone.

Pain exploded through Vince's face and head.

Through Sue's, too.

She thought, *Shit!*

But she heard Glitt crying out through the roar of the gunshot.

Did we get him? she wondered.

Vince thought so. In spite of his terror and pain, he seemed to think he'd wounded Glitt, if only in the leg. He wanted to pull the trigger again, but he couldn't find it. He realized that his hand was empty. He'd dropped the gun.

I'm gonna die! He's gonna . . .

Glitt pounded the phone against his face again.

Whimpering, Vince fell to his knees.

Sue thought, *Ow!* The floor striking his knees hurt almost as much as the blows to the face.

I oughta take a hike before . . .

She felt herself start to slide out.

No! I'm staying! Can't miss this!

Vince caught a knee in the face. It crushed his nose and knocked his head back.

His agony was Sue's agony.

Don't bail out!

Vince toppled backward.

Hang on tight! Ride 'em, cowboy!

He slammed the carpeted floor. Then his head bounced, and his mind flashed as if a firecracker had gone off inside.

Sue grunted.

Vince didn't. He lay sprawled on the carpet, his body limp, his mind vague. He was no longer aware of Glitt or anything that had just occurred. His mental commentary was gone. All that remained was a dreamlike scene in which he struggled deep in murky water. Something was after him. Something horrible and merciless that dwelled at the bottom. It was coming up for him. Gaining on him. He had to reach the surface. He would be safe there. But he knew that he didn't stand a chance. Any moment now, it would grab him by an ankle and drag him down and . . .

Glitt picked his legs up by the ankles.

In Vince's dream, tentacles wrapped his ankles and started dragging him down.

He cried out.

But he stayed unconscious.

Sue stopped paying attention to his dream, and focused on what Glitt was doing. She couldn't see, because Vince's eyes were shut. She could feel, though. Glitt was dragging him by his ankles.

Out of the den, and up the hallway.

The dragging had rucked up the back of Vince's warm-up jacket. His bare skin rubbed the carpet. It hadn't felt bad, at first. But now it burned as if the carpet had turned into a bed of coals.

Not that Vince cared.

Vince, in a dreamworld of darkest horror, was oblivious of the carpet burns.

No skin off *my* back, Sue thought.

She laughed a little, in spite of the pain.

Ain't even my pain. It's all his. And I aim to enjoy it.

"You killed Neal, you filthy bastard. Now yer gettin yers."

Vince's body made a turn.

Where we goin'? Sue wondered.

Vince's hip bumped into something. A door frame?

Sue wished he would open his eyes.

Not that she wanted his dream to end. So far, it was a doozy. The creature kept dragging him down, and he knew he was doomed. In the black at the murky bottom, it would do unthinkable things to him.

Sue tried to figure out what *sort* of things, but Vince didn't seem to have any specifics in his mind. He just seemed to expect the worst, and the worst was horrible beyond the power of his imagination.

What does he think it's gonna do, eat him?

Worse than that.

What could be worse than that?

Sue wasn't so sure that she wanted to find out.

Meanwhile, Glitt seemed to be making some sort of a U-turn with Vince's body. A few seconds after that, the carpet stopped. A cool, smooth surface slid under his back. The smoothness was broken by strips of narrow cracks.

There was a difference in the air, too.

An empty feeling, a dankness.

We're in the john.

With a mixture of fear and glee, Sue figured out where Glitt was probably taking Vince.

To the bathtub.

Hey, hey, Vince ol' boy. Guess what? Yer in for it now. He's gonna do unto you like he done unto Elise.

This oughta be good.

Glitt suddenly let go. Vince's legs dropped. The heels of his shoes pounded the tile floor.

The jolting impact saved Vince from whatever horror awaited him at the bottom of the water. He gasped, opened his eyes, and immediately knew that he was lying on the floor of his master bathroom. The overhead lights were on. He saw Glitt looming over him, down past his feet.

What's he doing here?

While Vince tried to piece things together, Sue studied Glitt.

This was the same guy she'd seen with Neal in the parking lot just before hell broke loose. She and Marta had figured he must be Glitt, but they hadn't known for sure.

The top of his head was bandaged. His thick, tangled beard made him look like some sort of crazy wino or hippie.

Looks nuttier than Manson.

He wore a long-sleeved black shirt. And black leather trousers so tight that they seemed to hug his long, bony legs. An inch or so of leather was gouged out of the left side, just below his knee. The furrow slanted downward from the front. Sue could see raw, pulpy flesh inside it.

Ya got him, Vince. A piece of him, anyhow.

Blood ran down from the wound, coating the leg of his pants and the side of his left boot, making a small puddle on the tile floor.

For a while, he did nothing except stand there and glare at Vince.

Vince had managed to figure things out. He felt shriveled and sick with fear, but his mind worked fast, trying to figure a way out.

He'll want his money. That's the thing. Promise him the money— promise him anything!

Why'd he bring me in here? This is where he killed Elise.

He just wants to scare me. He might be a sadistic maniac, but he's not gonna throw away a chance at half a million bucks.

"Wanna bet?" Sue asked him, though she knew he couldn't hear her thoughts.

"Vincent, Vincent," Glitt said. As he spoke, he squatted down.

"I thought . . . you were a burglar," Vince said.

"Not me. I'm a killer."

"I mean . . . I wouldn't have . . . shot you."

"Sure," Glitt said. Reaching down with both hands, he picked up Vince's left foot and pulled its shoe off.

Vince's fear surged. "What're you doing?" he gasped.

Glitt tossed the shoe aside and dropped the foot. "You didn't come up with the money, Vincent."

"It got stolen. Wasn't my fault."

"No fooling?" Glitt asked, but he didn't sound interested. He picked up Vince's other foot and removed the shoe.

"This afternoon," Vince explained. "They robbed me. Took it all. A guy, couple of cunts."

"Real nice language, buster," Sue told him.

"Look what they did? See?" Lifting a hand, he pointed at his chin. "That's from the prick's gun. See? He hit me with it."

"Terrible," Glitt said, and lowered Vince's bare foot to the floor.

Still squatting, he reached for the knife at his hip.

Vince whimpered.

Glitt pulled the knife out of his black leather sheath. It had a wide, shiny blade.

Vince's bowels curdled.

"They *robbed* me, Les! What was I *supposed* to do? The banks were closed. But I'll get *more!*"

"Really?" Glitt asked, but he didn't sound interested.

He lowered the blade of his knife between the second and third toes of Vince's right foot. With his other hand, he clutched the ankle.

"Leslie? Hey. I'll get you the money. Honest! I swear to God!"

"When?"

"Monday!" he blurted. "The minute my bank opens."

"Great," Glitt said, with no enthusiasm. Then he slowly slid the blade, slicing into the tissue between Vince's toes.

Ouch! Sue thought.

"No!" Vince squealed in his mind. He tried to jerk his foot away, but Glitt held on. The blade kept gliding, slicing deeper. "No!" Vince blurted. "Please!"

Glitt's eyes were gleeful. Grinning, he inserted the blade into the crevice between Vince's third and fourth toes. He pressed it gently against the skin at the bottom, then drew it very slowly toward himself.

Sue cringed.

Vince, squealing, flinched and shuddered.

Sue began to wonder if *she* could stand it.

Ain't my foot.

But she felt every bit of Vince's pain, anyway. Every bit of his terror.

Gettin' payback in spades, the bastard.

The knife went away. Sue felt like sighing with relief.

Vince raised his head and gazed at his bloody foot. He sobbed. Then he said, "Don't hurt me anymore. Please!"

"You tried to get me whacked."

"No! Not me!"

"Couldn't come up with the dough, so you hired a carload of assholes to gun me down."

"No! I didn't. Are you kidding? I wouldn't do a . . ."

"Don't move," Glitt said, and stood up.

"I'll get you the money."

"Really," Glitt said, and moved over to the side. He climbed down a few steps into something, walked out of sight, then returned and climbed up to floor level—with a thick bar of soap in his hand.

"What's that for?" Vince asked. But he knew what it was for.

"You're gonna be screaming your head off, Vince. We can't have the neighbors hearing you. Bad enough you shot your fucking gun."

The mention of the gunshot raised Vince's hopes for a moment. His hopes sank, however, when he remembered that he'd shut all the windows and doors to keep Glitt out.

How did he get in? he wondered.

"Like it matters," Sue remarked. *"He's in and yer up Shit Creek."*

Vince also realized that his nearest neighbors were on a cruise down the Mississippi.

A good chance that *nobody* had heard the gunshot.

Glitt straddled Vince's chest, crouched, and held out the soap. "Open up wide and say, 'Ahhh.' "

Vince started crying.

He didn't *want* to open his mouth, but Glitt would hurt him if he didn't.

He opened wide.

He didn't bother saying "Ahhh."

Glitt pushed the soap in.

It felt *huge* inside his mouth. Waxy against the edges of his teeth. Slick against his tongue.

Real nice, Sue thought.

The feel and taste reminded Sue of when she was a kid. A few times, she'd let a bad word slip out within hearing range of her parents—or a tattletale. And then her father would take her into the bathroom and jam a bar of soap into her mouth.

No matter what color, no matter what scent, they all tasted pretty much alike.

Vince had never gotten the soap treatment, but he was aware that Glitt had done this to Elise. He'd heard about it on the news, read about it in the paper. And he'd admired Glitt for coming up with such a handy, effective gag. A washcloth would've sufficed, but a bar of soap showed *style*.

Now, he wished he'd never had such thoughts. They'd tempted Fate. This was payback for *enjoying* the soap gag when it had been used on Elise.

Because of the soap, Vince could hardly breathe. He was sucking air in through his nostrils.

Sue feared she might be suffocating.

I can hang on if he can. Just gotta remember to bail out if he starts to crump.

She wondered if she should get out now.

No, no, no! It's just startin' to get good!

Glitt, still squatting over Vince, waddled backward. As he retreated, he pulled down the zipper of Vince's warm-up jacket.

Vince didn't like it. *What's he doing that for?*

Then Glitt pulled down Vince's warm-up pants.

No! What's he doing? Oh, God, no!

Vince grunted into the bar of soap and shook his head emphatically.

The tile floor felt cool under his back and buttocks.

He still wore something; Sue could feel straps and a snug pouch.

"You never impressed me as being a jock," Glitt said. Reaching out, he hooked his fingers under the elastic band around Vince's waist. He tugged it upward, made a couple of slashes with his knife, then tossed Vince's jockstrap aside.

"Guess you're not real glad to see me," Glitt said, grinning through his beard.

He fingered Vince's penis.

In his mind, Vince shouted, *"Leave me alone, you dirty bastard!"*

But he said nothing. He wept.

He's trying to make me hard, the dirty . . .

The hand went away.

"Let's get you into the tub," Glitt said, "before we make any more messes."

Chapter Nine

Sue writhed in the passenger seat. Her head thrashed about. She panted for breath. A couple of times, she laughed. Every so often, she flinched and cried out.

Marta kept glancing at her.

Nothing to worry about. She's safe here. She isn't getting hurt.

But the thoughts didn't reassure Marta. Her fingers gripped the steering wheel so hard that they ached. She had a tight knot in her stomach. Every muscle in her body seemed to be rigid.

She can come back whenever she wants to. Obviously, she doesn't want to. Not yet.

What if she can't? Maybe something's wrong and she wants to come back but . . . ?

With a sudden shriek, Sue lurched in her seat as if trying to throw herself backward.

Marta jumped and gasped, "Christ!"

Then she looked around. No other cars were nearby.

Sue was flinching, jerking, panting for air.

Marta reached out and put a hand on her shoulder. "Take it easy," she said. "You're all right."

"Ahhh!"

What's going on?

Sue bucked and gasped, "No!"

"Sue?" Marta shook her shoulder.

"No!" A moment later, her body convulsed and she let out a scream that sent ice up Marta's spine.

"That's it!" Marta said. Bundy Drive looked clear behind her, so she hit the brakes and stopped. With her right hand still on

Sue's shoulder, she leaned sideways and reached for the bracelet. She found it high on Sue's right arm.

She started to slide it down.

But stopped when she noticed that Sue seemed calm. The torments had apparently ended. Sue was still breathing heavily, but she no longer shuddered or flinched or cried out.

"Okay," Marta muttered.

She raised the bracelet until it was again snug around Sue's upper arm, then settled back into her seat.

"You all right?" she asked.

She got no response. Expecting none, she stepped on the gas pedal.

Sue turned her head. Eyes wide, mouth drooping open, she looked stunned.

"You're back?" Marta asked.

"Couldn't take no more," Sue gasped. "Judas Priest." She turned toward the windshield. "Where are we?"

"On Bundy, coming up on San Vicente."

"So . . . a couple more minutes?"

"Less than five, probably."

"Lord." She rubbed her face with both hands. Then she lowered her hands to the black cape that shrouded her lap and thighs. "What's this?"

"A cape."

"Huh?" She lifted it. "My skirt." She sounded puzzled, wary. Marta glanced over. It was still spread open.

"My skirt's torn," Sue said, and flung the cape over her shoulder into the backseat. "Who went and tore my skirt?"

"I had to leave you alone for a few minutes while I went up to Neal's room. Somebody came along and did that."

"*What?*"

"A caped crusader. He thought he'd found himself a girl-friend."

"Yuck! He tore my skirt? What'd he *do* to me?"

"He didn't rape you."

"Well, there's a blessin' in disguise. What in tarnation *did* he do?"

"Kissed you and felt you up, I guess." Marta swung onto San

Vicente. "Let's not talk about it, now. We're almost there. I'll tell you everything later. What was going on with *you?*"

Head down, she put a hand between her legs. "Well, I reckon I was gettin' molested . . ."

"Were you *in* someone?"

"I'm all sticky."

"Sue!"

"Okay, yeah, I got in Vince. It's just like we figured; he hired them guys to hit Glitt. Now Glitt's got him in the bathtub, and he's . . . doin' stuff to him."

"What sort of stuff?" Marta asked.

Sue didn't answer for a few seconds. Then she said, "I don't wanna talk about it."

"Torturing him?"

She gazed out the windshield and nodded.

"You were inside Vince while he was being tortured?"

"I took it for as long as I could. I wanted him to pay . . . Ya know? For gettin' Neal killed. I wanted to *feel* all the pain he was gettin'. And I kinda liked it for a while. I mean, he was hurtin' like ya wouldn't believe. Deserves every bit of it, too. But then I just couldn't stand it no more."

"I could tell you were suffering."

"Makes me sick, just thinkin' about . . ." She shook her head. "Glitt'll do things to *us,* too." She faced Marta again. "If he gets the upper hand on us, we're gonna wish we'd been born dead. I mean it."

Marta slowed down and turned onto Greenhaven.

Almost there.

"Our gun's loaded," she said.

"Vince, he had himself a gun. But he only got off one shot, and all it did was scratch Glitt's leg. And that was it. All she wrote. Vince was as good as dead, after that."

"*Is* he dead?"

"Nope. Or he wasn't, anyhow. He was screamin' his head off when I bailed out. Glitt's not gonna finish him off any time soon, either. Havin' too much fun playin' around with him." Using both hands, she drew the edges of her skirt together. "Damn pervert," she muttered.

The headlights, pushing ahead, lit the rear of a white Subaru parked at the side of the road. Marta's stomach seemed to fall.

She stopped behind the Subaru.

She shut off the headlights, the engine. Then she faced Sue. "So, they're both in the bathroom?"

"Yeah. Up till a few minutes ago, anyhow. And Vince, he ain't goin noplace. He's tied up in the tub. There to stay. Glitt was standin' in it, havin' himself a ball. Still there, I bet."

"Ready?"

"Never gonna be ready for this."

"I don't think we can just leave," Marta said.

"I know."

"We'll never have any peace."

"I know."

Marta slipped the key case into a front pocket of her shorts, then drew the pistol from between her thighs. "Let's go," she said, and opened her door.

They met in front of the Jeep.

"Where did Glitt get in?" Marta asked.

"I don't know."

They headed for the small, front gate.

"Does he have a gun?"

"Don't think so. Vince had that six-shooter, only I think it's still in the den. Glitt's got a knife. And . . . and some pliers. He got hold of Vince's eyelids with 'em, and . . ." She grimaced. "I can't think about it. He's got himself a screwdriver, too. And a cigarette lighter—been usin it to heat up the screwdriver . . ."

Marta led the way through the gate. Sue followed, close behind her.

"He's gonna use that stuff on us, we don't kill him."

"We'll kill him," Marta said.

"We better. But look, I don't wanna get taken alive. Not by him. So ya gotta promise to shoot me. Shoot me, and save a bullet for yerself."

Marta wrinkled her nose. She would've liked to make a remark about sounding like bad movies—but she knew that Sue meant it.

Sue had been there.

It made Marta feel ready to throw up.

"Nobody's going to get shot except Glitt," she muttered.

"Bullets don't put him down."

"Sure they do. All it'll take is one in the right place."

"I don't know."

Their voices went silent as they neared the front door. Marta tried the knob.

Locked.

They turned away and walked through the front yard. The soft grass felt good to Marta. It was wet, and the bottoms of her socks were soon soaked.

The front windows of the house appeared to be shut and unbroken.

"How'll we get in?" Marta whispered.

"Maybe round back," Sue said.

They stepped around the corner of the house, then walked through the small orchard of fruit trees. Their feet made no sounds in the grass, but Marta could hear Sue's quick breathing. And her own.

Though the night was mildly cool, Marta felt trickles of sweat sliding down her body. The pistol grips were slippery in her hand.

At the back of the house, she stopped, leaned forward, and peered around the corner. The surface of the swimming pool looked black except for a few shivering silver specks of moonlight. Nobody swam. The diving boards at the far end stood abandoned. The concrete surrounding the pool was gray like a field of dirty snow. Nobody sat at the table.

Marta saw no one around.

She stepped onto the concrete. After the softness of the grass, its hardness hurt her feet. She felt as it were trying to spread open every cut.

She heard Sue wince a couple of times.

When she came to the first glass door, she gazed into the house. No lights were on. She saw her own vague reflection as if looking at a black mirror. And she saw Sue at her side, slightly behind her.

She could see nothing of the living room.

"Can't see a thing," she whispered.

"The drapes are shut."

Marta almost found it amusing, but didn't. She stepped over to the door handle, gripped it with her left hand, and gave it a sideways tug.

She expected the door to stay shut.

But it flew open so fast that it almost leaped from her hand. She held on and wrenched it to a halt.

Sue eased against her, put an arm across her back, and whispered close to her ear, "Don't go in. Hang on a minute. I'll kiss the bracelet and make sure Glitt's still in the john."

"Don't." Marta turned around. Face-to-face with Sue, she leaned forward until their bodies met. "We shouldn't split up," she whispered.

"Stay with me. We'll do it right here."

"But *you'll* be gone, off in Glitt or something. I'll be stuck alone with your *body*."

"Try and take better care of it, this time."

"Very funny. Just forget the bracelet, okay? Something could go wrong."

"We gotta know where he's at." With that, Sue put both her arms around Marta and hugged her.

Marta kept the pistol down against the side of her leg. With her left hand, she caressed Sue's back. "I don't want to lose you," she whispered. "You're all I have, now."

"Ya got Neal's baby."

"Maybe."

Sue tilted back her head and gazed up into Marta's eyes. "And maybe we still got Neal."

"We don't," Marta said. Her throat was tight, and her eyes suddenly felt hot with tears. "You saw him. He's dead. You said they weren't even trying to save him."

"But what if he kissed the bracelet just before he died?" In the moonlight, Marta saw Sue's eyebrows rise. "What about that?"

"Fat chance."

"Might've."

"Did you see him do it?

"No. But he was outta sight after he got knocked through the glass. He could've done it then."

It seemed far-fetched. But then, *everything* about the bracelet seemed far-fetched to Marta. She could hardly believe that such a thing worked, at all. It sounded like complete nonsense. Obviously, though, it *did* work. Sue had proven that by knowing Marta's two secrets. Neal had proven it by finding the hidden sack of money.

"If he kissed it," Sue said, "he mighta gotten out and into somebody else. He might be in somebody right now. That's if he didn't get sucked back into his own self when I pulled the bracelet off him. But somebody was gonna take it, anyhow. I figured we oughta have it. Thing is, I wasn't thinkin' that he mighta gone off on a body ride. Didn't think of that till just now. So I didn't figure it'd make any difference to him. Anyhow, maybe he was already dead by the time I took it off."

"What difference would that make?"

"If he was dead, he *couldn't* get back into his own body. He'd *have* to find someplace else to stay."

"Are you sure?" Marta asked.

"I ain't sure of anything, comes right down to it. I'm just hopin' he got out in time."

"Is there any way to find out?"

Sue shook her head. "I don't know."

"Glitt was right there with him. What if he's in Glitt?"

"He wouldn't go into Glitt on purpose. I don't think so, anyhow. But it mighta happened by accident."

"If we kill Glitt, and Neal's *in* him . . ."

"I guess it'd kill off Neal. Or trap him, or . . ."

Marta groaned.

"More likely he got in you or me. That's what I'd do if I was him and knew I was about to go toes up."

"My God," Marta whispered.

Then, neither of them spoke. They held each other. Marta felt Sue's warmth, her heartbeat, the heat of her breath. And she wondered if Neal might actually be dwelling inside her own body, or inside Sue.

It didn't seem terribly likely.

But it seemed possible.

If he'd been alert enough to think of the bracelet as the bullets were hitting him, he *would've* kissed it. Or at least given it a try. Maybe he'd wanted to kiss the bracelet, but hadn't been able to bring it to his lips.

But maybe he did kiss it.

Maybe Neal had bailed out—fled his body like a fighter pilot ejecting when a missle has blown a wing off his jet . . .

Maybe he's in me right now.

"Hi, Neal," she said to him in her mind.

Or in Sue.

If he's in Sue, Marta realized, then he is holding *me* right now. He can see me, hear me. He can feel my body against him, just as if *he* is hugging me.

Marta's tears returned. "We'll never be able to know?" she whispered to Sue.

"I don't think so."

"Then . . . we'll have to live as if he *is* in one of us."

"I know."

"We'll have to stay together."

"Yeah."

"And we'll have to . . . *do* things for him. Make it so he has a really great time. Just in case."

"Yeah. It oughta be great." Sue hugged her very hard.

Marta tried to stop weeping. After a few moments, she said, "I just hope he *is* in you or me."

"I'll bet he is."

"If he's in Glitt . . ."

"We gotta kill Glitt, no matter what. Neal'd want that, don't ya think?"

"I think so."

"Me, too. But look, I wanna make sure where the bastard's at, anyhow. So the thing is, I'll kiss the bracelet and pay him a visit. Maybe when I'm in him, I'll be able to tell if Neal's in there, too."

"Is that possible?"

"Who knows? This ain't exactly ever happened before. Not that *I* know of, anyhow."

"Just be really careful, okay? And don't stay away for long."

They parted. As Marta rubbed the tears from her eyes, Sue took a few steps away. She sat down on the concrete, then stretched out on her back. Her skirt was wide open where the Creeper had split it up the middle. She drew its edges together and tucked them between her thighs. "Don't go in till I get back," she said.

"You can count on that. But hurry. Please. I don't like this much."

"This time, try and keep the perverts off my body."

"I'll try."

"*Adios,*" Sue said. She turned her head, raised her right arm slightly, and kissed the bracelet. Immediately, her arm flopped onto the concrete.

"Hurry back," Marta whispered.

Chapter Ten

Sue didn't bother with the open door. After rising out of her body, she stayed outside the house and sped along the back wall. In what seemed like half a second, she banked hard to the left and soared through the plate glass door of the master bedroom.

She slipped through the glass as if nothing was there. As she rushed over the bed, she saw a strip of light at the bottom of the bathroom door.

How come it's shut?

She slowed down.

Had Glitt shut the bathroom door while she'd been in Vince? She didn't think so. Of course, the doorway had been out of sight the whole time. It couldn't be seen, at all, from Vince's position inside the tub.

Glitt *had* disappeared in that direction a time or two.

Don't worry about it, just go on in and make sure he's there.

As she glided closer to the door, however, Sue had an urge to turn away.

She had a pretty good idea of what Vince would look like; she could live without seeing that. And the last thing she ever wanted to do was see Glitt again.

She wished she'd never set eyes on him.

Bad enough that Glitt looked like such a spook, but now she knew a few things about his tastes in perversion. Until a while ago, she wouldn't have believed that a person could *think* of such things, much less *do* them to anyone.

Now she knew better.

On the other side of this door . . .

She hovered in front of it, her dread growing.

Do it! Ya can't chicken out!

Moaning, she glided through the door. On the other side, the bathroom was brightly lighted. Glitt and Vince were out of sight; she shouldn't be able to see them from here—not if they were still in the tub.

Here goes . . .

She headed for the tub. Along the way, she passed over a few small puddles of blood, Vince's shoes, his warm-up suit and his jockstrap.

Then she turned her eyes to the mirror over the sink.

She saw no trace of herself.

Invisible girl . . .

But suddenly glimpsed the reflection of a raw red shape, arms stretched out as if it wanted to hug her. She jerked her eyes away from the mirror, but not nearly fast enough. In the moment before looking away, she saw that the thing had a crusty, hairless scalp. Pits where its eyes should be. A screwdriver handle for a nose. Teeth huge and white because there were no lips.

And in that moment, she also saw nobody else.

Where's Glitt?

Not trusting the mirror, not *wanting* to believe what it showed, Sue glided toward the tub. She fixed her gaze on the floor to avoid seeing Vince again.

A bloody towel on the floor near the tub.

Down at the bottom of the tub, Vince's bare feet. Some fleshy pieces of him, some meaty parts of him, and lots and lots of blood.

Nobody's feet except his.

Glitt was not in the tub.

Sue found her gaze sneaking over to Vince, climbing his shiny red ankles and shins.

Don't! Don't look! Gotta find Glitt. No tellin' where the dirty . . .

She veered away from Vince's remains. Rushing through the wall above the toilet, she suddenly found herself in the dark garage. There, she swung around and plunged back into the house. She was in the bedroom again.

No Glitt here.

She swerved through the doorway. The corridor ahead of her was long and dark.

No sign of Glitt.

He's gotta be down there. But how come he quit messin' with Vince?

At the time Sue had fled from Vince, she'd expected Glitt to continue working on him for another half hour, at least. Maybe even for an hour or two.

Havin' himself a fine ol' time. How come he quit?

Hope he don't know we're here.

Maybe it's just 'cause Vince up and died on him. That'd take most of the fun out of it, Vince being dead.

Maybe, or maybe not.

Sue made a quick detour through the guest bathroom, then continued down the hallway toward the den.

Anyhow, Vince didn't die on him. Glitt polished him off, stuck that screwdriver in his nose.

How come? Why'd he do that when he was havin' himself such a grand time?

He knows we're here.

Does not. How could he?

Don't matter. Just find him.

In the grayness of the moonlit den, Sue saw the revolver on the carpet where Vince had dropped it.

But no Glitt.

She wondered if he might be hiding behind the bar, the way Vince had done.

Not Glitt.

So she didn't waste time checking there. Instead, she returned to the hallway and drifted on into the living room. It was somewhat darker than the den. The furniture made black clumps in the gloom.

She saw no Glitt.

Marta looked as if she hadn't moved at all from her position just outside the glass door. Her silhouette was black against the pale, moonlit drapes.

If he ain't in the kitchen, I'd better see if I can find his car. Can't let him . . .

Marta's right arm came away from her side.

Her pistol looked like a knife.

That's kinda . . .

Reaching high, Marta used the point of the knife to sweep the curtain out of her way.

Huh?

That ain't Marta!

Sue hurled herself through the living room, aiming at the back of the dark figure, and slammed into Glitt as he took a stealthy step over the threshold of the sliding door.

He was almost within reach of Marta. Two or three more steps . . .

"*Turn around!*" Sue shouted at her.

But she heard the warning only inside her own mind.

The fingers of Glitt's right hand ached from their fierce grip on his knife.

"*Marta! He's right behind you! Turn around! Shoot him!*"

Glitt was breathless, his heart thudding fast, his body oily with sweat, his stiff penis pushing against the front of his leather pants.

His mind rambled.

Oh, this is my night, oh yes. Whoever she is, she's mine. All mine. Stick her in the back? Yeah, yeah. That'll take the starch out of her. Start with a quick one in the back, then turn her around and go for the goodies.

Hope she's not a fucking dog.

"MARTA!"

Chapter Eleven

Marta waited, her back to the open door, her eyes on Sue's body.

Can't be very comfortable, lying on the concrete like that.

Come on, Sue. Get back here. What's taking so long?

Had something gone wrong?

Maybe she went into Glitt and found Neal.

God, I hope not. It'd be better if he never got out of his own body, than . . .

"LESLIE GLITT!" Sue didn't sit up, didn't open her eyes, just suddenly yelled it at the sky in such a loud, rough voice that Marta, stunned, could hardly believe it had come from Sue. "Police! Drop the knife, Glitt! Step away from the woman!"

Marta whirled around, bringing the pistol up from her side.

She didn't really expect to find someone behind her.

But she was still in the midst of her turn when she glimpsed a black shape so close to her that it might have been her own shadow.

She squealed with fright.

The knife struck.

She fired.

In the next moment, Glitt was staggering backward as the pistol tumbled toward the concrete and Marta flung her right hand high.

Black against the moonlit night, her fingers were hooked like claws. A hunting knife stuck out of the back of her hand.

She cried out, "Shit!"

Glitt had fallen onto his back. He was starting to push himself up.

Marta swung her hand down. She only meant to bring the knife close to her body so she could grab it with her other hand. But she didn't pay attention and slapped it against her belly. The knife point, jutting from her palm, poked through her shirt and stabbed her.

She yelped. Her hand jumped away from her stomach. Then she clutched the knife with her left hand and jerked the blade out.

Knife clutched in both hands, she raised it overhead and dived at Glitt. She landed on him, her face in his belly, and pounded the blade into the middle of his chest.

He grunted.

"Marta!" Sue blurted. "Get off him! I got the gun."

Leaving the knife in his chest, Marta pushed herself off Glitt and scurried backward away from his legs.

He lay sprawled on the concrete.

He didn't move.

Sue didn't fire. She stood near his feet, her legs apart, her knees bent, her right arm straight out but angled downward, pointing the pistol at him.

"You'd better do it," Marta said.

Sue nodded, but didn't shoot.

Marta got up and stood beside her. She felt blood spilling down her hand, heard it splashing the concrete.

Sue glanced at her. "Y'all right?"

"He stabbed me in the hand."

"Looks like ya stabbed *him* in the heart."

"Shot him, too. Doesn't mean he's dead." Keeping her eyes on Glitt, she jerked open her shirt. There were quick, soft popping sounds as several buttons gave way. She pulled the shirt off, wrapped it quickly around her right hand, and clenched her fist to hold it in place. "We'd better make sure he's dead and then get out of here. Somebody might've called the cops."

"Call 'em for sure if I go ahead and pump him full of holes."

"We'll be gone."

"We don't gotta bother if he's already dead."

"This is Rasputin, remember?"

"I know. I know, all right. But that don't mean we gotta shoot him. There's quiet stuff we can do."

"Like what?"

"Like cut his head off."

"You're kidding."

"What's he gonna do without his head? If he *did* live through it, which ain't real likely, he'd be blind as a bat."

Marta found herself smiling. She couldn't *believe* she was smiling at a time like this. She looked at Sue and shook her head. "You're nuts."

"Got a better idea?"

"What would we use, the knife?"

"How about an axe? I seen one in the garage."

"No good," Marta said. "We can't split up. And if we both go, we'd have to leave him. He might pull a disappearing act."

"Reckon we'll just have to use the knife."

"If we don't do something quick, the cops are going to show up and bust us."

"Yeah. They'll run *you* in for indecent exposure."

"They'll run us *both* in. God only knows what they might charge us with. And they'll probably end up searching my apartment. When they do that, they'll find the money. We'll have a shitload of explaining to do. Plus, they won't let us keep it."

"They won't?"

"Are you kidding? Not a chance."

"Well," Sue said, "they ain't here yet. We better do something."

"I wish we had a silencer."

"I've seen 'em use pillows and stuff in the movies. How about if we shoot him through a sofa cushion? One of us can run into the living room right there, and . . ."

"No splitting up," Marta said.

"Course, if we got us a pillow we wouldn't *have* to shoot him. Just smother him with it."

"Who needs a pillow, then? Why not strangle him with our bare hands?"

"Better still," Sue said, "we got us a pool right here. Why not drown him like a rat?"

"Drown him like Rasputin."

"Yeah!"

"Give me the gun," Marta said. "I'll cover him. You take his boots off."

After passing the pistol to Marta, Sue squatted at Glitt's feet, tugged off his right boot, and flung it behind her. Marta kept her eyes on Glitt, but heard the boot splash into the pool. A few seconds later, his left boot followed.

Glitt never moved, never made a sound.

"Put his feet together," Marta said.

While Sue shoved his feet toward each other, Marta clamped the pistol under her right armpit. Then she used her left hand to unbuckle her belt. She spread her legs to keep the shorts from falling down, and whipped the belt out of its loops around the waist of her shorts.

"Take this," she said.

Sue looked over her shoulder, nodded, and grabbed the dangling belt.

"Strap his feet together."

Marta drew the pistol out from under her arm and aimed it at Glitt while Sue bound his ankles together.

"Okay, now let's drag . . ."

Roaring, Glitt pulled the knife out of his chest and sat up.

Sue yelled, "Ah!"

Marta yelled, "Shit!"

Glitt slashed at Sue. Lurching back on her knees to escape the blade, she lost her balance. As she fell backward, Marta fired. A moment later, Sue tumbled against her shins.

Marta stumbled backward, jerking the trigger again and again. Her shorts dropped. The pistol jumped in her hand, quick shots slamming through the silence, muzzle flashes lighting the night. Bullets punched into Glitt. He twitched as they hit him, but he was still sitting up, knife in hand, when Marta, tripped by the shorts around her ankles, tumbled backward off the edge of the pool.

Chapter Twelve

Sue, on her back with her knees in the air, heard a tremendous thudding splash and knew that Marta had fallen in. She raised her head. Framed by the V of her spread legs, Glitt sat just beyond her feet. He held his knife high like a mountain man about to attack a grizzly. But he didn't move. Water rained down on Sue, obscuring her view of Glitt and drenching her.

A couple of seconds later, the shower stopped.

Sue blinked water out of her eyes.

Glitt still sat there and didn't move.

If he's dead, how come he just keeps sittin' up?

'Cause he ain't dead. Just playin' possum, waitin' for a good chance to lay me open.

She bolted up and leaned forward hard, reaching with straight arms between her legs, stretching, going for the belt. With her right hand, she grabbed the buckle. With her left, she grabbed Glitt's right ankle. Then she flung herself back.

He skidded toward her on his rump.

Yer mine!

She scurried and squirmed her way backward, dragging him.

All the way, he remained sitting up, motionless, his knife raised—like some sort of weird, wax dummy of a wild murderer scooting on his ass toward a corner of Madame Tussaud's.

The way he looked gave Sue goose bumps.

But she kept on dragging him.

From behind came quiet, splashy sounds. Gasping sounds of Marta catching breaths.

"Stay back!" Sue yelled.

Feeling the edge of the pool under her rump, she gave Glitt's feet a last mighty pull and tumbled.

She saw herself facing the Man in the Moon.

He looked pale and astonished.

Marta shouted, "No!"

A moment later, Sue's back smacked the surface of the pool. The cool water spread open, took her in, closed down over her. The moon dimmed and rippled. Then she heard a muffled splashing sound.

Chapter Thirteen

As Sue started to fall backward off the edge of the pool, her feet flying up, Marta saw Glitt on the other side of them. Thinking he was about to plunge the big knife down and bury it between Sue's legs, she yelled, "No!"

But Glitt didn't strike. Just sat there as if frozen.

At the same moment Sue's back struck the water, his rump dropped off the pool's edge. He plummeted. Marta heard a thunk when the edge caught the back of his head. His head jerked forward as if kicked from behind.

Then he disappeared into the black water.

Except for his right hand.

He held the knife out of the water. Its dripping blade gleamed like silver in the moonlight.

Get that knife away from him!

As Marta went for it, the upthrust hand and knife turned and began gliding toward the deep end of the pool. She held off. She stared.

No sign of Sue or Glitt.

Just the hand, cut off at its wrist by the black surface of the water, taking its knife on a voyage. The wrist glided silently. Behind it was a wake of shiny ripples.

He can't be alive! Why doesn't he drop the knife?

He *must* be alive, Marta told herself.

He doesn't drop the knife because he still has uses for it.

She pictured Sue down below, towing him by his feet.

He's just waiting for the right time.

Marta swam in from the rear. Both her hands were empty; she'd been holding Neal's pistol in her left, and her stabbed right hand had been wrapped with his shirt. The pistol and shirt were lost.

She reached out with both hands.

Her right grabbed Glitt around the wrist. Pain erupted from her wound. She hissed, but held on.

Her left clamped the top of Glitt's fist and wrenched it sideways.

It twisted *easily*.

It twisted too easily, and too far. Marta heard crackly sounds.

She opened the limp fingers and took the knife.

He's dead. Must be.

But what if he isn't?

That's his big trick, making people think he's dead when he isn't.

Marta let go of Glitt's wrist. His empty hand glided along, fingers drooping.

She switched the knife to her right hand, gritted her teeth against the pain as she clenched it, then took a deep breath and went down.

Under the water, she was blind.

She reached out with her left hand.

When she found Glitt's hair, she grabbed it. She pulled herself forward. But couldn't find the rest of him. Not at first. The water beneath his head felt empty until she leaned backward and brought her legs up.

She realized that he must still be in a sitting position.

She matched it. Felt his shirt against her breasts, the slippery seat of his leather pants against her lap, his leather legs against her thighs.

Sorry, Sue. I don't mean to scare you.

She spread her legs, raised them, hooked her feet over the top of Glitt's knees, and thrust downward.

She met resistance.

But not from Glitt; she was sure of that.

The resistance came from Sue, struggling to keep her grip on his ankles.

Marta won.

With Glitt straightened out and latched fast against her body, she punched the knife into his belly. She split him open from belt to chest. Then she slashed his throat.

Chapter Fourteen

They climbed out of the pool and stood side by side on its edge. Water ran down their bodies. Gasping for breath, they gazed at the black surface. Its ripples flashed moonlight.

There was no sign of Glitt.

"Ya think we done him in?" Sue asked.

"If he makes it through this," Marta said, "we'll start calling him Lazarus."

"We better get goin'."

"Yeah."

But they didn't move. They stayed on the edge and watched the pool. Marta held the knife in her left hand. Her right hand dripped blood onto the concrete by her feet.

"He's a goner," Sue said after a while.

"I'd say so."

"We better get goin'. The cops're gonna show up."

"Yeah. But I dropped Neal's gun in there."

"So?"

"I have to get it," Marta said.

"No, ya don't. What're they gonna do, arrest him?"

"I just don't want to leave it behind. Anyway, we might need it some time."

Sue scowled down at the pool. "But *he's* in there. We can't even *see* him. What if he grabs ya?"

"He won't," Marta said, and jumped off the edge. Water splashed up, then rained down on her. Standing in the chest-high water, she began to feel around the tile bottom with her feet.

"If Glitt grabs ya," Sue said, "don't go blamin' me."

"I won't."

"Back in a sec," she said, and hurried off.

Marta continued searching for the pistol, wandering this way and that, sliding her feet around.

Suddenly, the pool lights came on.

Glitt, his bandaged head almost touching her knees, gazed up at Marta through the clear bright water. His wild bush of beard swayed gently in the currents. His teeth were bared as if he'd died snarling, ready to bite. The ragged red edges of the slash across his throat shivered as if stirred by a soft wind.

Marta saw bullet holes in the front of his black shirt. And she saw where she'd sliced him up the middle—guts bulged out through the split.

Though startled to find him so close to her, she hadn't screamed. She'd flinched and gasped. Then, unable to look away from him, she'd moaned.

She didn't scream until his left arm swept up from under his side and he thrust the pliers up through the water, their jaws spread.

Screaming, Marta bashed his head with her knee and flung herself backward.

The steel jaws of the pliers clashed shut an inch in front of her left nipple.

Then Marta lost her footing. She fell and went under, but only for a moment. Terrified of Glitt coming for her, she planted her feet on the pool floor and stood up fast.

Glitt was down near the bottom, face up, a couple of yards away.

Sue lurched to a halt on the edge of the pool. "What happened? Y'all right?"

"He tried for me."

"Good thing I turned on the lights, huh? He might've got ya." Bending over slightly, Sue stared down at him. "He sure looks crumped."

Marta moved closer to him.

His ankles remained bound together by the belt. But his arms were now stretched out away from his sides. Both hands were empty.

The pliers lay on the bottom of the pool. They were shiny in the lights. They appeared to waver and wobble as if made of flimsy rubber.

Beside the pliers, also wavering, was Neal's automatic.

"Watch him," Marta said. Then she ducked under the water and grabbed the pistol. She came up quickly. Glitt looked as if he hadn't moved. She stepped to the pool's edge and reached the weapon up to Sue.

As Sue took hold of it, Marta said, "Go to the garage and get the axe. I changed my mind."

Chapter Fifteen

After they finished with Glitt, they shoved his body back into the pool. Water burst up and splashed them. Sue picked up his head by its hair. She swung it underhand and let go. It flew high over the pool, tumbling.

It didn't splash.

It went too far and landed on the other side, hitting the concrete with a nasty *thonk*.

Sue muttered, "Oops."

They both watched the head roll to a stop.

Then they squatted over the pool and washed their hands in the water.

When they were done, Sue used the front of her shirt to wipe the handles of the knife and axe.

Marta picked up Neal's pistol and shorts. She dropped the pistol into one of the big front pockets. But she didn't bother putting on the shorts. "Okay," she said.

"Ready?" Sue asked.

"Yeah, let's beat it."

"Aren't ya gonna put 'em on?"

"They won't stay up. Let's go."

Marta in the lead, Sue close behind her, they ran to the corner of the house and through the dark orchard.

So much time had gone by since the gunfire that they hardly expected to encounter police. But they worried. They listened. They heard no sirens, no racing engines, no slamming doors, no footfalls, no urgent voices.

They heard only their own rough breathing and the quiet metallic sounds from the pockets of Neal's shorts: the clatter of loose .380 rounds clicking against each other and the pistol; the tinkling of her keys.

At the front gate, they stopped.

They listened.

Marta stepped out to the street and looked both ways. "We're okay," she whispered. Then she raised the shorts in front of her and dug into one of the pockets. She pulled out her key case. "You drive, okay?"

"Sure."

She tossed the keys to Sue.

As Sue climbed into the driver's seat, Marta leaned over the passenger side. She dropped the shorts and snatched up the Creeper's cape. Standing up straight, she unfurled it. She swept it behind her body, wrapped it around her front.

It stuck to her damp skin.

Sue, starting the engine, looked back at her. And smiled. And said, "Super Marta."

To which Marta sang out in a whisper, "Here I come to save the day!"

And thought, *Oh God, if only I could've saved Neal*.

As Sue thought, *You oughta be here, Neal. It ain't fair*.

Wrapped in the black cape, Marta climbed over the top of the door and dropped into the passenger seat.

Sue stepped on the gas. The Jeep took off with a lurch.

Later

Chapter One

In the days that followed, two major incidents vied with the O.J. Simpson murder trial for news coverage in the Los Angeles area.

The lesser incident involved a shoot-out in which a carload of gang bangers opened fire on a young man named Neal Darden, who was apparently out late at night returning rental movies to Video City. In an unusual twist of events, the victim happened to be armed. Though fatally wounded himself, his return fire and the resulting auto crash caused the deaths of all four of his assailants.

Neal Darden became an overnight hero to many citizens of Los Angeles. Others considered him a vigilante and no better than those who had killed him.

Nobody connected Neal's death to the butchery that occurred the same night in the nearby community of Brentwood.

Those killings weren't discovered until the next day when a young woman dropped by to pay condolences to Vince Conrad over the recent death of his wife. Conrad's wife, former Olympic diving great Elise Waters, had met her own grisly demise at the same house earlier in the week.

The woman, Pamela Goodwin, an actress who'd worked with Conrad on the recent film *Dead Man's Tale*, entered the property just before noon on Friday and discovered the remains of an unidentified white male in the backyard swimming pool. Inside the house, she found the body of Vince Conrad. Like the stranger, he had been horribly mutilated.

The police claimed to be working on several leads.

Pressed for more information, they stated that certain similarities in the crimes indicated that Vince and the stranger had most likely been victims of the same killer or killers who had butchered Elise Waters the previous Sunday night.

They refused to say more.

But several grisly details of the killings leaked out.

There was talk of another Manson family on the loose.

Gun sales in Southern California soared.

Time after time, on radio talk shows, callers remarked that they'd like to see the torture-killers run smack-dab into a guy like Neal Darden.

Chapter Two

Neal's funeral was to take place near the home of his parents in Larkspur, some four hundred miles north of Los Angeles.

Marta and Sue decided to avoid it.

Neither of them had ever met his parents, and this didn't seem like a good time to introduce themselves.

Particularly since the services were certain to be mobbed by gawkers and the press.

They were also worried about the police. Rumors floated about that females as well as males may have been involved in the Brentwood slayings. Though nobody seemed to be suggesting a link between Neal and the homicides at the Conrad house, the police might be keeping quiet about a few things. Marta and Sue thought it could be risky to show up at Neal's funeral.

Especially since pictures were sure to be taken.

Pictures were taken, all right.

CNN carried live coverage. The funeral was covered on the nightly news by every network. Within a day or two of the funeral, *A Current Affair*, *Hard Copy*, and *American Journal* all devoted stories to Neal.

Though some of his neighbors were interviewed for the magazine shows, nobody seemed to know the name of his mysterious girlfriend who apparently worked for an airline.

One of Neal's neighbors, a young woman named Karen who lived down the block, told an interviewer that she'd known Neal well. "He was such a sweetheart," she said, blinking tears from her eyes. "I'm going to miss him."

"That must be the gal he slugged," Sue said.

"The one who gets it on with her brother?"

"Yeah, that's gotta be her. Lyin' through her teeth."

"Who says she's lying?" Marta asked. "Maybe she really does think Neal's a sweetheart."

"Reckon it's possible. To know him was to love him."

Chapter Three

One night, after brushing her teeth, Marta entered the bedroom and found Sue crying. The bedside lamp was on. Sue was covered to the waist by a sheet. Her back was bare, her face buried in a pillow.

Seeing the bracelet on her right upper arm, Marta thought at first that she might be away on a body ride. Ever since Neal's death, Sue had been using the bracelet again and again to escape from her misery. Maybe she was crying, now, in response to the grief of a stranger.

Marta lay down beside her, and gently rubbed her back.

Sue turned her head.

Not off riding, after all.

"You okay?" Marta asked.

"I'm just sad, that's all."

"Neal?"

"Yeah."

"I miss him, too."

"I hardly even got to *know* him. It ain't fair. Three days. That's all we ever had. I figured we'd spend our *lives* together. But all we had was just three days."

"I know," Marta whispered. "I know." She glided her hand up the smoothness of Sue's back and gently squeezed her neck. "At least we'll have his baby."

"*Yer* gonna have his baby, not me."

"Maybe you'll have one, too."

"I ain't gonna hold my breath."

Trying to smile, Marta said, "You might try holding it till after you get your next period."

"I want *Neal*."

"Come here," Marta whispered.

Sue turned onto her side, and Marta slid in against her. As they held each other, Sue continued to cry. Marta cradled her head with one hand. With the other, she stroked her back. Sue's tears soaked through the chest of Marta's nightshirt.

After a while, Marta said, "Maybe he *is* inside one of us."

"I sure hope so." Sue sniffed. "I think about it all the time."

"Me, too."

"I . . . I talk to him, you know? In my head. Do you do that?"

"I sure do."

"But he don't answer."

"I know," Marta said. "But he can't."

"Wish he would, anyhow."

"Wouldn't that be great?"

"Do ya look at yerself in mirrors?" Sue asked.

"So he can see me? Sure. I do a lot of stuff like that. Thinking maybe he's in there. Yesterday, I danced naked in front of a mirror."

"Did ya?" Sue sniffed again. She no longer seemed to be crying.

"For Neal. In case he's in me."

"What else have ya done?"

Shrugging, Marta felt the wet place on her nightshirt pull at her breast.

"Fool around with yerself?"

Marta blushed. "Hey."

"I do. Wanna keep him happy."

"I know," Marta said.

"You do it, too?"

"Yeah."

Sue laughed softly. Her breath felt hot through Marta's nightshirt. "One thing for sure, he ain't in both of us."

"Not likely."

"So either you or me's goin to a lotta trouble for nothin'."

"Maybe both of us," Marta told her.

Neither of them spoke for a while after that. Marta wished she hadn't said it. She held Sue gently against her.

Then Sue said, "Sometimes, I'd swear he's in me. I can *feel* him inside. Makes me feel real good, and I don't even miss him for a spell. Only thing is, then I get to thinkin' how maybe he ain't in me, after all—and how I'm just pretendin' he is."

"I know. That happens to me, too."

"Like I'm kiddin' myself."

"Yeah."

"Then I feel just so empty and lonesome . . ."

Marta lowered her face down against the tickle of Sue's hair, and kissed the top of her head. "It's all right," she whispered.

"It ain't that I don't love *you*."

"It's all right."

"It's just . . . I miss Neal so *bad*."

"I do, too," Marta whispered.

"If I only just knew for sure about him . . ."

"I'll do it," Marta said.

Sue stiffened slightly, raised her face and met Marta's eyes. "Will ya?"

"If you're sure you really want me to."

She suddenly smiled. "Yer the greatest!"

"I know."

Letting out a soft laugh, Sue rolled onto her back and slid the bracelet down from her upper arm. "Y'always said ya'd never do it."

"I changed my mind."

Sue pulled the bracelet off her hand.

Marta took it and stretched out on her back. She slipped the gold, coiled snake over her bandaged right hand.

Sue, turning onto her side, propped herself up on an elbow. She had a wonderful eagerness in her eyes.

"Just try not to be too disappointed if I don't find him in you," Marta said.

"C'mon and do it."

"You haven't found him in me or anyone else you've tried," Marta reminded her.

"Not yet, but I'll keep lookin'."

"All I want to say is, it doesn't prove much. Even if he *is* inside you or me, maybe it's impossible to detect him."

"Well, see if ya detect him in *me*."

"Just . . . he might be in you, even if I don't find him. Remember that. So don't . . . abandon your belief. Okay?"

"I won't, I won't. C'mon and do it!"

"All right. Here goes."

Marta took a deep breath, let it out slowly, then raised her hand above her face and kissed the bracelet.

Chapter Four

Sue smiled as Marta's arm flopped to the mattress.

"Howdy," she greeted Marta in her mind. *"How ya like it in here?"*

She expected no answer, and didn't get one.

"Any sign of Neal? Well, take yer time. Scout around. No hurry. Just relax and enjoy yerself."

See how she likes *this*, Sue thought.

Getting to her knees, she straddled Marta's hips.

"Look how beautiful y'are."

Maybe they're both in me right now, she thought. Looking down at Marta with my eyes, both of them in on everything I think, both of them feeling everything I feel.

Or maybe it's only just Marta.

"*How ya doin? Have ya run into Neal yet? If yer in there with her, Neal, howdy. Hope yer havin' a good time.*"

Wish I was in there with 'em.

Wah, this is better. This way. I'm in charge of the fun.

It suddenly occurred to her that Marta probably hadn't found Neal.

Would've come out and told me.

"*He ain't in there, is he? Never mind. Just stay put, okay? This here's yer first body ride, and I aim to make it a good one for ya.*"

She bent down and gently kissed Marta on the lips.

"*How's it feel to kiss yerself? Weird, huh? I was in Neal one time, he did this sorta thing to me. It'll be great. Don't come out. Just relax and enjoy yerself.*"

Sue sat up and scooted backward. Kneeling above Marta's thighs, she grabbed the nightshirt with both hands and tugged it up. It took her a while, but she finally managed to remove the nightshirt entirely. She tossed it aside.

Now Marta was naked under her.

They both were naked.

"*Look at ya now,*" Sue said in her mind, and roamed Marta with her eyes. She lingered here and there, giving Marta plenty of time to enjoy the view. "*See how beautiful y'are?*"

She bent down, put her face between Marta's breasts, and pushed them gently against her cheeks. It was like having her face in a smooth, soft valley.

"*Oh, ya feel so good.*"

I don't have to tell her that—she can feel it for her own self.

Turning her face, Sue made her way with kisses up the side of one breast. At the top, she took the nipple between her lips. She flicked it with her tongue.

Marta moaned and started breathing hard.

"*Ya like this? Just relax. Whatever ya do, don't come back. Not till we're done.*"

She released the nipple and licked it.

Marta squirmed underneath her.

Sue slid her cheek down the side of Marta's breast, slid her lips up the other breast and sucked it deep into her mouth.

Marta shuddered.

And suddenly grabbed Sue under the arms and pulled her up and kissed her hard on the mouth. Her tongue thrust into Sue's mouth. Her hands roamed feverishly up and down Sue's back. She squeezed Sue's buttocks.

Then she rolled over and Sue found herself on the bottom. Marta squirmed on her, heavy and hot. Kissed her eyes, her mouth again. After pushing herself up a little, she slowly crawled backward and kissed the sides of Sue's neck, her throat, her shoulders, her breasts. She lingered at Sue's breasts, brushing them with her lips, licking them and sucking on them.

Sue thrashed and gasped and pushed her fingers through Marta's hair.

Marta crawled backward a little farther.

She swirled her tongue around Sue's navel.

And kissed her way down, and down.

Later, still sprawled on her back, Sue gasped, "Holy smokin' mackeral."

Marta, sitting across her hips, was panting for breath. Her hair was a damp tangle, her skin flushed and shiny. Drops of sweat fell off the tip of her nose, the end of her chin, and the nipples of both her breasts. They splashed softly onto Sue. Her buttocks felt slippery.

Though she looked as if she'd just finished running a mile or two, she smiled down at Sue and said, "I've been . . . wanting to do that for . . . a really long time."

"Well . . . Whew!" Grinning, Sue reached out and picked up a pillow. She used it to mop the sweat off her face. "Want it?"

Marta shook her head.

"Ya *like* to drip on me?"

"Sure do."

Laughing, Sue tossed the pillow aside. Then her laughter died. "Reckon ya didn't find Neal in me," she said.

"Afraid not."

"Well . . . I didn't really figure ya would, I guess. But like ya said, it don't mean he ain't here. Or in you. He's *gotta* be in one of us, don't ya think?"

"I'm sure he is," Marta said.

"Oh, well."

"Oh, well," Marta echoed, and smiled strangely.

"So anyhow, how'd ya like being inside me?"

"Not bad."

"*Not bad?* Up yers!"

Marta laughed. Then her face grew serious. Leaning forward, she put her hands on Sue's shoulders. "You want the truth?"

"Naw, just lie to me."

"The truth is, I wasn't in you at all."

"*What?* Ya were *fakin'*? But I saw ya kiss the bracelet!"

"You saw *Marta* kiss the bracelet."

Sue frowned. "What're ya talking about?"

"I'm not Marta. Marta's still in you. I'm Neal."

"Yer nuts."

A big, wide grin split Marta's face. "Howdy in there, Marta."

Chapter Five

"Yer *Neal?*"

"Yep."

"Sure ya are."

Marta grinned down at Sue and said, "The one and only."

Sue gaped at her. "If yer playin some sorta trick on me, Marta . . ."

"Marta's in *you* right now. I'm in *her* body. I've been inside Marta all the time—ever since the shooting."

"Ya kissed the bracelet?"

"Just before I died."

"My God," Sue murmured.

"I've been everywhere with you two. It's been . . . a hell of a ride. Marta?" he said as if speaking to Sue. "You're a terrific host . . . hostess. I hope you don't mind having me aboard."

"It's really you?" Sue asked, and dug her fingertips into his thighs.

"It's really me."

"So . . . yer *alive!*"

"Well, something is. My body's sure as hell dead. But my new one's just dandy." Grinning down at Sue, he took hold of Marta's breasts. He lifted them a little and gazed down at them. He squeezed them gently. "These are beauts."

"Up yers," Sue told him.

"I love yours, too. I love everything about you. About both of you. This is all so incredible. And now . . ." He shook Marta's head. "I was happy just to be alive, you know? To survive the ambush. And I thought it was pretty great to be inside *you*, Marta. I *still* think it's great. And I'm in here with my own kid . . . with *our* kid. It's all like some sort of fabulous miracle. The only thing was, I hated being stuck in here without any way to communicate. You've both been so sad. I just couldn't stand it. I *had* to find a way to get through and tell you I was in here. But I couldn't. I just couldn't." Tears suddenly filled Marta's eyes. "Nothing worked. Nothing. I *prayed* for a way. But I figured it was useless. I figured I was trapped in here for the rest of my life—the rest of *yours*, Marta—which would've been fine with me, if only I could find a way to let you know I was here. And then you kissed the bracelet."

"Me?" Sue asked.

"Marta."

Sue laughed softly. "How'm I s'posed to know if yer talking to me or her?"

A corner of Marta's mouth curled up. "We'll figure out something. Anyway, *Sue*, are you going to let me finish my story?"

"Sure. Let her rip."

"When you, *Marta*, kissed the bracelet and went into you, *Sue*, it was as if I'd suddenly been left alone in a car. Like the driver had stepped out and left the engine running. And left *me* at the wheel. All of a sudden, it was as if I owned your body, Marta."

"Soon as she left it?" Sue asked.

"Yeah." Marta's head nodded, and a very un-Marta-like silly grin appeared on her face.

"What'd it do, take ya five minutes to figure out how to run her?"

"Oh, that. The thing is, I was sort of stunned at first. For a while, I didn't know *what* was going on. Then the way you were messing around with me . . . I had a hard time thinking about much of anything."

"Gotcha goin' pretty good, huh?"

"Yeah. But then I got you."

"That's for sure." She patted Marta's thighs. "So, the deal is, yer livin in Marta from now on?"

"Far as I know."

"And any time she goes off on a bracelet ride, yer gonna be left in charge of her body?"

"Looks that way."

"Wow!"

He smiled down at her through Marta's face, and then the smile changed to a look of solemn tenderness. "It's me."

"Marta?"

"Yep, I'm back."

"Isn't this great?"

"It's pretty spectacular. My God. He's really here. I can't believe it."

"Being crumped, he sure looks a lot like you."

A smile broke out on Marta's face. Easing herself down, she kissed Sue gently on the mouth.

Then she whispered, "He's with us."

"Yer like all of a sudden two people."

"Sort of."

"Three, if ya count the kid."

Marta nodded. "And now that I've been inside you, I feel as if . . . I don't know. I liked it in there. A lot. You're a little bit odd, but . . . nice."

"Well, hope ya drop in often."

"You can bet on it. I'll probably be going on a lot of body rides from now on. I didn't think I'd like it, but . . . it's pretty neat. I suddenly want to try out *everyone*. And that'll free up Neal. I think he's got some writing to do."

"And some other stuff," Sue added, grinning.

"If I leave you two alone together, you have to promise not to damage the bod. I don't want to come back and find out that you've been rough-housing. No scratching or biting . . ."

"We'll be good. Won't we, Neal?"

"You're going to start talking to him while *I'm* here?"

"Why not? He's in ya. Yer *both* of ya."

Marta stared for a long time into Sue's eyes. Then she whispered, "Life is going to be very strange, from now on."

"It's gonna be *great!* Now, how about givin' the bracelet another kiss? C'mon over and jump in me, and we'll check in with Neal."

"Okay. Then I think we should all have a big celebration. Find out what Neal wants to do. I mean, maybe he wants a cheeseburger, or something."

"Beer."

"Ask."

"I don't gotta ask. Ya forgettin' he's *inside* ya? He knew ya were gonna ask me to ask him that before ya even got around to askin' me."

"But *you* don't know he wants beer."

"Betcha a thousand bucks."

"That's pretty steep."

"We got us half a million."

"Okay, you're on. A thousand bucks says the thing he wants most *isn't* beer."

"Yer on."

Smiling down at Sue, Marta spoke to Neal in her mind. *"Now we get to see who's side you're really on. Back me up, here, pal. You'll be glad you did."*

She kissed the bracelet.

RICHARD
LAYMON
BLOOD GAMES

They meet for one week every year, five young women, best friends since college, in search of fun and thrills. Each year they choose a different place for their reunion. This year it's Helen's choice, and she chooses the Totem Pole Lodge. Bad choice.

The Totem Pole Lodge is a deserted resort hotel deep in the woods with a gory, shocking past. Helen has a macabre streak and she can't wait to tell her friends all about what happened at the lodge and why it's now abandoned. But Helen and the others are in for a nasty surprise. The resort isn't quite as deserted as they think. And not all the gruesome events at the Totem Pole Lodge are in its past. The worst are still to come....

RICHARD LAYMON

NO SANCTUARY

Rick will do anything for his girlfriend, Bert. He'll even spend his vacation in the wilderness with her, even though it's the last place on Earth he wants to be. But Rick will follow Bert to hell and back—which is just what he's about to do.

Gillian is on vacation too, but her pastimes are decidedly weirder than Rick and Bert's. She likes to break into people's homes and live there while they're away. Too bad for her she picked the home of a serial killer—a particularly nasty one who likes to take his victims out to the wilds so he can have his fun without being interrupted. Rick and Bert have no idea how wild the wilderness can be. But they're about to find out.

RICHARD
LAYMON
DARKNESS, TELL US

It starts as a game. Six college kids at a party. Then someone suggests they try the Ouija board. The board that Corie has hidden in the back of her closet and sworn never to touch again. Not after what happened last time. Not after Jake's death. . . .

They are only playing around, but the Ouija board works, all right. Maybe too well. A spirit who calls himself Butler begins to send them messages and make demands. Butler promises them a hidden treasure if only they will follow his directions and head off to a secluded spot in the mountains . . . a wild, isolated spot where anything can be waiting for them. Treasure or death. Or Butler himself.
